CW01019607

IMMORTAL REVENGE

IMMORTAL REVENGE

by F. Anne Fischer

REFRACTED PRESS

Copyright © 2022 by Refracted Press, LLC
All rights reserved. This book or any portion thereof
may not be reproduced or used in any manner whatsoever
without the express written permission of the publisher
except for the use of brief quotations in a book review.
Printed in the United States of America
First Printing, 2022
ISBN 979-8-98664-9245
Refracted Press, LLC
8 The Green, Suite A
Dover, DE 19901

Chapter number artwork, licensed and © Graphics
Factory.com

Author photo © Olga Popova Photography

Cover art by Lily Dormishev

To you, dear reader, without whom this book would just be images in my mind

1

October 13, 1645

John tied his horse's bridle to the gate and looked around for any sign of a disturbance. The mare, which was usually the most docile horse in his stable, had reared up when she reached the fence and refused to enter the yard. Her sudden stubbornness made him wary, and he stayed as low to the ground as possible as he crept past the hedges running along his property. He saw nothing out of the ordinary in the yard, so he shifted his attention to the stables.

He slid silently through the stable door with his riding crop clenched in his right hand, and placed himself behind one of the stalls, where he could observe without being noticed by anyone inside. He knew immediately that something was wrong. Four matched white carriage horses were kept to the left of the door, with four hunters used by him and his wife on the right. He could not see or hear anything wrong, but every one of them was pacing in its stall and whinnying. He cautiously circled the entire stable without finding any cause for their distress, so he went back out into the yard.

There were no other places near the stables where any person or large animal could hide, so he made his way toward the root cellar, which was located a short distance away in the direction of the house. Fifteen feet from the stone steps leading down into the cellar, he froze. The ground was still muddy from recent rains, and in the mud were footprints leading away from the cellar and straight across the yard toward the wooded area beyond. His children frequently ran that direction to amuse themselves away from the strict glare of their tutor, but the prints seemed too large to belong to either of them. He stayed hidden in the shadow of the building for several minutes, listening, but heard nothing. He crept forward again but stopped dead at the top of the staircase.

A strangled, grating noise that sounded like a cross between a sob and a high-pitched scream escaped his throat as he half ran, half fell down the stairs, landing on his knees on the stone that filled the gap between two small, dark-haired boys lying on the ground. He felt their faces and arms, desperately shaking them to try to elicit some response that would indicate that they were still alive. His sons' bodies were still warm, but there was no other sign of life. There were long purple bruises on their necks and faces, and on the parts of their arms that were visible. John's chest heaved as he sat down on the steps, still feebly trying to shake them awake.

Hours later, John's steward came to look for him, since he had not returned to the house as planned. The sight that met Joseph's eyes in the stairwell caused him to stagger backwards into the yard. After a few minutes, he recovered enough of his composure to return to the top of the stairs. John was sitting on the fourth step, staring blindly at the stone wall in front of him, with the bodies of the children still lying on the ground below him. As Joseph went to offer his master any assistance he could, he glanced at the wall and was nearly overcome by a wave of nausea. He had suddenly noticed what John, who had been looking at it the whole time, had not seen. Even though there did not seem to be any open wounds on either child, the wall behind them was smeared with blood.

"My lord," he said softly. John did not move. Joseph grasped his master by the shoulder and shook him slightly. Very slowly, John turned his head to look at him. Joseph took an involuntary step backwards, nearly tripping up the steps. The clear blue eyes that had always reflected his master's intelligence and spirit were completely blank.

"What do you want?" John asked tonelessly.

Joseph swallowed hard. "My lord, have you checked the rest of the cellar?"

"For what?"

"I...don't know. But there's blood on that wall."

John's gaze followed Joseph's pointing finger, his brain finally seeming to register what he had not been able to see before. He rose stiffly and walked down the steps, carefully placing a foot on each one as if he expected it to give way under his weight. It seemed to Joseph that it took several minutes for him to manage the four steps to the bottom of the stairs. At last, he turned the corner and walked out of view. There was a brief silence, followed by a soft thump.

"My lord?"

Nothing. Joseph ran quickly down the steps and hurried into the cellar. As his eyes adjusted to the dim light, he felt as if all of the air had been crushed out of his lungs, and an instant later he found himself kneeling on the floor, retching violently. When he finally staggered to his feet again, he kept his head turned away from the center of the room while he fought down the last waves of nausea. He steadied himself against the door until he felt sufficiently in control of himself to turn back around. His master lay unconscious on the floor. His mistress lay several feet away in a pool of her own blood. It had flowed from a deep, violent gash that stretched the entire width of her neck and oozed onto the stone floor. Smaller puddles of it dotted the floor around the body. On the ground next to her lay a sickle, the blade also coated in the thick red blood.

Joseph fought back the bile rising in his throat again and ran out of the cellar to the stables. The head groom had returned from a trip to a neighboring estate and was leading John's mare toward the stable with a puzzled expression on his face. At the sight of the steward, the animal jerked from his grasp and galloped back toward the gate. The groom swore and made to go after the horse but stopped at the sound of Joseph's voice, reverberating with the horror he had just seen. Joseph choked out a brief description of what he had found and enlisted the groom's help to move their master out of the cellar and carry him up to the house.

For the next week, John hovered between consciousness and unconsciousness. The doctor visited twice a day, but during the periods when John was awake, he sent him away without seeing him. When John was not awake, there was little the doctor could do except advise the servants to keep their master quiet and call him if there were any signs of a worsening condition.

John was not able to leave his room for the funerals and sent away most of his meals untouched. His cousin was sent for to look after the estate. John's valet and Joseph did everything they could to keep the other servants away from their master, but they found it increasingly difficult to silence the whispers running through the servants' quarters. Suspicions that he had murdered his wife and children were discussed in hushed voices when the maids encountered each other in the halls. As weeks passed, the whispers started to hint at madness as well. And as John's consciousness returned, the doctor was barred from his bedroom increasingly often.

He continued to call and leave various medicines for the patient. At first, the valet attempted to administer them, but over time even his fortitude failed. With John's strength returning, it was becoming obvious that a change had come over him. He had always been a strict and rigid master. Now he was also moody and vicious. He snarled at his cousin's well-meaning suggestions and threw anything close by at any servant who dared to attract his notice.

Then, two months after the funerals, John's valet was startled to find his master up and dressed for riding when he brought him his breakfast. He begged him to return to his bed and let him call the doctor, but John flung the loaded tray at him and drove him from the room. Joseph summoned the courage to accost him on his way to the stables and beg him to return to bed while the doctor was called, but John thrust him aside.

"I don't need a doctor. I need to know what happened out there. I've already waited too long."

2

Renphor handed his ID and the papers he had just finished filling out to the landlord. While the man looked over them, Renphor sat staring out the window, grimacing at the view of an overflowing dumpster in the alley and peeling paint on the house across the street.

"Ryan Callaghan. So, you're a student?"

Renphor nodded.

The landlord squinted at the ID, which he was holding between his thumb and forefinger. "Bit old for that, ain't ya? You're about …" He stared at the date for a while. "Twenty-four?"

"About that." Renphor smiled.

The man looked suspiciously at him. "Why do you wanna live here? The school's across town."

"Because it's cheap."

"I guess if that's all you care about…" He looked Renphor up and down, plainly unimpressed.

Renphor was used to this. He was a few inches below average height, and his pale skin and blond hair combined to make him look frail and ill. He had chosen the age on his ID as the upper limit of what people would believe, but he actually looked more like a teenager. The landlord continued to stare at him for several minutes, until Renphor raised his eyebrows slightly and asked, "Anything else?"

The landlord looked at the cash in his hand. "Nah. The place is yours. Here's the keys. If the neighbors give you any trouble, try the cops. It ain't my problem."

Renphor took the keys the man was holding out to him. "Thank you."

The rental consisted of a single room, with a communal bathroom down the hall. It had obviously been shut up for a while and smelled strongly of mildew and something else Renphor decided not to think about. He didn't intend to spend much time here anyway. He needed an address to give to the university, and it was as good a place as any to keep his books and the few clothes that he owned. He walked over to the window to open it and get some fresh air, and hopefully neutralize some of the smells in the place. He tugged at it, but it didn't budge. Scowling, he examined it more closely and discovered that it had been nailed shut. He gave it a hard yank, and it flew open to the sound of splintering wood. There was no screen, of course. Place would be full of bugs in no time, and the buzzing would drive him half-mad.

Having dealt with the window, he took stock of the rest of the room. The overhead light had apparently lost its shade a long time before. It now consisted of a single dusty bulb attached to an alarmingly frayed wire. He made a mental note not to keep anything in the room that he would mind losing in a fire. The walls were badly in need of paint, and the floorboards appeared to be peeling. This seemed a bit odd, so he knelt down to take a closer look. At some point, they had been covered with contact paper to look like wood. It had been attached over linoleum. Considering the condition of everything else in the room, he was surprised anyone had bothered.

Renphor decided he would need to trash-pick something to use as a desk and chair, since he might want to use the place to study on occasion. The neighborhood wasn't a bad location for hunting, either, if he was careful about it. He generally didn't do so near his home base, but he was pretty sure that no one would notice another unsolved disappearance or two. He pondered whether he should pick up a mattress and decided to think about it later. Right now, he wanted to head to the bookstore to buy his textbooks and supplies for the semester. He also needed to stop by the rare books library, where he had accepted a part-time job. The work seemed interesting, and it would help pay for his rent and some of his books. Leaving the key lying on the floor, he walked out of the room and down the front steps of the building to the street. Several of his neighbors eyed him suspiciously as he left. He smiled at them and strolled off down the block, hands in his pockets.

He returned late in the evening, after buying his supplies and scouting out the locations for this semester's classes. He contemplated simply ducking down an alley and jumping himself back to his room but decided against it. He had to be seen coming and going occasionally, and he needed to learn the transit routes to his new place. The ability to jump eliminated the necessity of using traditional methods of transportation, since he could cross almost any distance in a matter of seconds, but it was likely to become known to a few people that he lived across town. It would look odd if he had no car and no knowledge of how to get there on SEPTA. He got off the bus ten blocks from the rooming house and walked the remaining distance to familiarize himself with the area. Since the fire escape was closer to his room than the front entrance, he walked around the back of the building to go upstairs. As he started toward the steps, four men suddenly appeared in front of him.

"Look what we have here, gents—it's our preppy little college boy." The four started to surround him.

"Didn't know we needed one of those 'round here," one of the men snarled.

8

"We don't, but the fucker moved in anyway."

Renphor leaned against the cast-iron railing of the fire escape.

"Looks mighty comfortable, don't he?"

"Nothin' to say for yourself?"

Renphor shrugged. "I didn't think you were looking for a response."

"Smartass, huh? What we're lookin' for is cash. Hand over whatever you've got."

Renphor laughed at this. "If I had any cash, would I be living here?"

"Must've paid for all that somehow." One of the men pointed at the bag that was full of Renphor's textbooks. "Come to think of it, we'll take the credit cards, too."

"I don't have any credit cards, either. At the moment, my wallet contains my ID and fifteen cents. Anything else I can help you with?"

His eyes narrowed as one of the men pulled out a gun and pointed it at him. Renphor hated guns. They couldn't do any permanent damage, but he had been shot in the chest a few decades earlier by a man in the midst of a psychotic episode, and it had hurt like hell.

The ringleader of the little group finally spoke. "You're no use to us at all, then. Get rid of him." He looked at the man holding the gun as he spoke.

Renphor didn't quite dodge in time, and the bullet ripped through his shirt and grazed his side. Roaring with fury, he leapt at his attacker, wrenching the weapon out of his hand. He slammed the gun into the side of the man's head and watched him drop to the ground. Startled, the others stood immobilized for a moment before one of them recovered his senses and dove at him. Renphor grabbed the man and threw him hard into the dumpster. He crumpled at its base, his head twisted at an odd angle.

Renphor turned around and advanced on the two men who were still standing. In his anger, he had neglected to maintain his shield, and the moonlight reflected off a pair of long white fangs. The two men took one glance at the elongated teeth and the red glow in his eyes and left in a hurry. He thought about pursuing them but decided against it. He guessed, correctly, that they would warn others in the neighborhood to stay away from him after that.

He examined the tear in his shirt with annoyance. The wound was superficial and had already begun to heal, but the shirt was beyond repair. He glanced irritably at the two men lying on the ground. The one by the dumpster was undoubtedly dead. Renphor poked the other in the side with his foot. Getting no reaction, he knelt down next to him. After confirming that the man was still alive, he stood and glanced up at the buildings surrounding the alley. Lights shining in half a dozen windows across the courtyard told him that a few of the neighbors were home. He hadn't fed recently, but it wasn't worth the risk of being seen. He picked up his packages from where he had dropped them when the gun went off and walked unhurriedly up the steps of the fire escape to his room.

3

John Elder bent over an ornately carved table in the middle of his library, deeply absorbed in a tattered, yellowed piece of parchment. Three more sheets of parchment lay beneath the one he was studying. His finger moved slowly down across a series of diagrams that covered the page. After about half an hour, he leaned back in his chair, exhaling slowly as he ran his hand through his black hair. A slim brunette walked into the room a few minutes later and found him still staring into the distance. She walked around the table and looked down at the parchment.

"I didn't know you knew Arabic," she said.

His lip curled disdainfully, revealing one sharp fang. "I don't. And it isn't." He leaned over to continue his study of the first diagram as he spoke, quickly becoming engrossed in it.

"So what language is it in?"

He tapped impatiently on the table. "Aramaic. Did you need something, Julie? This is quite complex, and I need to focus on it."

She ran her hand across the carvings on the side of the table, feeling each of the grooves in the elaborate design and completely ignoring the question. After a minute, he went back to what he was doing.

"Looks like a waste of time to me, John," she said.

He scowled at her. "What makes you think so?"

"I don't have to be able to read it to see how complex it is. Four pages covered in diagrams and the accompanying text. You don't have enough power to work it, and I can't imagine that you ever will." She started to walk away, but he called her back.

"What do you mean?" he asked.

"You've been too selective about the arts you were willing to study. Your protective shields are strong, but a lot of your other skills are rudimentary. Based on the pictures, I'd say that doesn't exactly fall into the shield category. What is it, anyway?"

He was scowling at her by the time she finished. "It's a fire vortex. Once you've widened the funnel, you can throw pretty much anything into it and send it straight to oblivion. And it is outside of the 'arts' that I usually study, but Renphor must be destroyed somehow, and he doesn't seem to be susceptible to anything else. It will just take me a bit of time to catch up on the skills I need to work it."

"Maybe it should tell you something that you've been after the same man for four hundred years, and you're no closer to him than when you started. Further, in fact, since you were actually able to locate him before." She walked toward the door but paused on the threshold. "He won't be susceptible to that, either, because you'll burn yourself up trying to control it. And if you really want to destroy him, you should probably focus on figuring out where he is first. You've had no news of his whereabouts for over a century."

"I'll find him," John replied. He looked up, intending to go into more detail, but discovered that he was talking to himself. He could see his mate disappearing up the marble steps in the main entrance hall. He returned his gaze to the parchment but changed his mind almost at once and stood up to follow her.

A short time later, another man appeared suddenly next to the fireplace. His gold-colored eyes glinted with interest as he looked around the room, taking in the floor-to-ceiling shelves double-stacked with books and the beautifully detailed uphol-stery on the chairs that sat on either side of the fireplace. His heavy cloak was inappropriate for a Philadelphia summer, but he didn't seem to notice the heat. As he strolled toward the table where the parchment lay, he heard John clear his throat from the doorway. He smiled slightly as he turned to face him.

"Stefan."

"You don't look pleased to see me, John."

"What do you want?"

"Just making the rounds. I haven't heard from you in sev-eral weeks. You know I like to keep abreast of things that are going on around me."

His eyes fell on the parchment that John had left spread out on the table when he had gone to search for Julie. Following his gaze, John made a hasty movement to retrieve it, but Stefan was faster. His hand shot out and held two of the sheets in place. He walked slowly around the table and examined them closely.

"Dear, dear. We are getting ambitious, aren't we? After Renphor again?"

John drummed his fingernails on the table and ignored the question. Stefan laughed—a low, rasping sound that held no real mirth.

"Don't blow yourself up, John. I'd have a hell of a time explaining that. Do you really think you can perform that trick?"

John pulled the parchment from under Stefan's hand and rolled it up, tying it with a piece of string. "It will take some work. Unless you care to teach me?"

"Certainly not. I suspect it would be useless anyway—I doubt you have the power."

"In other words, you can't do it either."

Stefan sneered as he ran his finger through the flames of the candles John had been using to read the parchment. "I can. So can the other twelve from the first generation. I've only ever heard of one person below the first generation that can produce a working version, however."

John glared but remained silent. Stefan stayed for half an hour longer, discussing local gossip and other unimportant topics. John was meticulously polite, but his eyes kept wandering to the parchment on the table. Stefan interjected a question into his narrative anytime John seemed to be distracted, forcing him back into the conversation. John finally snapped at him.

"Do you honestly expect me to believe that you care about some fifth-generation twit's choice of a mate?"

Stefan's lips curled unpleasantly. "Of course not. I'm only discussing it because I know that you don't care either."

John stood up so abruptly that he knocked his chair over, but Stefan remained languidly stretched out on his seat in front of the cold fireplace. "Would you like me to leave, John?"

John clenched his teeth. "Of course not, Stefan. You're always a delight to entertain."

Stefan laughed mirthlessly. "It's a good thing you can't have an apoplexy, John. Straining this hard to be polite would probably send you right off. Don't worry, I have a far more interesting appointment in half an hour, so I'm going now."

Renphor arrived in Stefan's rooms just as he was starting to dial his phone.

"You're late." Stefan tossed the phone back in the drawer and shut it with a snap.

Renphor bowed. "Apologies. I was in the middle of something and lost track of time."

"Care for cards?"

Renphor stared at him. "You know I don't have anything to bet."

"You could bet that ring." Stefan pointed to a gold ring with intricate carvings that circled the little finger of Renphor's right hand.

"Not on your life."

Stefan stood and moved toward a wide round table that sat some distance from the fire. "No matter. I'm bored, so I'll play anyway."

"What are we playing?" Renphor scowled at the seating arrangements, which placed him on the side nearer the fireplace, where there was a fire burning in the grate despite the August heat.

"Piquet."

"You know they've invented several new games in the past few centuries?" He reluctantly sat down as he spoke.

Stefan ignored him and dealt the cards. They played for close to an hour in silence. Stefan was deeply focused on the game, while Renphor spent most of the time between turns staring incredulously at the medieval tapestries that Stefan had recently hung around the room. They seemed entirely out of place in the mostly seventeenth-century decor. His inattention notwithstanding, Renphor was by far the superior player, so at the end of the first partie, the score was even. Stefan finally spoke while dealing the cards again.

"Are you actually capable of creating a fire vortex, or was that another rumor?" he asked lightly.

Renphor glanced up from his hand, an arrested expression in his eyes. "Who wants to know?"

"You're the only person I know who's more suspicious than I am. Call it idle curiosity on my part."

Renphor looked dubious but didn't argue the point. "I am." He went back to arranging the cards in his hand.

"Who taught you?"

"No one. Found a series of diagrams in an old stack of parchment a few decades ago. Taught myself."

Stefan nodded. "Any idea where those diagrams are now?"

"Why, haven't you figured out how to do it yet?"

"Don't be flippant."

"I put them back where I found them. You know I like to travel light."

Stefan's eyes narrowed. "Where did you find them?"

"Rolled up and stuffed behind an entire row of books on charms in the hidden library in Athens. Rather careless, actually. I'm surprised no one had thrown them out."

"So it's unlikely that anyone would notice if they disappeared?" Stefan tapped his index finger on the arm of his chair.

"Doubtful, since no one seemed to be aware that they were there in the first place."

They relapsed into silence as the game went on. Renphor waited until they had finished two more deals before deciding that Stefan was not going to volunteer any more information. As he watched the other man gather up the cards in disgust, he leaned as far back as the chair would allow. "Who has it?" he asked.

Stefan looked up at him. "What?"

"The parchment."

He half expected Stefan to ignore the question, since he was clearly irritated at having lost and was wholly focused on smoothing out the edges of the deck before shuffling, but he finally spoke. "John Elder."

Renphor closed his eyes for a moment, sighing. "When did you find out?"

"A few days ago."

"And has he figured it out yet?"

"Not yet, but he's working diligently."

Renphor suddenly snorted. "I didn't think he had that much power."

"He doesn't. He's a persistent man, though. He'll get there eventually."

"I believe you."

"What is this vendetta between the two of you?" Stefan asked.

Stefan had dealt the cards, and Renphor pretended to be engrossed in his hand. He shuffled an ace from one side to the other and back again as he spoke. "Acquit me. I don't do vendettas."

"Fine. From whence springs John's hatred?"

Renphor leaned his weight on the arm of the chair and considered his host. Finally, he sat up and made a discard. "Best ask him. I don't pretend to understand what goes on in that mad brain of his."

Their conversation for the rest of the evening was focused on the cards. Stefan insisted that his guest remain through eight more games, of which he only managed to win two. Renphor finally rose to go at around two o'clock in the morning, after flatly refusing to deal the next hand.

"What's the hurry?" Stefan eyed him angrily.

"Need to feed."

Stefan's lip curled in annoyance, but he nodded at his guest as he stacked the cards one by one into a pile. Renphor watched in amusement for half a minute before shaking his head and disappearing from the room.

5

John spent most of the week following his acquisition of the fire vortex diagrams studying them and trying to break the spell down into its component parts. He had broken it down into sections and was taking one section at a time until he had at least a basic mastery of each of the required skills. After that, he thought he would be able to put them together successfully. Monday morning found him back at the table in his library with the parchment. The surface of the table had also acquired a number of books and measuring implements that he had been using to work out the steps.

He tried to tune out the activities of his mate while he worked, with limited success. Julie was sitting in front of the fireplace, attempting to get comfortable on one of the upholstered chairs. She tried leaning to one side, then the other, finally curling her legs up under her so that she had somewhere to rest the magazine she had been pretending to read for the last hour. There was also a book lying on the table next to her, but it was marked at page ten. She finally tossed the magazine aside with a grunt and stood up, stretching and looking irritably at the chair. John's focus shifted to her as she stood.

"What's with you today?" he asked shortly.

She glared at him. "Nothing. Has it occurred to you in the past week to think of anything other than that stupid parchment?"

He glanced at the diagram in front of him. "Is there any-thing else that needs to be considered at the moment?"

"It's been four hundred years, John. Get over it." She stalked off in the direction of the hall, but he called her back.

"This is about more than just my own family, Julie. Ren-phor is a powerful symbol of everything that's wrong with our kind. He's self-centered, cruel, and manipulative, and yet many in the lower ranks look up to him simply because of his power. If we can get to him, maybe it would send a message that acquir-ing more black magic and a larger group of serfs isn't the solu-tion to everything."

Julie closed her eyes, sighing heavily. "Where on earth do you come up with this stuff? From everything I've ever heard, Renphor is a loner. You're probably right that some of the plebes look up to him, just as they would to any powerful, high-ranking vampire. Get rid of him and they'll simply shift that ad-miration to someone else. And it isn't likely to be you, since you don't offer anything that might appeal to them. You're chasing smoke and mirrors, trying to regain your humanity by pretend-ing you're something other than what you are."

He stood and took her hands in his, smiling down at her. "Is there something wrong with trying to be as normal as possi-ble? We seem to be doing alright so far. We have a beautiful, in-telligent, well-adjusted daughter who sees nothing odd about our family life. We have our house, and each other. What do you think we're missing?"

She did not return the smile. "*I* have a perfectly well-ad-justed daughter, John. You seem to have forgotten that she also had a perfectly human father who wasn't you. And you're putting her at risk with this nonsense." She stabbed her finger at the stack of parchment next to him.

He released her hand quickly and stepped away from her. "I'm trying to eliminate the risk to her. And to you. None of us are safe with Renphor on the loose."

She looked coldly back at him. "If you weren't so stuck on your own obsessions, you'd realize that Renphor doesn't care about you. All this talk about how powerful he is—why didn't he come after you centuries ago if you think he places as much importance on this supposed feud as you do? He isn't going to bother with you, or with us, as long as you leave him alone. If he gets wind of this, though, and he will, he's going to come after you at your weakest points. That would be my daughter first, followed by myself."

John stiffened. "He doesn't know about our daughter. I've been very careful about that."

"Have you? Stefan knows."

"Stefan doesn't interfere."

"No, and he has no qualms about passing on information either, if he thinks he can gain anything from it. In spite of all of your grand schemes, the few times you've been able to get any accurate information about Renphor, it's been thanks to him. Stefan is perfectly capable of having mentioned to any number of his friends that you segregated a substantial portion of this house for the sole purpose of housing your human step-daughter."

John tapped the back of the chair impatiently. "I have spies everywhere, my dear. I'd know if Stefan had betrayed the secret. And I'd know if Renphor were getting close enough to pose a threat to you."

"Really? Where is he at this moment?" John was silent. "You don't even know what city he's living in. He could have been living downtown for the last century. It's been longer than that since you've gotten any good information from your 'sources.'"

"I'd certainly know if he were living in Philadelphia."

She paced around the room a few times, finally coming to a stop in front of the table. "Don't become a danger to me or my daughter, John. I'm warning you."

John clenched his jaw. "I'm going to win this battle, Julie. Renphor has power, but no strategy. And I have right on my side."

Julie laughed derisively. "And how have you worked that one out? Last time I checked, showing off at church every Sunday doesn't cancel out making a deal with the devil."

He looked up quickly, stung by her words. "What do you mean? You know I didn't have any choice."

"You didn't have a choice about the conversion, but it was certainly your choice to go on existing afterward."

He gaped at her. "What are you suggesting? That I should destroy myself?"

"I'm just pointing out the hypocrisy of the whole thing, John. Now, if you don't mind, I'm going for a walk."

6

A week after his meeting with Stefan, Renphor found himself leaning against a tree, staring at the high stone wall that enclosed John's property. He was trying to look nonchalant while examining a heavy cast-iron gate. He had passed by it without realizing he had done so on his initial trip around the house, and even after noticing it, he had assumed it was an older, unused entrance. It had certainly been designed to draw attention away from it. Poison ivy and other vines wound their way around bars that looked like they had been rusting away for decades. However, on examining the metal more closely, he discovered that the rust was not as bad as he had originally believed. In fact, most of it seemed to be spray-painted on. Running his hand along the hinges, he found that they had been well-oiled despite their unused appearance. The gate was certainly well designed for keeping humans from taking too close of a look, but it wouldn't deter a vampire.

He had spent the previous day circling the perimeter of the property, trying to find an entranceway he could easily break through. He had started at the more obvious gate at the north end, only to find that it had been completely closed off. The tightest protective shields he had ever encountered were wrapped around the entranceway and for several hundred feet on either side. The shields were like a force field, making it difficult for him to even approach the gate. He decided that this must be a decoy to deter anyone who might be trying to break in, since the gate appeared to be unused. A heavy chain was looped several times around the bars and attached to a padlock.

He had returned this evening, hoping to gather more information, and on his second trip around the house had come across the neatly camouflaged gate at the south end. This was obviously the entrance that the residents used regularly. The gate here was also sealed with a protective shield, but it was not otherwise locked. The shield was not quite as strong, but after taking a few experimental taps at it, he decided that it would be strong enough to keep him busy for a while. He was reasonably sure that he could smash through it if he wanted to use brute force, but that would consume a considerable amount of energy and alert the occupants to his approach. He was still contemplating his next move when he heard footsteps coming around the corner. Quickly scaling the tree, he peered at the gate through the branches, hoping that his quarry would not decide to look up.

From his vantage point, Renphor watched as a small, gray-haired man walked around the corner and toward the gate. Oblivious to the poison ivy, he ran his hand down the crack in the center, and it swung easily open. He disappeared through it as a sleek black Jaguar rounded the corner and drove in behind him. Renphor caught a glance of the driver—a black-haired man who appeared to be in his early thirties. Instinctively, he bared his fangs, letting out a low hiss. He glimpsed a woman in the passenger seat, but the car disappeared up the dark lane before he could get a better look. The gray-haired man reappeared, nimbly swinging closed the heavy iron gate and running his hand down the crevice one more time.

Renphor waited for half an hour before sliding noiselessly out of the tree and moving back toward the gate. He ran his hand down the crack as the other man had done, but it had no effect. He hadn't really expected it to, but it had been worth a try. He wondered how visitors were admitted. Not that the knowledge would help him much, since he certainly couldn't ring the bell and announce himself. He needed to come up with a better plan.

Scowling, he jerked quickly to the side and disappeared, reappearing a moment later in his own room. He sat down on the bare mattress that was shoved into the corner of his room and leaned back against the wall, staring into space. He wasn't entirely sure that the evening's work had yielded anything. So what if he had found the entrance to John Elder's house? It was set up like a small fortress. He would go back tomorrow to make another attempt at finding a gap in the protections that surrounded the place, but he was not optimistic.

There was always Stefan, of course. He made the rounds to anyone of any importance living in the city, just to make sure they remembered he was there. He would certainly insist on being granted access to Larch Hill, and would know who else had access as well. Stefan loved luxury, which largely kept him away from Renphor's spare dwellings, but he was certain to find more enjoyment in visiting John. Renphor's lips twitched as he imagined how John must feel about it. Stefan's summonses were certainly annoying, but it must be even more aggravating to get home and find the man lounging in your favorite armchair. Pumping Stefan for information was dangerous, though. In a congenial mood, he might tell him the security arrangements down to the last detail, but he would also be sure to tell John he had done so the next time Renphor annoyed him. If he went that route, he would have to act quickly on whatever information he managed to get.

He returned to the house the following night, to see if he could find anything he had overlooked on his prior visit. There were no gaps that he could find in the armor surrounding the place. He could not open the gate, and scaling the eight-foot wall led to nothing but an annoying fall when he ran smack into the shield at the top of the stones. He landed hard on the sidewalk below. After a moment he stood, rubbing his elbow and glaring upwards. Count on John to come up with something like that. Still, it was good to know. If he had tried to jump into the property and hit the shield from higher up, the fall might have put him out of commission for a while.

He was still hanging around the gate, trying to come up with an idea, when he heard footsteps approaching. He swung around to see who it was and found himself face-to-face with a policewoman.

"What do you think you're doing out here?" she barked at him.

"Just going for a walk," he said casually.

"At this hour?"

"Clears the head."

The woman eyed him up and down, a hostile gleam in her eye. "You know there's a curfew here for minors."

She scowled as Renphor laughed. "I'm hardly a minor, Officer."

"Prove it."

Renphor shrugged, pulling his wallet from his back pocket and removing his ID. The officer stared at it intently, turning it from side to side in the dim light, trying to detect a fake. Finally, she handed the ID back to him. "Find somewhere else to stroll from now on."

7

Renphor spent the next twenty-four hours mapping out a plan. He had a large piece of posterboard labeled "Larch Hill," on which he had sketched out a rough drawing of John's property, with the various defenses notated around the edges. A new spiral-bound notebook lay on the floor beside him with the first several pages covered in writing, most of which had been crossed out. He had created, and immediately discarded, half a dozen complicated plans for breaking through the shields without alerting John. He was sitting in the middle of his room, poking irritably at the drawing with a pencil, when his phone rang. He picked it up to check the number and scowled when he saw that it was Stefan. Renphor had been ignoring Stefan since their conversation about the fire vortex and knew that he couldn't continue to do so, so he reluctantly pressed the button to answer.

"What?" he asked shortly.

"My drawing room. Now." The line went dead.

Renphor rolled up the posterboard and slid the notebook into a gap between a Classical Greek textbook and a copy of the plays of Sophocles that sat on a slightly battered bookshelf.

His arrival in Stefan's apartment was sudden enough to startle a gangly redheaded man standing by the fireplace. He jumped, knocking an expensive-looking figurine off the mantel. Fortunately for him, Renphor had fast reflexes. He caught the falling figure easily and restored it to its proper place just as their host reached them.

"Thank you. I happen to be particularly fond of that piece." Stefan glanced coldly at the redhead as he spoke.

"Duly noted," Renphor answered.

Stefan's eyes narrowed. "I'm so glad you decided to grace us with your presence today."

"If I'd known there was an option, I would've stayed home."

"There wasn't."

"Glad I didn't misjudge the 'invitation.'"

Stefan started to raise his palm toward Renphor but suddenly changed his mind and walked away.

The redhead had been looking back and forth from Stefan to Renphor in amazed horror and had begun to inch slowly toward the door. It was twenty feet from the fireplace to the exit, and he had only covered about two feet of it by the time Renphor's gaze returned to him.

"Do I make you nervous?" he asked conversationally.

The other man stopped his sideways progress but didn't come any closer. "Any other time I've heard anyone speak to Stefan like that, they've been on the ground in seconds."

The corner of Renphor's mouth lifted. "I'm not that easy to hit. And I'm standing in front of one of his favorite ornaments."

Stefan rounded on Renphor. "You've moved again." He tapped the back of a chair impatiently. "Well?"

"Was there a question in there somewhere?"

Stefan hissed slightly. "Don't be obtuse. Why the move?"

"Cheaper."

"Why the hell don't you get yourself some money? In all this time, you must have had the opportunity."

Renphor eyed the ornaments on the mantel with disgust. "Why bother? So I can buy expensive rocks? Nearly everything I require can be obtained for free."

The redhead seemed to have concluded that there was no real danger and finally chimed in. "You seem to be about the only one who thinks so. You should see John's place."

Renphor stiffened almost imperceptibly. "John? As in John Elder? Have you been inside that ridiculous pile?"

Stefan watched them with interest but remained silent.

"Yes, of course. He's my maker, and my mentor as well."

Renphor smiled tightly. "His place doesn't seem very- …welcoming. I don't suppose you can get through the front gate without an invitation."

The man paused. "Well…it depends. I have access, and so do a few others. Most people need to go in with a member of the household, though."

"A little paranoid, isn't it? What if your friend from Europe drops by to visit? Do you have to leave him at home if you can't get ahold of Elder?"

"Yes, actually. Only John, his mate, and his steward have the ability to bring another vampire inside the perimeter. Julie's daughter has access to the front section of the house, of course, but humans are completely blocked out of the back."

He had been looking at the ceiling as he spoke, trying to remember all the details of the security arrangements, so he missed Renphor's surprised reaction to these words. By the time he finished what he was saying, Renphor's face was a complete blank. He strolled to the window and pulled back a heavy brocade curtain to look out as the other man inched around to talk to Stefan.

"Um, I really should be going—"

Stefan cut him off with a nod, still watching Renphor carefully as the redhead hurried from the room.

"There's no point in looking nonchalant." Stefan sneered. "That idiot just handed you the best piece of information you've gotten in years."

"I thought you weren't involved."

"I'm not."

"Then don't be. What did you want me for, anyway?"

"Nothing in particular. I wanted your input on something three days ago, but since you chose to ignore me, I decided to talk to you now."

Renphor gritted his teeth. "What was it that you wanted to know?"

"It's a moot point now."

"Does that mean I can follow that twit's example?" he asked.

"As you like. I am curious, though. Is there some reason you prefer to hang around with a bunch of teenage coeds these days rather than spend time with your own kind?"

"If you mean my college program—it alleviates the boredom. Occasionally I pick up something worth knowing. And hanging around with teenage coeds helps me to keep current. As for my own kind—I don't avoid the attractive ones."

"Ariliana, for example?"

"She's one of the options, yes."

"John will get you in the end, you know." Stefan said smugly.

"Will he?"

"Of course."

"I suppose you want me to ask why."

"Because you've no attention span for this kind of feud. You'll get distracted by a female, or a new spell, and you'll forget to pay attention to what he's doing."

Renphor grimaced. "I don't intend to sit around thinking about John for the rest of my existence. Or even for the rest of his. I'll have to rely on the fact that I'm stronger than him to save me, I suppose. Are we done now?"

Back in his own room, his eyes traveled around, mentally comparing his surroundings to the ones he had just left. Shrugging, he walked to the bookshelf, pulled out the notebook and map, and dropped them onto a banged-up desk that leaned against one wall. He looked skeptically at the back of the rickety chair, testing it cautiously with his hand before perching on the front edge of the seat, and ran his finger around the map of John's property again. Picking up a pencil, he marked off the north side, where he had found the padlocked gate, and wrote "humans" next to it. At least now he understood the strength of the shields. John would not have wanted any of their kind to encounter his human stepdaughter.

Renphor sketched a few absentminded circles along the edge of a blank sheet of paper before writing down "Weak Points" at the top left of the page. He tapped the pencil on the edge of the desk, then began to jot down a list.

Mate—Julie? How much does she know?
Daughter—? No info
Red-haired idiot. Name?
Other friends?

He dropped the pencil impatiently. He still wasn't sure how he was going to get inside the house, since no one on his list would help him willingly. He had toyed with the idea of attacking John elsewhere, but there was no other place as convenient. At Larch Hill, there would be no risk of the battle being seen by humans, and if he could take John by surprise, he stood a far better chance of escaping the encounter unscathed. John was always on his guard while outside the confines of his own property. Renphor leaned back in the chair but sat up again quickly as he felt it start to give.

He glanced over the list he had made. Picking up the pencil again, he rested it on Julie's name for a while, considering. He flipped to the next page, wrote Julie's name at the top, then stopped. He had no information whatsoever about her. He made a note—*Can't assume she's as clueless as red-haired idiot. What are her habits?*

That was as far as he got for an hour. He finally stood up in frustration, deciding that there was no way he was getting anywhere sitting here at the desk. Before he left, he wedged the notebook back into place on the bookshelf, with more violence than was absolutely necessary.

Standing on the sidewalk in front of Larch Hill, he looked up and turned slowly on the spot, trying to find a decent vantage point for seeing over the high stone wall. An oak tree planted on the other side of the wall grew for at least another thirty feet above it, with branches that appeared to stretch well outside of the perimeter. They would probably fall outside of the shield and would give him a glimpse inside the property, at least. He examined a maple across from the oak. It was close enough to allow him to move from the branches of one to the branches of the other without having to jump directly from the sidewalk. It was a necessary precaution until he was certain of the extent of the shield.

He scaled the maple quickly and crept as far out on a long branch as he could. He paused for a moment, judging the distance between where he sat and the thicker part of the branch across from him. Looking down, he estimated that he was at least thirty feet in the air. Hoping that he was right about the shield, he tensed his muscles and sprang toward the oak branch. Coming to rest lightly on the branch, he smiled in satisfaction. This tree was taller and sturdier, so he was able to climb another fifteen feet before the branches thinned out too much to hold his weight. He crept slowly toward the trunk of the tree until he was stopped by the invisible shield surrounding the property. Having established the location of the shield, he moved through the branches until he was positioned in such a way that he could make out the house in the distance, down a half-mile-long lane.

He stared at the property, struggling to process what he was seeing. The mansion was enormous, built in an elaborate gothic style that was completely out of place in modern-day America. John had created an exact replica of his former ancestral home in Sussex, down to the stables and the root cellar that Renphor remembered vividly. The building had the appearance of having been added to over centuries, using varying styles and building materials, but Renphor was certain that it had been built in its entirety shortly after John had arrived in the country. The copy of the original stables stood about a hundred feet from the house and had been slightly modified at some point to house the beautiful car that Renphor had seen on his earlier visit.

Turning his attention back to the house, he noticed light coming from one of the front rooms. He watched with interest as it flickered and moved about. Was Elder really lighting the place with candles? The curtains had been drawn back, and he caught a glimpse of a slim woman sitting in a high-backed chair but couldn't make out her features at this distance. A sudden movement at the far side of the house diverted his attention. A tall man was creeping across the lawn away from the house, toward the wooded area behind the stables. Renphor flattened himself along the branch, watching as John crouched low behind a tree. He suddenly sprang, bringing down a deer that had wandered close to the edge of the woods. Losing interest, Renphor turned his attention back to the house and hissed in annoyance upon discovering that Julie was no longer seated in the chair. He waited another half hour to see if she too would come out to hunt, but he wasn't able to catch another glimpse of her.

Subsequent visits throughout the week didn't provide him with any more information than he had previously learned. His quarry never seemed to leave the house. In frustration, he finally gave up his surveillance and began considering other means of getting information about John Elder's mate.

8

John slid quietly into the room and stood watching his mate read a travel magazine. She pretended to be too engrossed in what she was reading to notice, but he could see that she hadn't turned a page in the half hour since he'd last been there. Sighing, he walked over to a chair opposite hers and sat down.

After a few minutes, he cleared his throat. "Julie?"

She didn't look up. "John."

"You've barely spoken to me in a week. Can we discuss this?"

She set the magazine down on the table, staring straight ahead. "I don't think there's much to discuss."

"There's a lot to discuss. Like why you suddenly think I'm endangering my family by doing essentially the same things I've been doing since before we met."

She finally looked at him. "It isn't the same, John. This time, you're trying to work a dangerous spell that's well beyond your abilities. Also new is the fact that it's likely to bring this little feud of yours back into the spotlight and get the gossips going. Renphor's left you alone for years. Why stir him up?"

John chose his words carefully. "I know you think I'm just asking for trouble, and that he'll continue to leave us alone if I don't attract his attention. But I know him, Julie. I understand him far better than you realize, after four hundred years. And I promise you that he won't miss a chance to take his revenge if he sees an opportunity. We have to constantly stay on the offensive."

"How can you possibly know that he hasn't found out about my daughter? How can you possibly protect her when she's living at school? We have no idea what she's doing or who she's with most of the time."

John shook his head. "Stefan's the only one outside of our inner circle who knows anything about that. I've given her a number of protective talismans that she has no idea she's carrying with her. And she's a sensible girl. Renphor couldn't follow her without her catching on, and she'd certainly let us know if something of that nature were going on."

"You claim to know so much about Renphor, but I haven't seen or heard any evidence of it. Who are his friends? What are his pastimes? I've never met anyone who admitted to being close to him. Having no one in his confidence puts him at a distinct advantage if he's really trying to avoid you."

John smiled patiently. "Everyone has confidants. No one is going to admit to you, or to me, that they're friends with him. I have several well-placed spies who get excellent information for me."

Julie twitched her hand to toss the magazine she had been reading onto the table, but in her irritation, she flung it too hard. It zoomed across the wooden surface and landed between the table leg and the wall. She snarled at it before turning her attention back to her mate. "How do you know that any of your information is correct? All of what you've been getting from your 'spies' hasn't led you any closer to his whereabouts. Do you really know who's on your side and who's on his?"

He frowned and took her hands in his to prevent her from fidgeting anymore. "You're really worried about this, aren't you? I can start including you in our meetings, if it would put your mind at ease. I have complete faith in the loyalty of all my friends."

"I'll certainly join you, if you're serious about the invitation. But you're still going to have to do better than that to convince me this is safe. No one else can possibly be as invested in this as you are, so why should they remain loyal if someone else offers them more?"

"Because it isn't just about Renphor. That's a personal fight that happens to help us toward a larger goal. But ultimately we have far bigger plans in mind."

They continued to argue for several minutes, until Julie suddenly stood up.

"Where are you going?"

"To retrieve that damned magazine," she grumbled as she crawled behind the table.

Julie spent another half hour attempting to read before giving up on the idea. Getting up from her chair, she opened the door and slipped softly out of the room. She knew that John was unlikely to come searching for her, since he would still be miffed about their spat. She managed to make it out the side door without attracting the notice of either her mate or his servant and walked quickly down the path through the woods to the front gate. Passing through it, she covered the ten blocks to the bus stop in a few minutes and sat down on the bench to wait. When the bus arrived she looked quickly around before jumping on, swiping her card, and taking a seat in the back where she could easily keep an eye on the other passengers.

An hour and a bus change later, she got off in front of what appeared to be a run-down building in an even more run-down area of the city. She noticed several men watching her from the shadows. *You'd be in for a big surprise if you tried it, boys,* she thought to herself. Running lightly up the steps, she pulled open the heavy oak door and stepped inside Stefan's private foyer. Within a few moments, she was greeted by Robert, Stefan's very correct servant.

"Is he available?" she asked.

"I will inquire, madam."

Robert disappeared up the steps but returned a minute later and motioned her to follow him.

Stefan put out his hand to Julie as she entered the room. "How's the bore?"

"Same as usual."

He started to pull her closer, but she stopped him. He stared at her in surprise.

"This isn't just a social call." She smiled at the expression on his face. "We can get to that later."

His features relaxed. "I seem to be running an information bureau. What is it that you want?"

She looked rueful. "Pretty much the same thing John's been trying to get out of you for years. I want to know where Renphor is."

"That is *not* a good idea." He walked away from her as he spoke.

She followed him. "Would he kill me outright, if he met up with me?"

Stefan considered this. "No…at least, it's not likely," he amended. "You're not seriously considering it?"

She flopped down on a nearby chair, apologizing for her treatment of his furniture when she saw the pained expression on his face.

"I don't know what I'm considering. I do know that John's going to get us all killed if he keeps going the way he is." She started to fidget with a feather quill that sat on the end table next to her but gave it an odd look and put it down when she realized what she was holding.

"I still haven't adapted to the idea of a ballpoint. What exactly do you hope to gain by finding Renphor?" Stefan asked.

"I don't know. It was just a thought."

He watched her for a while. "At the moment, he has a shitty little room in Frankford. I don't remember the exact address. Renphor's lodgings are never what you would call comfortable, so if I want to see him, I call him here."

"Frankford?" Julie felt like the bottom had dropped out of her stomach. "As in, Philadelphia?"

Stefan put his hand on her shoulder. "He's been centered here for a decade or so. Tends to move every year or two, to cover his tracks."

She swallowed. "So I was right about him not being interested in John. He could have wiped us out ten times over by now, if he'd wanted to bother."

Stefan shook his head. "It wouldn't be as easy as you think. John's shields are powerful. And don't go around thinking that Renphor isn't paying attention. He's certainly not as obsessed as John, but he's well able to look after himself."

She nodded. "What name is he using?"

"Julie, this is a really bad idea."

She stared at him mutely.

He sighed. "Ryan Callaghan. Don't get yourself killed."

"I'll be careful."

He pulled her into his arms again, and this time she didn't resist.

Julie stepped off the bus, looking cautiously around. John was unlikely to be lurking nearby, but she never felt entirely certain that she wasn't being watched when she returned from her visits to Stefan. She walked briskly around the corner to the front entrance of Larch Hill and pulled open the heavy iron gate without effort. She closed it firmly behind her as she stepped inside the perimeter of the property and then ran her hand down the crack in the center. Shutting her eyes for a moment, she took a deep breath before starting slowly up the long path toward the house. She was relieved to find the hall and John's library empty, but her relief was short-lived. He walked out of her sitting room just as she was heading toward it.

"Where were you?" he asked sharply.

She glared at him. "I thought you agreed to stay out of that room."

"I was looking for you. I know it's a large house, but it's still a bit strange not to run into your own mate for over twenty-four hours."

Julie had looked away when he started speaking and was still studying an oil painting when she answered. "I was on the grounds."

His eyes narrowed. "Hunting?"

"Walking."

"I know when the gate opens, you know. Who were you 'visiting' this time?"

She glared at him. "You act like I'm hiding a string of lovers behind your back. I was visiting Stefan, if you must know. I was hoping he'd help me knock some sense into you."

She could see him trying to suppress his irritation and barely managed to hide a smile. He had asked her to strike up a friendship with Stefan when the other man had shown more than a passing interest in her. At the time, John had wanted the connection far more than Julie had. Stefan and the other twelve first-generation vampires made up the ruling council, and John desperately wanted more influence over their deliberations.

"Is it really necessary to visit him weekly?" he asked.

"No, but it does provide a break in the monotony."

His eyes flashed. "I'm sure you could find some other way to entertain yourself."

"Not while I'm stuck living in this outdated mausoleum."

"Are you suggesting that we should give up a furnished mansion just to go find a more modern place to live?"

"Of course not. But you could put some effort into modernizing it. Little things like running the electricity through the entire house would go a long way."

"I prefer it this way. It's what I'm used to."

She clenched her hands but kept her voice level. "You're not the only one who lives here. For now, at least."

"Thinking of moving out? You seem to be forgetting the little fact that I made you, and am mated to you, which gives me certain rights—"

"Only so long as you're animate," she answered viciously.

"Trying to eliminate me again? That makes the second time this week."

She relented slightly at the obvious hurt in his voice. "No, but you really need to drop the medieval ownership garbage. It doesn't sit well in the twenty-first century."

He sighed. "So why do you say things to set me off?"

"Because you started flinging accusations at my head the second I walked in the door. I'm sorry that you don't like me visiting Stefan, but you and I both know that it would be extremely unwise for me to irritate him while you're running a subversive political group out of the ballroom and trying to learn a controlled spell without permission."

"Does he really require so much of your company to keep him happy?"

"No, what makes him happy is the knowledge that it's driving you crazy. I've no doubt that's why he called."

"Do you mean that he summoned you to his apartment?"

She had become extremely interested in a potted plant and addressed her response to it directly. "He called a few days ago. I didn't want to go too long without responding."

John crossed in front of the French doors and took both of her hands in his. "I appreciate the thought, love, but I don't think you need to be *quite* so accommodating. Besides, he doesn't know about the 'subversive' group, as you call it."

She pulled gently away. "Don't bet your fortune on it," she advised.

"And speaking of the spell, it's going far better than I had expected," he said cheerfully.

She spun around to look at him. "Have you figured out how to work it, then?"

He laughed. "I said it was going better than expected, not that there'd been a miracle. No, I can't work it yet. But I separated it into its basic components, and I've nearly mastered all of the pieces."

"Oh. That's good, then." She leaned wearily against the wall. "I think your idea about hunting was a good one. I can't seem to remember the last time I fed. I'm starting to feel a bit lethargic."

"I think it was Wednesday. You should look after yourself better."

She ran her hands through her hair. "Other things to think about, I guess. I shouldn't be gone long."

9

Renphor pulled up a chair in front of the desk and eyed the computer hostilely. It would be necessary for him to find information about John's mate without going through his regular sources if he was going to avoid attracting attention to what he was doing. He had considered various methods of getting what he wanted but had finally come to the inescapable conclusion that he was going to be forced to look for information online. He was proficient enough on the computer itself but viewed the internet with a vague horror. He was appalled by the idea that anyone could put anything online, true or false, and make it available to the entire world with a few clicks on the keyboard. Even so, he had picked up a fair amount of information about the internet from his classmates. He hoped it would be enough to execute a successful online search.

He decided to try the experiment at the public library rather than using the one at the university. Classes had barely started, and he was already annoyed with the behavior of the other undergraduates. Besides, he would rather make a fool of himself here than do it in front of some pimpled lab tech who he might run into on campus later.

It was around seven o'clock on a Monday night when he found himself staring at the screen, pondering where to start. He ran his tongue across his top teeth, clicking it in irritation over his lack of fangs. He made a habit of shielding them when he went out in public to avoid attracting attention, but he always found it vaguely unsettling to be without them. After a few minutes, he found a promising-looking icon and clicked it. The page that came up seemed to contain hundreds of lines of unrelated information. He began clicking on various links, trying to get a feel for what he was doing, but just when he had finally gotten the hang of it and was about to start his research in earnest, the librarian walked up to tell him that they were closing in ten minutes. Irritated, he turned off the computer and left without getting any information.

The next day, he showed up as soon as the library opened to continue his search. He was moving more quickly this time, but he soon realized that he was looking for a needle in a haystack. Searches for John Elder had brought up information on an author, an eighteenth-century English architect, several professional businesses, and even an Irish cricket player but had not given him any information about the man he was trying to research. His searches for Julie had been even more useless, bringing up only a few businesses and some links to social networking sites. He had been hoping to find some reference to activities that she might participate in without her mate. Possibly newsletters, or even some link to her daughter—but he had drawn a complete blank. After four hours of getting nowhere, he leaned back in the chair, running his hands through his hair and staring at the screen in front of him. Shutting down the computer, he left the library and searched out a bench where he could sit and think.

It was a particularly nice day for early September—sunny with a slight breeze, and without the extreme humidity that the city had been suffering under all summer. Renphor had never really adapted to weather in the western hemisphere, even though he had left England nearly two hundred years before. He sat on the bench for an hour, enjoying the sun and trying to clear his head. He had not completely wasted his morning with his fruitless search for John Elder's mate. His newly acquired skill with search engines had allowed him to dig up several sources of used textbooks that were far cheaper than what he normally paid, so he would be able to save a significant amount of money the following semester.

Shortly after he sat down, he noticed a man behaving strangely on the other side of the street. He was part of a couple sitting on a bench, and he was waving both arms wildly in the air. It took Renphor a few minutes to realize that the man was attempting to get his attention. Looking more closely, he realized it was the redhaired man he had met at Stefan's apartment. Sighing, he crossed the street to greet his new acquaintance. He perked up as he approached the bench and recognized his companion.

"Ariliana, my lovely. So nice to see you again." He kissed her hand before propping himself against the bench.

The dark-haired beauty laughed. She started to speak, but he silenced her with a look. Turning to the man, he put out his hand.

"I don't believe Stefan introduced us properly. I'm Ryan." Ariliana looked quickly up at him but remained silent.

The man shifted slightly on the bench to shake hands with Renphor. "Nelson Davies. Do you always fight with Stefan like that?"

Renphor laughed. "Frequently. We get on each other's nerves."

Davies shuddered. "You're braver than I am. Last time I annoyed him, he blasted me across the room."

"We've known each other for a few centuries. I shouldn't have acted like that in front of a witness, though. I don't doubt I'll pay for it somehow down the road."

Ariliana sat stock-still on the bench, listening to the conversation, until Davies addressed her directly.

"So you two know each other, do you?"

She spoke at last. "*Ryan* knows most of the vampiresses in the city. Don't you?"

"Only the attractive ones." He grinned.

Davies looked from one to the other. "Not honing in on your territory, am I?" he asked Renphor.

"No. I don't have territory. She does what she likes, as do I. Now, if you'll excuse me, I have a few things to take care of this afternoon."

He bowed slightly to both of them and walked off in the direction of Market Street.

Ariliana caught up with him five minutes later.

"Okay, Ren, what the hell was that about?"

"What?"

She frowned at him. "Cut the sweet and innocent look. I know you better than that. You wouldn't cross the street to talk to someone like Davies without a very good reason, and you definitely wouldn't use a fake name unless you're up to something."

Renphor smiled. "Nothing new for you, I'm afraid. He's one of Elder's satellites. He's absolutely no use to me if he knows who I am. Out of curiosity, what does he have to offer you? Seems a bit of an idiot."

"He's more than a bit of an idiot. But he happens to be a rich idiot, and the last guy who was paying my rent ran off to Italy for some reason."

"I can't imagine why you bother with me."

"Connections," she answered. "And you're good in bed."

"Thank you. Care to help me out a bit with the idiot?"

She eyed him speculatively. "What's in it for me?"

He looked bored. "The aforementioned—status and sex. Were you expecting more?"

"Not really. You're a pain in the ass, Ren. What do you want?"

"Information. As much as you can get about Elder. Security. Social circle. Social calendar. Whatever."

"Why the sudden interest in Elder? I thought that feud died down a century ago."

"I have my reasons. Will you do it?"

She sighed. "I guess so. I'll call you when I have anything."

10

Julie crossed in front of John's worktable, eyeing the parchment as she went. She looked quickly around to see if Joseph was lurking anywhere before circling around to the chair and settling down in it. She pulled the top page closer to her and maneuvered the candelabra so that it cast as much light as possible on the parchment. She couldn't read Aramaic, so the written instructions told her nothing, but she studied the intricate diagrams with interest. She was able to pick out several steps that seemed to belong to simpler spells that were within even her limited capabilities. She was helped along by the slanted English comments scrawled along the side of each of the pages, which gave her some clue as to the contents of the more complete instructions. She studied them with interest—they seemed to be notations made by a previous owner of the parchment. It certainly wasn't John's writing. There were four large pieces of parchment, and she spent two hours going slowly through each of them. At the end of the fourth page, she paused with a puzzled expression on her face and began slowly going back through it all again. She finally laid the third and fourth pages side by side and then overlapped them so that she could read the notes in the margins as one continuous thought.

Half an hour later, John came into the room to find her sitting upright in the high-backed wooden chair, staring into space. She didn't notice him until he was standing next to her.

His appearance startled her so much she nearly toppled out of her seat.

"John!"

His eyes narrowed as he looked from her to the diagram in front of her.

"Interested after all?" he asked coldly.

She shrugged. "Thought there must be something extremely fascinating about it."

"You don't know Aramaic." He rolled the parchment up as he spoke.

"No, but the notes in the margins are in English."

John sneered. "What good does that do you? There's nothing particularly perceptive about them."

"I realize that, but they do help for someone who can't read the actual document. And besides—"

He cut her off with a wave. "I don't have time to spend on the observations of someone who was obviously having trouble understanding what he was looking at. It's the substance on the pages that's important."

"Yes, I understand that no one is going to figure out how to work it based on those notes—they're really just a summary. But, John—"

He walked away without letting her finish the sentence. She stared after him for a few minutes before announcing that she would be in her sitting room if he wanted her.

Taking the seat his mate had recently vacated, John sat for a few minutes, staring into the candle flames. Finally, he stood up and walked to the fireplace to pull a heavy cord that hung from the ceiling next to it. Joseph immediately appeared in the doorway.

"Joseph, I want the car."

The servant bowed and left the room without a word.

Half an hour later, he was walking up the marble spiral staircase to Stefan's apartment, behind the efficient manservant, Robert.

His host smiled silkily at John as he entered the room.

"John—I had no idea I was to have the pleasure this evening. To what do I owe the honor?"

John bowed. "Does there have to be a specific reason? Julie isn't very good company this evening."

The smile widened. "Odd. She's always excellent company when she visits me."

John gritted his teeth but ignored the insinuation.

"What do you want, John? I'm not fool enough to think you came here for a social call." Stefan pulled open the drawer of a small end table and removed a deck of cards. Tossing it carelessly on the table in the center of the room, he seated himself in one of the adjacent chairs. "Piquet?" he asked.

"If you like."

"What shall we play for?"

"Information."

Stefan paused in the act of shuffling the cards. "About anything in particular?"

John smiled. "The fire vortex. Renphor's whereabouts. My mate's activities when I'm not with her. Take your pick."

Stefan sneered. "Not well thought out, John. I'll take number three. And it won't do you a bit of good."

John leaned forward. "What has she been up to?"

Stefan smirked. "You haven't won yet."

They played in silence for several hours. At the end of this time, John had not won a single round, and his frustration was boiling over. It was now three in the morning, and Stefan laid his cards on the table and declared himself done playing for the evening. John leaned back, staring at his host through half-closed lids.

"I don't suppose you ever intended to give me any information, did you?"

Stefan smiled unpleasantly. "I never gratuitously give out information, John. I merely collect it until it can be of use to me. Advice is still free, however. On the fire vortex—give it up. You haven't the power to operate it effectively, and if your execution is less than perfect, you'll do more harm to yourself than you will to your opponent. While you're at it, give up on Renphor. He's stronger than you, his sources of information are more...reliable, and he's infinitely more adaptable. And you might want to stop stalking your own mate. All it accomplishes is her annoyance."

John slammed the chair back so hard that it teetered on two slender legs before settling back down on the floor. "Thank you for the advice. I hope you won't be offended if I don't follow it."

"No. I won't even be surprised. Good night, John."

Stefan watched as John marched stiffly out of the room. Smiling to himself, he reached under the table, pulled out two cards, and added them back into the deck.

An hour later, a soft knock sounded on the door of Julie's sitting room.

"Come in."

She laid the magazine she had been reading on an end table as she spoke. John opened the door a crack and slid in.

"Julie..."

She glared at him.

"Sorry if I've been a bit obsessive lately."

"A bit?"

"Look, if I could just—"

"John, give it up. Seriously. Please."

He frowned at her. "Why?"

She stared out the window. After a few minutes, he turned to leave, but she called him back.

"He's stronger than you, John. Are you really prepared to sacrifice everything over something that happened four hundred years ago?"

John stared at her, his mouth slightly open. "You really think I should just let it drop, don't you?"

She closed her eyes. "Yes. A forlorn hope, I'm sure."

John walked slowly around to a chair facing his mate and sat down. He weighed his words carefully before speaking. "Julie, I understand why you're worried, but I swear I'm keeping your safety foremost in my mind. I'm not about to sacrifice what I have now over revenge for what I lost. But I owe them something, too. Can't you understand that?"

"Did you get anywhere with Stefan?"

John grimaced. "No. I don't know why I bothered, to be honest."

She traced a pattern on the table between them with her finger to avoid meeting his eyes. "You said you'd invite me to the next meeting. When is it?"

"We have one tonight, actually. In the ballroom, at eleven. Will you come?" There was more enthusiasm in his voice than she had heard in days. Since she couldn't bring herself to mirror it, she simply nodded as her finger continued its steady progress around the table.

11

The three girls giggled as the bartender passed their beers across the bar with a wink. He had thrown three other underage girls out right before they walked in, but Arabella had looked at him under her eyelashes and claimed to have lost her ID, and he had served her without question. She thanked him and slid off the barstool, and the girls headed toward the back, away from the bouncer, so as not to encourage him to come to his senses and throw them out.

"Arabella, I wish I'd known you three years ago." The girl in the middle grinned at her roommate. Her gray eyes danced with glee as she smiled at the beer in her hand. Of the three girls, she was the one who looked older than twenty-one. Her spiky black hair accentuated her already angular features, and that combined with her height generally made her look older than she was.

"Why?" Arabella looked at her innocently.

Sam grinned. "One look at you and that bouncer didn't even bother to ask for my or Cissy's IDs. You're like a skeleton key to drinking establishments."

Arabella laughed. She wasn't as tall as her roommate, but the combination of thick, naturally wavy brown hair that fell halfway down her back, a perfect figure, and ocean-blue eyes caused heads to turn wherever she went. She sat down in a corner with her back to the next table, and Sam took the seat opposite her. Arabella sipped her beer and determinedly ignored the three men at the next table, who hadn't taken their eyes off her since she'd sat down. Sam rolled her eyes in their direction but said nothing.

Their third companion flopped into the chair between the two. "Well, Ella, looks like you've found yet another group of admirers." She gritted her teeth as she cast a sidelong glance at the next table. Narcissa was loud and flirtatious, and she received a fair amount of attention when she wasn't with Arabella. She leaned to her left and said in a low voice, "Sam, do we always have to bring her out with us?"

Sam shot back, "What's the matter, Cissy, are you jealous?"

Narcissa laughed derisively. "No, but I get tired of her attitude."

"Her attitude? You're tired of not getting any attention. Look at it this way—you talk to way more guys with her around. Most of them don't have the nerve to start a conversation with Ella."

Narcissa pouted. "Like I'd want her sloppy seconds."

Arabella had been hunting through her purse for her wallet during this interchange. She accidentally glanced in the direction of the next table and quickly looked away again.

"I suppose you aren't going to give them the time of day, either. It's a complete waste of time introducing you to men. You never do anything with them." Narcissa took an angry slurp of beer.

"What would you like me to do with them?" Arabella asked. Sam choked on her drink.

"You could try sleeping with one or two of them. Or is Miss Pristine too good for that?" Narcissa wasn't a regular drinker, and the small amount of alcohol she had consumed had already loosened her tongue.

Arabella blushed. "Really, Narcissa. You act like I'm weird for not sleeping with every guy who buys me a drink. I'd be the campus slut!"

"Instead of the only virgin on campus," Narcissa retorted.

Arabella slammed her beer on the table. "So what do you want me to do? Take up with the next reasonably attractive guy that I find on the street?"

The three men at the next table looked hopefully at her.

Sam tried to calm her friend down, but Narcissa jumped in. "Why don't you? First guy we see when we walk out of this bar, you promise to sleep with by the end of the day tomorrow."

The men shifted at the table, as if planning to make a hasty exit. They received a look from Sam that caused them to sit back down in a hurry.

Arabella glared at Narcissa. "Fine. As long as he's single, I will."

Sam stammered slightly as she spoke. "Ella, you're not serious?"

"Yes, I am. I'm tired of her jabs about me being an iceberg. Now, I'm leaving. You can come with or not. I'm not in the mood anymore." Arabella stood up quickly, knocking her chair over in the process. Sam leaned over to pick it up as Arabella stormed out of the bar. She abandoned her drink and quickly followed her roommate.

"Can we at least agree on some parameters for this, Arabella? I mean, you can't just go around picking up any guy..." She trailed behind her friend as she spoke.

"I already gave you the parameters. First guy..." She stopped in the middle of the sidewalk, staring at a bench fifty feet in front of them. "There you go. Ryan Callaghan."

Sam's mouth fell open. "No. Fucking. Way."

Arabella stared at her. "Why not? He's not bad looking, and he doesn't spend half his life being drunk and stupid like a lot of guys do."

"True, but he's also a complete weirdo. I don't trust him."

Arabella shrugged. "See you back at the apartment." She walked toward the bench.

F. Anne Fischer

Sam started to go after her, but Narcissa, who had come out of the bar shortly after them, dragged her down the street in the opposite direction.

▼▼▼

Renphor was lounging on the bench reading a copy of *Canterbury Tales* under the light of a streetlamp when Arabella flopped down next to him.

"Hi, Ryan."

"Hello." He continued to read as he spoke.

"Must be an interesting book."

"It is." He finally looked up and completely forgot about the book, which fell out of his hand. "Arabella, right?"

Arabella giggled. "You dropped your book. And you look like you've just seen a ghost."

Renphor ignored the book, deeming it irrelevant. "I'm not convinced that I haven't. What are you doing down here by yourself at night?"

"My roommates are jerks. Aren't you in my English Lit class?"

"Um, yeah." He glanced at the book on the ground. "I take it you haven't started the reading list yet."

"Oh, is that one of them?" She looked at him guiltily. "Actually, I haven't even looked at the list yet. I can never seem to get motivated until I'm forced to..." She trailed off.

A smile crept onto Renphor's face. "Tell you what. I've finished most of them. You meet me for coffee tomorrow night at the Griffon, and I'll give you all the information you need."

"Would you really?" She beamed at him. "That would make the first week back so much better."

"I'd be delighted. Nine o'clock?"

"Sure."

She got up to go, but a mischievous grin appeared on her face. Before he realized what she was going to do, she leaned

56

over and gave him a quick kiss. "Thanks again!" she said and ran down the street toward the entrance to the bar.

Renphor stared after her for a long while before picking the book back up off the ground and hunting for his page.

He finally gave up on his reading at around one in the morning. He packed up his books thoughtfully, occasionally glancing down the street in the direction Arabella had gone. Once he had everything safely stowed in his bag, he stood, stretched, and looked cautiously around him. There was absolutely no one on the street at this hour on a Thursday morning. He jerked to the side and a moment later was standing in front of the bookshelf in his room. Pulling the books from his bag, he stuffed them onto the shelf, pausing with his hand resting on the folder of information about Larch Hill that he had stowed there for safekeeping. He was about to pull it off the shelf when his phone rang.

"What?"

A sultry voice answered on the other end. "Do you ever bother to be polite?" Ariliana asked.

"Rarely. What's up?"

"I have some information for you. Nelson is about as dumb as a person can get."

"No surprises there. What have you got?"

Ariliana started off explaining about the protections surrounding the house, but Renphor cut her off.

"I got most of that myself from Davies. Did you get anything more about his personal life?"

She was silent for a moment, and when she spoke again there was a definite edge to her voice. "I'm not sure why you bothered with me, if you were doing so well on your own."

"Cut the crap, Rilla. I don't have time for you to get into a snit. I have things to do tonight and I haven't fed yet."

She went on, somewhat sulkily, to explain all the information she had managed to obtain about John's family. There wasn't much that he hadn't already gotten. Nelson did not know the name of John's stepdaughter, but even though the information he had provided didn't seem like much, it seemed to satisfy Renphor. He was smiling broadly as he hung up the phone.

12

Julie wandered into the grand ballroom at ten thirty that night and watched curiously as Joseph set up chairs for the guests. They were the only furniture in the room and looked rather forlorn sitting alone in the center of the massive space. An ornate high-backed chair that reminded Julie of a throne sat in the middle of the room. A smaller one sat next to it. As she watched, the servant pulled four more chairs around the first two. She grimaced at the sight of them. All were upright, wooden, carved to within an inch of their lives, and upholstered in a hideous chintz fabric that gave her the strong impression that someone had thrown a handful of bluebirds at a clump of azaleas.

John joined her ten minutes later. She had gotten bored with watching the setup by then and stood staring out of the window at the heavily wooded property below. He walked softly up behind her and put his arm around her waist.

"Something interesting?"

She shook her head. "You could do so much more with this property."

"I thought you liked the wilderness."

"To a point."

She walked away from the window and sat down next to the throne. John took his seat beside her.

"So when do they arrive?"

"Any minute now."

Within moments, Nelson shuffled in and headed for the seat furthest from John. He noticed Julie when he was halfway to his seat and stopped to stare at her with his head to one side.

John beckoned him to a chair. "Hello, Nelson. You've met my mate."

Light seemed to dawn on Nelson. He loped over and shook Julie's hand vigorously before arranging his spidery form in the chair next to her. He was followed shortly by a married couple named David and Jennifer Edwards, who pushed the two chairs across from him closer together before sitting down in them with their hands clasped. Julie looked at the empty chair.

"Who's still missing?" Julie asked.

John looked around. "Stella."

Julie grimaced, but since Stella chose that instant to make an entrance, John wasn't looking at her.

Nelson and David also stopped midconversation to stare at Stella, and even Julie had to admit to herself that the creature wafting across the ballroom was stunningly beautiful. She had blond hair framing a heart-shaped face, and deep blue eyes. Julie was certain that she would have had a perfect rosy complexion while alive, but her extreme pallor did not detract from her looks. She watched irritably as Stella sank dramatically into a chair. She was tempted to toss a sarcastic comment in the woman's direction, but she was diverted from this purpose by Nelson's reaction to the new arrival. She watched in amusement as he spent several minutes trying to surreptitiously shift his chair so that he would be facing more toward Stella than his host. Since simply turning the chair would be too obvious, he tried lifting it up and turning it slightly every time John looked at one of the other guests. On the final attempt, one of the legs caught before the others, and the chair made a telltale crunching noise. Julie looked down quickly to hide a giggle.

"Now that everyone is … situated,"—John glared at Nelson, who looked at his knees—"we can start. I know that several of you have other ideas and agenda items, but I'd like to start with Renphor and cover the rest of it next week."

Jennifer started to protest, but he cut her off with a wave of his hand and continued, "We're farthest along on that, so I'd like to keep it moving. I already have a network of friends who give me any information that they get about him, because they know that I want it for personal reasons. If I start questioning them about other things, they might get wind of what we're really doing. Destroying him would be a coup that could bring some of the power seekers over to our camp, without tipping our hand too soon."

Jennifer compressed her lips but nodded agreement, and John went on. "We still need to get a better lead on someone who knows Renphor well. Ideas?"

Everyone stared at each other for a few moments without speaking. David finally broke the silence by clearing his throat. John turned his head to look at him. "David?"

"I feel sort of dumb bringing this up now, but, um…"

"Go on."

"Are Jennifer and I the only ones here who have no idea what Renphor looks like? I mean, I could be sitting next to him on the train every morning and not know it."

"Are there a lot of vampires on your train?" Julie asked innocently.

"None, but—"

John gave his mate an annoyed look and cut David off. "Do the rest of you know what he looks like?"

Nelson and Stella shook their heads. He looked at his mate, who shrugged.

"Not a clue, John. None of the stories you've told me included a description."

John leaned back in his chair, drumming his fingers on the arm.

"Okay, here goes. Renphor is fairly short, by modern standards. He looks like a very young man. Blond hair."

"Eyes?" Nelson had pulled out a notebook and was scribbling down everything John said.

"Anytime I've seen him, they've been blazing red. I honestly don't know what they look like when he's not angry, or when he's shielded," John admitted.

"Any idea how he dresses?" Julie asked.

John shook his head. "It's been a hundred years or so since I saw him."

"Do you have a picture?" Jennifer asked.

Everyone stared at her. John gritted his teeth.

"No. He hasn't been in the frame of mind to pose for one on the few occasions that we've met."

"It's a good point, though." David came to his wife's defense. "Maybe there are some in general circulation."

"I'll put the two of you on that. See if you can come up with one."

David and Jennifer nodded.

"Nelson? Ideas?"

Nelson took a while to respond. "I could check the phone book."

"How about asking some of your friends?" John suggested and moved on to Stella.

"I might give Stefan a try," she suggested.

John avoided his mate's gaze and nodded. "Worth a try."

Julie didn't quite manage to hide a snort. The rest stared at her.

"Sorry. Swallowed a bug."

Jennifer's eyes got bigger. "Eww. Gross."

Once everyone had their assignments, the meeting broke up quickly. By eleven thirty, Julie and John were once again alone in the ballroom. John had returned to his chair to think, but Julie walked slowly around the room, running her hand across dust-coated mirrors.

"Why did you build this room, anyway?" she asked.

"Because it was there in the original."

She looked curiously at him for a minute before coming back to the chair next to him.

"What do you mean?"

He jerked his hand around, indicating the house in general. "This entire place is an exact replica of my English estate. I even kept the name. Sentimental nonsense, but I wasn't really thrilled about leaving all of it behind."

It was unusual for John to be so expansive about his past, and Julie decided to seize the opportunity. "So why did you?" she asked.

"The locals were starting to develop strong superstitions about the place. No confirmed news of births, deaths, or marriages in two hundred years. Sightings of the occupants—maybe once in a generation. I played myself off as my own heirs for a while, but no one's descendants look that similar after that many years."

"I would think you'd have the same problem here," she said.

He stood suddenly and walked to the window, staring out into the woods. "I'm nobody here."

She followed him to the window. "So this place is an exact replica?"

"Not exact. The original wasn't walled in like this one. It was a necessary precaution to keep my human neighbors from running smack into visiting friends. Since I was planning to make this my permanent home, I didn't want that kind of attention on the place."

Julie suddenly waltzed across the room and twirled herself around the chairs still set up in the center. John stared at her, his mouth hanging slightly open, before starting to laugh.

"What are you doing?" he asked.

"We have a ballroom—might as well use it." She continued her solo dance for a few more steps before he joined her. She laughed as he spun her quickly around before dipping her almost to the floor.

13

At eight o'clock the following evening, Arabella found herself staring into her closet and not coming up with anything. Sam leaned against the door frame.

"What do you wear to seduce a guy?" Arabella asked.

"Personally, I don't. But in your case probably anything you want," Sam answered.

"Be serious, Sam. What the hell am I supposed to wear? And why on earth did I agree to meet him at the Griffon? Everyone I know will be there!" She dragged three shirts out of the closet and flung them on the bed as she spoke.

"Couldn't think of anything else on the spot?" Sam suggested.

"I could've thought of something this morning. He stopped me on the way out of Lit to confirm our plans. I could've asked him to change the place. What do you think of this?" She held up a black top with a V-neck.

"I think you would look stunning, as usual. And I also think that it won't advertise your intentions to the entire café, which is probably a good thing."

"Right." Arabella pulled on the top and a pair of jeans and headed to the bathroom to fix her hair and put on enough makeup to look like she wasn't wearing any. "Where's Narcissa?"

Sam muttered something to herself.

"What was that?"

"No idea where she is," Sam answered aloud. "Should I walk you down?"

"Could you? Then if he doesn't show…"

"What are the odds?"

Arabella laughed at this. "Probably slim. He seemed pretty into the idea."

They walked down to the coffeehouse and got to the door just as Renphor arrived from the other direction. He looked curiously at Sam, who said quickly, "Don't worry, I'm not staying. I'm just her escort as far as the door." She was already walking away as she spoke. Renphor pulled Arabella's hand through his arm. She looked quickly at him, startled.

"You did kiss me last night. I figured that meant this counted as a date." He smiled at her.

She blushed. "Of course it does," she responded as they walked into the café.

They stopped just inside the door and looked around for a table. The place was packed and extremely noisy. Arabella started to fidget as she realized that a heavy silence had started at the tables around the door and was slowly spreading through the room as people noticed her and Renphor standing by the door. She made a valiant attempt to act like she didn't notice but shifted nervously from one foot to the other. She glanced sideways at Renphor and was startled to see that he seemed completely unfazed by the attention.

They found a table in the back of the room. Renphor flopped into the chair and stretched his legs out along the wall. Arabella sat bolt upright, fidgeting with the spoon on the table in front of her until the waitress came over.

"What can I get for the two of you?"

"Just a decaf coffee. No cream," Arabella said.

The waitress looked at Renphor.

"Water."

She blinked at him but jotted it on her pad before walking away. Arabella looked at him curiously.

"Do you always order water at a coffeehouse?" she asked.

"I always order water everywhere."

"Why?"

"I have some weird dietary restrictions. It's just easier not to eat anywhere but home."

"Is that why you're so pale?" Her eyes widened as she realized he might take offense to the comment, but he laughed.

"Part of the reason, yes."

She relapsed into silence, trying to think of another conversation starter.

After a few minutes, Renphor said. "So, are we going to talk English Lit or sit and stare at each other?"

She jumped. "Sorry, I forgot about that for a second."

He leaned toward her. "It wasn't meant as a reminder. I'm perfectly okay with either suggestion."

"Wouldn't it get boring after a while?"

"Maybe for you."

She tried to respond but ended up tripping over everything that came out of her mouth. He finally took pity on her and pulled a book out of his backpack.

They sat for the next two hours going over the booklist. Renphor flirted outrageously with her the whole evening. She didn't know how to respond at first but eventually got her footing and even started to respond in kind. He seemed cheerfully oblivious to several very dirty looks he received from neighboring tables when Arabella giggled at his more pointed comments. They finally got to the end of the list a little after eleven.

"So, should we call it a night?" he asked.

She considered him for a moment. "Are you going to walk me home?"

He raised his eyebrows at this. "I wasn't intending to let you walk alone at this hour."

"In that case, let's get going." She jumped up from the table and grabbed his hand, half pulling him out of the café. He stopped her on the sidewalk.

"In a hurry to get somewhere?"

She nodded.

"Why?"

"Because the coffee shop is so public." She blurted out. Realizing how this must have sounded, she blushed and quickly added, "Not that I don't want to be seen with you, but it does hinder…um…other things." Arabella's face was fiery red by this point. She looked at the sidewalk and then became fascinated by a streetlamp.

"Where do you live?"

She glanced at him. He looked perfectly grave, but she had the impression that he was laughing at her all the same.

"Six blocks that way." She pointed in the direction of her apartment. "You don't live on campus, do you?"

"No." He turned left and started walking slowly in the direction she had said she lived.

"Do you live with your parents?"

He smiled slightly. "That would be rather difficult. My mother died when I was seven. Never knew my father."

"Oh. I'm sorry, I didn't mean to—"

"It was a very long time ago."

"You're older than most of the other students here, aren't you?"

He nodded. "I'm…twenty-four."

She slid her hand into his as they walked, and his fingers wrapped around hers. She couldn't think of much else to say for several minutes, until a thought suddenly occurred to her. "How do you pay for off-campus housing? I mean, if you don't have anyone to help you…" She stopped abruptly. "I keep putting my foot in it, don't I?"

"I don't mind. I work about twenty hours a week in the rare books library, which brings in a little bit, plus a couple of scholarships. I have an extremely cheap room in another part of the city."

"Where?"

"No place you're likely to have been. Not a particularly good neighborhood, but it works for me."

"Aren't you afraid you'll get mugged?"

He laughed. "They tried—twice. They got two dollars in change and a pocket dictionary. Gave up after that."

Her curiosity was starting to overcome her embarrassment, and her date didn't seem to mind the very personal nature of her questions. "It still seems crazy to me. Even if the room is cheap, you still have to pay for food and stuff."

"I have very few expenses."

She suddenly stopped and laughed.

"What's so funny?"

"We've walked right past my apartment." She giggled again.

"Which one?"

She pointed halfway up the block they had just walked through, and they turned and retraced their steps to her front door. She fumbled a bit with the lock but managed to get it open on the second try. He looked questioningly at her as she opened the door.

"Can you come in for a bit?" she asked shyly.

"I haven't anyplace more interesting to be," he responded.

She turned on the light when she walked in and looked around. The apartment seemed to be empty. Both of her room-mates had left the doors to their rooms open, and it was obvious that they hadn't come home yet. She wondered if they had gone out someplace together but doubted it after the fight she had overheard that morning. Sam was still furious with Narcissa over the scene in the bar the night before.

He interrupted her thoughts. "So, what are we doing here?"

"I want to ask you something about a...thing...I'm work-ing on." She led him back to her room, which was down a short hallway, away from the other two.

"So how do you get the master suite?" he asked. Her room was not only the largest but had a private bathroom as well.

"My stepfather pays about two-thirds of the rent," she answered.

"Stepfather?"

"Well, sort of. He and Mom aren't actually married. But we've lived with him since my father died eighteen years ago."

"So I take it he and your mother knew each other beforehand."

"Apparently they met before I was born. Mom wouldn't give him the time of day while she was married to my dad, but after the accident..." She shrugged.

He smiled at her as she stretched out on the bed. "It's good that she was able to find some happiness after the tragedy."

"Maybe. I don't know. She likes him well enough, I guess, but he's definitely more into her than she's into him. I don't think she's ever gotten over my father, frankly."

He lay down on the bed next to her. "So, what are we doing here again?"

She smiled mischievously. "An experiment."

"Oh? Of what variety?"

Arabella could feel the blood rushing to her face again. She mumbled a few disjointed words and became very interested in the books on the shelf behind his right shoulder. Renphor put one finger under her chin and turned her face toward him. He kissed her lightly at first, then, as she didn't resist, he pressed himself into her and pushed her back onto the bed.

She tensed as he pressed on top of her, and he pulled back slightly. She smiled and wrapped her arms around him, pulling him tightly against her. He slid both his hands under her shirt and pulled it off over her head, then moved his hand down to the button of her jeans.

Renphor got home around six o'clock the next morning. He had taken his time coming back, enjoying a long walk through the deserted city streets before jumping himself back to his room. He looked around with a slightly disgusted expression on his face. There was a faint aroma of something very nasty that seemed to be seeping through the walls from the room next door. One of these days he would have to go over there and figure out what was going on. He could get rid of the tenants if he had to, but there was always the risk that the replacements would be even worse. He flopped down on the chair, which protested but held firm, and started shifting some papers around on his desk. Half an hour later, he was still sitting there, staring at the far wall as he idly switched the desk lamp on and off. There was a sudden noise on the fire escape, which caused him to turn quickly toward the window. He smiled to see Ariliana climbing over the window ledge.

"Rilla. How lovely to see you."

She returned the smile, but hers seemed a little forced. "Apparently I'm lucky to catch you in. I'll never understand why you spend so much time at that school."

"For several reasons. But we've been over this."

She moved toward him. "So did I waste my time?"

He finally gave up on the lamp and stood to face her. "No. My evening was interesting, but not entirely satisfying. I could use some supplemental entertainment."

She laughed. It was a deep, melodious sound.

"So where were you that was so unsatisfying?"

"Up to my own devices."

"Who is she?"

"Jealous? No one you would know."

Her eyes narrowed. She moved closer to him but stopped dead a foot away as she caught the scent on his clothing.

"Human. Why on earth would you want to do a thing like that?" she sneered.

He shrugged. "I generally take what's offered."

She smirked. "Where did you leave the body?"

"Who says there was one?" He smiled at the startled expression on her face. "Too beautiful to get rid of. Besides, she is young enough and intelligent enough to have some potential. I'm sure I can find a good use for her."

A spark of annoyance showed on her face. "If that's the kind of help you're looking for—"

He cut her off. "I'm not in the mood for drama, Rilla. Get over it or get out."

"You're such a sweet companion, Ren. And here I was being nice enough to drop by to tell you all about my evening with Nelson."

He looked up quickly. "Did you get anything new?"

"Not much," she admitted. "John's up to something, but idiot boy started going on about you and I couldn't get him back on track. Seems to have gotten the idea that you're the root of all evil."

He laughed loudly at that. "Don't tell me you disagree?"

"I do. I can think of several other people who work much harder at it. I won't even mess with you by telling you the physical description he gave me."

There was a gleam in his eyes now. "Torture, Rilla. You must tell me what description John has passed on to his minions."

"Curiosity killed the cat, Ren. Let's just say they're never going to pick you out of a crowd." She dodged the hand that he had put out to grab her.

He grinned and leaned against the wall, watching her. "Did Davies have anything else of interest?"

"Not really. He went on a bit more about John's genius in protecting the place. Apparently it's a small fortress. Really medieval stuff."

"He's a bit young to be medieval. That's more my era. Victorian, more like. Although he's too old for that. Perhaps he's just an ass?"

Ariliana laughed. "You're impossible. Are you really medieval?"

"Mm-hmm. John isn't, though. Early sixteen hundreds. Anything else?"

She shook her head.

"It'll do for now. Now, come here." He put out his hand. She started to drift seductively toward him but gasped in shock when she suddenly landed on the mattress with him on top of her.

"Christ, you can move fast."

He smiled. "When I feel like it."

14

Sam always got up earlier than her roommates, so she generally took it on herself to make sure they both got to their morning classes on time. She started toward Narcissa's door first but changed her mind and veered off to the kitchen. She put together a quick breakfast, and after throwing coffee and eggs on a tray, she knocked softly on Arabella's door and went in.

"Good morning, princess."

Arabella rolled over and opened her eyes. She stared at the bed next to her. "I must have been out of my mind. And what are the chances that I'll ever see him again?"

Sam sat on the bed next to her. "Probably decent, since he's in one of your classes."

Arabella picked up a note that was lying on her nightstand and read it before handing it to Sam. "What do you make of this?"

Arabella—
Had to study for a test for my 8:30. Would much rather have stayed where I was. Please call me. 215-555-0143
R.

"I think he wants you to call him," Sam answered.

"Obviously. But for what?" Arabella picked at the eggs.

"Honestly? I think he really likes you."

"How do you figure?"

"Because there are no obnoxious 'thanks for the good time' comments anywhere on the thing."

Arabella had rediscovered her appetite and was shoveling the eggs into her mouth at high speed. Sam watched her in astonishment. "Worked up an appetite, did we?" Arabella choked on the last bit of egg. "Must've been some evening."

"It was." Arabella blushed but smiled at the same time.

"Glad to hear it. On a different topic, let's talk about the lovely Narcissa for a moment. If I know the little bitch at all, she's already been on the phone with half of her acquaintances, letting them know that you spent the night with Ryan Callaghan, of *all* people. This whole setup has been a plan to bring you down to the level of us mere mortals, and I'm afraid you've given her all the ammo she needs."

"How could she already have called people? She doesn't get up before seven."

"She didn't need to wait around to verify the results—all she needed was for him to be seen coming in here. So…get ready for the backlash, sweetie." Sam smiled tightly.

Arabella stopped in the middle of lifting the coffee cup to her mouth and set it slowly on the tray. "What do you think Ryan will do?"

"I don't know. Never talked to the guy before last night. Hopefully he's not your garden-variety asshole about the thing, but you can't count on that."

"I don't suppose I could just stay in the apartment all day." She sighed.

"Worst thing you could do. Not only confirms that you slept with him but broadcasts the fact that you're ashamed of it."

"I'm not, really."

"Good. Makes it easier to keep your chin up. Now get ready for your eight thirty."

Arabella started to get out of bed but stopped midway. "Oh God, he's in my ten fifteen!"

Sam laughed at the horrified look on her face. "I thought you liked the guy. I would think you'd be glad to see him."

Arabella stared at her, wide-eyed. "What am I going to say to him?"

"You seemed to be doing alright last night. I'm sure you'll think of something. Now get moving, or you'll be late for class."

Renphor had purposely stayed away from his room after leaving for his eight thirty class, just in case Ariliana decided to hang around and wait for him. He finished his exam early, so between nine thirty and ten fifteen, he found a bench in the middle of campus and parked himself on it with a book. He had been sitting there for about ten minutes when he looked up to see four burly men led by Rick Stevens, captain of the football team, approaching the bench. He rolled his eyes and kept reading. They stood towering over him, looking as mean as possible.

"Callaghan, I want a word with you," Stevens barked at him.

"Oh? And what do they want?" Renphor didn't look up from his book.

All four glared at him. "I heard a rumor about you and Arabella Flynn. Is it true?" Stevens's face was beginning to redden.

"Depends on what rumor you heard."

"I'm not going to repeat it! That girl belongs to me, and you better watch your back if you're going to go messing around with her."

Renphor laughed derisively. "Is she aware that you own her? Because she seemed to be under the impression that she was a free agent yesterday."

"We're not together yet. But everyone knows we will be."

Renphor finally lowered his book and regarded him coldly. "I see. And were you planning to let her in on this?"

Rick pointed his finger at Renphor. "Just what do you think you were doing at the Griffon last night?" he asked.

"I believe it's generally referred to as a date."

"And what about afterward?"

"Afterward?"

"Come off it, Callaghan. Three different people told me she invited you into her apartment. Did you sleep with her?"

Renphor stared at him, expressionless. "I believe that would be my business, Stevens. Now I suggest you and your little friends go entertain yourselves elsewhere and stop spreading garbage about a girl you claim to care about."

Rick stared back, but Renphor had picked up his book again. Rick sneered. "That answers that question, anyway. If you'd actually gotten to first base you'd be broadcasting it to the world." Renphor didn't answer, and all four of them walked away.

He lowered the book slightly to watch them go. The four men didn't look at him again, so they didn't see the faint red glow that had appeared at the back of his eyes.

15

John walked slowly along a small stream, using a stick to smack cattails out of the way as he went. This part of his property was the farthest point from the house, and he frequently came here when he wanted to think things over. The point where he stood was only about twenty-five feet from a heavily traveled road, but the property was elevated at this end, and the high stone wall that surrounded the estate was at least five feet thick. For someone facing away from the wall, it was as if you were standing in the middle of an extensive forest.

His thoughts were rudely interrupted by the sound of a male voice calling his name from about a hundred yards away. He turned to see David Edwards waving and walking in his direction. Sighing, he leaned against a nearby tree and watched David's approach.

"John. I had a heck of a time finding you. Julie was nowhere to be found, and all Joseph could say was that you were somewhere on the grounds. Tried the other direction first, but I ran smack into some kind of weird invisible wall."

"It's called a shield, David. It's for keeping out uninvited visitors."

"Oh. Well, anyway, I wanted to catch up with you about what everyone's been doing."

John looked mildly interested at that. "Walk with me," he said and started moving in the direction he had been traveling before the interruption.

David walked silently for several hundred feet before John finally got impatient and told him to get on with his story. David cleared his throat several times.

"Well, um, let's start with Stella." He looked at the treetops for inspiration and nearly tripped on a root as a result. When he managed to steady himself, he looked at John, who was waiting patiently for him to go on.

"She's certainly zealous. And you do have to give her credit for a certain amount of resourcefulness. I mean, it's been less than two weeks, and she's already gotten in to see Stefan." He cast a nervous glance in John's direction.

"And?"

"She thought things were going well. He seemed perfectly happy to entertain her all evening. What?" he asked in response to John's snort.

"Nothing. Continue."

"Anyway, she said they talked for a few hours. But as soon as she tried to turn the conversation around to Renphor, things got really ugly. He asked her if she thought he was a complete idiot, told her he was well aware that she was one of your satellites, and ended up ordering her out of his rooms with instructions never to come near him again."

David had said this last sentence all in one breath, and he still seemed to be holding on to the last of it while he waited for John's response. John scowled at the tree in front of him. "Apparently I should've asked Julie take that part of the assignment after all."

David blinked at him in surprise. "Julie? But how would she—"

"Stefan has a certain...fondness...for my mate. She could probably get the information out of him if she really wanted it, but she's a little resentful about the time that I devote to finding Renphor. What about the rest of you?"

"Well, Nelson is trying. He's had two fairly large parties and invited all sorts of wealthy, connected people. He's got enough money to pull that kind of thing off." John nodded, and David went on, "The problem is that he either doesn't know people with the right connections, or he had no idea how to go about the thing. He's gotten nothing—not so much as a single person who admits to knowing Renphor, let alone having any idea where he might be living."

By this point, they had reached the part of the pathway that ran into the shield David had discovered earlier in the day. John had no intention of giving the other man access to that part of his property, so he turned around and headed back in the direction they had come, with David trailing behind him.

"And what about your efforts?" John asked.

This time, David looked at a clump of weeds for inspiration. "Well, Jennifer and I ran into sort of the opposite problem from Nelson. We decided to hang out at one of the clubs downtown. Stefan's place, actually." He gulped a bit before going on. "The first guy we talked to apparently knows Renphor pretty well. The problem was that he also figured out pretty quickly that we're friends of yours. He got really annoyed about the whole thing. If he has a picture, he sure as hell won't give it to us."

John smacked viciously at a cattail, narrowly avoiding smacking David as well. David dodged his swing, but he looked a bit rattled by the encounter.

"And Renphor now knows that we're after a picture and will see to it that any that exist are destroyed."

They walked silently for a few more minutes until David finally spoke. "I know you have your reasons for focusing so heavily on Renphor, but I think you should give some consideration to what Jennifer was saying the other day. Our core agendas are supposed to be democratization and vampire and human relations—maybe we need to find other ways to promote them. If we get a larger base following, you might have more access to him."

John stared at the stream, mulling things over. "Perhaps. Put some thought into it. We can talk it over at the next meeting."

David thanked John for seeing him and made a hasty exit in the direction of his car. John continued along the streambed for another ten minutes but finally gave up. David's visit had shattered his concentration, so he decided to spend a few hours reading to get his focus back.

Julie found him several hours later, deeply engrossed in a book about etymology of the Modern Greek language.

"Looks thrilling," she commented.

He looked up from the book and smiled. "No, but certainly interesting. And useful. So many of our ancient texts were never translated from the original language." He marked the book and closed it carefully.

"What have you been up to all day?"

"Reading." She grinned. "Nothing as educational as that, though. Regency romances, in fact."

He shook his head but refrained from telling her what he thought of her choice of reading material.

"John, are you seriously planning to devote all of your time and energy to Renphor for an unspecified period of time?"

He swiveled his chair around to face her. "Bored?" he asked.

"Very."

"It shouldn't be long now," he assured her, turning back to his book as he spoke. A minute later, he heard the door close softly behind her.

16

John circled the large ballroom, greeting each of his guests in turn. He had decided to throw a ball shortly after his conversation with David, and Joseph had spent the better part of the last two weeks polishing crystal chandeliers and brass candle holders. He didn't seem to mind the work, and the results were astounding. Silk brocade curtains, ornately embroidered, were tied back from four long windows at one end of the room. Mirrors lined the opposite wall, in a manner reminiscent of the Galerie des Glaces at Versailles, although the room at the original Larch Hill predated the palace by two decades. The long wall that contained the entrance to the room also provided space for a small orchestra and a pianist that John had hired for the occasion. The fourth wall of the room displayed an impressive antique tapestry that he had brought with him from his original estate in England. The combined effect was a blaze of light and color that transported the attendees back in time to an era of wealth and privilege that had not existed for centuries.

The guests were also richly adorned. Many of them had chosen to wear their ceremonial robes for the occasion, and glittering reds, deep blues, and rich greens that indicated which of the original vampires they had descended from sparkled in the candlelight. The attendance exceeded a hundred people, all of whom had either rank or fortune, and most were blessed with both. Many had rearranged prior engagements out of sheer curiosity—the ballroom at Larch Hill had been used only one other time. That was in the mid-1800s, shortly after John's relocation to America, and the attendance then had been restricted to those who had also emigrated overseas in search of more territory, or the select few who possessed the ability to jump the distance from Europe. Guests who had not spoken to their host in centuries had traveled halfway around the world for the chance to dance in John's ballroom.

John had been watching his mate closely while she danced with a blond-haired man in an emerald-green robe. The man had wandered off, and Julie leaned against a marble pilaster while she watched the guests twirl around the room. John excused himself from a small group of friends and made his way toward her.

"Enjoying yourself?" he asked.

She smiled at him. "Yes, it's delightful. It's like a scene out of one of my old period novels, except that the costumes are slightly off."

He grinned. "And not really constructed for dancing. Blasted sleeves keep getting in the way."

She nodded. "I'd noticed." She flicked the long, pointed sleeve of her crimson robe out of the way as she spoke. "But you haven't really told me why you've gone to all of this trouble."

"You said you were bored. I thought you'd enjoy the chance to mingle with some new people."

"Mmm. I believe I'll go have a word with Jane—I haven't spoken to her in ages." She walked purposefully away from him. Whether she was really planning to talk to Jane or was just looking for an excuse to leave, John never found out, since she was waylaid by Stefan a moment later and led off to an alcove.

John watched them through narrowed eyes for a moment before walking over to a group of slightly bored-looking men. One of them leaned conspiratorially toward his host. "Is there anywhere without dancing? There's a creature here in a royal-blue robe who's on a major mate hunt. I don't know how much longer I can dodge her."

He laughed at this. "Lady Elmsworth, no doubt." He pointed to a door that was partially concealed behind the orchestra. Lowering his voice, he said, "There's a card room over there. I'm keeping it somewhat quiet, since I don't want every man in the place trying to escape, but if Elmsworth is after you…"

The other man thanked him and moved quickly away. After looking around to see that his mate was still engaged with Stefan, he slipped quietly out another side door. Stella, David, and Jennifer were already seated in a room barely large enough to hold a round table with chairs and a small desk. It was dimly lit by a single candelabra. John slid into the last vacant chair.

"I would have thought a few of you would be out circulating. How can you get any information if you're in here talking to each other?"

"We were, but you told us to meet you here at four. It's five past," Jennifer answered.

Stella chimed in. "I've been having trouble shaking Davies. Once I got rid of him, I figured I better get out of the way before he found me again."

John nodded at her.

"Why isn't Nelson here, anyway?" David asked.

The other three looked at him. "Because this particular task required finesse," John answered bluntly.

"Why did you decide to hold this thing in the middle of the night, anyway? Midnight seems like an odd time to start a party."

"A couple of the guests have some light sensitivity issues. I wanted to give them travel time after dark."

"You invited plebes?" Stella looked shocked.

"No. A few fourth-generation friends who had incompetent makers." John glared at her.

"How are you doing with that fire thingy?" Jennifer asked in a hushed voice.

"It's coming along alright, but it doesn't do me any good if I can't find Renphor. Any luck?"

The other three looked at each other but seemed reluctant to speak. Finally, David broke the silence. "Not a word, John. I managed a few glancing references, as did the others, but no one seems to have any idea where his home base is."

Jennifer chimed in to back up her husband. "I had a guy tell me that he was pretty certain Renphor was living in a cave in the Alps." The others looked at her disdainfully. "What? I'm just passing the information along."

"Well, I've done a little better than you. There's a man in a turquoise robe, answering to the name of Philip Avery, who has been fairly close friends with Renphor in the past. Stella, I'm assigning him to you, since he'll respond best to a beautiful female."

Jennifer scowled. "Nothing for me, then?"

"I do have something for you. There's a petite blonde in a black-and-gray evening gown. Looks completely out of place, so you won't be able to miss her. Name of Rose Everett. Used to be a fairly regular lover of Renphor's. Seems a bit put out with him and would definitely respond to any female who showed her any kindness. She's right up your alley." Jennifer nodded mutely. Stella smirked.

John addressed David last of all. "You've got more of a group assignment. Make your way into the card room—"

"There's a card room?"

"—behind the orchestra. There's a blue-and-green tapestry over half of the door. I've only told about a dozen people about it. All powerful and well placed. All old enough to have known Renphor before he went underground. Well, all except one, anyway. Hang out there and schmooze."

"Are we really supposed to latch on to the same person for the rest of the evening?" Jennifer seemed to be appalled by the idea.

John gritted his teeth. "This ball will probably go on for another four hours, since no one seems to be slowing down yet. If you lose your assigned person, keep circulating. There are plenty of people here, from all kinds of society. There have to be at least a couple who can help us."

John rose from his chair. "Follow me out at fifteen-minute intervals." He slipped quickly back into the ballroom, leaving the others looking at each other in consternation.

"Which of us gets to sit here for the next forty-five minutes?" Stella asked glumly.

John had been correct in his guess about the length of the ball. Those guests who were unfortunate enough to be sensitive to sunlight had started to leave before four o'clock, but the rest of the party kept going at full force until the musicians packed up at eight. Stella, Jennifer, David, and Nelson stayed behind for another hour after the music stopped, closeted in what had been the card room with their host. Julie joined them half an hour later, while they were still reviewing the evening's events. They jumped when she walked in.

"Did I miss the meeting invite?" she asked.

John stood and ushered her to a chair. "Sorry to exclude you, but I didn't want both the host and the hostess to disappear while there were still guests lingering around."

"So I drew the short straw." She grimaced as she flopped into the chair. "So what did all of the little spies find out this evening?"

John ignored the comment and picked up where he had left off. They were still short on solid facts. Stella had gotten a great deal of information about Renphor's lodgings in Cairo. She had been excitedly making mental notes when Philip had mentioned that he had really enjoyed visiting him there during the golden age of archeology. Unfortunately, when Renphor had moved in 1920, he had left no forwarding address.

Jennifer had run into a similar brick wall with Rose. She had been easily persuaded to talk about her trysts with Renphor, since it was obvious that they had been the high point of an otherwise dull existence. He had met her when she was just barely eighteen and trying to decide whether she should go to college or marry the nice local boy she'd been dating. Renphor had converted her within a few weeks of their meeting. For a short time afterward they had spent nearly every day together, but he had gradually grown more distant. She had seen him off and on over the following ten years, but it had been nearly three decades since their last encounter.

Nelson, who had not been given any specific assignments, had not gotten any new information. He had made friends with several men he had never met before, but their discussion had been mostly about racing and the English countryside.

David had fared the best of all of them. The long-standing feud between John and Renphor had come up naturally in the card room, following quickly on the surprise of the guests over John opening his house to so many strangers. David had gleaned from them that Renphor was frequently to seen in Athens and Rome. John smiled at this information and congratulated David on managing to gather it without sounding suspiciously curious. He sent them all home after the discussion and wandered happily into his study to look for a European atlas.

He was only vaguely aware of his mate's sigh of relief when the door closed on the last of them. Looking around a moment later to ask her a question, he was surprised to find her gone.

17

Renphor rolled his eyes as Stefan's number flashed onto his phone screen, but after five rings he picked it up with a sigh.

"I want you in my drawing room in five minutes," Stefan barked without preamble.

"For what?"

"The pleasure of your company. Don't tell me you have something better to do?"

"I do, as a matter of fact."

"What?"

"None of your business."

"Didn't really care, anyway. Postpone it."

The call ended abruptly. Five minutes later an extremely irritated Renphor stood in the middle of Stefan's drawing room.

"Did you call me here for any purpose other than to be annoying?" he asked shortly.

"Perhaps. Cards?"

"If you insist." Renphor slouched into a chair at the card table. Stefan sat across from him, smiling unpleasantly.

"I wonder that you continue to obey my summonses, if you find them so irksome," he said icily.

Renphor looked up from the pack of cards he'd been shuffling from one hand to the next. "Thus far, it hasn't been worth the effort it would take to overthrow you," he said lightly.

Stefan regarded him narrowly. "If I thought you meant a word of that…"

The corners of Renphor's mouth tilted up. "It's a well-known fact that I'm too lazy for politics, Stefan. You waste your time and mine with this constant need to know what I'm doing. None of it is of any interest to anyone but myself, I assure you."

Stefan took the cards from Renphor's hand and dealt them in silence. Neither spoke to the other for the next half hour, as they concentrated on the game. There was no betting involved, since Renphor steadfastly refused to gamble, but they took out their hostility toward one another on the cards. It was Stefan who finally broke the silence.

"Any luck at Larch Hill yet?" he asked casually.

"I have a few avenues of inquiry—nothing particularly solid yet. I don't think there's any hurry."

"No, I don't suppose there is."

Renphor looked over the tops of his cards at his opponent. "How's the fire vortex coming?"

"As well as can be expected. He's still trying to work through the components."

Renphor nodded but didn't respond.

"So what stimulating activities did I prevent you from undertaking this evening?"

Renphor picked through his cards, moving them from one side of his hand to the other. "Nothing in particular."

Stefan glared at him. "Indeed. Funny that you gave me quite the opposite impression over the phone."

Renphor hid a smile. "Thought I might develop more of a campus social life."

Stefan scoffed. "I'm sure you'd fit in beautifully with the coeds."

"I'm doing alright so far."

"Oh?"

He laughed at the incredulous expression on Stefan's face.

"Just a bit of a diversion. I was deciding whether or not I wanted to bother finishing my current program this year, when I ran into a perfectly lovely reason to hang around."

Stefan studied him through half-closed eyes. "So I was right about you getting distracted. It seems to have taken less than a month, too, which beats my original bet."

Renphor yawned, purely for theatrical effect. "Who's getting distracted? I can't sit and think about John all day—I'd turn into almost as big of a bore as he is."

"You'll get completely wrapped up in this new diversion, and John will have worked out the fire vortex and tossed you into it before you accomplish another damned thing. Who is she?"

"It will take John years to create a vortex that strong. You know damned well how much energy it takes to maintain one and he's never been any good in a head-to-head fight. That's why he always whacks me from behind with something and takes off in the opposite direction." Renphor made a violent discard.

"Perhaps. But you didn't answer my question."

"Did I hear that the council passed the new secrecy regulation they were babbling about at the last open assembly?"

Stefan went rigid and stared glassily at his cards. "They did."

Renphor nodded. "Thought they would. Asinine of them, of course—we've had a pact of secrecy for centuries without needing any laws to back it up. It's just a way to placate the plebes."

"It's the plebes' fault that someone decided we needed the law. Parading around bragging about all of their wonderful powers, when most of them are nothing more than light-sensitive humans on a large dose of steroids."

"Only because they're too ignorant to realize that they need to study. The core powers don't get really diluted until you go down nine or ten generations. The cutoff after the fourth generation is completely arbitrary."

Stefan gritted his teeth. "Just because you've met a few exceptions, it doesn't disprove the general rule. Fifth generation is almost universally the point where the weaknesses and mutations start to creep in." He went on in this vein for the next hour, while Renphor quietly played his cards. The result was that at the end of the evening's play, Renphor had won decisively.

Renphor rose from the table around midnight, saying that he had to hunt. Stefan looked angrily at the cards spread out in front of him before sweeping his arm across the tablecloth and gathering them willy-nilly into the small drawer he had opened on the side of the table.

As he stood, Renphor bowed slightly to him. "Do let me know when you want me to drop by again." He disappeared too suddenly for Stefan to call him back.

Stefan stood next to the table, fuming and staring at the place where Renphor had been a moment before. "Slippery pain in the ass," he muttered to himself. He stalked across the room to a grotesquely ornate sideboard and pulled violently on the bell cord that hung next to it.

18

John mentally checked off the contents of two bulging suitcases that stood in the front hallway. Joseph was picking through a small carry-on, tutting about all the things his master had chosen to omit.

"There's no point in making that noise, Joseph. I'm not going to be bothered with all of that when I have no one to act as valet anyway."

"I could go—"

"No. You will stay here and look after Julie."

"Going on a trip?"

John jumped at the sound of his mate's voice directly behind him. "Yes. Didn't have time to hunt you down earlier, since my flight is in three hours. I'm heading to Athens, and then to Rome, to follow up on the information that I've gotten. Apparently Renphor fancies himself something of a scholar," John sneered.

"How long are you planning to be gone?"

"I'll be back by Halloween. If I can't get anywhere by then, I'll have to try for more information here."

"Halloween! That's a whole month away."

John nodded. "I'm sure you'll find something to keep yourself busy with while I'm away."

Julie leaned against the door frame and watched Joseph attempting to fit several rolled pieces of parchment into the carry-on.

"Taking the fire vortex with you?"

"Yes, I don't want to miss out on the practice."

"I suggest you refrain from practicing on the plane. I'm pretty sure it's against FAA rules. Do you need a ride to the airport?"

He smiled at her. "That would be lovely. Thank you."

She grabbed her car keys from an end table as the three of them headed out to the car. Joseph backed away from the trunk after stowing his master's bags, and the Jaguar swung easily out of the driveway and turned toward Route 95.

After swearing at the airport traffic for half an hour, Julie finally managed to maneuver the car in front of Philadelphia International's terminal A. "I think this is the end of the line for me, unless you want to pay for short-term parking," she said.

"I'm good from here. Thanks for the lift." He unloaded quickly and pushed his way through the glass doors to the ticket counter.

Julie sat in the car for a few minutes, braving the displeasure of other unloading passengers, before heaving a deep sigh and easing the car out of the loading area.

John landed in Athens the following morning, looking far more chipper than his fellow travelers. He had arranged ahead of time to meet an old friend of his who had lived in the city for more than three centuries, so once he navigated customs, he was able to step out of the airport and into a waiting car. Within a short space of time, it delivered him to a narrow house in the heart of the city, within walking distance of the National Library. The man who had sold him the fire vortex diagrams had told him that he'd found it in the secret room in this library, so he intended to start his search there.

He was greeted warmly at the door by Petros, who he had met years before while traveling in the country for research.

"John—it's been far too long. You need to leave that drafty house of yours more often." Petros clapped him on the back and led him into the house.

John smiled tightly. "Travel has its appeal, but I spend so much of my time in study."

"But there is so much more to study here. I have a vast library even in my basement, which is still nothing compared to the hidden room at the National Library. And where is your lovely mate?"

"Not along this trip. Do you have access to that hidden room, by the way?"

"Of course. But first, come up to your room and settle in."

He led John up a narrow staircase to a bright front room with white plaster and an expansive view of the city. John set his suitcases down carefully next to an end table and walked to the window. He smiled at the beautiful view below him.

"I believe you're right, Petros. It has been far too long."

The two men decided to take a walk amongst the ruins and catch up on old times. The conversation drifted easily over such topics as Petros's research of the ancient Greek texts and the ways in which John was keeping himself occupied. At length, it was Petros who introduced the topic of Renphor, and in a fashion that was not particularly pleasing to his guest.

"I hear tell that you become more and more obsessed with this vendetta of yours, John." There was genuine concern in Petros's voice, but John scowled in displeasure at the words.

"I don't know that I focus on it any more than I ever have," he answered stiffly.

"No? I understand that prior to your ball, you hadn't been seen publicly with your mate in more than ten years, outside of a few official functions. That's no way to keep a lady interested, my friend. And ladies who find themselves permanently tied to the object of their disinterest get strange ideas into their heads."

They were passing through a deserted temple, and John stopped to examine a crumbling statue of Dionysus.

"Pity to see places like this falling to ruin," he commented. Petros stared mutely at him. John sighed. "Don't concern yourself about my mate. I assure you she isn't likely to do me any harm."

They wandered on for another hour in silence, until Petros finally spoke.

"And how is the search for Renphor coming along?"

"Not as well as I would like. It's hard for me to get information about someone who has no standing in society—we don't seem to know many of the same people."

Petros considered this comment carefully.

"It is not wise to underestimate Renphor, John. Just because he doesn't operate in the same social spheres that you do, it does not diminish his rank, his connections, or his power." He spoke quietly, and John pretended not to hear. Instead, he launched into an explanation of the information he had received about Renphor's frequent presence in Greece. He planned to search any of the libraries that Renphor might be interested in and see what kind of information he would have had access to. That might give him an idea of what kinds of weapons he might be up against.

"And if you walk around the corner and run smack into him between the stacks?"

"Even better."

"Are you prepared for a confrontation?"

"I will be soon. I brought along something that I want to show you. I'm obviously missing something, and I was hoping you could help me with the last bit that I need to complete the spell."

Petros nodded. John felt irritation rising in his throat at the expression on his friend's face. Petros had not been openly dismissive of his plans, but John read disapproval in his eyes. He would just have to visit the libraries alone. They spent a few more hours climbing silently among ancient marble ruins and the debris left behind by long-dead gods, then returned to the house.

The first thing John did on their return was to unpack the parchment from his luggage. Carefully unrolling it, he brought it down to Petros. Petros, after a brief frown upon discovering the contents, bent over it carefully. They studied it together for an hour, neither wanting to speak and break the other's concentration. It was finally Petros who spoke.

"Where's the rest of it?"

John stared at him. "What do you mean?"

Petros had the pages lined up on the table. He pointed to the notes that ran down the sides, moving his finger slowly from the bottom of the third page to the top of the fourth. With this simple action, John discovered what he had been overlooking for months. The last word of the final sentence on the third page was missing, and it didn't continue on the fourth. He was missing part of the spell.

He leaned back on the chair, slowly exhaling. Petros leaned back as well, watching him.

"I take it this is the cornerstone of your offense?"

John nodded.

"Not a bad plan. The missing part seems to move you from a ball of fire to an actual vortex, so we'll just have to work that part out on our own."

Petros practiced for about an hour. With John's help, he was quickly able to reach the point where he could produce a ball of flame. After that, the two sat in silence, trying out various tactics and combinations of spells to see if they could produce any result. Once or twice Petros seemed on the verge of success, but it always fizzled quickly and left them right back where they had started from. Finally, in frustration, John decided to start his tour of the libraries.

He went out armed with the directions that Petros had given him to the hidden room in the National Library. The entrance was almost perfectly concealed in the wooden stacks. Walking slowly along the perimeter, he searched for the mark that Petros had told him would be there. He looked skeptically at the small symbol when he finally found it. There was no sign that the shelves here were not every bit as solidly placed as the ones in the rest of the room. Glancing around to make sure he wasn't observed, he slid his hand experimentally down one of the panels and stepped back as a small section swung away from the wall, revealing a staircase down to an underground level. The door swished closed behind him as soon as he stepped through, causing him to jump.

"Don't mind that, it opens alright from this side as well." A cheerful voice called from the bottom of the steps.

John peered down the steps. "What?"

"The door. Everyone gets a little panicky the first time. Think they're going to get trapped inside."

"Oh. What do you do at the library, then?" John slowly descended the steps, taking in the strange figure before him. The man was barely five feet tall, and his skin looked like the gnarled bark of an old tree. Wisps of white hair stuck out from his head with abandon, and his eyes appeared almost yellow. Odder than all of this, considering where John met him—the man was human.

He had been returning John's shocked gaze with one of amusement, but now he responded cheerfully to the question. "I'm something of an expert on ancient languages and have a great deal of experience with magical texts. I have a room at the back of the library, and they bring food in for me. Since I haven't had any human contact in nearly sixty years, no one thinks of me as a threat."

"Sixty years? Then you couldn't have been an expert when you were first brought here. You'd have to be over a hundred!"

The old man cackled wildly in response. "Oh, but I am. As near as I can figure, it must be other humans who cause humans to age so rapidly. I was nearly fifty when I moved here, and I'll probably stick around at least another forty years. My name is Bartholomew, by the way. What can I help you with?"

John pulled out a list of topics that he had jotted down, all of which had to do with improving his mastery of the fire vortex. Bartholomew nodded as he looked down the list.

"You'll want to start back here." He beckoned John to follow him and walked briskly toward a back section of the library. John trailed behind, staring around him at the aging volumes. He briefly lost track of Bartholomew when he stopped to examine a small book bound in green leather. Realizing he'd lost his escort, John walked slowly in the direction he thought the man had gone, peering down stacks of books as he went. When he reached the third row, he was startled to encounter a dark-haired man staring back at him. He excused himself hurriedly and started for the next row just as Bartholomew's head popped out from the end of a row ten feet away.

"This way!" he chirped. John followed him with relief.

He soon found himself set up at a quiet table in the back, with three or four tall stacks of books, manuscripts, and a few odd parchment scrolls. He pulled a battered notebook out of his pocket and picked the top book off the stack.

He spent three days immersed in the library, jotting down notes. At the end of that time, he had several ideas he was anxious to try out. He tracked down Bartholomew to put the books away and prepared to leave.

"Thanks for the help. I'm impressed that you were able to find so much useful information."

The old man smiled. "I've a very good memory. I pulled a very similar list some fifty years ago for another American vampire."

"Oh?"

"Yes. A blond one...Renphor. That's it. Only he had a stack of diagrams of his own that he'd brought with him."

John twitched involuntarily. "Has he been back since?"

Bartholomew rubbed his chin reflectively. "Not a lot. At least not recently. Used to come in pretty regularly a few decades ago. No idea what he got up to, since he preferred to help himself once he'd figured out the layout."

John bowed and thanked the man for all his assistance. He walked slowly back to Petros's house, turning the new information over in his mind.

He stayed two weeks in Athens, visiting all the other libraries that were likely to have information during the day and working with Petros on the vortex at night. By the end of this time, they were able to produce the fireball with ease but still couldn't expand it to anything other than a small, whirling ball of flame.

"Which will do little more than burn down the house if it lights on something flammable," John commented drily.

Petros entreated him to stay a few more weeks, but John was adamant that he needed to move on to Rome. He did not like to be away from home for more than a month at a time, since the protections he had put around the place would weaken over time. He bid a fond farewell to his friend, who promised to spend time with the complicated notes he had taken and send word to John if he made a breakthrough. Half a day later, after dealing with traffic and airport delays, John was in Rome.

19

Two days after John left for Athens, Julie found herself wandering through his library, trying to find some way to pass the time. She pulled several volumes about spell work off the shelves, only to shove them back in disgust upon realizing that they were written in some language she didn't know or contained spells far beyond her capabilities. She finally flopped down in John's chair and stared at the books in disgust. Joseph found her there a few minutes later.

"Is there a problem, madam?"

"Not really, Joseph. Just thinking how personal a library is." She suddenly sat bolt upright in her chair. "The library!"

"Madam?"

"Sorry, Joseph. I'm going out for a few hours."

Within minutes, the car swung out of the gate and turned right toward the city. She left the gate open—Joseph had followed her down the driveway, and she knew he would close it behind her. She managed the drive in under twenty minutes, pulling into a parking space near the public library just before nine o'clock. By the time she had paid at the kiosk and made her way to the front door, they were just opening for the day. After confirming the location of the public computers at the information desk, she headed up the stairs to grab an empty seat in the middle of a row.

She smiled as she sat down in front of the computer. She ran her fingers happily along the keys and watched with satisfaction as the screen lit up. It had been over two years since she had touched a computer because John refused to have one in the house. He even forbade his mate from having a smartphone, since he believed they were dangerous and addictive. Her daughter had a laptop for school, but even she did not have internet access on her computer when she was at home. Julie browsed happily for a while, looking up a few video clips and reading some articles. When she looked at the clock, she was startled to find that an hour and a half had passed. She decided it was time to get down to business.

She only had two pieces of information from Stefan—the name Ryan Callaghan and the fact that he lived in Frankford. She tried a few broad searches, but they brought up too many hits to be useful. She even took a stab at a few searches under his real name but came up completely empty. She was not particularly surprised by this—even if he didn't have excellent reasons to avoid leaving a digital trail, most of the vampire world wasn't yet on the internet. She tapped her fingers impatiently on the table, trying to remember all the tidbits that she had heard about Renphor over the years. She finally remembered someone telling her that he spent a fair amount of his time studying at various universities. Starting her search on the website of the university her daughter attended, she immediately hit on a photograph of three men from the Classical Studies department. She enlarged the photo until she could get a clear view of the faces. Her gasp caused two people that were sitting further down the row of computers to glare at her in annoyance. Two of the men in the photo were obviously human, but the third was an extraordinarily pale blond, whose green eyes were tinged with red that didn't seem to have been caused by the camera. He was definitely a vampire, and the physical description fit the one that John had given. She had a moment of panic at the realization but calmed herself down by considering the odds of any two of the thousands of students at the university running into each other.

After jotting down all the information she had obtained, she logged off the computer and left the library for a café across the street. There she took a table as far in the corner as she could manage and annoyed the waiter by ordering nothing but a small water. Julie had met a few of the professors at the university through her daughter, so she flipped through the names on her phone and dialed one of them who she knew fairly well. After fifteen minutes on the phone, she hung up and stared at the address she had written down for a building in Frankford. She pulled a blank sheet of paper out of her notebook and carefully copied only the address onto it. Then she threw out all the other papers she had been using for her research and tucked this one carefully into the side pocket of her purse.

Realizing that her meter was set to run out any minute, she paid for her water, left a generous tip for the waiter, and ran down the street to the Jaguar. She smiled to herself as she slid behind the wheel. In five hours, she had discovered what John had been trying to find out for the last century. And she had done it using the very technology he had repeatedly scorned. She drove home to Larch Hill, turning everything over in her mind. She was in possession of Renphor's address, and the very thought terrified her. If she used it to find Renphor, she had no idea what his reaction would be. On the other hand, if she did nothing with it and John found out about it, he might very well kill her himself. Stefan hadn't thought that Renphor would harm her, but it was entirely possible that he would try to ransom her. Would John pay? And what if he didn't?

When she got home, she poked her head into the library to discover Joseph dusting the ancient volumes. She told him she was going up to the top of the tower and disappeared quickly from the room. She sat there for hours, turning things over in her mind and trying to bring herself to some kind of decision. At the end of a few hours, she was confused, exhausted, and hungry. She went back downstairs to hunt, trying to make her mind run on any topic other than Renphor.

20

The day after his conversation with Stefan, Renphor sat on the steps outside of the building where Arabella had her anthropology classes, waiting for her to appear. It was a gorgeous fall day, and neither of them had any afternoon classes, so they had decided to take a walk down Kelly Drive and along the Schuylkill River. She came out of the building just as he glanced at his watch, wondering what could be keeping her. "There you are. I was beginning to think you forgot to meet me."

"Of course not. Or did you think I stood you up?" She smiled engagingly at him.

He stood and took both her hands in his. "I certainly hope not. You're the best thing that's happened to me in years."

Arabella blushed and became fascinated by a twig that was stuck to the base of the bench. He watched her, smiling slightly, as she tried to pick it out from under the bench with the toe of her shoe. He finally interrupted. "Are you ready?"

She looked up quickly. "Of course."

Arabella had suggested a side excursion to the art museum before remembering with disappointment that they were closed on Mondays. She cheered up again when Renphor reminded her that they would have all winter to visit the museums, but the season for walking along the river would be ending in a few weeks. They held hands as they strolled along the walkway, keeping well out of the way of the bicyclists and runners. Every ten minutes or so, Arabella would stop so they could watch the rowers for a while before continuing on their leisurely way along the path. She chatted about her childhood and her family as Renphor listened.

"Do you remember your father at all?" he asked at one point.

Arabella shook her head sadly. "Not at all. Mom kept some photographs, but they're mostly tucked away in a box in the coat closet. My stepfather doesn't really like to have them around."

"Doesn't that bother your mother?" he asked.

Arabella looked thoughtful. "I'm not sure if it does or not. Mom still gets pretty upset when the subject of Dad comes up. I think she might be perfectly happy to keep all of that tucked away most of the time."

"Has she kept his side of the family tucked away too? Surely you have aunts and uncles who like to see you occasionally?"

She laughed. "Except for Christmas, I usually do holiday dinners with Dad's side of the family. Mom doesn't have any family left, and Dad's relatives have been mad at her ever since she took up with my stepfather, so I usually go alone."

"Really? No family bonding over the holiday table?"

"No family bonding over any table, actually. I usually ate in the living room as a kid. I'm not sure I've ever seen either of them sit down to a meal other than Christmas."

Renphor tried to keep one ear on what Arabella was saying, but his brain was chasing a fleeting tidbit of something he had heard. Her words started to blur together, until she finally stopped in the middle of the sidewalk and stared at him. "It's really annoying when you check out like that in the middle of a conversation," she said tartly.

He jerked out of his reverie. "What were you saying, pet?"

"Never mind." She pulled away from him and walked down to the river, staring over the water. He followed her after a moment, putting his arm around her waist and turning her toward him for a kiss.

"I'm afraid I'm easily distracted, pet. Don't take it personally, okay?" He grinned sheepishly, and Arabella's scowl became less pronounced.

"I'd love to know what you were thinking about."

"Nothing of interest, I assure you."

She looked curiously at him, and he turned down the path to prevent further questioning. They walked on in silence for a while, enjoying the warm afternoon and the sun reflecting off the water. By the time they returned to their starting point it was nearly dark, and Arabella was anxious to get home and have her dinner.

Renphor left Arabella at her door around six o'clock, saying that he needed to spend some time on a translation he was working on for one of his Greek classes. He promised to return later in the evening and strolled around the corner in the direction of the library. As soon as he was out of her sight line, he ducked down an alley and disappeared from view.

Renphor did not go to the library but instead returned to his room. He pulled his phone out of his pocket and dialed Ariliana's number, tapping his foot while it rang. After seven or eight rings, she finally picked up, sounding less than thrilled to talk to him.

"What do you want, Ren? I've got company."

"Sorry to interrupt. It's not idiot-boy Davies, is it?"

"As a matter of fact—"

"Even better. Is he out of earshot?"

"Yes, why?"

"Did you find out anything more about Elder?"

"What's it worth to you?"

"The same thing it always is."

He heard a heavy sigh on the other end of the line. "Did you know he's left the country? He's traveling in Europe for a month. Greece and Athens, from what Nelson told me. Might be the perfect time to break into Larch Hill."

"It would be, if the whole reason I wanted to get in there weren't to get to John. Won't do me much good to break in while he's in Europe. What's he doing there, anyway?"

"Looking for you."

He laughed derisively. "Where the hell does he get his information? He must have the worst informants in the history of the world."

"You've met Nelson. If any of his talk is true, he's the star of the show," she said drily.

"Satan save us. Did you happen to find anything out about his mate?"

Renphor listened with increasing interest to what Ariliana told him. When he hung up the phone, he was laughing. He went quickly to the shelf and extracted the notebook where he had written all his information about Larch Hill. Flipping to the list of John's weaknesses, he put a checkmark next to the item for John's daughter.

21

In the five weeks since their first date, Renphor and Arabella had spent a good part of every weekend together and usually several nights during the week as well. Once the weather started to get colder, they spent most of their time at her apartment. Their first real argument had occurred three weeks after they started dating, when he had flatly refused to tell her where he lived, saying it wasn't a safe place for her to go. The argument had lasted for nearly a week, but he had ultimately ended it by simply ignoring her every time she brought it up.

Arabella's roommates were not as easy to reconcile to the situation. Sam, who had seemed fairly complacent toward him in the beginning, became less and less cordial. Based on rare comments that Arabella let drop, he gleaned that she thought he was taking advantage of her naivete, since this was her first serious relationship. Narcissa didn't seem to be speaking to anybody if she could avoid it and made frequent snarky comments about charging him rent. Since Arabella was paying twice as much as the other two combined, the rest of them ignored her.

Sam did say something to Renphor one Sunday afternoon in October when she found him lounging on the couch watching a movie with Arabella nowhere in sight.

"Have you actually moved in with us, or are you still keeping your own room?"

"Oh, I still have my own place. I never spend much time there, though."

"I'd noticed. But you haven't explained why you're sitting here by yourself."

He tilted his head backwards over the arm of the couch to look at her. She took a hasty step backwards, and he realized too late that he'd let his shield waver for an instant.

"I'm not sitting here by myself. Unless you're an illusion?"

She was still staring at him, transfixed. "No, I'm definitely here," she said slowly.

He turned over and looked thoughtfully at her. "You don't seem so sure."

"Sorry, I just got a little rattled. Trick of the light. Unless you happen to be a demon of some sort?"

"No. Definitely not a demon."

"Any way to prove that?" She started to walk toward her room as she asked the question.

"Humans can't see demons."

Sam stopped abruptly and stared at him. "How would you know?"

Renphor shrugged and went back to watching the movie.

Narcissa walked in a few minutes later and glared at him lounging on the couch.

"I don't suppose an actual resident of this apartment could get a chance to sit on the couch and watch what I want to watch," she asked bitterly.

"Of course. What did you want to watch?"

Since this effectively prevented her from starting an argument with him, Narcissa flounced into her room without answering and slammed the door. He stared after her for a moment with a bemused look on his face, then shook his head slightly and turned back to the TV.

Arabella came in shortly afterward. She was wearing a light jacket, which she flung casually across the back of a chair before plopping down on the floor in front of the couch.

"Would you rather sit up here?" Renphor asked.

"No. I like the floor better, actually. That couch is pretty awful."

"Agreed. Let me join you." He swung his legs off the couch and slid down on the floor next to Arabella.

"What are you watching?" she asked.

"No idea. It happened to be on. I started in the middle, so I didn't catch the name."

"You could check the guide."

"That would take the mystery out of it."

She handed him the remote. "It's the red button marked 'guide.'"

"Ah. So what have you been up to this morning?"

Arabella described the history society's meeting she had just come from. They had decided to stage a series of "faires" that would reenact various periods of English history, and charge admission to raise funds. They planned to start with the Middle Ages, then work their way forward through the twentieth century. She asked Renphor if he would help with the first one, which was supposed to replicate the early 1400s.

"What are you expecting me to contribute?" he asked.

"Well, you must know something about that period."

He was startled for a moment but managed to keep his voice even as he answered. "What gives you that idea?"

"You were reading Chaucer when I first met you. You must have picked up something."

Renphor relaxed against the front of the couch. "As I recall, you were supposed to have read that too."

"Are you sorry I didn't?" She looked up at him through her eyelashes.

"No." He started to kiss her but was interrupted by Sam coming back out of her room. She frowned at him before heading into the kitchen. He watched her for a moment, then got up and followed her.

She jumped when he walked up behind her.

"Now what have I done to irritate you?" he asked.

"Nothing." She didn't look directly at him when she answered, and he looked at her skeptically. She shrugged and went on, "I don't see what Arabella sees in you, frankly. She seems to think you're some kind of saint, and the more I see of you, the less I believe it. You don't deserve her."

"I'm not disagreeing, but what's actually bugging you?"

"Your habits weren't exactly saintly before you met her. And I swear there's something inhuman about you." She looked at him suspiciously.

He laughed at this. "Are you accusing me of being nonhuman, or inhumane?"

"Nonhuman." She looked away from him as she spoke.

His eyes glinted for a moment, and he didn't quite manage to keep the edge out of his voice when he answered. "And what exactly does that make me?"

She started to back away from him, and he noticed her hands were shaking. "I don't know. I don't know what I was talking about. It just came out of my mouth." She backed quickly out of the kitchen and through the living room, shutting her bedroom door softly behind her. He followed more slowly and eased himself back onto the floor next to Arabella.

"So, what are you planning for this 1400s shindig again?" He didn't meet the searching look that Arabella gave him and was relieved when she didn't ask about his conversation with Sam but launched into an enthusiastic description of the event instead.

The general plan was to mimic a medieval celebration of some kind. Several of the members had wanted to show everyday life, but they had decided that this plan would be more complicated than showing a single event. The most popular idea was that it would be a wedding, and the visitors would be treated as guests.

"Were you planning for a nobleman's wedding, or a commoner's?" Renphor asked.

"A nobleman's. We can have more fun with the costumes that way." Arabella's eyes danced at the thought.

"What is it about women that always attracts them to the thought of a wedding? Even the sensible ones."

Arabella cocked her head to one side. "Are you counting me in the sensible group, I wonder?" He grinned at her but didn't respond.

Scowling, she went on, "Anyway, can you help out?"

"Of course. What do you need me to do?"

She looked at him for a second, then answered hesitantly, "Would you mind coming to some of the planning meetings? Help us come up with some ideas? I know you're not big on the committee thing..." Her voice trailed off, and her eyes seemed to be focusing somewhere over his left shoulder.

"Still with me?" he asked.

"Sorry...my mind was wandering around a royal wedding." She grinned.

"And you complain about me drifting off into neverland. To answer your question, I suppose I could stomach a planning meeting or two. It would make your roommates happy, since they wouldn't run into me on your couch."

Arabella sighed. "They really ought to get over it."

Renphor smiled at her. "I do see their point. But it's so damned depressing at my place."

"Don't worry about it. I'm paying more than enough for this place to cover an additional person."

Renphor grimaced. "No, you're not. Your stepfather is. Since you told me he's doing so on the condition that he approves your choice of roommates, I don't think he'd be at all happy to find he's been supporting me as well."

"He'd be ok with you sitting on the couch, at any rate. And he's bound to find out about you eventually. I'd really like to just introduce you and get it over with. And you and my mom would get along great."

Renphor stood quickly. "I have to head to the library this afternoon. I have a ridiculously long paper to write. In Greek. Should I come back this evening?"

"Don't you always?" Arabella asked crossly.

He gave her a tight smile. "I generally do, but I figured it was still polite to ask."

22

Julie fitted her key into the lock of Arabella's apartment and smiled. At eight a.m. on a Saturday, she didn't really expect to find anybody awake, but she figured it improved her chances of finding Arabella at home. She was startled to find Sam awake and sitting in the living room in front of the TV. She sat bolt upright as Julie walked in.

"Mrs. Flynn!"

"Hi, Sam. Where's Arabella?"

"She's not home. Out with Ryan—she didn't say where."

Julie inhaled sharply. "Ryan?"

Sam rolled her eyes. "Ryan Callaghan. Hasn't she told you about him?"

"Not yet." Julie sat slowly on the recliner across from Sam, gripping the arms of the chair with both hands. She tried to calm herself down by remembering how many hits had come up under that name when she searched for it. Sam was starting to look at her strangely, so she forced herself to speak in a level voice. "Why are you up and about so early?"

"I was *supposed* to be going shopping for winter clothes with Arabella," Sam answered sullenly. Before Julie could ask any more questions, Sam's phone rang. She grabbed for it, and Julie watched as she grimaced at the other half of the conversation. She hung up after about five minutes.

"She's on her way home now, apparently," Sam said.

Julie nodded. "Was she out this early, or this late?" She was still struggling to fight the panic rising in her chest.

"Early, believe it or not. I don't think she's ever even been to his place, let alone slept there."

"I see. So what aren't you telling me?"

Sam fidgeted a bit. "I probably shouldn't tell you any of this, but—"

"But what?"

"Frankly, I'm sure Narcissa will find the opportunity if I don't, and she'll be a lot bitchier about it."

Julie leaned back into the chair as Sam told her about the somewhat unconventional beginnings to Arabella's relationship. When she had finished, she sat staring at her hands for a few minutes before looking at Julie.

"I don't mind her picking the guy up for a fling, but flings aren't supposed to last for months. I can't understand what she sees in him." Sam stopped, staring at a picture on the wall while Julie mulled over what she'd heard. She chose her words carefully as she continued to question Sam.

"So what's really bothering you about him? I agree the circumstances behind the meeting are a bit off, but I can't imagine you're still holding that against him after this amount of time."

Sam scratched her head. "It's tough to describe," she said slowly.

"Try."

Julie hadn't intended to sound terse, but the word came out as more of a command than a request. Sam stammered slightly as she started an explanation of Renphor's quirks. The fact that she had never seen him eat. The questions that he simply refused to answer. His apparent lack of any existence before starting school. She paused at the end, seeming to struggle with something.

"Anything else?"

"You'll think I'm nuts."

Julie smiled tightly. "I assure you, whatever you may say, I've heard weirder."

After a bit more encouragement, Sam reluctantly told her the story about the red glow she had seen in Renphor's eyes. "It must've been a trick of the light, but I don't understand how it could've been. The light source was at the wrong angle. I don't know what it was about it, but it really threw me off. Mrs. Flynn? What's the matter?"

Julie came back to herself and looked intently at Sam. "Go over it again. All of it," she said shortly.

Sam retold all her concerns to Julie, this time remembering a few other items she had omitted. As she talked, Julie stood and began pacing around the room. By the end of Sam's tale, she had come to a decision.

"Do you have his phone number?"

Sam shook her head.

"Damn. And I don't suppose Arabella will tell me either." Julie frowned, ignoring Sam's surprised expression.

At that moment, they heard the key in the lock, which ended the conversation. Arabella came in looking very flustered and quickly dropped her purse on the table.

"Mom! I didn't know you were coming over this morning. Sam, I'm really, really sorry. I completely lost track of what time it was. Are you totally pissed at me?"

Sam shook her head. "Where's demon boy?"

Arabella glared at her. "*Ryan* had some work to do this afternoon. Since you and I had plans, he didn't bother to come back with me."

Julie smiled slightly at the conversation. "Ryan? I don't believe I've heard about him."

Arabella blushed. "My boyfriend. He's really sweet. You have to meet him sometime."

"I certainly intend to. I'll leave you two to your shopping. Arabella—call me later."

Julie turned the conversation with Sam over in her mind as she drove home. There was no doubt in her mind that Arabella had fallen into a relationship with Renphor. But if Renphor had really gotten enough information to find Arabella, he must have an extraordinary source. She didn't think Stefan would have told him, but she couldn't think of anyone else who could have. Even if she wanted John to know, he was out of the country for another two weeks. She briefly debated phoning him, before thinking through the possible implications of throwing John and Renphor together in Arabella's presence. From her conversation with Sam, she didn't think that Arabella was in any immediate danger. Renphor had obviously devised some use for her, or he wouldn't have spent all those weeks keeping her on a string. She would need to plan carefully if she wanted to talk to him without endangering herself or Arabella any further.

23

John had discovered a great deal about the vortex in Greece but hadn't come across anyone besides Bartholomew who could remember having met Renphor. The books that were housed in the hidden libraries in Rome tended more toward magical theory than practical applications, so he didn't expect to find as much useful information about the fire vortex here. On the other hand, he was more likely to run into other vampires, since the ruling council's seat was located in an underground chamber across the Riva Ostiense from the Vatican. Greece was the milieu of the scholars, who spent their time in study and kept largely to themselves. If you wanted to know about society, Rome was the place to be.

He was once again met at the airport. In Rome, he would be staying with his friend Angelo, whom he had barely spoken to in nearly fifty years. He was looking forward to the visit—Angelo had a large number of friends, and since he had come for company rather than study, he fully expected to enjoy himself.

He was staying at a house a few miles outside of the city, but Angelo's butler knew how to jump and was easily able to transport them around town. John refused to learn to jump, and was not a fan of the practice in general, but relaxed his rule so as not to offend his host.

"I wonder that you never learned to jump yourself," John said on his second day there.

Angelo grimaced. "I tried once. It really didn't work out very well. Since then, I decided it would be safer to pay someone to handle the technical part."

They had been invited to attend a party that night, and John was genuinely looking forward to it. The guest list included several powerful friends who he had not seen in years. He had brought along his formal robes for the occasion and was glad to notice on his arrival that most of the guests were similarly attired. He enjoyed the shifting colors that well-made formal robes emitted. The blood-red fabric of his own let off a dull glow in the darker card room and shimmered brightly in the main ballroom under the vast number of candles in the gilded chandeliers.

His appearance at the party caused quite a stir, since apart from his own recent ball it had been over a century since he'd made an appearance at any private party. The ball at Larch Hill had consisted mostly of American vampires, with the rest of the guests being those with the means to cross the ocean on a whim. The party in Rome was much more diverse.

He was hailed in French within a few minutes of entering. Excusing himself from Angelo, he walked over to greet a tall thin man with brown hair. "*Salut*, Michel. What brings you all the way from France?"

Michel grinned. "You know it is not so very far these days. What brings you to Rome? Business or pleasure?"

"A little of both," John admitted. "I have some research that I'm working on, but I'm delighted to see everyone again. It really has been a long time."

He followed Michel into the card room, where every game of chance that had ever been invented seemed to have a representative table. He sat down to play piquet.

"What, no poker?" a small man chided at his elbow.

"I've never learned, and it doesn't look like this is the place to try." He eyed a large pile of bills in the center of the poker table. The man laughed his assent and moved away to find someone else he could fleece.

John was used to people shying away from discussion of Renphor in his presence and was therefore surprised when the topic was introduced and vigorously discussed almost immediately upon his joining the table.

"Still chasing Renphor?" a hefty man wearing a red smoking jacket asked him.

John smiled. "Always."

"What is the disagreement between you two? Four hundred years is a long time for a feud. Even the Hatfields and the McCoys gave up well before then."

"That's because the principals died off." John replied.

The others laughed and continued playing their cards. John waited a few minutes before reopening the conversation. "Renphor seems to have been even quieter than I for the last century or so. Or is it just that no one's talking about him in front of me?" he smiled.

A blond man across from him answered. "The latter. I wouldn't exactly call him social, but he surfaces once or twice a decade at some fancy event."

John nodded. "So he hangs around Rome a lot?"

The other man shrugged. "Rome, Paris, Geneva, Athens, Prague. Anywhere his whims take him. Mostly around cities with major universities. He seems to have even more of a passion for study than you do." John snorted, but the other man ignored him. "I guess you can be pretty footloose if you can travel from one side of the globe to the other in an instant."

"I can't imagine that even Renphor is reckless enough to go globe-hopping on a whim. The amount of energy that would burn would be astronomical." John leaned back in his chair, drumming his fingers on the table and rearranging his cards by turn. He spoke more to himself than the others at the table. "He *must* have a home base somewhere."

The blond man laughed at this. "Not one that anyone's figured out. He obviously keeps his official robes somewhere, since he doesn't get new ones before each function." The others laughed, and he went on, "but as near as anyone can figure, all he has is a storage space."

John shook his head. "He must keep clothing somewhere. And books, if he does all of that studying."

The hefty man nodded. "I think he does, actually. I'm pretty sure I heard Stefan mention an apartment, but whoever he was talking to pressed too hard for more details, and he clammed up. It's one of the enduring mysteries of the age— where the hell does Renphor call home?" he grinned.

John looked perplexed. "Why would Stefan care about telling people where he lives, if he knows?"

A thin man on the other side of the table finally spoke up. "Because he doesn't want his stuff destroyed. Renphor has the fiend's own temper from what I understand. He's powerful enough to wreak holy havoc on Stefan's apartment before anyone could stop him, too. It's better not to mess with him unless you can't help it."

"If he's so powerful, I wonder why he's the one in hiding."

Two of the others laughed, but the thin man looked grave. "I don't think he is hiding. Just likes to be left alone, and when you publish your address, some fool is always knocking on your door, asking for a favor." He shook his head glumly.

"You seem to be well versed on his personality," John remarked.

The other man inched slowly away from the table as he responded. "I've talked to him a couple of times when we ran into each other around town."

They played for a while longer in silence as John mulled over the information he had gotten from the other three. None of it was very helpful. He abruptly left the table an hour later and hunted out Angelo to tell him he was going for a solo walk along the river and would take a cab home.

Angelo shook his head. "I would offer you my valet's services, but you would need a phone in order to call him after your walk."

"That does rather rule him out, doesn't it?" John replied.

He made use of a changing room on his way out and concealed his robes inside a bag he had brought along for the purpose. Wandering the streets of Rome in shimmering red robes would draw exactly the kind of attention he wished to avoid.

Back in his regular street clothes, John strolled slowly, enjoying the night air. His acute sense of smell picked up all the scents he remembered from his first visit as a young man. These mixed with more modern exhaust smells and the more subtle scents that his vampire senses could now detect. His mind wandered over the information he had gleaned from the other cardplayers. He had guessed that Renphor could jump, since it was an almost universal ability in Stefan's line, but he had not been aware that he was an expert. Cross-continental jumpers were rare, since it required a significant amount of skill and energy.

He started forming new strategies in his mind, based on the information he had been given. Stefan seemed to be the key to finding Renphor's home base. He had previously thought there must be plenty of people who knew it, and they just weren't talking. But getting information from Stefan was an unreliable strategy. He continued his solitary walk, through the gardens and past the Colosseum, until he noticed that it was getting light. He took a cab to Angelo's house. Since his host wasn't back yet, John spent a few hours with the vortex until his return.

He remained two more weeks in Rome, visiting with Angelo's acquaintances some nights and meeting up with old friends of his own on others. Everywhere he went, the story he had heard the first night was reinforced. Everyone assumed Renphor had a home base. No one knew where it was. At the end of his visit, he reluctantly boarded a plane home, and within eight hours he was in the passenger seat of his own car, telling his mate everything he had found out during his trip.

24

On the Tuesday following Renphor and Arabella's conversation about the festival, he left her apartment far earlier than usual. She had some work to finish up and didn't want any distractions, so he decided to take an early-morning stroll around the city while it was still warm enough to enjoy one. A few blocks from her place, he became aware that someone was following him. Not wanting to turn around and advertise the fact that he had noticed them, he resorted to glancing in windows in the hope of catching a reflection. Using this tactic, he was able to figure out that his pursuers were part of the group of goons that generally hung around with Rick Stevens. Renphor sighed. He debated shaking them off but decided they would be back the next day, and the day after that, until they managed to force a confrontation.

Knowing that they would hang back until they were out of sight of the main road, he ducked down a side alley that ran behind a line of row houses and a closed restaurant. He was amazed at how much restaurant debris still lingered. It looked as if the trash collectors had given up on the route several months before the place had closed. Any food scraps had long ago been picked over by rats and other animals, but there were still paper remnants and bits of plastic bags strewn the whole way down the alley. After half a block, he ran into a dead end. He turned and found himself confronting four men who looked more like three-hundred-pound gorillas. A quick assessment told him that he was facing off against a significant portion of the football team's starting lineup. Stevens was not among them. Renphor was unable to hide a sneer.

"I see your fearless leader chose to miss this little meeting. Why is that, I wonder?"

The largest of the goons answered. "Like he'd waste his time on you."

Renphor sized up the four men, including the baseball bats they were carrying. What had been mild irritation at the start was turning to pure rage. He disliked bullies, and given his size and apparent strength, they had obviously not intended to give him a fighting chance. His original plan to extricate himself as quickly as possible evaporated. These assholes needed a good lesson. He cracked his knuckles and smiled slightly.

"Well? Are you actually planning to murder me, or just break a few bones? You seem to be rather over armed for the project."

Another of the goons smiled. "We can't let you live, can we? If you go and tell on us, someone might believe you. We'd be kicked off the team."

"Ah. Interesting. I don't suppose it occurred to you that several people probably saw you wandering around campus with those bats? Since even the laxest of referees wouldn't go for deadly weapons on the field, someone might question you about them if they were to find me beaten to a pulp."

"If? You think you might get away?" The third goon leered.

Renphor laughed at this, causing all four men to cast puzzled looks at one another. They stood staring at each other for a few minutes, unsure of how to handle the situation. The fourth, and apparently stupidest, finally got tired of waiting. He charged Renphor with his bat held high. Renphor barely seemed to move, and the others had dropped their bats to their sides to watch when the man was suddenly hurled backwards as if he

had been flung from a giant slingshot. The force of his momentum knocked over one of his comrades, and the two of them
landed in a heap about fifteen feet from Renphor. The bat,
which had flown out of his hand on impact, smashed against the
wall an instant later. Both men had hit the ground with enough
force to be knocked unconscious, and the sight of their inani-
mate forms stunned the other two into inactivity for a long moment.

Finally getting over their shock, the remaining goons ran at
Renphor. He jumped himself out of the way when they were
inches from him and laughed as they tried desperately to stop
their forward momentum before hitting the brick wall at the end
of the alley. There was a sickening crunch, and both men fell to
the ground. They managed to stand again after a few minutes
and helped each other get their balance. Renphor leaned against
the opposite wall, smiling languidly at the two as they staggered
up. Enraged by the sight of him, they charged again. When they
had covered half of the distance to the wall, he darted forward.
Their reflexes were much too slow to allow them to stop in time,
and as they passed him, he grabbed them both and smashed
their heads together hard. They collapsed a few feet from their
friends. Renphor looked at the heap of men in disgust before
turning on his heel and walking away.

When the campus newspaper reported the story about the
attack the next day it glossed over the bats that had been found
at the scene, and the fact that the men had been attacked down
a dead-end alley, where they couldn't possibly have had any legit-
imate business. One or two people who were familiar with the
tension between Rick and Renphor were bold enough to make
snide comments to Arabella, but she told them tersely not to be
ridiculous. Fond as she was of Renphor, she wasn't besotted

enough to believe that he had taken on four men twice his size and emerged without a scratch.

Throughout the following week, Arabella noticed some of her classmates whispering behind their hands and turning away from them as she and Renphor walked past. Renphor ignored them completely, and most of the time Arabella looked straight ahead and feigned deafness. She became less reserved when the two of them found themselves alone in her apartment a week after the incident.

They had been sitting on the couch, watching *Pride & Prejudice*. He was completely engrossed in the movie. When she was in a happier state of mind, she found this very funny, but a fencing lesson shown on the screen recalled the attack to her mind, and she wasn't able to put it back out of her head. After watching Renphor for a few minutes, she cleared her throat hesitantly. He started and looked at her with a puzzled but slightly amused expression. "Did you want to say something?"

"Were they really looking for you the other morning?" She had meant to approach the question with a little more preamble and blushed slightly at having blurted it out like that.

"Yes. But there's no need to look so guilty about it," he said soothingly.

Arabella paled slightly. "Why were they trying to beat you up? Because of me?"

"It seems the most likely explanation. Don't let it worry you."

"But it does worry me. I don't want you to be in danger because of me." Her head drooped, and she stared at her hands.

Renphor put his finger under her chin and lifted her head so she was looking him in the eyes. "My pet, believe me when I tell you that I am far more of a danger to you than you are to me." He smiled at her, but she noticed a hint of bitterness behind the smile.

"Why would you be a danger to me?"

"For a dozen different reasons." He was looking at the movie again as he answered and did not meet her eyes. She started to press the issue but realized that the invisible wall that sometimes seemed to wrap around him had gone up again. Arabella sighed and rearranged herself on the couch so that she could lay her head on his shoulder. He put his arm around her and gave her a slight squeeze.

The following Saturday was Halloween, and Renphor spent the morning lounging on the couch in Arabella's apartment, watching old cartoons. Sam walked past him but stopped before she got to her bedroom door. She stared at the TV for several moments before looking at Renphor.

"Er, demon boy, do you know you're watching *Scooby Doo*?"

"Is that what it's called?"

She laughed in spite of herself. "You could change the channel, you know."

"I did know that, thanks." He continued to watch intently.

"But you never do."

"I'm perfectly happy with whatever is on."

Sam shook her head in disbelief, then changed the subject. "Are you and Arabella going to the party tonight?"

Renphor looked at her at last. "What party?"

"Didn't she mention it? I would have thought she would have been all over you to go. She's a complete nut about Halloween."

"She didn't, actually. I'll have to ask her about it. Who's hosting?"

Sam realized too late why Arabella hadn't mentioned the party. "Oh. Um. Why don't you ask her about it?"

She started to shuffle toward her room, but he reached over the arm of the couch and grabbed her wrist to stop her. Sam jumped at his touch.

"Jesus, your hands are cold!"

"I know. Who's hosting?"

She tried to pull away from him and realized with a jolt that his fingers were clasped around her wrist like steel clamps. She sighed. "Troy Brown. That's quite a grip you've got, by the way."

"Thank you. Troy Brown as in one of Rick Stevens's satellites?" His voice was very level.

She nodded. He let go of her at last and went back to watching the program. Sam stared at him for a moment, rubbing her wrist where he had held her. He hadn't applied any noticeable pressure and had certainly left no mark, but she could still feel the cold sensation from his hands even after he released her. She shivered. "Is all of your skin that cold, or is it just your hands?" She regretted the question almost as soon as she had asked it, but he seemed highly amused. He put out his arm again. "See for yourself."

She tentatively felt his arm above the wrist, and then above the elbow. Finally, she put her hand on his neck. Her eyes met his, and she was startled to notice that he was on the verge of laughter.

"You should see the look on your face," he said.

She stared at him. "That's just not normal. How does Arabella stand it?"

"Doesn't seem to bother her."

Sam backed slowly away from him before retreating to her own room.

Arabella came out of her room shortly afterward.

"What are you grinning about?" she asked.

He explained the conversation with Sam as she flopped on the couch next to him.

"So, why didn't you mention the party?" he asked.

She looked surprised. "I didn't think you'd want to go."

"Am I even invited?"

She waved this away. "Other people bring dates. I don't see why not. But wouldn't it be weird for you?"

"No, I think it would be quite—interesting."

"It's a costume party, though. What would you go as?" She had never seen him wearing anything other than the white shirt and jeans he had on now and couldn't fathom where he would come up with the pieces for a costume on short notice.

"I don't know." He suddenly grinned. "Yes, I do, actually."

She looked at him curiously. "What?"

He kissed her. "You'll see."

Arabella tilted her head. "Do you have time to buy the costume?"

"No need. I've got everything I require. How about you?"

She thought for a moment. "Yes. I have a costume I started to make last year and didn't wear. I should be able to finish it in a couple hours."

He smiled at her. "In that case, I'll leave you to it. What time should I pick you up?"

"Eight."

Renphor arrived promptly at eight o'clock. Arabella and Sam both stared at him when he walked in.

"Hey, demon boy?"

"Humans can't see demons."

"So you keep saying. But I think you might have missed the point of a costume party."

He was dressed in the same clothes he had been wearing when he left the apartment that morning.

"Did I?" He smiled, revealing two long white fangs. Sam staggered backwards slightly as she noticed that the red glow was back in his eyes.

"That is totally fucking creepy. Where did you get those teeth, and how the hell do you get your eyes to do that thing without going blind?"

"That's my little secret. Arabella, my pet, you look stunning."

Arabella was dressed in an elaborate Victorian dress. Sam, who hadn't felt like making as much of an effort, was wearing a store-bought maid's costume. Arabella smiled at him.

"What teeth?" He smiled again to let her see.

"Those are impressive." She reached out her hand toward his mouth. He grabbed her hands quickly.

"No touching."

"What are they made out of?"

"Bone? I have no idea."

She giggled. "Are you trying to tell me they're real?"

"Of course." He put his arm around her.

"So why haven't I seen them before?" She kissed him on the chin.

"Magic. Shall we get going?" He guided her toward the door, with Sam following behind.

Renphor and Arabella got back to the apartment around midnight. Arabella had gotten tired of listening to rude comments about her boyfriend mixed in with blatant sexual innuendo, and had suggested they leave. Sam had gotten bored early and left a couple hours after she arrived, so she was already lounging on the couch in her pajamas by the time they got back. She was eating a bowl of popcorn and watching *Saw III*. Arabella shuddered.

"I don't know how you watch that stuff," she said.

Sam shrugged. "It's all fake. Besides, you just walked in with the creepiest thing I've seen all evening." She looked pointedly at Renphor.

Arabella scowled at her before addressing Renphor. "I guess you have to take out those fangs."

"What fangs?" he asked, smiling. There was no trace of the elongated teeth. Arabella stared, eyes wide.

"What did you do with them?"

He pulled her close to him. "I told you, it's Magic."

Sam looked curiously at him. "Did you enjoy the party? I noticed Troy was acting mighty chummy."

Renphor laughed. "You could call it that. Badgered me into joining their stupid arm-wrestling competition."

Arabella was aghast. "They compete for hundred-dollar stakes!"

He grinned. "I noticed." He pulled a wad of cash out of his pocket as he spoke. Arabella's and Sam's mouths both fell open.

"You won all of that?" Arabella gasped.

"One would think you didn't have any confidence in me." He put the money back in his pocket. "Now let's watch the rest of this excellent movie Sam found." He pulled her over to the other side of the couch and sat down. She curled up next to him but continued to cast curious glances in his direction until they went to bed.

26

John returned from Rome on Halloween afternoon and spent the rest of the day wandering listlessly around his library. Because he refused to feed on human blood, the scarcity of prey inside the city limits had caused him to get off his normal feeding schedule. The combination of that and the long journey home had sapped his energy levels. His lethargy hadn't lasted long, however. By the following day, he was back at the table in his library. Julie found him sitting there, irritably flinging bits of fire from his fingertips. She watched him for several minutes, casting an occasional glance toward the shelves piled high with books or the silk curtains. "Have you considered practicing that little skill outdoors?" she asked at last.

"It's raining."

"So much the better."

He glared at her. "What's that supposed to mean?"

She considered a spark that had landed on top of an enormous old globe in the corner of the room. "Apparently you've forgotten your fire prevention methods," she answered. He turned his head to follow her gaze and quickly rose to swat at the smoldering ember that was still perched on Greenland. He began pacing the room.

"For the life of me, I can't work out how to complete this spell. Petros and I worked on it for two weeks. The fireball starts out good and strong, but then it just fizzles out. I'm missing the page that explains how to intensify it." He poked pettishly at the diagram, then hastily patted it down as a lingering spark dropped off the end of his finger and landed on top of the stack of parchment.

She eyed him grimly. "Missing a page, are you? When did you figure that out?"

"Petros found it. He was trying to figure out if the side notes would provide anything useful, and he realized there was an incongruity between where the third page ended and..." His voice trailed off. "Why the devil didn't you tell me?"

"I started to. You acted like I was some subspecies of idiot for looking at the parts I could actually read. Since you're so much smarter, I figured you'd find it on your own eventually."

He opened his mouth to answer, but he was interrupted by Joseph's quiet entrance into the room. The servant stood stiffly at the corner of the table until John acknowledged him.

"Mr. Davies to see you, my lord."

"Show him in." As Julie rose to leave, he said irritably, "Going somewhere?"

She waited until Joseph was out of the room before speaking. "I'm not hanging around to chat with that idiot. The cat has better conversational skills," she said, heading for the French windows.

He considered calling her back, but Nelson had been shown into the room before he had a chance to do so. Frowning in the direction she had exited, he motioned his visitor to a chair.

Nelson perched on the edge of the wooden chair, bouncing up and down as he prepared to deliver his news. John suppressed the urge to squelch him and turned the chair he had been using around to face his guest.

"I take it you have some information for me?" He was interested in spite of himself.

Nelson smiled broadly. "I finally met someone who knows Renphor. He gave me some information about him."

John waited expectantly. Nelson finally took the hint and went on.

"He said he saw him in Paris two weeks ago." Nelson seemed absurdly pleased with this revelation. John sat stock-still for a moment.

"And?" he asked coldly.

Nelson looked confused. "Well, we just need to go there to start our search. Once we pick up his trail, we can follow it to wherever he went next, right?" John cast an icy look in his direction, and he faltered on the end of the sentence.

"This acquaintance you were speaking to. Did he happen to mention that Renphor was *staying* in Paris?"

"No...but how far could he have gotten in two weeks? He must have spoken to someone there who knew where he was headed." Nelson sounded defensive. John closed his eyes and leaned back in his chair. He sat motionless for several minutes while Nelson watched him anxiously.

"Davies, how on earth have you survived this long without stepping into a volcano?"

Nelson's mouth dropped open. John sat up quickly, his usually bright blue eyes blazing orange with rage. Nelson crawled so far back in the chair that he seemed to be trying to disappear through the back of it.

"Renphor is a jumper, Nelson. Do you know what that means?"

Davies nodded. "Of course—"

"Apparently not. It means, my good fool, that his location in any particular city at any particular time means *nothing*. He could have run into this acquaintance of yours in Paris at noon and been happily lounging on a South American beach an hour later. I need his home base, not anecdotes of how he spent his afternoon two weeks ago!"

"Paris to South America is a bit of a stretch, isn't it?"

"No."

Nelson slumped against the back of the chair as John began pacing the room. He ignored the fishlike motions Nelson's mouth was making as he apparently formed and discarded several ideas without speaking. John's patience finally wore out. "Get out. I can't deal with any more of your idiocy today. I have things to accomplish."

The dejected informer slunk out of the room as quickly as possible. John picked a set of brass scales up off the table, examining them closely before smashing them against the tall bookcase across the room.

27

On the Monday after Halloween, Renphor found himself with nothing to do. Arabella had plans for most of the evening, so he couldn't spend the evening with her the way he normally would have done. His last class was at five o'clock, so he decided to spend some time studying at the library after it ended. Since he had nothing urgent to get done and needed to return to his room for a few things, he decided it was a good time to be seen using the bus system. He would get off at the stop about a quarter of a mile from the rooming house and walk the rest of the way. It was already dark by the time the bus reached his stop, and his senses had heightened as the last of the light faded away. He was aware of being followed almost as soon as he got off the bus. Realizing that his pursuer was human, he ignored it at first, but after a few blocks he started to feel irritated by the intrusion.

Renphor glanced casually into the windows across the street so that he could see behind him without turning his head. He grimaced, realizing that he was being followed by Rick Stevens, and that he appeared to be carrying some kind of weapon. It looked a bit like a tire iron, which the man was unsuccessfully trying to conceal between his arm and his body. *Typical*, he thought. Rick undoubtedly meant to whack him with it before he could fight back. Renphor pretended to stop in a doorway to tie his shoe and observed his pursuer's behavior with amusement. Rick had frozen to the spot for a second before scurrying into a doorway. Renphor sneered. It almost wasn't worth playing when the adversary was this stupid. He sighed and continued toward his rooming house. Several people eyed him hostilely as he passed, before casting confused glances in the direction of Stevens's slinking form. Renphor couldn't decide if they had noticed the sad attempt at concealing the weapon or if Rick just looked that out of place in this neighborhood. One of his less antagonistic neighbors tried to give him a visual warning, but Renphor just smiled and nodded in the man's direction.

They continued in this fashion until they got to the run-down building where Renphor lived. He passed the front steps just as the landlord was coming down them. The landlord had developed a much friendlier attitude toward him in the months since he had first rented the room. Renphor suspected that this was largely due to his almost unheard-of habit of paying his rent consistently and on time.

"Yo, Callaghan, looks like you got a friend," he said softly.

"Subtle, isn't he? I believe I'll walk around back to the dumpsters. Anyone back there?"

The man shook his head and quickly went back inside. Renphor bypassed the entrance to the building and walked around to the back steps. He pretended to start up them but spun around as he sensed Rick quickly closing the gap between them. He took in the raised weapon and the livid look on the man's face without seeming to move. Rick got to within a few steps of his quarry, who still stood motionless on the steps, but seconds before the tire iron would have made contact with its target Renphor flicked his fingers toward him and Rick suddenly flew backwards and cracked his head hard on the pavement.

When Rick opened his eyes a few minutes later, Renphor was standing next to him. "Get up." Rick stood unsteadily. He looked dazedly around for a weapon to protect himself, but he had lost the tire iron and there was nothing else in sight. "Not very sporting, Stevens. Coming after an unarmed man with a blunt instrument."

F. Anne Fischer

Rick was still dazed. "Unarmed? But...what...how...?"

Renphor laughed derisively. "Always so hung up on appearances, aren't you? There was no need for me to actually touch you to knock you across that alley."

Rick shook his head to clear his thoughts and immediately put his hands up to his temples. "What happened to my head?" he groaned.

"No idea. Probably smacked it on the ground. Least of your worries, anyway." An unpleasant look had started to creep across Renphor's features as he spoke.

"What do you want?" Rick's voice shook, and he took an involuntary step backwards.

"You have once again pissed me off, and this time we're alone and I happen to be hungry." Renphor was staring intently at his prey now, considering his approach.

"H—hungry?" Rick stumbled backwards as Renphor smiled, revealing the two long fangs that everyone had admired at the Halloween party.

"Hungry. Look at it this way—death by vampire is a fairly interesting way to go. Not that anyone will ever know, of course."

"You expect me to believe that you're really a vampire? What are you doing dating Arabella, then?" Some of Rick's jeering manner had returned.

"Arabella is none of your business. And it doesn't matter what you believe, since your life expectancy is about thirty seconds."

Rick started to sneer but instead gasped in shock as Renphor made one quick movement and sank his fangs deep into the man's throat. Rick struggled in his grasp for a few seconds but quickly went limp. Renphor drank as much of the blood as he could while Rick's heart continued to pump it. When the flow stopped, he removed his fangs and snapped the neck quickly backwards before dropping the body on the ground. He ran his tongue around his fangs and lips methodically to make sure he hadn't missed any of it.

After checking his clothes for any telltale signs of blood, Renphor pondered the body lying on the ground in front of him. He hadn't really been hungry, since his normal feeding night was Thursday, but since dinner had so obligingly followed him home, he had made an exception. Now the first order of business was to get rid of his adversary's remains somewhere far from his own building. He paused for a moment, looking around to make sure none of the neighbors had gotten curious, before picking up the body and disappearing into the night with it.

A few days later, Arabella was sitting alone in the cafeteria when Sam flopped down next to her. "Where's demon boy?"

"Sam—"

"Okay, okay. Why isn't Ryan with you?"

Arabella shrugged. "Not much point in him coming to the cafeteria. Just wastes a chair. He had some work to do on a paper for Lit, so I figured this was a good time."

Sam laughed. "Are you always so helpful with his schedule?"

"What do you mean?"

"You basically just told me that you'd given your kind permission for the man to do his homework while you ate. Nice of you."

Arabella blushed. "That isn't what I meant. I don't run his schedule."

"No need to get all embarrassed. I'm certainly not concerned about his happiness." Arabella started to answer, but Sam cut her off. "Did you hear about Rick Stevens?"

"What about him? Still making an ass of himself over losing his spot on the football team?"

"Cold-hearted, aren't we? If he is, he's at least doing it where no one can see him. He's disappeared. None of his friends have seen him since Monday night."

Arabella regretted her flippant tone at once. "Disappeared? Do you think something happened to him?"

"Nah. I think he couldn't handle not being top dog anymore, so he took off to look for greener pastures."

"Has anyone talked to his parents?"

Sam laughed. "I thought you used to talk to the guy? He hasn't spoken to his parents since freshman year. They wouldn't have a clue about his whereabouts. Doesn't talk to the rest of his family either. Got in a snit because one of his cousins was sole beneficiary in his grandparents' will and blamed everyone for plotting against him."

Arabella was only half listening to Sam's explanation. She stared straight ahead, lost in thought.

The Friday after the disappearance, Arabella and her roommates decided to go out to Han Dynasty for dinner, to try to lighten their moods. The restaurant was unusually empty when they arrived, but they still chose an out-of-the-way table at the back so they could talk in peace. Narcissa wedged herself as far back into the corner as she could, leaving Sam and Arabella to take the seats facing away from the middle of the restaurant.

"Seriously, Cissy, you've been acting like a nut all week. What does Rick's disappearance even have to do with you?" Arabella asked.

"I was friends with him. People know I was friends with him."

"We don't even know what happened to him, Cissy. The police just issued a statement saying there was no indication of foul play," Sam said reasonably.

"They were all over it for a week, and suddenly just closed the case? Am I the only one who thinks this is suspicious? They were practically following Arabella around for three days."

"There was no 'practically' about it. I caught one of them staring through the window of my study room the last time I went to the library." Arabella rolled her eyes.

Narcissa looked close to tears. "And you're still allowing that freak to hang around you."

"Narcissa, I will not listen to this."

"You're crazy, Ella. Rick's car was found ten blocks from his place. Troy told them he was planning to go there to confront Ryan. *There was already an unsolved murder right behind his building.*"

"And what does a murder of some random guy in a bad section of the city have to do with the fight between Ryan and Rick? I don't even know how you're making that connection."

"I'm trying to point out that he's a psychopath," Narcissa whined.

Sam finally chimed in. "Come off it, Cissy. You know I'm not part of Ryan's fan club, but pretty much everyone agrees that it would take someone with mobster-level skills to have committed the murder you're trying to pin on him, and to have disposed of the body that effectively. It's just not reasonable."

"Thanks for your support, Sam. I think," Arabella said. "Plus, Cissy is leaving out the fact that absolutely no one saw a man answering to Rick's description within five blocks of Ryan's place."

"And aren't we supposed to be here to get our minds onto some topic other than Rick? I suggest we do so starting now," Sam said.

28

It had been a week since any of John's adherents had shown their faces at Larch Hill. After his somewhat painful encounter with their ringleader, Nelson had spread the word that John was in a bad mood. They had agreed amongst themselves to avoid John until he summoned them, or until one of them had actually run into Renphor on the street. Then they considered this for a while and decided that they would stick with the first part of this plan and avoid the second part at all costs. John's description of Renphor's personality and habits had convinced them all that he was likely to blow them to pieces in the most public way possible if they had the misfortune to encounter him while alone and unprotected, and the closer they felt themselves drawing to their quarry, the more nervous they were becoming.

Julie was fairly well informed about the general feelings of the group, having run into Nelson at Stefan's apartment a few days earlier, so she was startled when Stella wafted into John's study unannounced. She stopped dead on the threshold, staring at Julie. Julie stared back for a few seconds before waving her uninvited guest into a chair.

"What do you want?" she asked without preamble.

Stella stiffened. "I prefer to speak to John," she answered haughtily.

Julie shrugged. "Suit yourself. He won't be back for at least another two hours, but you're welcome to wait." She stood as she spoke and picked up her book.

"Where are you going?" Stella asked.

Julie continued her leisurely path to the door. "My plans for the evening didn't include entertaining John's…friends. If you want to sit here for hours like an idiot, figure out how to entertain yourself."

She closed the hall door behind her with a bang.

John had spent a fruitless evening trying to pump Stefan for ideas about the fire vortex and finally returned around midnight. He was shocked to find Stella running her hand pettishly along the shelves of antique manuscripts that lined his walls and steered her forcefully back to her chair.

"I didn't think you were much of a reader," he commented drily.

"I'm not." She sulked. "But Julie was too rude to stay and keep me company while I waited, so I've had nothing to do since nine o'clock."

"You've been here for three hours? Alone?" He looked nervously around the library.

"I told you. Julie made a few very rude comments to me and then walked out." She looked up at him from under her eyelashes.

John compressed his lips but refrained from commenting on his mate's behavior in Stella's presence. "What was it that you wanted to talk to me about?" He took the high-backed chair opposite the one he had given to Stella.

"I have some real information about Renphor," she stated triumphantly.

John sat up abruptly. "You're sure?"

She nodded. "You remember that you asked me to talk to Philip Avery at the ball?"

"Of course. What about it?"

"I got into a conversation with him at another party. Apparently he's seen Renphor in the past week, and I managed to, um, convince him to give me a little information."

John was familiar with Stella's methods of convincing men to do what she wanted but chose to let it pass. "Go on," he said.

"Anyway, it seems Davies wasn't so far off after all." She paused, but John stared at her impassively. "Apparently Renphor is based in Paris. He's not sure of the exact address. Thinks he might actually be living in the sewers."

John twitched slightly. "A fitting location," he responded. "But also a difficult one. How sure is he of this information?"

Stella fidgeted in her chair. "He says he sees Renphor at least once a month, and they've talked several times about how much they both enjoy living in Paris. Avery is only there part of the year, of course, when his business requires it."

John stood and nodded to her. "This is extremely useful, Stella. Thank you. I will follow up with a few friends who live in Paris and see if I can get any more definite information about where he's set up camp."

She stood as well and moved closer to him. "I'm so glad I could be of use." She slid her hand up his arm and looked up at him through her lashes. "I'm surprised Julie hasn't done more to help you with your search. She seems to be content to sit around in all this luxury you provide and never do anything to earn it." She glanced around her as she spoke, an avaricious look in her eye.

"Oh, Julie is helpful where she can be," he answered lightly. "It's a little harder for her to get information from people, since they can't have any doubts as to her motives."

He held on to Stella's hand for a moment before escorting her to the door. Once she was out of sight, he went in search of Julie. After finding her sitting room empty, John went up the tower to look for her there. As he came through the trapdoor, he saw her put a marker in her book and set it calmly to the side.

"What did the blond nitwit want?" she asked coldly.

"You might have found out for yourself, if you'd chosen to fulfill your duties as hostess."

"Doubtful, since she told me pretty unequivocally that she preferred to talk to you."

"You could at least have stayed with her."

"I don't intend to waste my evening entertaining your...friends."

"She's a useful informant."

"She's a pretty harpy who's after as much as she can get. And apparently she's already gotten plenty from you."

John bit back a retort, knowing that he was on shaky ground where discussions of Stella were concerned. There was too much truth in Julie's words for him to make a convincing argument to the contrary.

"You shouldn't have left her alone in my library, at any rate. God knows what she might have gotten up to."

"Well, I wasn't putting her in my sitting room."

"Anyway, she had some really good information about Renphor. Came from a reliable source, too." He recapped the conversation for her as he paced around the top of the tower.

"Paris!" was all she said.

"Yes—why do you seem so surprised?"

She smiled. "I'm not surprised—just relieved. The farther he is from my family, the happier I am."

"Does that mean you don't want to accompany me there?"

She had started to reach for her book again but stopped with her hand in midair at his words. "You're going to Paris? It's been years since I was there—"

He took her hands in his and looked at her eagerly. "So come with me."

She grimaced. "And spend my time roaming around the sewer system?"

"Of course not. We'll be spending most of the time visiting various friends and acquaintances, sounding them out for information. You can do as much sightseeing as you want during the day. Come with me, Julie! It'll be fun."

"When are you planning to go?"

"As soon as possible. Tomorrow, if I can get the tickets."

He watched her for some indication of her thoughts as she sat staring into space, tapping one finger on the cover of her book. "How long were you planning to be gone?" she asked at last.

"Two weeks at the most."

"Alright," she finally answered. "Arabella is wrapped up in her schoolwork, so I don't see any reason for us not to go for a few weeks."

John grabbed both of her hands, kissing the fingertips. "Go figure out what you want to pack. I'll work on transportation."

29

The Sunday after Rick's disappearance, Renphor found himself lounging on the chair beside Arabella's desk, waiting for her to finish getting ready. Arabella had coerced him into going out to breakfast with her, even though he never ate anything at restaurants. She told him she was in the mood for eggs benedict and said they were too much work to make for herself, and he finally acquiesced. Just as she was coming out of the bathroom, they heard a slight commotion in the living room. Arabella was looking toward the door and didn't notice Renphor stiffen or observe the red light that had suddenly appeared in his eyes.

From the next room, they heard Sam's voice. "Mr. Elder! I didn't know you were coming to visit."

Renphor shot across the room to the window so fast that Arabella turned to the chair to speak to him before she realized that he wasn't there. She looked around in confusion. "How the heck did you move that fast?" He shrugged. "My stepfather is here."

"So I gathered."

"Are you going to let me introduce you?" There was an edge to her voice.

He smiled. "Not a chance." Without giving her time to respond, he unlatched the window and made a hasty exit onto the fire escape.

Arabella walked into the living room a minute later. "John, I didn't know you were going to visit today."

He smiled at her, attributing her obvious irritation to his unannounced arrival. "I'm sure your mother told you that we're leaving for Paris soon. I figured I would take you and Sam out for some breakfast before we go and catch up on what's going on in your life."

John looked at Sam, who had started to say something to Arabella, but she suddenly closed her mouth again.

He glanced from one to the other. "Now, what's going on?"

Arabella answered. "Nothing. I had originally planned to go out to breakfast with Ryan, but something came up."

Sam blinked but continued to hold her tongue.

"Will I do as well?" he asked tentatively.

She smiled suddenly. "Better, I think. Sam, are you coming?"

Sam nodded and looked around for her coat and purse. They left in a group, but halfway down the hall he noticed that the two girls had fallen behind, and circled around to wait for them. They quickly stopped their whispered conversation and hurried toward him.

Over breakfast, John brought the conversation back around to Arabella's boyfriend. "I didn't know you were dating anyone. Tell me about him."

"He's a Classical Studies major. He helped me out with some of my reading assignments for English Lit our first week back, and we really hit it off."

John pretended not to notice Sam's grimace but made a mental note of it all the same.

"So what do the two of you do?"

Sam choked on her egg. Arabella shot her a look.

"He likes old movies, so we watch a lot of those. And walks in the park."

"And never talking to other human beings…"

"Sam!"

"Sorry."

"Sounds like a man of deep thoughts."

Arabella giggled. "Some. Some not so much."

John raised his eyebrows, but Arabella had become serious again.

"It's nice hanging around someone sensible for a change. The rest of the guys in my classes are more—"

"Toddlers," Sam interjected. "I'll give Ryan that much. He's weird, but he's definitely an adult."

Arabella frowned at her friend and gave several more points in her boyfriend's favor. John decided that Sam was suffering a jealous fit because she had lost her friend's exclusive attention.

"So, do you and this wonderful guy do anything else together?"

"Not much, neither of us have much money..."

John smiled. "Is that a hint?"

Arabella picked at her eggs. "I could use a little more. I know you've been really generous, but I'm going to need interview clothes and stuff soon..."

"Alright. An extra hundred a week, but don't tell your mother."

Arabella beamed at him. Sam scowled and tore her toast into shreds.

Arabella pulled the key out of her purse, commenting as she did so that she would have to come up with some way of entertaining herself for the day. She jumped as Renphor suddenly spoke directly behind her. "Why?"

He schooled his face into a conciliatory look as she spun around. "So you've decided to rejoin us, have you?" she asked tartly.

He nodded. "Are you totally pissed off, or do you still want to head to the park today?"

She sighed. "It's too nice a day to sulk inside, so I suppose I'll forgive you."

Sam shook her head. "Too easy. And how did you happen to know when we'd be back?" She eyed him hostilely.

"Lucky guess."

He followed them into the apartment and spent some time smoothing Arabella's still-ruffled feathers. By the time they were ready to leave, she was perfectly happy with him again, much to Sam's irritation.

"You're a pushover, Ella. You're not even making him explain himself for disappearing out a window."

Renphor smiled tightly. "I wasn't about to let John find me in the girl's bedroom."

Sam opened her mouth to retort but was cut off by Arabella. "He doesn't owe you an explanation. He can give me one later." She looked pointedly at him, and he nodded.

Arabella opened the refrigerator door and stared inside. "How long are we planning to be out, anyway?"

"How long do you want to be out?"

Arabella looked out the window as she mulled it over. "I think it's going to be gorgeous. We could plan on the whole day, if you want?"

"Whatever makes you happy."

"In that case, I'll pack something for lunch."

Ten minutes later, they headed out the door. Arabella slid behind the wheel of her green Toyota as Renphor jumped into the passenger seat.

"Do you ever plan on learning to drive?" she asked curiously.

He laughed. "What would be the use? I can't afford a car."

She blinked. "Yes, but after you graduate, I assume you'll get a job. Won't you?"

"I wasn't planning on graduating anytime soon." He didn't quite meet her eyes as he spoke.

"But you're a senior—what will you do after this year?"

"Grad school, I guess. Anything to keep living off the government's money." He smiled at Arabella's shocked reaction. "I had enough of making it on my own when I was younger. I'm enjoying the chance to coast for a bit."

"You must have had one of the lousiest childhoods on record."

He smiled sadly, playing on the obvious sympathy he had seen on her face. "It was a long time ago. So what are we planning on doing once we get to the park?"

"Hiking a bit, I suppose. You don't happen to own a bike, do you?"

"Never ridden one. Why?"

"Because it would be fun to ride around the park, but if you don't know how…"

"I could always learn, I suppose."

She shook her head at him. "I can't imagine making it into your twenties without learning how to ride a bicycle."

"So teach me. Might be an entertaining way to spend the morning."

This put Arabella in a very good mood. "In that case, we'll have to go somewhere that rents bikes."

Renphor was extremely entertained by the bicycle. He initially attempted to learn the correct way to ride it but quickly grew frustrated and switched to less conventional methods. This caused Arabella to give him a very strange look when he dismounted and forgot to drop the bike. She stared at it, startled, until he realized that he was still holding it up through the energy field he had been using. He dropped it quickly, and to his relief Arabella decided that the kickstand must have been caught partially down.

Once Renphor had mastered staying up on the bike, they set off down one of the trails. They rode for several hours over rough trails, until Arabella confessed that she was exhausted.

"I don't know where you get your stamina." She had panted at the top of a particularly steep hill. Renphor had simply smiled and offered to race her to the bottom. An hour into their explorations, she had questioned him rather closely about his familiarity with the woods. He dismissed her questions by saying that he'd spent a lot of time there walking by himself before they'd started dating. They finally returned the bikes to the rental shop around lunchtime, and he strolled up the trail a bit while she ate her lunch.

They spent the afternoon walking some of the more level trails, since Arabella was worn out from the cycling they had done that morning. He cast annoyed glances toward the trees as the smaller prey animals scampered away from him in terror. After an eight-point buck exhibited similar behavior, Arabella cast a curious glance at him.

"Ryan, have you ever had a pet?" she asked.

"What brought that up? No, I haven't. I'm not nearly settled enough."

"Not even as a child?"

"No—my family had other things to focus on when I was a kid."

"I can't imagine not having pets." They walked for a few minutes in silence before Arabella spoke again. "And now, can you explain to me why you'd rather go out a window than meet my stepfather?"

He grinned sheepishly. "I didn't think the timing was very good."

"And what was wrong with it?" she asked shortly.

"Well, it's pretty much the reason I gave you this morning. Your stepfather strikes me as being a bit…old-fashioned. I didn't think finding me in your bedroom would be a great introduction."

The look she gave him was unsettlingly dubious, but she didn't comment further, and he decided to be grateful to have gotten off so lightly.

▼▼▼▼

John came back from breakfast in a better mood than he had been in since his return from Rome. Julie looked up from her book as he came into the room whistling.

"What's up? You haven't been this cheery in a decade."

He smiled at her. "I just had breakfast with Arabella and Sam."

"Breakfast?"

"Well, they did, anyway. Did you know Arabella has a boyfriend?" He turned to remove the cat from his seat. The cat, unhappy at being disturbed, took a swat at him. He swatted back. Julie stared at them in amazement.

"Are you seriously having an argument with ten pounds of fur? Just put her on the floor and be done with it."

He had succeeded in claiming the chair and sat down quickly to avoid losing his advantage. Once he had settled himself, he returned his attention to his mate.

"You didn't answer the question."

"About Arabella's boyfriend? Sam mentioned something. Did you meet him?" She looked hopefully at him.

"No, but we talked about him. Seems like a nice guy. She's certainly happier than I've seen her since she started school."

"So, she told you a lot about him?"

"As much as teenagers generally do."

"She's not a teenager. She's almost twenty-one."

John's hands twitched irritably. "Not much difference, is there? Apparently he's majoring in Classical Studies. Not particularly useful, I'll grant you. Maybe he's planning to go into research. Or become a professor. Anyway, from what I could glean, he treats her like gold. Sam didn't seem as enthusiastic, but then she's used to having Arabella pretty much to herself."

Julie blinked. "Did she tell you that she doesn't like him?"

He shook his head. "No, but it was fairly obvious. She clammed up as soon as Arabella started talking about him."

Julie suddenly stood and walked over to the bookshelf. She examined the rows of books and rolls of parchments lining the shelves. Running her hand over them, she pulled out a book seemingly at random. She jumped as she turned around to find John directly behind her.

"Looking for anything in particular?" he asked.

She shook her head. "Just seeing what there is to see. I really need to start picking up some skills apart from the basics."

He took the book out of her hand, laughing as he read the title out loud. "*Basic Attack Spells*. Planning to get into a battle? There's nothing here that you need." He placed it back on the shelf. Since his back was turned, he didn't notice the red glow that came into her eyes when he took the book from her, and it had vanished again by the time he turned around.

"I don't know why you bother to have any of this," she said shortly.

"What do you mean?"

"You don't practice any of the more useful arts because you're worried about their origins, and you won't let me learn anything at all. So what is the point of keeping volumes of information about them?" She glanced at the shelves stacked floor to ceiling with all manner of materials.

"Keeping it out of the hands of others." He smiled.

"Ridiculous."

30

John's preparations for the trip had taken a few days longer than he had hoped but he and Julie were in Paris by Thursday. Julie flopped on the king-sized bed as soon as they entered the hotel room and lay there, flat on her back with her arms out, for several minutes. John stowed the suitcases and lay down next to her. She gave him an irritated look and turned her back on him.

"What have I done this time?" he asked shortly.

"If you'd learn to jump, we wouldn't have to deal with that nonsense of airports and taxis that we just wasted ten hours on." She continued to stare at the wall next to the bed as she spoke.

John sighed. "What are ten hours to a couple of immortals? And it isn't as easy as you make it out to be. Even most experienced jumpers can't hoist themselves across the globe. Particularly if they need luggage."

"Stefan can."

He gritted his teeth. "Stefan is first-generation. Not everyone has the power or the stamina to cross the ocean and back as nonchalantly as if they were walking into the next room. In fact, only a few are that adept."

She sat up. "I know that, but you belong to a strong line of jumpers. You should be able to learn easily enough, and even if I never got strong enough to go cross-continental on my own, you could take me as a ride-along. And you don't need luggage if you can leave your house in Philadelphia and arrive a minute later at a party in Paris."

"I'm still third-generation, and—"

"And you were made by one of the most skilled jumpers in the world," she finished. He froze.

"Who told you that?"

"Stefan. Didn't you know?"

He waved his hand to dismiss the idea. "Of course I knew. I don't understand why you'd be discussing it with Stefan, though."

"Perspective. You only ever talk about Renphor in terms of how to get rid of him. Stefan's comments are slightly less biased, which gives me a better idea of what we're really dealing with."

She stood and started unpacking her suitcase as she spoke. John watched her hang up three cocktail dresses before he had enough control of his temper to answer her. "Only slightly less biased?" he asked tersely.

"Yes. He doesn't particularly like Renphor either, but his dislike doesn't amount to a vendetta."

John grabbed a small black notebook from his luggage and placed himself as far away from his mate as the room allowed. Sitting down at a table near the window, he started to flip through the pages and jot down names on the hotel stationery.

He watched Julie through narrowed eyes as she picked up her phone and dialed a number.

"Who are you calling?"

"Arabella."

"Why? You don't call her when we're home."

"I call her all the time when we're home. You just don't happen to be in the same room with me when I do it."

She turned away from him to talk into the phone, even though he could still hear every word she said. This irritated him, but he refrained from commenting. He listened intently to the conversation and was surprised to hear that his mate seemed genuinely concerned about her daughter's welfare and asked some very searching questions about her activities.

"What was that all about?" he asked as she ended the call.

"What do you mean?"

"You act like she's in danger of immediate annihilation."

Julie rolled her eyes and picked up her book from the nightstand.

Contrary to John's original plan, it had taken several days before they had found themselves in company with any of the Parisian vampires that he claimed as friends. He finally received an invitation for an evening party on the third day, while Julie was out on another excursion. He fretted around the hotel room, waiting for her to return, growing more aggravated with each passing hour. She finally wafted in around eight o'clock in the evening.

"Had a good time?" he asked tersely.

"Very. I have so much more energy to explore than I did the last time I was here. Even at twenty-one, as a human you eventually run out of steam after so many steps. I was so busy trying to catch my breath that I missed some of the views. Pity I can't still enjoy the food, but I guess everything is a trade-off."

"Did you really need to stay out so late?"

"Yes. I was watching the sun set over Sacré-Cœur. It was magnificent. You look somewhat overdressed for sitting in the hotel."

"We're going out, so get yourself changed. An invitation to cards by none other than Philip Avery."

"Philip Avery?"

"Do you listen to anything that I say?" he asked shortly. "Avery is the man who gave Stella the small amount of information that we have about Renphor. If we can coax more out of him, we could have everything we need to act by the end of the evening."

"Except a working fire vortex. And how do you intend to coax him? Not through Stella's methods, presumably, unless you expect me to sleep with him."

"I do not. Although it couldn't hurt to try for a little more charm than you use with me."

She turned toward the closet without comment and selected a dress for the evening. They maintained a cold silence until they had finished all their preparations and were in the elevator to the lobby.

"Will anyone that I know be there?" she asked.

John's brow creased. "I don't know. The list seemed pretty short, and most of the names belonged to people that I haven't seen in decades." He noticed the look on her face and amended, "He only listed the men. A lot of the women that hang around his salons are much younger—you may have met some of them."

Four hours later they were on their way back up the hotel elevator. John had a furious expression on his face, while his mate simply looked intensely bored. He slammed the key card into the slot so hard that he nearly broke it in half. Once inside the room, he gave vent to his feelings.

"Could he have wasted our time more effectively if he'd planned it? All that time, and I didn't get one word out of him about Renphor's existence, let alone his whereabouts!"

"He did plan it, John. One of his chirpy little satellites repeated what Stella said—Philip generally spends at least one evening a month in Renphor's company. He knew perfectly well that his comments to her were what sent you off in a sudden rush to Paris, so soon after you'd gotten home from Rome. Now he's just messing with you."

John stared at her, his temper rising. "To hell with him, then! If Renphor's in Paris, there must be other people here who know where. We just need to find them."

They stayed a full week in the city, circulating through different social functions. They had been last-minute additions to the guest list at some. Others had been arranged in their honor when the hosts had learned of their presence in Paris. All of them left Julie bored and John frustrated. She continued to leave every morning on various sightseeing expeditions. John refused to accompany her, choosing to remain behind in the hotel, mapping out elaborate strategies and rereading his notes about the fire vortex. He finally booked their flight home, deciding that his questions had been pointed enough to have revealed his purpose to any of Renphor's acquaintances who he might have encountered, and therefore rendered any continued investigations useless.

31

The day of the medieval festival turned out to be ideal. It was sunny and unseasonably warm, so that both the guests and the actors would be perfectly comfortable for the entire day. Renphor had been in a particularly conciliatory mood since his exit through Arabella's bedroom window, and he had willingly helped with the setup for the day. Arabella had even managed to convince him to dress in period garb and help the committee members who were working the stands on the day of the festival. He regretted this decision when she showed him the outfit she'd picked out for him. It was a long purple tunic with gold accents and a gold belt. He grimaced at the sight of it.

"What's wrong with it?" she asked.

"Not my style."

She giggled. "Glad to hear it. You start running around campus dressed like this, and you really will get attacked down a dead-end alley."

Renphor looked at her speculatively. "You don't think I was attacked?" he asked.

Arabella looked surprised at the question. "Of course not."

"Why 'of course not'?"

She stared at him. "You didn't have any injuries three hours later. If the four of them had really gone after you, you would at least have had a few bruises."

Renphor smiled. "Ever seen a bruise on me?"

She looked confused. "No—but you must get them. Everyone does."

"I'm not everyone."

Arabella continued to dress in silence. Her hands shook slightly as she pulled her dress over her head, and she cast occasional furtive glances in his direction. After several minutes, she continued the conversation as if it had never been broken.

"Anyway, if you say you weren't, then I believe you."

"When did I tell you I wasn't?"

"You told the police…" Her voice trailed off.

"What I choose to tell the police and what I tell you are two different things."

She stood motionless, watching him. After swallowing several times, she asked, "Were you attacked?"

"Yes."

The conversation for the next twenty minutes consisted of requests to be handed one or another piece of costume that had somehow gotten away from its proper owner.

The festival was in full swing by nine o'clock. The food and entertainment were a hit with the attendees, and the atmosphere really did seem to have taken on a medieval feel. Renphor had been designated as a floater, so he spent several hours drifting from station to station. On a trip between the refreshments tent and the games area, he sat down on a bench to take a break and watch what was going on around him. He was tracking a middle-aged blond who seemed to be wandering aimlessly amongst the stalls and so did not immediately acknowledge the woman who sat on the bench next to him.

"Contemplating lunch?" She finally spoke.

He smiled. "Not in this crowd. Still, she looks like a fairly easy mark. You?"

"I ate at home."

He turned at last to see who it was that was sitting next to him. A thin brunette of medium height and build was watching him through slightly narrowed eyes.

"I don't think we've met?"

"No."

He waited expectantly, but she didn't elaborate.

"What do you want?" he asked at last.

"To know exactly what you are doing with my daughter."

"Your daughter?"

"Arabella. I believe you're rather well acquainted."

"You could say that."

"What are you up to?"

"One would think you didn't trust me." When he smiled again, his fangs were clearly visible.

"Do I look like a fool? I'm grateful that you've left her unharmed so far. But it also means you've worked out some use for her."

"You know who I am?" She nodded. "How did you find out?"

"I asked Stefan a few questions a while back. What city you were living in. What alias you're using. When Arabella started raving about her new boyfriend, it wasn't too difficult to put the pieces together."

"Stefan gave you that? Interesting. He generally doesn't give out anything that will shorten the game."

"In this case, he knows it will just create more of a tangle."

Renphor leaned slowly back against the bench and contemplated the clouds blowing across the sky. A slight smile played across his lips as he weighed his options.

"Does John know?" he asked softly.

"What do you think?"

His lips twitched. "Why haven't you told him?"

"I don't want Arabella mixed up in this—John's problems are his concern."

He felt a jolt of surprise but didn't respond.

"I'll ask again—what do you intend to do with Arabella?"

He looked fixedly at her for several moments before making up his mind on a response. "She's no use to me dead. Beyond that, I can't promise anything."

"I guess I'll have to take that for now." Julie stood up and faced him. Holding out her hand, she said, "If you do convert her, will you promise to keep her under your protection?"

He blinked at her, then answered slowly. "To the best of my ability. I've grown rather used to her presence, to be honest. There's a certain je ne sais quoi about her." He stood and took the hand that she held out. "Do you intend to say anything to John?"

She regarded him for a moment. "No."

He watched her disappear into the crowd, an arrested expression on his face. Once she was out of sight, he walked slowly toward the games area, mulling things over as he went.

Renphor spent the night after the festival with Arabella, thinking through his strategy regarding John while she slept. She finally rolled over and opened her eyes around eight the next morning.

"Good sleep, princess?" he asked.

"Very. How about you?" She put her arms around him and pulled herself closer.

"As well as ever," he responded.

"Ryan?"

"Hmm?"

"Who's Randall?"

He started, staring at her. "Where did you pull that name from?"

"You said it yesterday, when you were talking to Tom about the carvings that you did. Something about having carved children's toys, I think."

He leaned against the headboard, and stared out the window, turning over his options. Finally, he answered. "Randall was my son."

Arabella froze. "Your son?"

"His mother and I were extremely young. About sixteen, when he was born. We were both staying in a shelter and just sort of ended up together."

He noticed that her breathing had become very shallow and tightened his arm around her shoulders.

"Why haven't you ever talked about them before? Where are they?"

"They died. When I was nineteen. Car accident."

"Oh." She took his right hand in hers, examining the gold ring that circled his middle finger. "Your wedding band?"

"An heirloom that belonged to my wife. It's supposed to have magic properties." He clasped his fingers around her shaking ones.

"Were you in the car too?"

He shook his head. "I was out of state at the time. Nobody was able to reach me until after the funeral." He stood up quickly and walked over to the window. Arabella watched him in concern.

"What was her name?"

"Anna."

He only half noticed her curl into a ball on the bed, staring at him. The lie had hurt more than he cared to admit. He stood staring into the city streets, wondering for the millionth time what had really happened to the family he had left behind. He realized that his fingers had clenched onto the curtain, smashing it into a wrinkled mass, and quickly released it.

"I need to get going. I have a project meeting in an hour for my senior seminar." He got dressed quickly, kissed Arabella goodbye, and left before she could ask any more questions.

32

John was still in a foul mood when he and Julie got home from Paris, but it evaporated quickly. After considering the matter, he realized that he had picked up some potentially useful information. The only thing that he regretted was the loss of practice time, since Julie had strongly dissuaded him from attempting the fire vortex in their hotel room. He made up for it after their return by spending twelve hours a day in the courtyard trying different combinations. He had received a letter from Petros while he was away that contained several promising suggestions. Three days after they got back, he was sitting in the garden trying one of them out when the fire vortex suddenly expanded from a ball of flame the size of a volleyball to a whirling vortex that was at least two feet across. It startled him so much that he jerked backwards. The flame went out, but the success was enough to encourage him. He spent the rest of the day trying to reproduce what he had been doing when it had happened, until he realized that he was completely exhausted by the effort. Remembering that he needed to feed more often than usual while he was studying this intensely, he took off through the woods toward the back of his property in search of dinner. He took the opportunity while he was there to walk around the grounds, inspecting his defenses to make sure no gaps had appeared while he was traveling. As a result, he did not return to the house until well after midnight. His sudden entrance into the library startled Julie, who was examining the shelves of books with interest.

"At it again?" he asked coolly, removing *Defensive Spells and Shields* from her grasp and putting it back on a shelf above her head.

"I don't see what objection you could have to me defending myself."

He smiled down at her. "From what, my dear? You've no enemies that I know of."

"But you have. And if they're half as determined as you, they wouldn't have any qualms at all about coming after me to get their revenge."

"But how would they get to you? I have you very well protected, you know. Apart from the residents, only five people have access to enter the grounds without me, and the only one of those five who isn't a member of our inner circle is Stefan. Surely you don't think he intends to harm you?"

"No. I don't trust his intentions, but I'm reasonably certain he prefers that I remain in one piece. But I can't stay on the property all the time."

"When you leave, you're protected by several shields that are designed to warn me of danger and deflect any attacks."

"And track where I go." She flopped into an armchair, glaring at him.

He sighed and sat down across from her. She didn't meet his eyes as he spoke. "I've told you, even if I wanted to, I couldn't track your daily movements. I could probably find you if you were in danger because of the energy burst it would create, but that's it."

"And by the time you got to me, I'd have already been turned into dust."

"Unlikely. If someone was really trying to get to me, they'd be more likely to kidnap you."

The muscles in her jaw worked for several seconds before she got up and quickly left the room. John sighed as he watched her go. His melancholy mood didn't last for long, though. As he sat staring into the fire, Joseph entered softly behind him and cleared his throat. John turned.

"Well?"

"Nelson and Stella, my lord."

"Show them in."

His visitors entered the room a moment later, and John waved them to chairs near the fireplace. He sat down between them, looking from one to the other.

"I take it this isn't a social call. What have you found?"

Nelson fidgeted and looked into the fire. Stella shook her head at him.

"It isn't anything that we've found. I heard about what happened in Paris, with Philip Avery. Since it was my lead, I thought I'd come by and...well...apologize. For sending you on a wild goose chase like that. I should have known Philip was up to no good. If there's any way we can make it up to you, we will."

John smiled at both of them.

"There is something you can do for me. The Paris trip wasn't a complete waste. I met a man there who knows Renphor slightly, and he was pretty certain that he's using an alias. See if you can dig out someone who might know what it is. It's almost impossible to keep a thing like that secret for long. You're bound to run into someone on the street who ends up calling you by the wrong name, and then the whole thing comes out."

Stella smiled. "I know just where to start, too. There's a guy in the Social Security Administration who owes me a favor. If Renphor has a US identity, he might know. Most of the fake identities go through him. Or so he says. It's worth a shot, anyway." She stood up and headed for the door. Nelson jumped up nervously, staring from her to John and back again.

"Nelson, there's a job for you, too. Several of the men I ran into in Rome seemed to think Renphor was fairly attached to an American vampiress. Thought she was probably a plebe but couldn't come up with a name from anywhere. You're a member at a couple of the gentlemen's clubs—do the rounds and see if you can come up with anything."

Nelson nodded glumly and quickly followed Stella out of the room. John smiled as they went. Their unexpected visit had saved him the effort of calling another meeting, which left him more time to work on the fire vortex. He had some minor instructions for David and Jennifer, which he could easily jot down and send off with Joseph. Gathering up the parchment from the table, he hurried out to the courtyard to practice.

33

The Thursday following the festival was Thanksgiving. John and Julie had surprised Arabella by telling her that they intended to accompany her to dinner at her paternal grandmother's house—something they hadn't done since she was sixteen and able to drive herself there. The house was a little less than an hour north of Larch Hill, but it was a pain for them to have to eat food that may as well have been paste, and Julie's mother-in-law never scrupled to show her dislike of John. The second part had been their main excuse for the last five years.

It had been Julie's idea to go this year, and John was highly annoyed about it. He had some writing that he wanted to finish and was hoping to hear some news from either Stella or Nelson. He had sent David and Jennifer some small items to research about the fire vortex, but it was more to keep them busy than anything else. He had not yet replicated his earlier success, but he was now consistently able to form the beginning of a vortex from the small ball of flame before losing control of it. He still found himself tiring easily as he tried to work the spell, and he determined that he would need to spend some time making it more efficient once he had mastered the basics.

Both John and Julie were sullen during the trip, still fuming from their fight about whether or not they should go at all. They picked Arabella up at her apartment that morning, and after the initial affectionate greetings, the three sat staring out the windows as they drove. John, wrapped up in his own thoughts, didn't notice that his stepdaughter was uncharacteristically silent until he caught a glimpse of her in the rearview mirror and realized how miserable she looked. This temporarily startled him out of his own melancholy.

"What's wrong, petite?" he asked solicitously.

"Nothing."

Julie looked away from her window at last. "Then why so quiet? You haven't spoken two words to anyone since you got in the car. We'd love to hear what you've been doing for the last couple of weeks."

"It's not my fault you ran off to France."

John smiled. "You couldn't expect us to take you with us in the middle of the semester. It was mostly a business trip anyway."

"I don't care about that." She was still looking out the window as she spoke.

Julie smiled understandingly. "What did he do?"

John looked surprised. "Who?" he asked.

Julie glared at him. "Ryan, of course."

Arabella stared at her mother. "How did you know—?"

"Because you're obviously not really mad at us, so the only other person who could cause this amount of angst is the boyfriend."

Arabella fiddled with the window mechanism for a while before answering. "Nothing, really." She looked at her mother. "But seriously, can you see any reason why he wouldn't come along to dinner today? I know he can't really eat the food, but would it be so terrible to meet my family?"

She looked like she was ready to burst into tears. Her mother answered soothingly. "I can think of several reasons, sweetie. You've only been dating a few months."

"Yes, but—" Her eyes met John's in the mirror, and she clammed up. For the rest of the trip, she relapsed into a brooding silence.

▼▼▼▼

Arabella's cousin had made the trip from Rochester with her husband and two small children, and Arabella filled the time before dinner by playing with them. At dinner time, she was seated across from her cousin Kathryn. Kathryn seized her opportunity almost as soon as John had finished saying grace.

"So, Arabella, I hear you finally convinced some guy to date you." She punctuated the statement with a shrill laugh, which caused John to wince.

"Where did you hear that?" Arabella asked.

Kathryn seemed to be at a loss. "Grandma asked, when you came in—"

Arabella cut her off. "I'm seeing someone."

She went back to pouring the gravy, and John hoped that was the end of it, but Kathryn couldn't seem to help herself. Her voice changed to a tone of sympathy. "It's a shame he couldn't come with you today. I would have loved to meet him. I understand you've been very secretive about him." She tried to cast a conspiratorial look at her aunt. John gathered from the change in her expression that Julie's look of disgust was not what she had expected to see.

"He's not big on groups of people," Arabella said.

John decided to intervene in the conversation before the cousins went for each other's throats. "Pity. I would have liked to meet him too, but no doubt we'll all get another chance."

"I'm sure he'll come around when he feels comfortable doing so. Three months of dating isn't a very long time to build up the nerve for this bunch." Julie looked pointedly at Kathryn and her husband before sweeping her gaze around to cover their children, who were busily flinging mashed potatoes at one another while their parents weren't watching.

This effectively changed the topic of conversation, since Kathryn had to defend her offspring and John was busy glaring at the potato-covered toddlers.

Nothing more was mentioned about Arabella's boyfriend until after dinner, when John managed to separate her from the group.

"I don't like seeing you so upset. You gave me the impression that this guy was treating you really well."

Arabella looked up quickly from the magazine she had picked up. "He is. This is the only thing we argue about. Really."

He looked thoughtfully at her. "Sam didn't seem to think so."

Arabella rolled her eyes. "The things that annoy Sam don't bother me in the least."

"Such as?"

Arabella hedged. "Ryan's a bit…quirky. He's had sort of a rough life. He'd rather stay home or go for a walk with me than go out to parties and hang out with a bunch of people. Sam thinks it's weird because she can't imagine not wanting to be friends with everyone in the world."

John frowned. "So he's antisocial?"

"No…when we do go out, he's fine. I thought at first that he was shy, but that isn't it. He just seems to prefer peace and quiet over a lot of loud music and stuff."

John nodded. "Wise man. I can't say I agree with your mother, though. He should have made an effort to be here. When is he normally around your place?"

"Um…it depends on his schedule. He's got a lot going on with school, so I never know more than a day or two in advance when he'll be there." She picked up the magazine again and buried her face in it. John suppressed his annoyance at the obvious dismissal and went to find his mate.

On the ride home, Arabella pretended to fall asleep in the car. She had done the same thing as a child, and John recognized the act but decided to let it go while he was focused on the road. He did lose his temper when they got back to Larch Hill around nine in the evening and she walked immediately to her car. He insisted that she come back into the house, but she was adamant that she had to go, and after arguing back and forth for ten minutes she finally ended the dispute by getting in her car and driving away. John turned on his heel and stormed into the house, nearly slamming the door on his mate, who was following a few feet behind him. He apologized curtly and stomped off to his study.

When Arabella's alarm went off the next morning, she lay in bed listening to the silence of her apartment. Sam and Narcissa were both staying with their families through Sunday night, so she would have the place to herself for the better part of three days. She smiled at the thought. Climbing out of bed, she switched on the computer before jumping into the shower. She ate a quick breakfast and sat down with a steaming cup of coffee, ready to dig in on one of the three major term papers she was working on. She had even lied to Renphor, telling him that she was planning to stay with her parents for the entire weekend. This had been done more out of anger than a real urge to work, but she decided to use it to her advantage and not fess up until she had made some serious progress.

Two hours later, she found herself idly trawling various websites devoted to magical and mythical creatures. She had gotten distracted two minutes into her research by a link in an article she was reading and had quickly veered off course. Glancing at the clock, she sighed and reluctantly shut down a website devoted to "demons, vampyres, and other hellish creatures." Deciding that online research was a bad idea, she packed up her notebooks and headed to the library, where she resolutely stayed away from the computer until close to dinnertime. Looking through her handwritten notes, she smiled with satisfaction. She would have to spend the evening typing everything up, but she had completed all but the final edits on two of her three projects. She would come back tomorrow and finish the third.

34

The unseasonable warmth that they had been having the weekend of the festival gave way to a cold snap and freezing rain by the Friday after Thanksgiving. Since the weather was so miserable and he had no particular plans for the day, Renphor had decided to do some studying in his room. He was reading, leaning against the back of his chair with one foot resting on the desk, when a loud cracking noise came from the seat. Jumping up quickly, he kneeled down next to the chair to see where the noise had come from and noticed a long crack where the back of the chair was joined to the seat. He debated fixing it but decided it was probably easier to dig up another one. He sat carefully on the edge of the chair and flipped through the chapter he was supposed to be reading, his hand resting on the empty notepad next to him. A few minutes later he slammed the book closed.

Forgetting about the crack, he slumped backwards and found himself on the floor next to two halves of a broken chair. He picked himself up and grabbed the seat portion of the chair with both hands. His initial instinct was to rip it into pieces, but he changed his mind. Grasping it by one of the legs, he flung it hard against the wall and hissed as it stuck hard in the plaster.

"Not the result you were hoping for?"

Renphor spun around to see Ariliana standing just inside the window. He gritted his teeth.

"No. I wanted to see it smashed to bits. How long have you been standing there?"

"Not long enough to see what the chair did to you." She looked at the broken back lying on the floor. "Oh dear. Have we been dumped?"

Renphor took a deep breath. "Cheap fucking garbage."

"Well, if you'd spend some of the money you must have hidden somewhere—"

"What do you want, Rilla?"

She walked slowly toward him. "I just came for a visit. It's been almost three weeks since we've...run into each other. Maybe that's why you're so tense." She ran her fingers through his hair as she spoke, and down the back of his neck.

"I don't think that's going to help." He pushed her back to arm's length.

Ariliana stared at him. "What's your deal?"

"Things on my mind. Any more information from idiot-Davies?"

"No. Should I leave now, since you don't seem to have any other use for me?"

He leaned against the wall, eyes closed. "Don't get into a snit. I'm just trying to get some things sorted out in my head."

"A hard task, apparently."

He ignored the sarcasm. "Very. My brain is refusing to process a few things, and I need to get my mind around them if this is going to work."

She moved toward the window. "I don't know what you're doing with all this information, Ren, but I'm getting the feeling you're in over your head."

He smiled. "I frequently am. But this should come off as long as I'm careful."

Ariliana feigned nonchalance, but he noticed the glint of curiosity in her eyes. "What are you up to?"

"Nothing I'm going to share with you, my dear."

"Well, aren't we secretive. Why not?"

He grinned. "Nosy much? You don't want to be mixed up in this, I assure you."

She eyed him from her spot near the window. "You're going to get yourself killed this time. Not that you ever seem to care."

"If I didn't care, I would have kicked it years ago. I just don't suffer from your abundance of…caution." He walked across the room and grasped the chair by one leg. He yanked hard on it, pulling it out of the wall and sending it flying across the room. It smashed to pieces against the door.

"Much better."

"Had your revenge?"

There was no mirth in his smile this time. His fangs showed, and his eyes had a red glow in them. "Only against the chair."

"What exactly are you planning? I don't see how any of this is helping you to get closer to John Elder."

"I'm surprised you want to know. For someone who's so bloody cautious of their own skin, I'd think you'd want to be well out of it."

Ariliana's eyes had begun to develop a red glow of their own. "Nice of you, after I've been risking my neck to feed you information from Nelson."

He laughed derisively. "Very risky. The idiot's thick as a post. What harm could he possibly do to you?"

"Nelson? None. But I'm sure Elder would be happy to take his anger out on me if he found out about our…relationship. So what am I up against?"

He clenched his teeth. "Stay out of my affairs, Ariliana. Let's just say I found another path to John."

"Does it have anything to do with that pretty little human that's been following you around like a puppy for the past three months?"

"Mind your business. And if I find you anywhere near her, they'll pick up what's left of the pieces across the length of the Walt Whitman. Get it?"

"Who is she?"

"No one." He looked past her out the window and noticed red lights flashing in the distance. They were drawing nearer. "Damn."

She looked out the window, a bored expression on her face. "What about it? Must be a fairly common sight around here."

Renphor growled. "Damned neighbors. Call the cops if I so much as drop anything in here. They must've heard the chair."

Ariliana laughed. "What'd you do to piss them off?"

"Knocked a couple of their cronies through a dumpster when they tried to jump me. You'd better get out of here before they knock on the door."

"What about you?"

He laughed. "You know better than that."

"Forgot."

Ariliana went back out through the window onto the fire escape. Renphor watched her run down the alley and around the corner before turning out the light and disappearing from the room.

35

John looked up in irritation as Stefan suddenly appeared in front of him. "You know it's rude to drop in unannounced?" He went back to what he had been doing without rising.

Stefan suddenly raised his arm. Fire shot out of his fingertips, blasting the candelabra John had been using clean across the room. John stood slowly, turning to make sure the candles had gone out before facing Stefan. "What do you want?"

"Just a word." Stefan's upper lip curled into a sneer. "And perhaps you could tell me how I could possibly notify you in advance of my arrival when you don't have a telephone?"

He stood next to the table, idly picking up the various instruments that were strewn across it.

"You could let Joseph announce you like a civilized person, instead of just appearing in the middle of my library whenever the whim hits you." John rolled up the parchment before walking into the center of the room. "Would you care for a seat?"

Stefan looked at him through narrowed eyes. "No. I like it where I am." He continued to shift items on the table. Finally, he paused, his hand on a long metal instrument shaped almost like a gun but obviously constructed to shoot some kind of liquid. He picked it up, running his hand along the smooth metal.

"You know this is out of bounds?" he said softly.

John looked steadily at him. "Why? The council must know I have it."

"If I remember correctly, you were told to dispose of it two centuries ago. I can't imagine why you would want to risk censure to keep it. Your target doesn't seem to be the least bit annoyed by it. He only showed up at your hearing because the council forced him to, and then he could barely be bothered to testify."

"If he was so unconcerned, how did they find out that I have it in the first place?"

"Because even the most powerful vampire will sustain some damage from that little concoction that you sprayed all over him. As it happens, I ran into him at the healer's, collecting a salve for the wounds. Seemed to think the whole thing a pretty good joke."

John gritted his teeth. "From what I understand, he went to ground for three months after that attack. Made sure no one saw him. You seem to have been surprisingly lucky to have chosen the same healer as him and to have been there at the precise moment he arrived. And as to why I left it where it could be found, if you didn't wander in and out of other people's houses at will, I would have made sure to put it away first."

Stefan dropped the instrument back on the table. "Try to join us in the twenty-first century, John. If you'd get a damned cell phone, I wouldn't have to drop in unannounced."

"You know I don't like them."

"No, nor any other electronic device. You've got a forty-room pile that you still light with candles. It must drive Julie mad."

"I don't know what you're griping about, anyway. Your place is lit by candlelight too." John stared at him.

"Only the public meeting areas. It's atmosphere. I have perfectly functional electric lighting in my personal rooms, along with a computer, a television, and several other modern conveniences."

"Did you come over here to discuss electricity?" There was an edge to John's voice now. He had just had a similar discussion with Julie that morning, and it galled him to hear the same arguments from Stefan.

"Of course not."

Stefan moved behind the desk to where John had been sitting and casually unrolled the parchment the other man had been studying when he had come in. He noticed with interest that there were now additional notes in John's handwriting running down the margins. Sitting down, he looked around irritably for a better light.

"You knocked it over there," John commented.

Stefan reached out toward the candelabra, which flew into his hand. Replacing the candles, most of which had fallen out or snapped off, he ran his fingers over the wicks to relight them. He placed it on the table near the parchment and ran his finger down the diagram, smiling as he did so.

"You seem to have made some progress with this. It looks like there's a page missing, though. Where did you get the rest of the information?" he asked.

John made a vague gesture with his hand. "A friend helped me to work it out."

"I see. And how is the practical side of things going?"

"It's coming along. A little rough in places, but I'll get there."

"Will you, John? What's your plan B, by the way?"

"I've no intention of telling you."

Stefan laughed. "Afraid I'll go running to Renphor? Unlikely, I assure you. I don't particularly care who wins this battle, since either way it gets rid of one royal pain in the ass from my territory."

John looked up quickly at that. "Your territory?"

Stefan smirked. "Surely you know where he's living?"

John glared and said nothing.

"Dear, dear. We don't seem to have done our homework. Yes, John—I'll give you that much. Renphor is not only residing within my territory but within the limits of the city of Philadelphia. You could come around any street corner and find yourself face-to-face with him. Now why so twitchy?"

John's hand had tightly clenched the arm of the chair where it had been resting. "And Julie didn't think he was interested in me. Shows how much she knows."

"I don't think he is interested in you. This is where he happened to end up this time around."

John attempted to get more information from his visitor, but without success. Stefan stayed for an hour or so longer, discussing local gossip, before finally leaving for an appointment. John leaned against the back of his chair, staring reflectively at the row of books on the opposite wall.

The conversation with Stefan goaded John into calling another meeting much sooner than he had intended to. The ballroom had been returned to its regular barren state, and the chairs in the middle of the room were once again the only furniture. John sat in his high-backed chair at the head of the little group, feeling far tenser than he usually did at these meetings. Julie sat to his right, looking disinterested as usual.

Stella leaned forward in her chair, her voice somewhere between a coo and a whisper. "What's wrong, John? Something must have happened to upset you—we've only been working on our last batch of assignments for a few days."

John drummed his fingers on the arm of the chair, ignoring the look of loathing that his mate was casting toward Stella, and looking around at all of them. They leaned forward, anticipating important news.

"I have received very reliable information on Renphor's whereabouts. I've no reason to believe that this particular source would lie, since he is known to be a neutral party."

Nelson bounced up and down on his chair in expectation. John cast him a quelling look, which caused him to stop bouncing and perch on the very edge of the seat.

"Well? Are you going to tell us?" David asked.

John took a deep breath. "He's here."

Nelson looked around nervously. "Where?"

"In Philadelphia."

"Oh." Nelson slouched back into his chair. Jennifer gasped dramatically.

"Right here in the city?"

John nodded.

"So we could run into him at any time?"

He nodded again. She leaned back in her chair, twisting her hands together and casting nervous glances at her husband.

Stella looked at her with disdain. "What are the odds that Renphor would recognize any of us if we did run into him?" she asked.

"Slim," he answered. "I doubt he would trouble himself to take notice of anyone below his own station in life."

David looked affronted at this. "It's not like we're plebes."

"No, and we're not first- or second-generation, either. Apart from John, we're all fourth. The very bottom rung of nobility, so to speak," Jennifer commented.

John nodded. Nelson seemed to have been chewing over an idea, which he finally voiced. "It's a pity we don't have anyone higher-ranking." John cast him a venomous look, and he went on hastily. "I'm not just talking about getting rid of Renphor. That's important, but once we've done that, what then? We've got other initiatives, which we've really sort of neglected for years. The plebes might be more likely to follow us if we had someone from the second generation. Even if we had another third-generation member or two. Right now, everyone in our group was made by you."

John sneered. "That's a lost cause. Most of the higher ranks are far too happy with their power and riches to have any interest in submitting to more regulations. We'll have to content ourselves with the plebes we can recruit on our own merits until we get some real power behind us." He set his teeth as his mate looked up at the gilded carvings on the ceiling and smiled.

David weighed his words. "I see what you're saying, John, but Nelson has a point. We need more clout. And I'd like to start discussing some of those other initiatives. I still think too much time is being devoted to Renphor."

John turned to answer David, but Jennifer broke in. "Couldn't you just make a bunch more like us? Then we'd have more people to go out and spread the word, so to speak."

The others stared at her. John barely managed to hide the condescension in his voice when he answered. "A great plan, but a bit limiting. I've already made six of our kind. I can only make seven more."

"Oh. I forgot about that."

Stella snickered.

"Wait, who's the sixth?" Nelson looked around the group as if counting the people in the room.

"Joseph."

"Ohhhh."

"And as for our other initiatives…David, I thought you were going to think about that? Have you come up with any-thing?"

David fidgeted. "Not really, John. But I'd like a little more discussion to take place."

"I've already told you where my focus is. Bring me some-thing else that's useful in regard to your priorities, and we'll talk about it."

David sulked in his chair as John steered the conversation back to the search for Renphor. It went on for two more hours, with much emphasis placed on the importance of the assign-ments each of them had been doing. When the meeting finally broke up, Julie rose from her chair and went to the door to say goodbye to each of them as they left. John turned to her as Nelson, the last of the group to leave, finally disappeared out the door.

"Was it really necessary to demolish that table?" he asked pettishly. He pointed irritably to a two-inch square hole in the veneer of the table next to where Julie had been sitting.

"Probably not, but one of the mice seems to have started it for me. You know I can't resist picking at something that's sticking out like that. Where on earth did you get the stupid thing anyway? I can't imagine that it came out of an earl's residence."

John glared at her. "I picked it up after I moved to America. And long after I had to pass on the title, in case you've forgotten."

Julie shrugged. "I don't see that it makes much difference. It's still cheap."

John clenched his teeth. "As a matter of fact, it isn't. Or wasn't, prior to you putting a hole in it. I suppose I should be grateful that you stuck to destroying the furniture and didn't insert your own opinions of our agenda into the conversation."

"You should, but apparently you aren't. I think I've had enough of higher company for the time being. I'd like to have the rest of the evening to myself, if you don't mind." She left the room quickly. He watched her head toward her sitting room before veering off toward the portrait gallery.

He scowled at the detour and called out to her. "Why the devil do you need to spend so much time hanging around with *my* ancestors?"

"Someone should. I've no idea why you bothered to hang the damned portraits, since you're so averse to being in the same room with them."

"Because—"

"They were in the original house. I know."

"And they are my ancestors. However far I've fallen, I still owe them some kind of duty."

Julie rolled her eyes. "Flaming hell, you're a prig."

By the time John thought of an appropriate response, she had disappeared down the long hall. He slammed the door to the ballroom and stomped off to his library.

36

Arabella finished up most of her work Sunday morning as planned and decided to treat herself to one last solo lunch at a nearby diner before her roommates returned. When she got back, she found Narcissa curled up on the couch, watching a movie and nervously munching on a bag of pretzels. She leapt up as Arabella walked in and glanced wildly at the open door.

"What on earth is the matter with you, Cissy?"

"Is he with you?" Narcissa's hand shook as she spoke.

"Who, Ryan?"

"Yes, of course, Ryan!"

Arabella walked to Narcissa and put her hands on her shoulders, forcing her back onto the couch. "He isn't with me. Now what on earth is the matter with you?"

"Close that door, please." Narcissa glanced nervously at the doorway.

"Alright."

Arabella came back to find Narcissa out of her seat again, pacing back and forth in front of the couch.

"Narcissa, you need to sit back down. I'm going to call the medical center. You're having some kind of breakdown."

Narcissa sat down quickly and hugged one of the pillows tightly against her chest. "I'm not having a fucking breakdown, alright? Having a real fear for your life doesn't count as a breakdown."

Arabella stared at her. "Why are you afraid for your life?"

"Because of that freak you're dating. He got Rick already. I know he's after me."

"Narcissa, you really are having a breakdown. Why would Ryan want to hurt you? I know you don't get along with him, but neither does Sam, and she's not acting like this."

"Sam didn't supply Rick with his movements." Narcissa's eyes widened as she realized what she had just blurted out.

Arabella had been holding Narcissa's hands in a comforting grasp, but she released them and stood up when the words registered in her brain. Her face hardened, all concern wiped away.

"You're the one who kept telling Rick where he was, so that he could send his goons to try to take him out?"

Narcissa nodded miserably. "I was just trying to help you, Arabella. He's dangerous. I was afraid he'd hurt you."

"You weren't trying to help me. You were jealous because I had a boyfriend, and you wanted him out of the way."

Narcissa had started sobbing into the pillow. "It doesn't matter now. Are you going to let him kill me? Are you that mad at me?"

Arabella exhaled slowly. "He isn't going to kill you. He has no reason to kill you. He didn't kill Rick either."

"He did kill Rick. He's coming after me next, because I was helping him. God knows what he has planned for you."

Arabella sat down again, her anger dissipated by the pathetic sight in front of her.

"How on earth were you getting the information to give to Rick? Were you actually following Ryan around?"

"Yes. At least…I tried to. Every once in a while he'd just disappear."

"Disappear."

"He'd go around a corner into a blind alley, and then he'd be gone."

Arabella smiled. "Are you sure you're not just really bad at following someone?"

Narcissa took offense to this. "Of course not. How hard is it to follow someone down a dead end?"

Arabella let it go. "Really, Narcissa—I'm still not sure why you think he's trying to kill you. Why would he?"

"Look what happened to Rick," she answered dully.

"We don't know what happened to Rick, but the police said it wasn't foul play. Also, Ryan says it didn't involve him, and I believe him."

Narcissa stared at her in disbelief. "You're really that far gone, are you? Good luck to you, then. Whatever he does to you, you deserve."

"I could say the same for you, Cissy. You've been trying to get him killed for three months, and now you decide to throw a hysterical fit because you're afraid he might retaliate?"

Narcissa looked shocked. "They weren't actually going to kill him! Just—knock him around a bit to keep him away from you."

"And you call me gullible. They were carrying baseball bats."

"They weren't! I read the report—if he told you that, he's lying."

"I know the officer who was first on the scene. They could easily have broken every bone in his body."

"Doubtful, pet. I'm not that easy to damage."

Narcissa screamed. Arabella shot out of her seat. "Ryan! How did you get in?"

Renphor held up a set of keys with a pink puffball hanging on the end. "I believe these are yours?"

He smiled at the confused look on her face.

"Where did you find them?" she asked.

"In the door." He handed them to her. "You should be more careful. Not everyone is likely to be as benevolent as I am." He smiled mockingly at Narcissa as he spoke. She was looking up from her pillow now, staring at him in terror. "I must confess to overwhelming curiosity. What have I done to inspire that horrified expression?"

Arabella glared at Narcissa. "She thinks you killed Rick. And that you're going to go after her next."

Renphor laughed. "Why? Because she's been attempting to follow me around campus for three months and tell that other idiot everything I do?"

Narcissa's eyes widened. So did Arabella's. "You mean to tell me that you knew she was doing it?"

"Of course I knew. Don't ever go into the CIA. You'd never pull it off."

He sat down next to Arabella. Narcissa squeaked and scuttled to the other side of the couch.

"Now, you complete twit, listen to me. I'm not going to hurt you, however much you may deserve it. I'm not a murderer. If someone comes after me with a baseball bat, I will defend myself. Is that clear?"

Narcissa finally spoke. "I don't believe you. I know you were behind Rick's disappearance."

"And how would you know that?"

"Because he told me he was going to look for you. What happened to him after I left him in the park?"

"I neither know nor care. If I wanted you dead, I've had ample opportunity. You're not worth it. If you ever pull another stunt to try to hurt Arabella, I might reconsider, but you're safe for now. Now go away—I want to spend some time with my girlfriend."

37

On the following Saturday morning Arabella was lying in bed half-asleep, with Renphor rubbing her back as she nuzzled her head into his shoulder, when they heard voices in the living room. The sounds drifted slowly across Arabella's consciousness. She suddenly sat bolt upright.

"Fuck!" She leaped out of bed and yanked open her bottom dresser drawer in a single motion.

Renphor jumped at the sudden activity. "What?" He stared at her.

"I completely forgot—it's the first Saturday of December. My mother and I always go shopping today." She was hastily throwing on her clothes as she spoke. "Are you listening? Get dressed!"

Renphor smiled as he leaned against the headboard. "I don't dress as quickly as you. If I get up now, she'll walk in just in time to get more of a view than she wants."

Arabella's mouth dropped open. "You're not the least bit concerned?"

"No. Apart from going out the fire escape naked, not much I can do about it. If she finds me in your room, she's smart enough to figure out the rest."

Arabella finished dressing just as Julie walked in. She smiled weakly at her mother. "Hi, Mom."

Julie looked past her to Renphor, stretched out casually on the bed. Since he was sitting up, the covers only reached to his stomach, leaving his torso exposed.

"Are you still hanging around?" Her tone was cold.

"As you see. Did you expect otherwise?"

"Ryan, isn't it?"

He smiled slightly as he nodded.

"Were you planning to spend the entire day in my daughter's bed?"

"Not if she's not with me."

"Then go. I want to talk to her."

Renphor got up and started searching for his clothes. Arabella's mouth fell open as she looked from one to the other. Renphor eventually found everything and headed toward the living room but stopped at the door. "Are you coming back here tonight?"

Arabella closed her mouth and glanced at her mother.

"We should be done around dinnertime," Julie replied.

He left without another word.

Arabella finally broke what seemed to her like an endless silence. "Mom, I—"

"Don't bother. I don't care for your choice in boyfriends."

Arabella bristled. "Why not?"

Julie sighed. "I don't have any reason that would make sense to you, sweetie. I just don't trust him."

"You've only seen him for a few minutes." Arabella suddenly giggled. "And I don't think that was the best first impression."

The corners of Julie's mouth lifted. "On the contrary. I suspect I've now seen the best parts of him. But there has to be more to a relationship than that, you know."

Arabella sobered instantly. "There is more. I promise. He's really very sweet to me."

"Is he?"

"Yes, really. I keep trying to get him to come up to the house so you can get to know him, but he doesn't want to go."

"I'm not surprised. We can talk about it over lunch. Let's go, we're wasting good shopping time."

Arabella followed her out of the room.

Arabella and Julie returned to the apartment around six. Both were carrying stacks of packages so tall that they could only see by peeking through the gaps between them. Arabella laid her packages carefully on the table and started to flop onto the couch. She gasped when she discovered that the couch was already occupied. "Ryan!"

"Did I startle you? Sorry."

"I didn't expect you to still be here."

"I'm not. Still here, that is. I actually got quite a bit done today and got back here about ten minutes ago."

Arabella sat next to him. "How did you get in?"

"Ran into Sam as she was leaving. She let me in rather grudgingly, but I managed to convince her that you were expecting me."

"That's good to know. I'd hate to think my apartment was that unsafe."

Renphor smiled and took her hand. "My pet, anyone who wanted to gain quick access to your apartment would come up the fire escape and pry open your window in under five minutes. Be thankful this is a fairly safe neighborhood."

She sat upright, and he winced slightly at the pressure that she suddenly applied on his fingers. "You mean my bedroom window?"

"Precisely. Aren't you glad I spend so many nights here?" He looked mockingly at Julie, who had walked across the room to a comfortable-looking chair by the window. To his surprise, he realized that she was trying to suppress a grin.

"Can't you lock it down somehow?" Arabella asked nervously.

"I could, but it would severely limit its use for the intended purpose."

"Oh." Arabella looked at her mother. "I'm completely exhausted. Mom, I don't know how you do it. You seem to be able to go all day without wearing out."

"It's a question of stamina. I've had more years of practice."

Renphor eyed the packages on the table. "Presumably you had a successful trip."

"Very. I have a whole new wardrobe for winter," Arabella said.

"Did you need one?"

"Yes. Not everybody can wear the same outfit every day without anyone noticing." She eyed his white shirt and jeans.

"The trick is to possess so many other strange traits that no one pays attention to your clothing."

"I'll work on it. What are we doing this evening?" She leaned against Renphor's shoulder as she spoke.

"Since you're tired, we could watch a movie I suppose."

Arabella grinned. "*Pride & Prejudice* again?"

"If you want."

Julie chimed in. "One of my favorites."

"Ryan's too. You can stay if you want."

Julie looked quizzically at Renphor. "Seems an odd choice for you. And I think I'll take you up on that."

Renphor looked warily at her, but she did not meet his eyes as she grabbed the remote control.

It was a long movie and lasted late into the evening. Arabella had fallen asleep halfway through and was curled up on Renphor's chest, with one hand grasping his shirt collar. Julie occasionally cast annoyed looks in their direction but remained silent until Renphor spoke.

"There's nothing you can do about it, you know." His voice was sympathetic.

"I know. You know that she's in love with you, don't you?"

"Yes. It will make things easier for her in the long run, I think."

They sat in silence for a few minutes. Renphor pretended to focus on the movie while he watched Julie out of the corner of his eye.

"You intend to keep her, don't you?"

He smiled, as much to himself as at Julie. "Yes, I believe I do. You don't seem to find me as objectionable as John does. Once he's out of the way, I suspect we'll all get along fine."

"Where will you live?"

"I hadn't thought about it."

"Not at your place."

Renphor's eyes narrowed. "What would you know about my place?"

"As of now, the address. I don't trust John's shields—I'm never sure how much of my movements he can track."

"He can't."

She looked up quickly. "What do you mean?"

"Vampire 'magic' is all based on energy, and the control thereof. If you find yourself in danger, you might send out enough of a distress signal for him to find you, but he can't trace your day-to-day movements."

Julie exhaled slowly. "I didn't believe him about that. Thank you."

Renphor nodded. "To the original question—since you seem to be so invested, where do you suggest we live?"

She stood up and looked out the window. He thought that she was going to ignore the question, but she finally turned to him.

"You intend to kill John?"

Renphor nodded.

"And Joseph, too, I suppose."

"Unless he can be persuaded to get an existence of his own and drop this nonsense. I doubt it, though."

"So do I. I have nothing else in the world except Arabella. At least until I can get my life back in order, would you consider bringing her to Larch Hill?"

Renphor looked at her in surprise. "Certainly, if you wish it. It would be far more comfortable than any lodgings I've had until now."

"Your own choice, I suspect."

"Partly."

Arabella stirred and shifted her position slightly. She was not yet awake, but her movement put an end to the conversation, since neither Renphor nor Julie were in any hurry to admit her to it. They watched the rest of the movie in silence.

Julie entered the house as silently as she could but was not surprised when John called to her from his study. Sighing, she turned her steps away from the staircase and walked back to the heavy oak door. She paused for a moment with her hand on the doorknob before opening it and entering.

"It's almost one in the morning! Where on earth have you been?"

"With Arabella. We watched a movie and got to talking afterward."

"Until after midnight?"

She gritted her teeth. "Yes, John. She isn't twelve anymore. It's okay if she occasionally stays up past midnight."

"I don't really need sarcasm this evening. Stella came by tonight."

"Oh? Did she have anything intelligent to say, or was she just here to seduce you?"

"Must you really throw a jealous fit every time her name is mentioned?"

Julie turned sharply on her heel and walked back toward the door.

"Do you care at all what she had to say?"

"Only if any of it was new," she answered wearily.

He smiled at her. "As it happens, she had some very good information." Julie rolled her eyes, but John apparently didn't notice. "I know what alias he's using."

Her grip tightened on the doorknob. She tried to sound casual when she answered. "Oh? And what is it?"

"Ryan Callaghan. Now all I have to do is look him up."

Julie gasped, but John seemed to be too preoccupied with his own thoughts to notice.

"Do you have anything else to go on?" she asked.

He shook his head, but he seemed perfectly satisfied with the information he had managed to obtain. He was somewhat affronted that his mate didn't share in his enthusiasm. She left the room quickly after that, not wanting him to probe any more deeply into what was really on her mind. She attempted to settle down to a book but found herself pacing around her sitting room, casting the occasional glance at her phone.

38

Renphor slouched back against the new desk chair that he had acquired that morning. Someone had put it on the curb a day early, to be ready for the Monday morning garbage collection. He had gotten a few funny looks from passing cars while performing strength tests on the back of it, but he was reasonably certain that he wouldn't end up on the floor again. He flipped irritably through the pages of his English Lit text before closing it with a snap and taking a picture of Arabella out of his desk drawer. She had refused to give it to him when he asked for it, because she'd said it was the worst picture ever taken. He had sneaked it from the drawer when she'd gone to the kitchen for a drink of water—it was the only one he had ever seen where she was laughing. Running his fingers through his hair, he laid the picture carefully back in the drawer. A sudden voice behind him made him jump.

"Studying again?"

Renphor slammed the desk drawer closed. "Ariliana. And how do you always seem to know when I'm home, I wonder?"

She smiled as she walked toward him. "I don't. I buzz by whenever I'm in the mood, and once in a while I get lucky."

"I should put better seals on the place." Renphor went back to his lit book and opened it to the page he had been reading.

"Seriously? When did you start caring who wandered in and out of your room?"

"What do you want? I'm in the middle of something."

"I should've thought you could guess," she purred. She leaned over him and ran her hand down his neck. Renphor didn't look up from his book, but he felt her remove her hands quickly and assumed she had stepped away from him. "In a mood this evening, are we?"

"I'm always in a mood. Could you be more specific?"

"Did we have a fight with the girlfriend, Ren?"

"No," he answered shortly.

"I seem to have touched a nerve. Still, I don't see why it should make a difference to me." She put her hands around his neck and leaned in to kiss him. Renphor grabbed both of her wrists and forced her backwards. Ariliana, caught off-balance by the unexpected move, stumbled and nearly fell. She righted herself and glared at him, fangs bared.

"And I actually believed you when you said this human was just part of a bigger plan. If that's true, you're a lousy planner. You've gone and gotten attached."

Renphor leaned back against the chair with his eyes closed, a slight smile on his lips. "I'm not such a fool. Still, she is consummately entertaining. You, on the other hand, are more of a one-trick horse."

Ariliana released her breath slowly through her teeth. "I hope you weren't too fond of that one trick." She turned quickly on her heel and moved toward the fire escape.

Renphor laughed. "It was convenient. You're a fool, my dear. Do you think I can't find plenty of that kind of entertainment?"

She spun back around to face him. "I'm surprised you bothered with me, then."

"You were available. So are a lot of others. They're all after a bit of power too."

Ariliana's eyes blazed in anger. "And what about this human girl? What are you going to do with her when your little plan is done?"

Renphor looked mockingly at her. "I believe I shall keep her. I did promise her mother that I would."

Ariliana drew a sharp breath. "You mean to have her for your mate? After everything I—"

"You weren't seriously expecting me to take a plebe to mate? You're a bigger fool than I thought if that's the case. Now leave—I'm not in the mood for your temper tantrums tonight." He turned back to his reading. It was several minutes before he heard her move toward the fire escape and climb out onto the stairs. Renphor watched her go out of the corner of his eye. Sighing, he closed the book and stared out of the window that she had left open. After a few minutes, he stood and walked over to the bookshelf to get the notebook full of information about John. He pulled out his list of weaknesses and savagely drew a line through the entry for Nelson.

Stefan lounged idly in a red velvet armchair, reading an ancient leather-bound volume to pass the time. He was vaguely annoyed that he had not had any visitors that day. On days when he didn't want to see anybody, he was plagued with them. Today, when he had absolutely nothing to do, there wasn't a soul in sight. He tossed around the idea of forcing someone to come and play cards with him but discarded it. He wasn't really in that kind of mood. He had just picked up the book again when Robert suddenly appeared in front of him.

"Well?" Stefan asked.

Robert bowed. "A visitor, sir."

"I'd gathered that much. Who?"

"Female, sir. Wouldn't leave a name."

Stefan was intrigued but loath to admit it. "You've no idea who she is?"

"None. Shall I send her away?" Robert turned toward the door, but Stefan stopped him.

"No. Bring her here."

A few moments later, he ushered Ariliana into the room before bowing back out of it. Stefan looked her up and down and was sufficiently interested to offer her a chair.

"To what do I owe the honor?" he inquired.

Ariliana smiled. "Nice manners. But I doubt you consider it much of an honor."

"Perhaps not. Still, the interruption was not unwelcome this afternoon. And I certainly can't complain about the aesthetics." He eyed her pleasing form again.

She smiled at his obvious interest. "Plenty of time for that later. I have some information that might interest you."

"About?"

"Renphor."

He turned slowly away from the porcelain statue he had been examining. "And how do you know Renphor?"

"We've been friends for a while. At least we were. He seems a bit...distracted at the moment."

Stefan nearly yawned but decided it wasn't worth the effort. "And what do you want me to do? Get him back for you? I'm afraid I don't much care about Renphor's love life."

Her eyes narrowed. "Would you care if it involved a human?"

He paused. "That would certainly merit investigation, at the very least. Do you have evidence of this?"

"He admitted it. Not to having formed an attachment, though I'm sure he has, but to being tangled up with her."

Stefan stood and moved slowly into the room. "And what makes you think he's developed an attachment?"

She shifted uncomfortably, failing to make eye contact. "I don't think that would interest you."

"Jilted you? Dear, dear. Still, the information is interesting. I shall discuss it with him."

She eyed him warily. "You won't tell him I was here?"

"Not afraid of him, are you?" he mocked her.

She stiffened. "Laugh all you want. He's a hundred times more powerful than me. I heard that even you don't get on his bad side without a really good reason."

"It's rarely worth the effort. Still, for a plebe I suppose the scruples are wise." He smiled unpleasantly as her lips pressed tightly together. "You are power hungry, my dear. Barking up the wrong tree with Renphor—he doesn't bother with such things. You'd do far better with me."

Her eyes glinted. "Would I?" She moved slowly toward him. Stefan stopped her a few inches away by grabbing both her wrists. He forced them downwards as he pulled her closer to him. She looked at him for a moment, then dropped her eyes.

"You do understand the rules, don't you? I will call the shots, and you will like it. Understood?"

She nodded.

"Good."

He tilted her chin upwards and looked her in the face for a moment. "Yes, you will suit me well enough for the time being. I hope you aren't otherwise engaged this afternoon?"

She shook her head.

"What marvelous timing. Neither am I." He released her wrists and walked toward his private chambers, without bothering to see if she followed him.

39

Julie entered the study cautiously and looked around. Finding it empty, she softly closed the door behind her. She walked quickly to the shelves on the opposite wall and began running her eyes over the books to see what was interesting. Only two days previously, she had gotten into a vicious argument with John over her desire to study more advanced skills. He had finally agreed to teach her some more of what he knew on the condition that she stayed away from the information contained in his library, which could be dangerous to all but the most advanced practitioners.

She scanned the titles, skipping quickly over a whole section on herbs, as she was already a skilled herbalist. She was about to give up and move to another shelf when she noticed a small leather-bound volume with no title on the spine. It appeared to be very old—the leather binding was cracked despite a shield that had been put on it. Its presence on the shelf intrigued her. It was obviously something that John valued enough to preserve, so why had it been stuffed between two unimportant volumes on basic shields?

She carried it carefully to the table and set it down gingerly before taking a seat. The book crackled softly as she opened the cover, but it seemed to hold together, so she eased her fingernail under the first yellowed sheet and turned it over to view the writing on the other side. Her finger rested on the date at the top—April 7, 1630. The page was completely covered in what appeared to be an elderly woman's handwriting.

An hour later, John found her still bent over the table, with three quarters of the diary's pages turned over. She was so engrossed in what she'd found that she had not heard him enter nor noticed his presence until he spoke.

"What are you doing?" he asked sharply.

She jumped and looked up from the book. "John."

He reached out to take it, but she stopped his hand. "Why didn't you ever tell me about this?"

John sighed. "It belonged to my Aunt Beatrice. She wrote scores of them, but this particular one covered such an important part of my own life that I kept it."

"Your marriage?"

"Yes. The thoughts that she recorded about my own behavior weren't particularly complimentary, but she seems to have liked Sophia well enough." He smiled bitterly.

Julie laughed. "I think you're taking her words a little too much to heart. You seem to have behaved like any normal seventeen-year-old boy."

He sat down across the table from her. "I wasn't a boy. I was an earl, and owner of a large estate. And I had a wife by the time I was eighteen. She didn't approve of that, either. Thought I was too young, but at least she couldn't complain about my choice. Sophia's father was a duke, and a wealthy one at that. She was an only child. It all fit in quite nicely with my family's plans for me."

She glanced at an ornately framed portrait on the wall, depicting a dark-haired woman standing in front of a white horse. "And she also had the good sense to be stunningly beautiful, which I'm sure was perfectly alright with you."

John laughed suddenly, losing the melancholy look that had come over his face. "It was the only thing I cared about. Thank God they did approve, or I probably would have married her against my family's wishes and created a huge mess." His

smile didn't last long, since talking about his family always reminded him of his pain over their loss.

Julie changed the subject hastily. Pushing the diary toward
him, she pointed to an entry from December of 1630. "What
was this all about?" she asked.

"That's the irony of everything that's happened. Batty was
obsessed with the fear of vampire attacks. She reamed me out
time and again for wandering around the woods, and if I dared
come back after dark, she'd have a fit and go running to my
mother to have me punished. She got so bad in the end that they
locked her up. And I used to mock her mercilessly for believing
in such garbage." John shook his head.

"But there's more to it than just a fear of vampire attacks,
John. She's got pages of notes here on a family curse—she
sketches out the dates of death of every one of your male ancestors, dating back to the fourteen hundreds. For someone
who's supposedly insane, that's some meticulous research."

John leaned back in his chair. "She got most of it directly
from my grandmother. There was quite a bit of nonsense about
a family curse. And admittedly the heads of my family generally
died fairly young. I used to taunt Aunt about it when I was a
teenager. None of my ancestors died without a male heir. Pure
coincidence, of course, but I kept telling her I was going to live
until a hundred just by staying single." He smiled.

"She couldn't have believed you were serious?"

"Not entirely, but it still worried her. She was an extremely
proud woman. The continuation of the line was everything to
her. After my conversion, I tried to hide it from her for as long
as I could. Feigned an illness for weeks—only coming out of my
room in the dead of night. She figured it out eventually, though.
Begged me to take her life, since she couldn't stand the dis-
grace." He stared out the window as he spoke.

"Did you?"

After a pause, he nodded sadly. "One of my few human
kills. I made Joseph shortly after that, since he was determined

not to leave me, and it wasn't safe for him to serve me as a human. I would eventually have lost control and killed him as well."

They sat in silence for a while, Julie turning over everything that he had said, and John staring off into the distance. Julie spoke first. "Tell me about the suspicious deaths."

He started, having forgotten that she was in the room with him. "The deaths? No official record shows anything suspicious. The coroner's verdict was always natural death, or accident. The 'unofficial' accounts are more of an oral tradition, which we were always careful to keep within the family circle. It started with the first earl, who died in 1420, shortly after being granted the title. He was found in his study, with all of the doors locked and the fireplace poker lying on the ground next to him. It was a third-story tower room. Your favorite tower, in fact, although his view was of his fields. There was ivy growing outside of it, but not thick enough to support a man's weight for more than a few seconds. Certainly not long enough to climb the whole way to the top of the tower and go in through the trap, and you know that a man couldn't fit through those window slits. They ruled it a natural death—assumed he had seen something that shocked him into having a heart attack, and that he had grabbed the poker because he was frightened. That's the official record, at any rate. The family legend states that the butler, who found the body, said there were two puncture wounds on his neck spaced about an inch apart. The second earl inherited the title when he was ten years old. He married at twenty-two, had three children, and was found dead in the woods at the age of thirty, attacked by some kind of wild animal. And so it goes. Two hundred twenty years of my family line—ten generations of earls. Every one of them dead by thirty."

Julie tapped her fingers on the table. "So what did Renphor have against your family?" she asked.

John jumped. "Renphor? What's it got to do with him?"

"Your family is stalked by a vampire for over two centuries, and you just happen to have a run-in with one on your grounds? He's old enough, too."

John shook his head. "Doesn't fit. If Renphor were the source of the supposed curse, he would've killed me rather than my family. Our 'vampire' never went after the women or children."

"So something changed things when he got to you. No other scenario makes sense. If it was someone other than Renphor, they would certainly have confronted you by now."

John stood up quickly and walked to the bookshelves, running his hand along the spines. "But I don't believe that my family was stalked by a vampire. None of these accounts were ever written down. They were passed down from the older generation of women to the younger, always just after the most recent death. And there is a strong vein of insanity in the females of our line."

"Just the females?" She raised her eyebrows.

He grinned at her. "I don't think the men lived long enough to develop those kinds of problems. But we certainly had a higher number than your average family of aging spinsters locked in secret towers."

"I see. I still say Renphor is tied in somehow. Maybe something happened that he hadn't planned."

He picked up the diary and closed it carefully. "Don't you start going batty. This is how it starts, you know."

Julie watched him put the ancient book back on a high shelf, out of her reach. She rose quickly and headed toward the door. In response to John's question about what she was doing, she said she was going to spend some time on top of the tower with a good murder mystery.

40

Stefan leaned back into the red upholstery of his chair, staring into the fireplace with his fingertips pressed tightly together. It had been a week since Ariliana had first visited him, and she had revealed more than enough information in that time to cause Stefan real concern. She was obviously bitter, but if anything, that fact supported the truth of her story. If Renphor was really as deeply involved with a human girl as Ariliana said he was, it would be necessary for Stefan to rein in his behavior to keep things under control in his territory. Had it been anyone else, he would simply have had the girl killed, but he was well aware that his hold on Renphor was already tenuous at best. Stefan knew that Renphor's lack of involvement in the political upheavals that surrounded him sprang from apathy, not fear. He was perfectly capable of causing the maximum amount of trouble if anything annoyed him enough to push him out of his lethargic state.

He opened and closed the drawer on his end table irritably, without looking inside. For his own part, he didn't care who Renphor carried on a relationship with. It was the plebes who worried about exposure, since their vulnerabilities made them possible marks for the few humans who still partook in vampire hunting as a hobby. Still, the lower classes had their own sort of power. A plebe uprising in his territory would be almost as much of a headache as a battle with Renphor. He sighed, staring at the phone that he had finally pulled out of the drawer.

"Robert!" he barked for his servant.

The man materialized instantly next to his elbow. "Sir?"

"We will be entertaining a guest this evening. I do not wish to be disturbed by anyone else. Is that clear?"

"Yes, sir."

Robert disappeared into the shadows. Stefan stood up quickly and began to pace in circles around the room, finally dialing the phone on his third lap.

A few minutes later Stefan stood in the same spot, smiling slightly at the phone in his hand. Renphor's irritation at the summons had been evident, but he had agreed to the meeting with little resistance. It would be far easier for Stefan to get any information he wanted if Renphor was already annoyed. Renphor's worst failing was his temper—if Stefan taxed him about his behavior when he was angry, he was likely to fly off the handle and tell him everything he wanted to know and then some. Stefan started toward the fireplace but stopped midstride. Eyeing his porcelain collection thoughtfully, he turned and walked firmly to the other side of the room.

Renphor appeared suddenly in front of the card table. The scowl on his face informed Stefan that he had not been mistaken about his mood.

"What do you want?"

Stefan gritted his teeth but kept his tone level. "I hear interesting news of your...activities."

"I can't imagine that my activities are any of your business."

"They are when they involve a human girl who seems to be exercising an alarming degree of control over you. You know perfectly well what kind of problems that causes."

"Control? You shouldn't listen to malicious gossip."

He flopped into one of the Louis XIV armchairs as he spoke. Stefan winced but remained silent.

"I'm sorry—is this your chair?"

"Don't heed it. I prefer to stand."

"Good."

Stefan stiffened but managed to bite back a retort. "You don't deny the liaison?"

"No."

"What exactly do you mean by it?"

Renphor's lips curled. "Is that your concern?"

"Perhaps not. I could always bring the girl here and ask her, I suppose." He leaned casually against the door to his private apartments.

"You have the subtlety of a rhinoceros. The girl has numerous attractions beyond the physical. Frankly, the physical isn't so bad either—she's quite beautiful."

"Don't tell me you're drawn to her sweet nature."

Renphor laughed at this. "Hardly. I'm more drawn to her lineage."

"Oh?"

"Does the name Flynn ring any bells for you?"

Stefan started. "Yes. Does it mean anything to you?"

"I'm not in the mood to fence with you this evening, Stefan. You know perfectly well that John Elder is mated to one Julie Flynn. You are also aware that she has a daughter."

Stefan feigned indifference, but he leaned forward a little as he spoke. "What of Julie's daughter?"

"At the moment, she is well on her way to being quite hopelessly in love with me." Stefan let out a sharp bark of laughter. "Yes, it is rather amusing, isn't it?"

"And here I thought you were losing your grip. How in the name of Satan did you arrange that?"

"Lucked into it, actually. She picked me up on campus one night."

"She picked you up?"

"Off a park bench, in fact. She was in a towering rage at her entirely obnoxious roommate, who was tweaking her for being too virginal. The timing couldn't have been better."

"You always were the luckiest bastard on the planet."

Renphor stood. "Is this ridiculous conversation now over? I was in the middle of something when you called."

Stefan waved off the comment. "I don't care about your plots against John. Just be careful that you don't stir up trouble elsewhere. And don't let the girl catch on."

He opened the door that he had been leaning against but turned back with his hand still on the knob. "Renphor."

Renphor jerked his head in Stefan's direction. He had been about to start his jump and stopping midtwist knocked him off-balance.

"What?" he asked shortly.

"Out of curiosity. Are you planning to kill her, or convert her?"

"I'll figure it out when the time comes. No point in planning that far ahead until I know how things are going to play out."

At this, he jerked to the side and disappeared before Stefan could call him back again.

Stefan stood staring at the spot where Renphor had been, a slight smile curling his lips. "You always could be counted on to provide the entertainment, Renphor. Good luck to you."

41

The Sunday before Christmas, Arabella woke up already planning her study schedule for the day. Realizing that the sun wasn't even up yet, she rolled over to check the clock and groaned. She turned to the other side of the bed before remembering that Renphor hadn't come over last night. He had claimed to have some studying to do and promised to drop by later in the day. Sighing, she got up and dressed, wandering out into the living room just as Sam came out of her room.

"Morning, Sam. Why are we both up at six a.m. on a Sunday?"

"Beats me. Something must've made a noise. Is Cissy awake?"

Arabella shrugged. "You can check. I don't really care."

Sam shook her head as she opened the door to Narcissa's room. She paused for a moment with her hand on the knob before turning back to Arabella.

"Ever known her to be up and about at this time of the morning?"

"No, why? Is she?"

Sam shook her head. "She's not here. Odd. She didn't say anything to me about staying out all night."

"Maybe she decided to stay once she got to wherever she went, and actually showed enough consideration not to call in the middle of the night."

Sam smiled thinly. "I doubt it. The only reason she stays out all night is because she managed to hook up with some poor sap, and she never keeps that kind of info to herself. Anyway, it wasn't my turn to watch her. She can take care of herself. But if it wasn't her, what the heck woke both of us up?" She yawned as she wandered into the kitchen. "Guess I'll grab some breakfast. Wish I could go back to sleep, but it's never going to happen now—my brain seems to have jumped straight to my to-do list."

Sam and Arabella sat around talking over breakfast, putting off the inevitable trip they both needed to make to the library that day. It occurred to Arabella how little tension there was in the room with Narcissa gone, but she decided to keep this thought to herself. Sam had made it clear that she was tired of the arguing between Arabella and Narcissa. When they grabbed their books and headed out, there was still no sign of their missing roommate. Sam was beginning to worry, but Arabella assumed that Narcissa would turn up by lunchtime.

Renphor dropped by Arabella's apartment later in the evening. He noticed the tense look on Arabella's face as soon as she opened the door, and Sam didn't look much better.

"Demon boy! Don't suppose you've seen Narcissa?"

"Humans can't see demons. Have you misplaced her?"

Arabella put her hand on his arm. "Be serious, Ryan. Nobody has seen her since she left for the party last night. Sam was just going to call the police."

"Have you tried calling whoever she went out with?"

Sam answered, "I ran into the girl she was supposed to be with in the cafeteria. Cissy never showed up at her house, and she ended up leaving without her. It's only a ten-minute walk from our apartment to her place."

Renphor considered for a moment. "Her parents live in the city, don't they? Maybe you should try them?"

Arabella was appalled. "And scare the crap out of them when there probably isn't anything wrong?"

Renphor smiled. "My pet, who do you think the police are going to call first? Which is worse, a call from her roommates, or a cop on the doorstep?"

Sam picked up her phone. "Much as I hate to admit it, he's right."

She dialed Narcissa's home number and had a brief conversation with her mother while Arabella fidgeted around the living room, pretending to tidy up. Renphor watched the proceedings, smiling as she shifted everything from one side of the coffee table to the other three times. Giving up on his original plan to take her to a movie, he flopped down on the couch next to her.

She looked up at him, irked. "Aren't you the least bit concerned?"

Renphor snorted. "About Narcissa? Why would I be?"

She stared at him. "Because no one has seen her all day!"

"No loss, as far as I'm concerned." He got up and turned on the TV. Arabella handed him the remote, which he put back on the coffee table without using, and began watching the cooking show that had appeared on the screen.

"Taking up a new hobby, are you?"

"Why not?" Renphor answered casually.

Arabella stared at him. "Because you don't eat. Ever."

He didn't meet her gaze. "Nonsense. Of course I eat."

"What? And when?"

"Is this really an interesting topic?" He picked up the remote and began to study it intently. After about two minutes he hit a button at random, and the sound went off on the TV. Renphor blinked. "Odd."

Arabella laughed in spite of herself. "Not when you hit the mute button it isn't. Honestly, I don't know how you get through life."

"Quite easily, pet." He glanced up as Sam slammed her phone on the table. "Are her parents that irritating?"

Sam was glaring at the phone. "No, apart from her mother having hysterics. So I called the police, who weren't concerned at all. They told me it hasn't been enough time yet. College students stay out all night all the time, she's probably sleeping it off somewhere, blah, blah, blah."

Renphor spoke soothingly. "It's true, you know. She might just be...visiting."

Arabella shook her head. "She hasn't shown any interest in anyone since Rick disappeared."

Sam grimaced. "I can't believe she was dumb enough to think he was really interested in her. Anyway, I guess I should be glad that you didn't end up with that prick." She stormed off into her room.

Renphor smiled at Arabella. "So what are we doing tonight?"

"I don't think I could go out while Narcissa is still missing. Maybe we should just watch a movie."

Renphor at last showed some concern. "I sincerely hope she isn't missing long. Excuse me a minute—I just remembered a phone call I have to make."

Half an hour later, he and Arabella were curled up on the couch watching a movie when they heard a knock on the door.

Arabella jumped up. "Maybe Narcissa forgot her key." She half ran to the door, but the color drained out of her face when she opened it and found two police officers standing outside. "What happened?" she stammered.

The taller of the two men spoke first. "I'm Detective Dougherty. This is Detective Campbell. We understand that your roommate has disappeared." The man had brown hair and pale skin and looked much too young to be a police detective. Detective Campbell was somewhat shorter, with sandy hair and a red complexion.

Sam came out of her room and eyed them up. "Do you have any ID?" she asked curtly. The officers showed her their badges, and she waved them into the room. "I thought you wouldn't investigate this as a missing person yet. What changed your mind?"

"We got an anonymous call that convinced us otherwise. We just want to ask you a few questions about her activities last night."

The detectives stayed for half an hour, going over what Narcissa's plans had been and who she was supposed to be with. They seemed satisfied with the answers, asked them all to let them know if they thought of anything else, and left quickly. Arabella was relieved now that she felt like something was being done. Renphor was indifferent. Sam was suspicious of the sudden interest of the police.

"What do you think that anonymous caller said?" she asked as soon as the door closed.

"What do you mean?" Arabella asked.

"I think it's a really bad sign that they got an anonymous tip that convinced them to start looking into this right away. I'm going to call her parents again—they should know about this."

When the call ended fifteen minutes later, Sam looked even grimmer than she had before. She wandered across the living room and sat down on the couch next to Renphor.

He stared at her in surprise. "What did they say?"

She jumped and looked at him as if she'd just realized he was there. She started to stand up but changed her mind and leaned back against the couch. "I got her mother. She had hysterics again. Then her father got on the phone, yelled at me for upsetting her mother, and hung up. I'll let the police keep them updated from here on out."

Sam stared blankly at the TV. Arabella curled up as close as she could to Renphor without actually sitting on top of him and rested her head on his chest. Both of them eventually fell asleep on the couch, with Renphor still sitting between them.

42

Two days before Christmas, John was lounging in front of the fireplace in his library, pretending to read a heavy leather volume while he watched his mate out of the corner of his eye. She was pacing irritably back and forth across the carpet. He finally gave up on the book, setting it on the smoking stand next to him.

"Why so restless this evening?" he asked solicitously.

"No idea. Can't seem to settle on anything."

"Try a book," he suggested, picking his back up from the stand.

She gave him a disgusted look. "That's your best suggestion, when my whole problem is that my brain won't settle down to anything?"

"What is the problem, exactly?"

She flopped onto the sofa. "I already told you," she snapped. She stood up again and paced over to the bookshelves. Pulling things off the shelves at random, she flipped quickly through the pages before putting them back. The sixth book finally caught her attention. After flipping through quickly, she went back to a page in the middle and stared at it with interest. Still reading, she walked back to the leather couch and lay on her stomach, book propped against the arm. John watched her progress narrowly.

"Found something?"

She nodded vaguely. Realizing that was the only answer he could expect, he stood up and moved to look over her shoulder.

"Why are you reading a segment on jumping?" he asked sharply.

"Because I'd like to learn, and you can't be bothered."

"I can't do it, and you don't have the skills to make the attempt." He made a grab for the book, but she put out a hand to stop him.

"You can't do it because you won't try. I'm part of Stefan and Renphor's line too, in case you've forgotten. There's no reason why I shouldn't have the ability." She picked up the book and turned away from him.

"You'll never learn it on your own. You'll end up in pieces on the back lawn." He sat back down in the chair.

"What's your problem with it, anyway? You can't seriously consider effective transportation as one of the dark arts."

John clenched his teeth. "I have no interest in any gifts from Renphor."

"Don't be ridiculous. All of your abilities came from Renphor, one way or another. I see no reason to refuse to learn something really useful just because your bloodline is well known for it."

John slammed his book closed. "Do you understand what he did to me?"

She looked at him coldly. "Yes, I think I have some idea. Turned you into a vampire against your will? I have a bit of experience with that."

John's mouth fell open. "You can't say that I've mistreated you. I've given you everything!"

Julie sighed. "Yes, everything that you thought I should have. Ever think to ask me what I wanted? It certainly wasn't this."

"What complaints do you have? I've kept you fed, helped raise your child, kept a roof over your head—"

She cut him off. "I'm not from the seventeenth century, John. I was perfectly capable of handling all that on my own. You decided even while my husband was still alive that you wanted to add me to your possessions, so when the opportunity came, you didn't hesitate long enough to consider my viewpoint. Now, I'm not having this pointless conversation—if we're going to be stuck together for centuries, I might as well get over it."

She turned her back on him and propped the book up against the back of the couch.

Christmas Eve morning, John sat in the living room in the modernized part of the mansion, watching his mate's activities. She had forced him to put away the fire vortex and rounded up Joseph so that she could put up a Christmas tree and decorate the living room.

"Is there a reason for all of this sudden activity, my dear? Arabella won't be here until tomorrow."

"She's coming this afternoon."

John raised his eyebrows in surprise. "When did that happen?"

"She called me this morning. Said she'd had more than enough of the semester, and she was coming home early. So could you help?"

"Have you unchained the gate yet?"

"Joseph has orders to do so at noon."

John stood and looked around reflectively. The rooms that had been updated for Arabella to live in were furnished in an entirely different fashion from her parents' quarters. Soft electric lights glowed in wall sconces over a slightly ancient stereo system. An upholstered chintz couch and love seat surrounded a large television set, and a recessed alcove to the right of it that usually contained a stone sculpture was now filled with a large empty evergreen.

After two hours spent untangling lights from the cardboard meant to keep them in order and raiding boxes of ornaments for the best selections, John stood back to admire their work. The tree now sparkled brightly and dripped with all variety of ornaments.

"It's beautiful. But why did you anchor it to the wall like that?" He looked curiously at the length of heavy-gauge picture wire that ran from one side of the alcove to the other and was wrapped three times around the trunk of the tree in the middle.

"Bast." She nodded at the large black cat that was sitting very erectly in front of the television, with her tail wrapped around her front paws.

"Do you think she'd bother it over in the corner?"

"Are you kidding? It's irresistible. It smells like the outdoors and has lots of shiny dangly things."

"Fair enough. Where are the gifts?"

"I'll be right back."

Julie walked to a very solid-looking bookcase and ran her hand down the side. It opened noiselessly to reveal a candlelit hallway. She disappeared but returned within a few minutes with a pile of beautifully wrapped packages. She distributed these around the tree as John watched.

"Why on earth do you put that much time and effort into something that's going to be ripped to shreds in ten seconds?"

"If there's one thing I've got, it's time," she replied. "And besides, it's fun."

John knelt to examine the gifts. "And what could possibly be in the one for me that's appropriate to open around Arabella?" he asked.

"Like I'm going to tell you. You'll have to wait until tomorrow."

He got up and walked to a stack of CDs standing next to the stereo and pulled one out of the middle of the stack. A few moments later, medieval Christmas tunes came out of the speakers.

"We really should update that system. CDs are going the way of the dodo," Julie said.

"What for? Arabella's almost done with school, and she'll probably end up with a job in D.C. or New York. Even if she wanted to move back here after graduation, I'd discourage it."

Julie sighed. "I suppose you're right. I hate the thought of distancing myself from her, but she really needs to move away from all of this."

John looked out the window as she spoke and noticed a small green car pulling up the lane, just as Julie heard the sound of the tires crunching on the stones. Smiling, she ran out the door to greet her daughter.

John stood in the doorway, observing the scene in front of him. He had slipped quietly into the master bedroom from the other part of the house so as not to disturb Arabella's sleep, but she was already awake. The gas fireplace had been lit. The remains of Arabella's breakfast were on the coffee table, but the two women were already seated in front of the Christmas tree. Both of them were wearing old pairs of jeans and beat-up flannels. Arabella was pawing through the packages, occasionally rattling one.

"You're as bad as a four-year-old. Can't you wait an hour until you open them?" Julie scolded her.

Arabella grinned. "No."

Julie sat down next to her daughter and carefully examined a box with her name on it.

They both jumped at the sound of John's voice. "Couldn't even wait until I got dressed?" He had put on pajamas and a dressing gown to make Arabella think he had slept.

"We didn't open anything," Arabella answered defensively.

He smiled at her and pulled a small package from under the tree. "This one's yours."

Arabella shook the box hopefully and smiled at a faint rattling sound. She carefully peeled away the paper, her eyes widening at the sight of a black felt box. She opened it slowly and oohed softly at its contents. A narrow diamond-and-emerald choker lay on the black felt background.

"It isn't real, is it?" she asked nervously.

"Of course it is. A family piece—it isn't really your mother's style, so I thought you should have it."

"It's beautiful." She barely spoke above a whisper. "But where will I keep it?"

"The safe here." John indicated a portrait above the fireplace. "Or you can get a safe deposit box, if you prefer."

She laid the necklace carefully back on its cushion and closed the lid. "I think the safe is a good idea. I'll think about the safe deposit."

The rest of the gifts were opened to the sounds of Bing Crosby on the stereo. John received a large, ornate magnifying glass from Arabella and a small golden object that confused Arabella but caused him to grin widely. "But what is it?" she asked.

"Just a knickknack," he responded quickly. He shot a look at his mate that spoke volumes.

Julie received a garden planner from her daughter and a bronze-and-gold ring from John. She put it hastily onto her finger as Arabella reached for it and held out her hand to show it off.

The rest of Arabella's gifts consisted of books (not academic, per her request) and a few small items for her apartment.

They spent the remainder of the day singing carols and trying out their new gifts, until Joseph entered the room to tell them that dinner was ready. He had cooked a very small Christmas goose, mashed potatoes and gravy, cranberry sauce, and a beautiful apple pie. Arabella piled her plate high with food and laughed at the meager portions her parents placed on theirs.

"Couldn't you splurge a bit on the food for Christmas?"

Julie shook her head. "I'd only regret it later. Enjoy your dinner, sweetie." She gave her daughter a quick hug before sitting down to eat.

After dinner, they sat around drinking coffee and talking over Arabella's plans for her final semester until eight o'clock, when she got up and announced that she had to get back to her apartment.

"You're not staying tonight?"

"No. I have some schoolwork to do."

"Over the holidays?"

"Yes. I have a two-semester anthropology course, and I have a hundred-page paper to write."

"I believe that's known as a book."

"Not according to my professor."

She kissed him on the cheek and hugged her mother. "Thank you so much for my gifts." She gathered everything but the necklace into a paper bag and asked John to put his gift in the safe for her. Then she left quickly, running out to her car.

John looked at his mate, no longer hiding his irritation at his stepdaughter's sudden exit. "What was that all about?" he grumbled.

"I suspect she had another gift exchange to do tonight," Julie answered blandly.

"What do you mean?"

"The boyfriend. I couldn't get out of her what she had bought for him, but I have a feeling she's anxious to give it to him."

John was stunned. "She didn't mention him at all over the last two days. I figured he'd gone by the wayside."

"The opposite, I think. That's why she didn't talk about him—she didn't want to answer any questions about how serious they've gotten, because I don't think she's even had that discussion with him yet."

"Huh." John picked up his magnifying glass and smiled. "This will be really helpful for some of the manuscripts I've been trying to read." He looked at his mate. "And the gold scales are quite lovely. I've not had much time for alchemy lately, but I may have to try a few things just to test them out. Thank you."

43

The Sunday after Christmas, Julie found herself alone in the library. John had left for church early in the morning, since he had switched congregations again and wanted to get there early to check things out. He had been rotating through seven or eight churches since he'd arrived in Philadelphia, remaining at each just long enough for people to think that he was aging remarkably well, without realizing that he wasn't aging at all. He had attempted to take Julie once, but she had laughed in his face. She'd told him that she hadn't been devout before being turned into a monster, and it was probably a little late for religion at this stage of the game. He had argued with her for a while, but in the end she had flatly refused to go. He had long since given up on trying to change her mind, even though she had occasionally agreed to send Arabella along with him when she was a child. John had been hopeful that his stepdaughter would someday share his own religious views, but it hadn't seemed to take. When she had decided at the age of thirteen that she didn't want to go with him anymore, he had been furious. He'd tried to force her to capitulate, but Julie had backed up her daughter's decision, and John had eventually backed down.

On this particular morning they were planning a long service and had a church council meeting afterward, so with travel time she knew she would have at least five hours to herself. She had only been able to steal a few moments here and there to study the jumping diagrams over the past few days, since John's satellites had been in and out, invited by him to partake in various festivities. She had wasted additional time because he had attempted to hide the book from her several times, but she had always managed to figure out where he had put it. She had been elated at the chance to spend a few uninterrupted hours studying, but her cheerful mood hadn't lasted for long. It had been nearly half an hour already, and she still didn't even know what her first step should be. Either she really didn't have enough of the basic skills to manage it, or there was more to it than what was shown on the page. Knowing that it was counterproductive to allow herself to get frustrated, she closed the book and stared reflectively at the wall for a few minutes. Finally, she stood and walked quickly out of the room.

An hour later, Renphor appeared in his own room, where Julie had been awaiting his return. He turned toward his desk and jumped backwards across the room at the sight of her standing there. She put up her hands to prevent him from attacking.

"Sorry to drop in unannounced."

Renphor scowled at her. "What the devil do you want?"

She smiled at him. "Grouchy this morning?"

"I wasn't."

"Again, sorry I startled you. I would have called, but I don't have your number and figured Arabella wouldn't give it to me even if I asked, so I took a shot that you'd probably be through here this morning."

He looked slightly more relaxed but continued to glance out of the window as they spoke. "Why?"

She looked at the ceiling for a moment, then back at him. "I want you to teach me to jump."

"You're planning to sneak over here for lessons? How?"

"Same way I did this morning. John spends hours in church every Sunday. Even goes to confession a few times a week, although I suspect he leaves out a few key points."

"Probably. How did you get here?"

"Bus system. It stops right outside our gate. And there's a stop not far from your place too."

"I know." He stared at her for a few minutes before putting out his hand. She took it tentatively and was startled a moment later to feel herself being pulled toward him. She had a temporary sensation of being squeezed through a tube and suddenly found herself on the opposite side of the room. It was a short jump, but the odd sensation left her a bit shaken.

"Ever done that before?" he asked.

"No. I don't think I care for it, to be honest. But it's efficient."

He nodded. "That was just to get the initial shock out of the way. Come here." He motioned her toward him and grasped both of her wrists in his hands.

"We're going to do a few more ride-alongs. Only this time, I want you to focus on the sensation that's being created. Try to pinpoint where it's coming from."

"What happens if you screw this up?" she asked nervously.

"Inexperienced jumpers mess up all the time. Usually they just slam into a wall. Once in a while someone will get stuck inside of one and have to figure out the best way to extricate themselves. It can be annoying and occasionally painful, but there's nothing really dangerous about it. It sucks a lot of energy, which is the main reason so many people who have the ability don't bother to learn."

Julie's fears were somewhat allayed, and they spent the next hour hopping from one side of the room to the other.

They stopped when Renphor decided it was time for her to take a break. She flopped down on the desk chair, and he spread out on the mattress.

"So, now that I have you alone..."

Julie looked up quickly, and Renphor laughed.

"Don't worry, I wasn't going there. I'm just curious about what put you onto the fact that Arabella was dating a vampire."

"Oh, that. Sam did, actually."

"Really? She spends so much time avoiding me, I'm surprised she noticed that much."

"Sam's no fool. You've been pretty lax about trying to fit in, and she's convinced there's something off about you. Arabella might not notice, since she's used to John and me, but Sam picked up on it right away. And apparently you dropped your shield in front of her at some point."

He grimaced. "Not exactly. I did get a little too relaxed, and the light hit my eyes at enough of a slant that it broke the shield for a bit. I was kind of hoping she'd forgotten that episode."

"A forlorn hope. And the whole first date thing put her off a bit."

"She told you about that?"

"Yes. Figured I'd hear a garbled version from Narcissa if she didn't."

"Probably. Little bitch."

"Speaking of, what happened to the little bitch?"

"No clue. Contrary to appearances, I wasn't involved. And I don't care enough to look into it."

"Interesting."

She looked at her watch and decided she needed to get back.

"Same time next week?" she asked.

He nodded. "Just make sure you're not followed."

"I will."

She headed toward the fire escape but stopped as a new thought occurred to her. "If it takes so much energy, won't John be able to tell? You said—"

"Perhaps. Certainly not from what you were doing today, since that was mostly me. When you start doing solo jumps, maybe. So be careful."

She nodded. "I'll see you next week."

Julie got back to Larch Hill almost an hour before her mate. When John arrived, she was sitting at his desk, intently reviewing the diagrams on jumping.

44

Arabella had the apartment to herself for a few days after Christmas, but by New Year's Eve, Sam was back. Arabella could hear her moving around in the apartment by the time she crawled out of bed at nine o'clock that morning.

Sam poked her head through the open door to Arabella's room. "Where's the freak?"

Arabella glared at her. "Ryan wanted to spend the evening with me tonight, so he did his usual Thursday night stuff last night."

"So, what are you two up to?"

"Probably just going to sit around here and have some champagne. You?"

Sam grinned. "I'm going to a big jazz thing down by the river."

Arabella was impressed. "Really? Who are you going with?"

"Woman I met while I was home visiting my parents. Her name's Amanda."

Arabella's curiosity led her to pump her roommate mercilessly for information. Sam submitted to this good-humoredly for about twenty minutes before getting up to leave the room.

"Calm down, Ella. I just met the woman—don't start picking out wedding dresses yet."

"I'm sorry, Sam. I didn't mean to be pushy—I'm just happy for you. I know it's been a while since you and Emily—"

Sam cut her off. "I don't want to talk about that. Come help me pick out something to wear tonight."

"What time is she picking you up?" Arabella followed her roommate to her closet, and they started pulling out a collection of dresses.

"Seven. I should be home around two."

"Wouldn't it be safer to stay downtown?"

"With someone I just met on Saturday?"

Arabella blushed and looked away. "Guess not."

"Sorry, Ella. Didn't mean that to come out that way."

They spent the next few hours weighing the merits of all the dresses in Sam's closet. Arabella even added a few of her own to the potential pile. They finally settled on a red sequined dress with a slit up the side. Arabella helped Sam with her makeup, since she hardly ever wore any and wasn't very experienced in applying it. By quarter to seven, she made Sam stand up and stepped back so that she could get a better look at her.

"I almost wouldn't recognize you if I met you on the street—you look great, Sam."

Sam ran her hand self-consciously across the sleeves of her dress. "I never feel normal in a getup like this."

"Come out in the living room. We'll have to get a second and third opinion when our dates arrive."

Sam grimaced but followed Arabella out of the room.

Renphor arrived at Arabella's apartment just before seven. He ran into Sam in the living room.

"Have you got your own key now?" She asked.

"Yes, Arabella gave me a copy. Said she was sick of jumping up and down to let me in." He stared at her. "You look stunning. Who's the lucky gal?"

There was a knock on the door before she got a chance to respond, and she hurried over to open it. Arabella wandered in from the kitchen and looked curiously at the athletic-looking woman standing in the hall holding a bouquet of daisies.

Sam turned toward Renphor. "Demon boy, this is Amanda. Amanda, this is Ryan, and that's my roommate, Arabella."

"Nice to meet you," Renphor said.

Amanda looked at him curiously. "Demon boy?"

Renphor shrugged. "She has this strange idea that I'm some sort of demon."

Amanda blinked. "Any reason?"

"Ask her." Renphor walked over and flopped on the couch. He picked up the remote and stared at the buttons.

"Figured that thing out yet?" Sam asked.

"Partly." The TV came on, and Renphor settled into the couch.

Arabella looked nervously from one to the other and opened her mouth to speak twice before closing it again. Finally, she said, "Amanda, would you think I was horribly rude if I asked Sam to take a look at something before you leave? I have to finish a project tonight that I want her opinion on."

"Of course not. Better that than having you call her all night."

Sam followed Arabella back to her room, leaving Amanda and Renphor alone in the living room.

Renphor spoke first. "Be very careful tonight. I happen to like your date."

She traced her fingers across the surface of the table. "So do I, actually. Don't worry."

The conversation was cut short by the reentry of Sam and Arabella.

"You ready, Manda?" Sam asked.

"Whenever you are."

Amanda put her arm around Sam, who jumped.

"What's wrong?" she asked.

Sam shook her head slightly. "Nothing. It's just that your hand is really cold."

Arabella knocked over the vase of daisies on the table as the door closed behind them.

Sam climbed into Amanda's Jeep, while Amanda slid behind the wheel.

"The flowers were a nice touch. Where are we really going?"

Amanda smiled. "Exactly where we said we were—the Penn's Landing Hyatt."

Sam looked startled.

"You have to be able to tell them about the party."

"I guess that makes sense. Did you get any kind of read on him?"

Amanda shook her head. "Didn't get to talk to him long enough. What do you have against the guy, anyway?"

"You mean apart from the fact that he probably murdered my roommate, and the police aren't doing anything about it?"

"Why are you so convinced he did it?"

Her jaw dropped. "Are you seriously taking his side? What am I paying you for?"

"I'm not taking his side. I'm just making sure that I get all my facts straight. I don't want anyone's murder to go unpunished, but it doesn't do anything for my professional reputation to accuse the wrong guy, either."

Sam had to admit that she was being reasonable. She went through all the details of Narcissa's disappearance while Amanda maneuvered her way through traffic. There was a break in the conversation while she dealt with parking and they figured out where the party was being held, but Amanda steered her into a quiet corner once they got inside the event room. She let Sam talk herself out about everything and then sat watching her for a few minutes until she got slightly ruffled. "Well, what are your next steps?"

"Can't do anything more tonight. I'll have to hang around your place a bit and try to get a better read on things. Now, everyone else in this place seems to be having a good time on the dance floor. Why don't we join them?"

They danced for hours, and Sam was startled when she realized around one o'clock that the musicians were packing up.

"We can't have been here for five hours already!"

Amanda laughed. "'Fraid so. Should I take you home?"

"What else would we do?"

"Well…they do rent rooms here."

"What are you suggesting?" Sam was annoyed to discover that she was blushing.

"That we get one. I had a great time tonight—didn't you?"

"What about our professional relationship?"

"We may have to pretend we're dating for a while. Might as well get to know one another."

Sam stared at her for a few moments before grinning. "Let me call Arabella and tell her I won't be home."

45

Three weeks after Christmas, the temperature, which had been unseasonably high, suddenly plummeted into the single digits. Fires were lit in every room of Larch Hill to preserve the furniture and books from the frost.

John sat in the atrium, where the snow still lay heavy on the ground from an earlier storm. Even though the courtyard was surrounded on all four sides, a bitter wind from the north had somehow made its way over the roof and was blowing sprays of snow toward the house. John shivered. He generally tried to stay indoors as much as possible between mid-December and spring, never having cared much for the cold weather. The area where he was sitting was covered in grass during the warmer months but in the winter it was mostly mud. Heavily ornamented columns flanked the entryway into the house, and a slate patio wrapped around the perimeter of the courtyard. A section of the snow that started just in front of the chair and extended ten feet out from it had a glassy look indicating that it had melted and refrozen. He was facing away from the door, focusing hard on the fireball that had just shot from his hand, and didn't hear his mate approach.

"John."

"What!" He jumped at the sound of her voice and completely lost control of the fireball. Glaring at her, he blew on his slightly singed fingers.

"You do know that there is such a thing as a lawn chair, right?"

He looked at her, and then at the upholstered chair that he had brought out with him.

"I was going to be out here for a while. I wanted to be comfortable."

"Comfortable? In the dark and the snow?"

"Not really. But I didn't want to try this part in the house."

"Signs of sense at last. How's it going?"

"I have the expansion working now. I think it's just a question of practice and strength at this point."

"Really?"

He compressed his lips. "That attempt that you just saw was the first failure in an hour. I think I'm starting to get tired. Might be time for a break, and a feeding."

She nodded. "I'll leave you to that. I'm going inside before it starts to snow again."

He acknowledged her with a nod and stood up, stretching. He looked up, considering the sky, and picked up the chair to move it into the house with him before heading out the back door and into the woods in search of dinner.

Two hours later he was back in the atrium, this time with an old metal chair that Joseph had scrounged up out of the carriage house. The snow was starting to fall thickly around him, so he had left the diagrams inside and was seeing what he could do without them. The first couple of tries shot off his wrist sideways or fizzled immediately. He got up to retrieve his notes but stopped himself before reaching the door, and resolutely sat back down. Focusing his attention on the back of his hand, he slowly lifted it into place. A stream of fire suddenly shot from his fingertips and whirled in front of him. Slightly shifting the position of his hand caused the fireball to grow wider and a flaming funnel cloud seemed to descend from the center into nothingness. He dropped his hand after a second and fell back onto the chair with his eyes closed for a few minutes, to gather his strength before making another attempt. The same pattern of a quick spurt of energy followed by a period of rest was repeated over and over for the next three hours. At the end of that time, he was able to produce a consistent vortex three feet across and maintain it for ten seconds.

He finally went inside around ten o'clock. Joseph was standing just inside the door when he entered and took the banged-up chair from him.

"Have you been waiting here all this time to make sure that thing didn't make it into the living room decor?" he asked with a hint of amusement in his voice.

"No, my lord. You have a visitor."

"Oh. Who is it, and how long have they been waiting?"

Joseph explained that the stranger had refused to leave a name but had been very insistent on seeing John. He had put him in the front parlor half an hour ago and had come here to find his master. "I didn't really think it was safe to wander out into the courtyard while you were practicing, so I waited inside the door," he explained.

"You've left an unnamed visitor in the front parlor for half an hour?" John asked sharply.

Joseph looked at the ground. "Madam is aware of him as well. She offered to keep an eye on him while I came to find you. Neither of us cared to dismiss him outright, under the circumstances."

John walked quickly toward the front entrance and stopped at a closed door at the end of the hall. Turning the knob, he went inside.

A tall, angular man with gleaming silver eyes turned from his contemplation of the grounds to greet him.

"Aristotle! What brings you here?" John walked forward to greet his friend.

"I happened to be in the area. Summoned to visit Stefan, in fact, but much more interested in seeing you."

John pulled two chairs toward the fire and motioned the other man into one.

"Are you staying long? And where are you putting up?"

Aristotle made a noncommittal gesture with his hand. "I don't even know why I'm here yet. Could have to hurry back to Transylvania."

John grimaced. "Still living there, eh?"

"Of course. The tourists love me—some of them even have their children pose with me. And quite a surprising number of them are dumb enough to wander into the woods alone."

John gritted his teeth but said nothing. His friend noticed, however.

"Still set on this idea that we shouldn't live off humans? It's a lost cause, my friend."

"Then why have so many of our kind changed to a mostly animal diet?" John took the opening he had been offered.

"Because humans nowadays have all sorts of nasty little explosive devices that could blow even the ruling council to smithereens. This is not the time for us to jump out of the woodwork yelling 'surprise, we exist after all.' Unless you want to be subject to an attempt at mass extermination."

John examined his extremely comfortable surroundings. "Not particularly," he said.

"No, nor does anyone."

The two friends spent hours catching up on current events, and less current scholarly pursuits. John refrained from showing his companion the fire vortex. Aristotle worked in an information-gathering capacity for the council, and John was fairly certain that they would not condone his activities. It was better not to risk it becoming generally known, until he was ready to spring a trap for Renphor. He did attempt to persuade his friend to stay with him while he was in Philadelphia, but Aristotle was persistent in his refusal. He said that it was easier, given his work, to put up alone somewhere near the center of town. "I definitely want to see you again before I leave, if I can. Fifty years is much too long. What's your cell number?"

"I haven't got one."

Aristotle looked stunned. "Really? I thought that young mate of yours would have brought you up to date. Oh well—I'll try to drop by again."

John walked him to the door and watched him exit down the drive with a reflective look on his face.

John slid through the bookcase opening into the living room where they had celebrated Christmas with Arabella. Joseph had cleared away all signs of the festivities, and a light coating of dust covered most of the room. He walked over to a small stand with a cordless telephone sitting in the middle of it, on top of a lined yellow tablet. He picked it up tentatively and turned it over in his hand before pulling open the drawer and extracting a thick phone book. It was old, since the phone company had stopped issuing them years ago, but he hoped it would still have what he needed. He flipped to the yellow pages and began jotting down information on the notepad.

By nine o'clock, John had a list of addresses in front of him. He put it into his pocket and started back toward the book-case. Changing his mind halfway there, he went out the exterior door and slipped around the front of the house to the garage. The black Jaguar slid slowly down the drive and out the gate without alerting anyone in the house that John had gone.

Half an hour later, he pulled into a parking space in a nearby shopping center and got out his list of addresses. All of them were in the same general area, so he picked the first one he came to. Pushing through the door, he blinked slightly as his eyes adjusted to the fluorescent lighting. Once he'd gotten his bearings and taken in the array of electronic devices lining the walls around him, he stood staring at them with his mouth slightly open.

"How on earth are you supposed to pick one? They all look like little black wallets to me," he muttered to himself.

He walked tentatively toward the wall and picked up one of the phones. With his head cocked to one side, he started pressing images at random. The phone blinked on and off, and screens jumped in front of his eyes. Putting it back carefully on the shelf, he moved on to the next one. A few minutes later, a perky saleswoman in a ponytail and rhinestone glasses walked up to him.

"Do you need some help?" she asked, smiling.

"Um, yes. I'm afraid I'm a bit of a technophobe, but my friends are threatening to abandon me completely if I don't get one of these." He turned the phone around in his hand and shook it slightly.

She smiled and turned it back right side up.

"Do you have anything—simple?" he asked a little ruefully.

"Over here." She led him to a wall of phones that looked to him exactly like the one he had looked at, although he noticed that the prices were significantly lower. She picked one up and flipped it open, handing it to him. "This is just a basic phone. We sell it for our ol…less experienced customers." She smiled brightly and started showing him how to work the basic features.

John put his hand on his forehead. "Does it come with in-structions?"

"Of course."

He looked at the fifty-dollar price tag under the phone, and the long list of features. Then he stared back at the small piece of plastic in his hand and shook his head. "This one, then, I guess."

"Oh good. Now we just need to get you signed up for a plan."

She handed him a brochure with a color-coded chart showing all of the plans clearly mapped out. He bit his lip and stared at it for several minutes before pointing to the cheapest plan. "That one."

The saleswoman spent another fifteen minutes trying, in her cheerful way, to convince him to consider more minutes. She was certain that he would absolutely love the phone once he got used to it, but John was steadfast in refusing to purchase a more expensive plan. Finally giving up, she turned her back on him and stomped to the register.

He was impatient over the paperwork but finally got everything filled out. After paying cash for his purchase, he picked it gingerly up off the counter before walking back to his car. He stuffed the whole package in the glove compartment and drove back to Larch Hill, mulling things over.

The next morning, John sat at his worktable, tapping his finger impatiently on a set of notes next to him. He had written down all of the information that he had gathered about Renphor and determined that it was woefully insufficient. He cast an occasional glance at the drawer of the smoking stand.

Julie rose suddenly from her seat across the room and picked up her purse and keys.

"Going somewhere?" John asked.

"I have a few things to buy in town. Can't seem to focus on my book, so I might as well get it out of the way."

He watched her leave through narrowed eyes. An instant later, Joseph appeared suddenly from the shadows, then disappeared just as quickly on a signal from John.

He waited a few minutes to make sure both of them were gone before going to the smoking stand and pulling the phone and the instruction manual out of the drawer. He pressed the power button by way of experiment and was quite pleased to see the screen light up. Smiling, he flipped to the first page in the instruction manual and started to read.

Three hours later, the smile had been replaced by a pronounced scowl. He had gotten through the entire manual, reading several sections multiple times, and he still wasn't sure what he was supposed to do with the object in front of him. Sighing, he looked around at the array of books and instruments scattered around his library. He ran his hand over a replica of da Vinci's flying machine and a small ancient globe before staring back at the lump of plastic.

When Julie came back from her shopping expedition, he was still lounging in the chair, staring out the window. The phone was still in his hand, but the hand was draped over the arm of the chair and was being pointedly ignored. She cleared her throat, but John ignored her, so she walked over and lifted his hand, removing the phone from it.

"What is this?" she asked.

"I should've thought you could figure that out on your own."

"Let me rephrase. Why do you have a cell phone?"

"Because I couldn't stand the badgering anymore."

"Do you mean to tell me it's yours?"

He nodded. She pointed at the instruction manual. "That thing making you nuts yet?"

"How did you guess?"

"Because I've done this before."

She programmed her number into the phone and showed him how to call it. "That's pretty much it. I can program a couple of others in for you until you get used to it."

"Thanks."

She sat down in her chair while he fiddled with the phone a little more. Finally, he gave up and went back to staring out the window. "If you wanted to find a particular person living in the Philadelphia area, how would you go about it?"

"Internet," she answered promptly.

He glared at her.

"Directory Assistance?"

His scowl deepened.

"I don't know what else you want. You've tried networking and gotten nowhere."

He sighed. "We don't have internet access. Not even in the other part of the house. And it would be a royal pain in the ass to get it set up."

"True. I'm not sure how you even got the phone lines run without one of your acquaintances biting somebody."

"I increased the shields."

They sat silently for a few minutes until Julie spoke again. "You could go to the library."

He stood and paced around the room a few times before turning to her. "Come with me."

The central library would have been the obvious choice, since their resources were better, but John was reluctant to attempt to work the computers in such a public setting. They headed to a smaller nearby library branch, where they were more likely to be left alone. On Julie's instructions, John sat in front of the screen, while she pulled up a chair beside him. He was tentative at first, staring at the buttons and lights doubtfully. He thought the wireless mouse particularly odd and spent several minutes flipping it this way and that, pointing it at the screen and clicking the buttons. She finally tried to take it out of his hand, telling him he was making a scene. He noticed that the librarian was, in fact, giving him a very strange look, and immediately put the mouse back where he had found it.

She gave him a quick tutorial on the rest of the computer before pulling up the internet. She had him start by typing in a few basic searches. He smiled at her stunned reaction when he started typing rapidly on the keyboard.

"You know how to type?"

He nodded.

"But you write everything by hand!"

He smiled. "There's an old typewriter in an attic some-where at Larch Hill. At one point I was a bit more involved in human affairs than I am now, and it was useful. The keys on this are much easier, though."

He was slightly stymied when it came time to start search-ing for Renphor, however. A search for "Ryan Callaghan Phila-delphia" brought up over half a million hits. None of the infor-mation he had collected narrowed down the list much. Julie made several suggestions, but they were no more helpful than the things that he had already tried. Every attempt returned at least ten thousand hits.

"This is pointless." John leaned back in the chair with his arms folded over his chest. He was used to careful research in his library, and the glut of information combined with the blink-ing lights on the screen wore on his nerves quickly. Julie con-vinced him to give it another try, but after several hours, he sat staring blankly at the screen. "And this is your idea of efficient? How the hell am I supposed to sort through this mess?"

"There are nearly two million people living in this city. You expected it to be easy to find one with nothing to go on but a name? Do you have any other information about his current life? Anything from your network about interests, or hobbies?"

John shook his head. He stood up from the computer and walked away. On the car ride home, a tense silence prevailed.

He flopped back into the armchair when they got home. "I have to get information from someone who knows him. Not his address—I doubt any of his friends are that stupid. But some-thing."

46

A month after she had first asked Renphor to teach her to jump, Julie showed up for her fourth jumping lesson at the regular time. Renphor only half listened to her telling him about her close call with Joseph when she'd left the house—she had caught him trying to follow her. Since she'd been driving their only car, he'd had to make the attempt on foot, but between his speed and morning traffic, he had managed to stay with her halfway across the city. She thought that John had put him up to it. When she realized that Renphor's attention was entirely elsewhere, she stopped talking and snapped her fingers in front of his face.

He jumped and glared at her. "What?"

"I was explaining why I won't be back for a while," she said.

"John getting suspicious?"

She nodded.

"Just as well if you avoid all of us for a bit anyway. And definitely keep that menace of a mate of yours holed up in his mansion as much as possible."

She looked at him in surprise. "Why?"

He shook his head. "There's some…stuff…going on that makes things a bit precarious. John would just add another complication." He smiled suddenly. "You're almost there anyway.

Hopefully we can get you to the point that you don't need me by the end of today's session."

She spent the next half hour hopping solo from one side of the room to the other, until Renphor decided it was time for her to try some distance. He told her to aim for an abandoned warehouse a block away, and he would follow her to make sure she didn't miss the target. Five minutes later, the two of them were standing in the warehouse, grinning.

"Good job. Let's head back to my place. Now that you've got it, you can practice on your own." He took her hand but allowed her to lead the jump. She landed safely back in his room.

Once she had gotten her equilibrium back, she turned to face him.

"You don't need Arabella for this scheme of yours, you know. She's not the only one with unlimited access to Larch Hill."

He froze. "And if I fail? You know that kind of betrayal carries a death sentence?"

She nodded. He regarded her steadily for a minute.

"You'd really do it, wouldn't you?"

"Yes."

After a moment he looked away, staring at the photo on his desk.

"Sorry, but no. I want the girl."

He glanced out the window and snarled.

"What's wrong?" she asked.

"You were followed this morning. Joseph is prowling around by the car."

She hissed in irritation. "He wasn't behind me when I came into the building, so he doesn't know yet which one I'm in. I'll simply have to give him a bit of the runaround. Thank you."

He nodded absently.

"Renphor—one other thing."

"Yes?"

"Whatever happens—take care of Arabella."

He smiled slightly. "Go. Before he starts getting the idea to search the buildings."

Sighing, she jerked to the side and disappeared. A minute later he saw her walk out the door of an apartment building across the street and down the block from his rooming house. She accosted Joseph at her car, and Renphor could see that she had a few choice words for him. The longer the conversation lasted, the further away he cowered. She finally got into the car and drove off, leaving him standing in the middle of the sidewalk, looking extremely foolish in the formal evening dress he insisted on wearing to wait on his master and mistress at Larch Hill. He had left the house in such a hurry that he hadn't had time to change.

Renphor crossed the room, picking up the photo on his desk. He stared at it for a long time, a slight smile lifting the corner of his mouth. Finally, he tucked it into his planner and gathered up his books, heading out to finish some research he had to do for a class.

John was pacing around the room, his temper rising steadily as he waited for his mate to return. When she finally walked in, he exploded at her.

"Where the devil have you been? I got back from church early this morning and found the car gone and the whole household missing!"

"Maybe if you hadn't sent Joseph to spy on me, someone would have been here to tell you that I was visiting a friend!"

"I have no idea what you're referring to. And I'd love to know what kind of friend you've been visiting who's teaching you spells that you have no business knowing."

Julie froze. "What do you mean?" she asked quietly.

"I mean the energy bursts that I felt coming from you all morning. What on earth have you been trying to do?"

She sat down on the nearest chair, tucking her hand under her leg. "I wasn't doing anything. I was talking to Gayle, and we got into a political discussion. You know how wound up I get."

"Gayle doesn't live in Philadelphia."

"She was here visiting a friend."

Joseph had quietly entered the room and caught his master's eye. John nodded to him.

"Julie, excuse us for a moment."

"I beg your pardon?"

"I want to discuss something with Joseph."

This was too much for Julie. "You're not even bothering to hide it anymore, are you?"

"Hide what?"

"The fact that you care far more about what your little spies are up to than you do about anything I have to say. As long as I don't do anything you disapprove of, obviously."

"It's not a question of disapproval, but someone needs to protect you from yourself, since you clearly don't have enough sense to know your own limits."

"I'm perfectly capable of making decisions for myself, you know!"

"Not anymore. Joseph, bring the key to the tower." He spoke quietly, but Julie's mouth dropped open at his words.

"What are you doing?" she gasped.

His hand clenched around her arm and pulled her out of the room. "You are not going to go around scheming behind my back. Until you're in a more reasonable frame of mind, you will remain where I can keep an eye on you, even if it means that I have to keep you under lock and key."

He dragged her up the long marble staircase and across the hall to the iron tower door. Joseph followed slowly behind with the key, gaping at his master. John pushed Julie through the door and slammed it behind him.

47

The following Sunday found Sam stretched out on Amanda's couch, watching a show about buying and flipping houses. She wasn't particularly interested but was feeling too lazy to change the channel. She glanced over at Amanda, who was intently studying something on her laptop, with her elbows propped on the dining room table.

"Hey, Manda?"

"Hmm?"

"Have you actually done anything that I'm paying you for?"

"Yes. And in case you haven't noticed, you aren't paying me."

Sam jerked around to face her. "What do you mean?"

"I haven't sent you a bill."

"I thought you billed monthly."

"I do. I don't intend to send you one next week, either."

Sam was sitting very straight on the couch now. "Why not?"

Amanda got up from the table and took a seat next to Sam on the couch. "Because, as you may have noticed, we've developed a decidedly nonprofessional relationship." She ran her hand across Sam's back as she spoke, and Sam wriggled her shoulders to let her get a better angle.

"I thought that was all part of the cover." Sam grinned at her.

"So sue me." Amanda pushed her back against the pillows and climbed on top of her.

Sam pushed her away and sat up. "Just a minute, though. What have you done about that thing that Arabella's dating?"

Amanda sighed. "'That thing' doesn't appear to have been anywhere near Narcissa the day she disappeared. I haven't been able to find any evidence that they came within a mile of one another. She was supposed to be heading south to her friend's house, but anyone I've talked to who actually saw her said she was heading north. Are you sure she wasn't mixed up with something shady? Could she have been involved in drugs like the police indicated?"

"Wouldn't put it past the idiot." Sam frowned. She slid off the couch onto the floor. Amanda stretched her legs out and propped herself up on one elbow, watching her.

"What do you have against Ryan, anyway? I'll grant you he's odd, but if it doesn't bother Arabella, I don't see why you should have a problem with it."

"This goes beyond odd. I just get a really bad vibe from the guy. Like he doesn't really give a damn what happens to her as long as he gets whatever it is he's after."

"Which would be?"

Sam picked irritably at the carpet. "I don't know. She has a little bit of money, but it doesn't seem to be that. I don't think it's about the sex, either, though gods know she isn't holding back. I just feel like something's off."

Amanda slid onto the floor beside her. "Is there any chance you'll just let this go? I mean, I'll keep doing whatever research you want me to do, but I honestly don't think it's going anywhere. If you're trying to pin a murder on your roommate's boyfriend just to get him out of the picture, it isn't going to work. Even if they arrest him, they'll never get anything to stick, and you'll be in a worse position than you were when you started. There's no evidence to be found, and I don't think Arabella would take kindly to what you've been doing. If you're really determined to find Narcissa's killer—well, I don't think there's anything to be found there, either. They might eventually find her body in the river, but I doubt that, too."

During the course of this speech, Sam's expression dissolved from shock into horror. "There must be something to find! People don't just disappear into the ether! Even if demon boy wasn't involved, you have to find something!"

"Humans can't see demons." Amanda spoke automatically, but her words caused Sam to shoot backwards away from her.

"That's what Ryan always says." Sam's voice quivered.

"I know. Where do you think I picked it up from? What's wrong?"

Sam moved tentatively back toward her original spot on the carpet. "Sorry, for a second there I just thought…" She trailed off, shaking her head as if to pry something loose from it. After a minute or so, she relaxed and rested her head on Amanda's shoulder. Amanda put her arm around her.

"I think all of this is getting on your nerves a bit, babe. I promise to keep doing what I can, if you'll try to put it out of your mind. Agreed?"

Sam nodded into her shoulder. She eventually fell asleep that way, and Amanda watched her for a few minutes before sliding carefully out of her grasp. She tucked a blanket around her before going quietly onto the fire escape with her phone.

The phone was answered on the second ring.

"Ryan? It's Manda. Is Arabella with you?"

"No, I'm on my way to the library. What do you want?"

"Just wanted to update you. Sam still thinks that you killed Narcissa—I've almost got her convinced to stop badgering me for updates, but I don't think she's going to let it go without strong evidence to the contrary. Are you sure you don't have anything you can give me?"

"What kind of private detective are you? If you can't come up with your own evidence to convince your human girlfriend of what you want her to believe—"

"There's no need to take that attitude. I've come up with a number of things, and I've put a good bit of time into showing her that Narcissa was nowhere near you that day, but she's still suspicious of you. And you owe me two grand for my time, by the way. I've been neglecting a couple of other clients while I spend my time trying to prove that a vampire isn't a murderer. I'm sending you a bill."

"Oh? Where were you planning to send it to?" The silence that greeted this question was prolonged, but Renphor finally laughed and relented. "I'll bring cash the next time I see you. I don't want a paper trail. Particularly not in your apartment, with Sam hanging out there all the time."

"Alright. Look, I have to go, before she wakes up. I'll be around there on Tuesday and Friday." She hung up quickly and slid the phone into her pocket before climbing back through the window. By the time Sam was awake, she was back at the computer, studying the corporate bank accounts that she had been looking at that morning.

48

A week after John's fight with Julie, she was still confined to her tower prison. He had accompanied her onto the grounds once to hunt, but the door had otherwise remained locked. He stopped by to visit her, only to discover that she had put something heavy over the trapdoor to the tower roof. When she finally came downstairs an hour later, he was pacing back and forth across the sitting room. He bared his fangs in a grin as she glanced around him to the door.

"Joseph's on the other side of the door with the key."

"What do you want?"

"Did it occur to you to mention to me that Arabella's roommate disappeared?"

She sank into a chair. "Is that what you're on about? No, John, it didn't. Should it have?"

He felt his temper rising again. "Of course it should have! What are we going to do about it?"

"Nothing. The police are working on it. As far as they've figured out, she got herself involved in a drug deal and did something stupid. It's a bit stressful for Arabella and Sam, particularly since the police still occasionally show up at their apartment, but there isn't anything useful that either one of us can contribute."

"Nothing…she should move back home."

Julie suddenly became alert at this. "This is exactly why I didn't tell you before. Arabella is nearly twenty-one years old. She cannot run home every time something bad happens in her life. You were just going on a few weeks ago about needing to distance ourselves from her."

"I wasn't referring to situations where her life is actually in danger!"

She sighed. "It isn't. Don't be melodramatic, John. It's ridiculous at your age."

He knocked sharply on the exterior door. "I'm going over there."

"Do what you like," she sighed.

Renphor stretched out on Arabella's bed, enjoying the coolness of the sheets. She came out of the bathroom fully dressed and stared at him lying there.

"Comfortable?"

He smiled. "Very." He stretched out his hand toward her, but she sat down at her desk, just out of reach.

"You know your phone's ringing."

"Let it ring. Come back to bed."

She got up and kissed his forehead. "I can't. I've got to finish writing that anthropology paper."

"Maybe I can help. I know quite a bit about humans."

She glared at him, but her retort was cut off by the sound of a knock on the front door and she walked out of the room without responding.

She wrenched the door open just as she heard a second, louder knock.

"John! Um…just a second…I have to go check something in my room."

Arabella ran quickly back to her room, but Renphor was nowhere to be found. She stared at the empty bed for a few seconds. Then she checked the bathroom, the closet, and under the bed. She checked the window and found that it hadn't been opened. Perplexed, she sat down at her desk chair and looked around. The sound of John calling from the living room reminded her that she had only come back to her room to make sure Renphor got dressed quickly. She was heading back toward the hallway when her gaze fell on a pile of men's clothing on the floor. She blinked. Then she grinned. The grin turned into a giggle, and within a few seconds she was holding on to the bedpost, trying to control paroxysms of silent laughter. She pushed the clothes quickly under the bed when she heard John's footsteps in the hallway.

"Everything okay, petite?"

She composed her features before turning to face her stepfather. "Fine. I thought I'd left the water running in the bathroom sink, but it must have been upstairs."

He looked surprised but didn't comment.

"Is everything okay at home?" she asked, suddenly wary of her stepfather's appearance in her apartment on a Monday morning.

"Yes, why?"

"Because I haven't heard from Mom in over a week, and you don't normally drop by on weekdays," she answered bluntly.

"I came to see if you were okay. Your mother didn't tell me that Narcissa disappeared a month ago." She could tell that he was gritting his teeth as he spoke.

"Sam and I are okay. Narcissa has spent most of the year doing stupid, dangerous things. Apparently one of them caught up with her. What has mom been doing?"

He didn't meet her eyes. "She's been busy with her garden. You don't seem very worried about—"

She cut him off. "Gardening in January?"

"Planning her garden," he said lamely. "But you don't seem bothered about—"

Arabella cut him off again. "It bothers me that she probably got herself killed. But she and Rick set up a little scheme to beat up Ryan not that long ago, so I don't feel as sorry for her as I might otherwise."

"Rick?"

She recounted the story of the attack, picking out the pieces that she felt her stepfather should hear and disregarding those that he didn't need to know about. He looked deeply shocked.

"This Ryan must be something else, for you to stick with him through all of that. What is his last name, anyway?"

Something in his tone made her suddenly suspicious. "Ca—Carter," she lied.

She saw John's eyes narrow. "Ca-Carter? What does he look like?"

She looked at the wall behind him. "He reminds me of you, a bit," she answered cautiously.

He relaxed slightly. "Do you mean he looks like me?"

"Y…es. Yes, he does. Sort of. Same coloring, anyway." She looked out the window as she answered.

"Oh. So when do I get to meet this guy? Seems like you're pretty serious about him."

"I don't know. Our schedules can get a bit crazy. I don't see nearly as much of him as you'd think I would."

He showed an inclination to hang around chatting, but she hurried him out of the apartment by telling him that she had a class in twenty minutes. She leaned against the door, a grin slowly spreading across her face at the memory of the pile of clothes.

Sam came out of the shower a few minutes later to find her roommate bent nearly double in front of the door, laughing until tears ran down her face.

49

Renphor lounged casually with one wrist draped over the gilded arm of the chair while the other flipped cards over onto the table. Stefan regarded him with a slightly irritated look on his face.

"Could you focus for a minute?"

Renphor looked up. "On what?"

Stefan twitched. "On what I've been trying to say to you for the last half hour."

"The police are investigating my movements. What of it?"

Stefan took a deep breath and closed his eyes. "That depends on what they find. You know I don't like police investigations."

Renphor laughed. It was a harsh sound, from deep in his throat. "Coward."

A ball of light suddenly shot out of Stefan's hand toward Renphor. Renphor flipped himself behind the chair and crouched low to the ground, fangs bared. "Not bright, Stefan. You're so fond of the crap in this precious apartment. You start a firefight with me, and I promise you there will be nothing left but ashes."

Stefan lowered his hand slowly. His eyes had deepened to a shimmering metallic shade that looked like liquid mercury. "I should have taken you out years ago."

Renphor sneered. "Not good politics. Everyone knows I'm no real threat. Start killing our kind out of bile, and you'll have a full-scale revolt on your hands."

Stefan leaned back against the wall, eyes half-closed. "And if I convinced them that you were a threat?"

Renphor stood and flopped back on the chair. "Because of a police investigation that's only still going on because the girl's parents won't shut up about it?"

Stefan crossed the room slowly and sat in the chair opposite Renphor. "They aren't going to drop it until someone finds something. And they have enough influence to keep pushing the police not to drop it either."

Renphor looked at him in some amusement. "And you think they'll manage to pin something on me? They won't, I assure you."

"Mighty sure of ourselves, aren't we?"

"Very."

"Why?"

Renphor grinned. "You've yet to ask the most pertinent question."

Stefan gritted his teeth. "And what is that?"

"Did I kill her?"

Stefan stood impatiently, flicking the card that Renphor had been studying off the table. Renphor stared at the empty space for a moment before raising his eyes to Stefan. "Getting a bit childish, aren't we?"

"Stop talking nonsense. A girl who has been irritating you for months suddenly disappears. You call in an anonymous tip to someone in the police department—"

Renphor snorted. "Very anonymous."

"Shut up. You know exactly what happened to the girl."

Renphor smiled to himself and bent to pick up the card that had been knocked to the floor. He began slowly arranging the deck in front of him, watching Stefan out of the corner of his eye. He finally spoke very softly. "Of course I know what happened to her."

"So why would I need to ask if you killed her?"

Renphor continued the slow movement of the cards. "I always keep track of my adversaries Stefan. Everyone from John Elder right down to this ridiculous human."

"And you expect me to believe that you aren't responsible for her death?"

"She is responsible for her own death. She chose to follow me when she would have been far better off at home."

"And so you killed her."

Renphor's eyes shone with glee. "I didn't kill her. You did."

Stefan was silent for a full minute. When he finally spoke, his voice remained light, but there was an unmistakable bite to the words. "I beg your pardon?"

"She followed me right past your front door, Stefan. Gaylord picked her up."

Stefan's voice was sharp. "When was this?"

"Over a month ago. Any trace of her is long gone by now."

Stefan swept all the cards off the table with one fluid movement and leaned forward to glare at Renphor. "And you didn't tell me this? Why?"

Renphor smiled innocently. "You never asked."

Stefan was still glaring at Renphor a minute later when Robert slid quietly into the room. He cleared his throat, and Stefan turned his head quickly toward him.

"Well?"

"Mistress Ariliana, sir."

Renphor started and stared at Stefan with narrowed eyes. Stefan sneered at him. "Is there a problem, Renphor? Show her in, Robert."

Robert bowed and left the room.

"I believe I'll be going."

"No, you won't."

Renphor stiffened but didn't make a move to leave. Ariliana glided across the threshold but stopped dead at the sight of
Renphor standing there.

Stefan held out his hand to her. "I believe you know my
other guest?" he asked smoothly.

"Yes. We used to be...close...until he decided he preferred
human company."

"That's not quite how I remember it, my dear. The fact that
I got tired of you was completely unrelated to anything else I
was doing at the time."

Ariliana looked up sharply. "At the time? Does that mean
she's out of the picture?"

Renphor laughed. "I haven't the slightest intention of
telling you."

"No? With any luck, she dumped you for a ghoul. Once
you've developed a taste for the undead—"

"The problem with that is that the undead sometimes return the favor."

"Don't tell me you've gone and killed the girl? After all that
fawning over her photo."

"I haven't. She's still a more interesting companion than
you."

Ariliana started toward him, her fingers curled like claws,
but Stefan intervened. "You're not going to have your little
lovers' spat here," he said coldly. "Ariliana, did you come to visit
me, or to argue with Renphor? Because if it's the latter, you can
go back to his shitty little room and finish the discussion. I've no
interest in it."

Ariliana calmed down at once and moved toward him, her
hips swaying side to side. "I definitely came to visit you," she
cooed.

"I assume you've no objection to my departure now, Stefan?" Renphor drawled.

Stefan waved his hand in dismissal. Ariliana looked over his shoulder at Renphor. "If you ever get over this little human obsession, you could try calling me."

"When hell freezes over."

50

Julie was lost in thought when her phone suddenly rang and startled her into attention. She picked it up quickly. She wasn't sure if John had realized that she still had it, and she was in no hurry to have it confiscated. Stefan's smooth voice could be heard on the other end.

"Good evening, my dear. Could I speak to John?"

Julie was silent, thinking hard.

"Julie?"

"Sorry. I got distracted. I don't know where John is right now."

"Would you mind looking for him? It's important."

"I can't…you could call his phone. Aristotle finally talked him into buying one."

"Did he? What's the number?"

Julie gave it to him and tried to get off the phone.

"One moment. I'd also like to know where you've been for the past three weeks."

"I've been…busy. I should have called you before—"

"But you were afraid John was watching you?"

"I know he was. Is. That doesn't matter—"

"And you didn't want me to know that he'd locked you up in your own house."

Julie gasped. "How did you—"

"I dropped by for a visit the other day. John isn't nearly as good of a liar as he thinks he is. Why didn't you call me?"

"I have my own reasons. Please don't get involved, Stefan. I'm alright—I just need to work through a few things. I'll call you if things get out of hand."

"By which point it will be too late. I'll check back with you in a week."

"If you must. Thank you." She ended the call quickly, before he could say anything else.

Twenty-five minutes after he had received a peremptory and very annoying summons to Stefan's rooms, John pulled into a parking space in front of Stefan's club. He hit the locks on the Jaguar as he got out, shooting a suspicious look at several scruffy-looking young men who had emerged from an alley. They slunk back into the shadows as he passed.

Robert greeted him at the door and led him up the staircase. He was curious about Stefan's summons, since the other man rarely invited him to any kind of social gathering. He resisted the urge to ask Robert who else was present and strolled through the door half an hour to the minute after Stefan had called. He glanced around the room, grimacing. None of his particular friends were here, and among the assembled company were several people he cordially disliked. Stefan had stopped short of actually inviting Renphor, but John recognized several of his intimates among the assembled company. He bowed stiffly as his host crossed the room toward him.

"How marvelously punctual you are, John. Have you by some chance learned to jump since I last saw you?" He smiled unpleasantly. John gritted his teeth as several of the others smirked.

"I have not. You know perfectly well that I do not choose to study that particular skill."

Stefan laughed. "Always so predictable, John. It amazes me. And how is the family? I haven't heard from your mate in ages."

John's eyes narrowed as he saw one or two of the others were still eavesdropping on the conversation.

"Julie is fine. Occupied with planning her garden."

Stefan nodded and led John into the room, seating him at a card table between a man wearing a long black fur coat and black lipstick and one John had seen several times in Renphor's company. John pretended not to notice the makeup and introduced himself to the man in the black coat, who gave his name as Aelfred. He made small talk for a while and even dropped a few casual comments about the reforms he and his adherents were pushing the council to adopt. Aelfred seemed less interested than most, and John had pretty much given up on him when the conversation took an unexpected turn.

"What did Stefan mean by your 'family'?" he asked curiously.

"I can only assume he was referring to my mate," John said tightly.

The man to John's right, who Stefan had introduced as Gilbert, chimed in. "He doesn't ask me about my family, and he's quite fond of my mate." He had spoken softly, but there was heavy significance in the words.

John studied him for a minute. "Do you often waste your time trying to fathom Stefan? That way lies madness, I promise you. But then, maybe you're already on your way down that path."

"And you think the guy wearing the makeup and fur is a saner choice?"

Aelfred's head jerked up. "Oi—"

He stopped when he saw Gilbert's eyes had suddenly widened in shock as he stared over John's left shoulder. John turned quickly to follow his gaze, but there was nothing there. He looked curiously at several other guests who were staring at the same spot, before returning to his neighbor, who looked relieved.

"I suppose Renphor thought better of spending the evening with us, then?" John asked drily.

"Probably. I can't imagine even Stefan was insane enough to invite you both on the same night."

"I would think he'd enjoy the tension."

"Not enough to see his rooms destroyed."

John looked at him disdainfully. "I wouldn't dream of being that rude to my host."

Gilbert snorted. "Then you'd get fried. Renphor wouldn't think twice about it."

John's lips curled backward in a sneer. "Bad breeding."

"Good sense."

John rose pettishly and stalked to the other side of the room. Stefan glided over to him, a singularly unpleasant smile on his face.

"You don't look as if you're enjoying yourself, John. Perhaps I should have asked Renphor to stay."

"I would certainly enjoy reducing him to cinders. But not in your apartment, and not when he has this much—backup."

"You are too kind. How is the fire vortex coming?"

John looked quickly around to see if anyone was listening before responding to his question. "It's coming along," he replied softly.

Stefan smiled unpleasantly. "And how is the rest of your family?"

John hissed his displeasure. "Keep your mouth shut about that, Stefan, I'm warning you."

"And what, exactly, do you think you can do about it if I do choose to advertise your somewhat unorthodox homelife?"

"Throw you into a fire vortex. It'd be good practice."

"So you've gotten that far, have you? Interesting. Now all you have to do is find your quarry."

He walked away, allowing this barb to sink in. John decided this indicated permission to leave and promptly did so, driving back to Larch Hill lost in thought.

John arrived home about twenty minutes later and went directly to the tower room to talk to Julie. He wasn't thrilled to be giving her ammunition but felt she had a right to know what had occurred. He found her in the ground-floor reading room, although there were no books in sight. She sat crocheting a small doily, which he found sufficiently odd to ask her what the point was. She shrugged. "Keeps my hands busy. It'd be nice if I could watch a movie while I'm at it, but that's apparently too much to ask in the modern age." This was not an auspicious start to the conversation, but John decided it couldn't be put off. He perched himself on the chair across from her and haltingly told her of the gathering at Stefan's, and the blatant way in which the man had mentioned the existence of a family. Julie didn't react as badly as he had expected.

"Did he mention names, or specifics?"

John shook his head.

"Then they probably don't know any more than they already did."

He stared at her in amazement. "You're not concerned at all?"

She lowered her crocheting and looked coldly at him. "How do you expect me to react? There's nothing I can do about it from this tower, so there's no point in getting agitated." She lifted the doily again and went on with her work, pointedly ignoring him until he got up and left.

51

By late February, Sam was spending nearly as much time at Amanda's apartment as she was at her own. Early one Saturday morning, she rolled over and smiled at the woman lying in bed beside her. She had her eyes closed, but she didn't appear to be asleep, so Sam tapped her sharply on the shoulder to get her attention. She was going to ask about breakfast, but the words never made it to her lips. As Amanda opened her eyes, Sam found herself scrambling away from her. She didn't get far, since she was on the side of the bed that was pressed up against the wall. She lay there, breathing quickly, staring.

Amanda looked at her curiously. "What's the matter, babe?"

Sam forced herself to breathe more slowly. "Sorry. I think it must be a trick of the light." Amanda had blinked, and the red light Sam thought she had seen had disappeared from her eyes.

"What must be?"

Sam laughed shakily. "Maybe I have been wronging Ryan all this time. For just a second, I thought I saw that same red glow in your eyes that I saw in his. Must be me who's seeing things."

She waited for an answer, but Amanda just continued to stare at her.

"Manda?"

"Hmm?"

"Are you going to say anything?"

"I thought you had it all worked out on your own."

"A little reassurance would be nice."

She rolled over, staring at the ceiling. "Sam, how would you like to be with me forever?"

Sam's laugh was genuine this time. "Is that a strange marriage proposal, or just an overly dramatic way of gauging my feelings?"

"Why is it overly dramatic?"

"Forever? Have you unlocked the secret to immortality, or are you just planning for multiple reincarnations?" A slight smile lifted one corner of her mouth.

"Assume that either one is true. Would you want to spend the time with me?"

Realizing that she was serious, Sam took her face in her hands and smiled at her. "I would. Does that make you happy?"

Amanda looked more relieved than happy. "You have no idea how glad I am."

Sam grinned. "And why is that?"

"Because it means I don't have to kill you."

Sam leapt backwards again as Amanda smiled, this time revealing two very sharp-looking fangs. "Wha...what are those?" She pointed at the teeth.

"What do they look like?" Amanda moved closer to her.

"Fangs. Are they fake?" Sam tried to sound nonchalant but didn't think it came off very well.

Amanda laughed. "No. What good would fake fangs do?"

"I don't know. What good do the real ones do?"

"Oh, the real ones are good for biting things. You, for instance..."

Sam forced herself to breathe evenly, but her eyes darted around the room, looking for a quick escape. "Why? What have I done?"

"Nothing, except pay a bit too much attention. I'm afraid vampires have some pretty strict secrecy laws."

Sam didn't get a chance to reply. In one swift movement, the fangs were buried in her throat. She gasped in shock and pain, struggling to pull away, but she was held fast.

The bite only lasted for a minute, but when Amanda pulled away, Sam had gone ghost white and was shaking violently. She put her hand to the wound in her throat and nearly passed out when it came back covered in blood. To her horror, Amanda licked it off her fingertips. "That's just residual, you know. The wound has already closed."

"What have you done?" Sam asked hoarsely. She could feel a cold sensation starting to spread slowly from the place where Amanda had bitten her.

"I think we already covered that. It was either this or kill you. Now I'm going to turn up the TV, so the neighbors don't hear you screaming and call the cops."

Sam suddenly contorted in pain as Amanda rose and switched on the television at high volume.

Hours later she lay there, still naked, processing the fact that the pain had finally stopped. Amanda was facing away from her in a chair, her focus on the TV, so Sam slid quietly from the bed and moved toward her. Amanda turned before she reached her.

"Feeling better?"

Sam hissed at her. "Better? What the hell have you done, you miserable—"

Amanda stood up and pushed her back onto the bed. "I've already told you—it was this or kill you."

"Bullshit. You could have thought of half a dozen other solutions. You were just looking for an excuse."

"Sam—"

Sam jumped back up and dressed.

"And where do you think you're going?" Amanda asked.

"Home. Arabella will think another roommate has disappeared."

"You're not going home."

"The fuck I'm not!"

Amanda pushed her violently into the chair. "First off, you need to feed before you do anything else. Second, you're not going near your roommate."

"When the hell did you start calling the shots? And why do you care if I go home or not?"

"Because if you lose control and do something stupid, I lose a very valuable source of income. And possibly more than that, depending on how good he is in a fight."

"What are you talking about?"

"Ryan. He's been paying me to keep you out of his business. It almost feels like stealing, since I'd have happily done it for free after the first night." Amanda reached out a hand to her, but Sam moved out of her reach.

"What exactly are you telling me? That he's a vampire too?"

"Yes. And whatever his reasons are for hanging around Arabella, he would not be pleased if anything happened to her."

"So on top of destroying my life, you've just been using me for a fee?"

"Apparently you weren't listening. The idea was just for me to lead you down the wrong path. I was supposed to get a double fee out of it, but I got more attached than I intended to."

"How lucky for me."

"I'm sorry, Sam. I really am incredibly sorry. I wish you'd never gotten mixed up in this."

Sam sat down on the bed, still glaring at her. "How does a vampire end up as a private detective, anyway?"

Amanda's smile was bitter. "I started on the cleanup crew. There's a fair amount of investigation that goes into that, and I turned out to be really good at it. Most of our kind are smart enough to go for prey that won't be particularly missed. There are exceptions, and that's what the cleanup crew has to take care of. Whoever killed Narcissa was one of the exceptions."

"Wasn't that Ryan?"

She shook her head. "I don't think so. He strikes me as the efficient sort. But I'd bet my last buck that he knows who really did do it." She leaned against the wall, drumming her fingers on the bedpost.

"What makes you think he knows?"

"He knows pretty much everything that goes on in and around that apartment. I'm pretty sure he knows what Arabella's going to do before she knows it herself."

"So he is a creeper. I've always suspected as much."

Amanda grimaced. "You need to feed."

An hour later, they were back in Amanda's apartment. Feeding had taken some of the edge off Sam's rage, but she was still keeping pointedly out of Amanda's reach. She had come up with a plan to escape from her before realizing that she had no idea where to go or what to do next, so she had reluctantly returned to the apartment.

They sat in silence for an hour before curiosity got the better of Sam. "How old are you, Amanda?"

"Seventy-three."

"You've aged well."

"I'm actually fairly young for our kind."

"Hmm. So how old is Ryan?"

"You're mighty curious about him."

"I'm curious about him because I just found out there's been a vampire running tame in my apartment since last fall."

"I wouldn't say he was all that tame."

"Please. Even Rick Stevens was kicking him around like a soccer ball at the beginning of the year."

Amanda looked amused. "And what happened to Stevens?"

"No one knows, he just dis...oh. He's dead, I suppose."

Amanda nodded. "Which is another reason I don't think he killed Narcissa." Sam looked at her curiously, and she went on. "Stevens disappeared with barely a ripple. No one has even bothered to look for him. If Ryan could make the star of the football team vanish that easily, he could certainly have done a cleaner job with Narcissa. As far as I can figure, even her parents didn't like her all that much, although they're kicking up a hell of a fuss now."

Sam shuddered. "I never gave him credit for being able to orchestrate a birthday party, let alone something of that magnitude."

"I don't know that much about him, but I know enough not to underestimate him."

Renphor's phone rang, startling him. When he saw Amanda's number come up, he answered quickly.

"Manda. Do you know where Sam is?"

"Yes, she's here at my apartment, why?"

Renphor hung up the phone. His sudden reappearance in Amanda's apartment caused Sam to scream. Even Amanda looked surprised. Renphor stared at Sam until Amanda finally broke the silence.

"I didn't know you were a jumper."

"Not that difficult, really."

Sam spoke a bit shakily. "Hey, demon boy. Nice trick."

Renphor smiled. "Humans can't see demons."

"Can vampires?"

"Certainly. Actually, I'd prefer you take it easy on the demon comments. It's really quite an insult."

"Why?"

Amanda smirked. "You'll know once you've met one. Brainless jackasses."

"Oh. Will I meet one?"

"Not if you're lucky," Renphor added caustically.

Amanda suddenly came back to the earlier phone call. "What's with hanging up on me, anyway?"

"You should thank me. Ever been on the phone with someone who was midjump?"

She shook her head.

"Nastiest fucking noise you ever heard." Renphor flopped into a chair next to the TV, eyeing Amanda in a decidedly hostile fashion.

She swallowed. "You pissed at me?"

"A bit."

"How much is a bit?" She fidgeted.

Renphor barely seemed to have moved, but Amanda suddenly flew backwards and crashed into the wall, bringing most of the pictures down on top of her. After an initial moment of shock, Sam laughed and applauded. Amanda picked herself up very slowly and looked shakily at Renphor. "Anything else?"

"No, I think that'll do it for now."

"Okay. Sorry, Ryan. She was catching on to too much. It shouldn't mess up what you're doing."

"And how would you know that?" He stood up quickly, pacing to the other side of the room. "She can't come back to the apartment. Arabella's no fool, and I don't think I trust Sam not to do anything stupid."

Sam looked affronted. "Like I'd hurt my best friend!"

"You can't know that until you're around her. Did you think you could drink the blood out of a human being before today?"

Sam fell silent and stared out the window.

Amanda edged toward the door. "Ryan—do you think you could stay with her for a while? I have something that has to get done—"

Renphor didn't look at her. "Go," he said.

Sam and Renphor were left staring at each other as the door closed behind her.

After a few minutes of silence, Renphor finally spoke.

"How are you?"

"Of all the idiotic questions—"

"I know, but I couldn't think of a better one on the spur of the moment."

"I need help. I don't want to stay here with…her. But I don't know what else to do."

"It would be best for you to stay."

Her eyes flashed. "Stay here with that—"

"Sam—I understand that she handled things badly. But it's a delicate balance. Hanging around a vampire is always going to end badly for a human, one way or another. She didn't want to kill you outright and didn't feel like she had another choice."

"Don't you come out with a bunch of garbage about secrecy statutes." She glowered at him.

"Alright. Wait here for a quick minute." Renphor disappeared, but he was back less than five minutes later, with a stack of papers in his hand. He handed them to Sam.

"What are these?"

"Legislation on human and vampire relations."

She rolled over on the bed with her back to him and started to read.

52

Arabella stumbled sleepily into the living room on Monday morning, expecting to see Sam at her usual perch on the couch. She could never understand how her roommate managed to be so alert at six a.m. She found the couch empty, so she opened Sam's bedroom door softly and looked inside. The room was empty, and the bed still neatly made. Sam never made her bed until after she'd had her shower and breakfast, and Arabella hadn't heard the water in the bathroom or any noise from the coffeemaker. She peeked into the bathroom and the kitchen just to make sure. Neither had been used that morning.

She reached for her phone but stopped with her hand hovering over it. She finally pulled her hand back and stood with her robe wrapped tightly around her, shivering. She tried to pull herself together and sat down on the couch, thinking hard. The easiest way to set her mind at rest would be to call Sam, but it was still very early. If she had spent the night at Amanda's, which Arabella had to admit as a possibility now that her mind was starting to work again, they probably wouldn't appreciate the phone call. She finally picked up the phone and slowly dialed her mother's number.

Julie picked up almost at once.

"Mom?"

Julie's voice was sharp. "What's wrong?"

Arabella spoke quickly. "Nothing. At least, I think it's nothing, but my brain doesn't seem to be working. Sam didn't come home last night—probably because she was out with Manda, but she usually calls me if she's going to stay over there."

"Who is Manda?"

"Her girlfriend. Amanda Sharpe." There was a long silence at the other end of the line. "Mom?"

"Sorry. Did you say Amanda Sharpe? What does she do for a living?"

"She's a private investigator. That's an odd question."

"How long have they been together?"

"Since New Year's. I know I'm overreacting, but I've been jumpy since Narcissa disappeared."

Julie's next words caused Arabella to start shaking again. "You're not overreacting. Is Ryan with you?"

"No, he said he had something he needed to take care of last night, so he couldn't come over."

There was a pregnant silence on the other end of the phone.

"Mom? He wouldn't do anything to Sam. He likes Sam. Mom?"

Julie spoke very slowly. "Arabella, listen to me. I don't know exactly what's going on. But I know this much—you can't trust anyone right now. And I mean anyone. Go with your own instincts. Try not to call me unless you're in immediate danger. Even then, I might not…I think that I could get to you. But I can't be sure."

"Why can't you come over now?" Arabella's voice was rising with terror.

"Because it would put both of us in danger. Don't worry too much about Sam. She probably spent the night with Amanda, like you said. But please be careful. I have to go. I love you." She hung up, leaving Arabella staring at the phone, gulping for air. She curled into a ball on the couch and lay there, shaking violently. She stayed there for a long time, until she finally decided that the only way to keep herself sane was to do something. She got up and got a shower and managed to choke down a few eggs and some juice. She sat back down on the couch with the phone in her hand and had just started dialing when she heard a key in the lock, and the door swung slowly open. Arabella let out a piercing shriek.

Renphor jumped and slammed the door behind him. "Jesus, Ella, what was that about?"

Arabella stared at him, wide-eyed. "What do you want?"

He blinked. "I told you I'd be here at nine. What's going on?"

She swallowed several times, trying to calm down. "Sam didn't come home last night."

Renphor started to walk toward her, but she shrank away from him. He stopped in his tracks. "Are you somehow connecting that with me?" he asked coldly.

"No…I don't know…you weren't here last night."

"Have you called her, by any chance?"

Arabella shook her head, not meeting his eyes. "It was early, and I didn't want to wake her—"

"So you figured you'd wait until lunchtime to see if anything serious had happened?"

There was heavy sarcasm in his voice, which caused her mouth to drop open. He pulled out his phone, found Amanda Sharpe's number under the received calls, and dialed.

Amanda finally picked up the phone after four or five rings. Renphor spoke quickly. "Manda? Put Sam on."

"What for?"

"Because Arabella's freaking out over the fact that she hasn't checked in for twenty-four hours, that's why."

Arabella shot him an annoyed look, but he ignored it. A few seconds later, he handed the phone to her.

"Sam?" Arabella smiled in relief. "No, not freaking out, exactly. It was just a little too much like the morning Narcissa disappeared. When are you going to be home?" Arabella frowned as she listened. "The Bahamas sound nice. The apartment is going to be a bit empty being here by myself, but I guess I'll survive for a few weeks. You're what? I see. No, I'm not worried about the rent. I'm sure John will cover me for three more months, but…" Arabella scowled. "No, he isn't moving in. Anyway, have a good time with Manda. Talk to you later." She hung up the phone and handed it back to Renphor.

"Why not?" Renphor asked.

"What?" Arabella looked startled.

"Why aren't I moving in?"

She hugged her arms around her chest and stared at him. "I told you—John insists on approving my roommates."

"And also, you don't trust me not to murder you in your sleep. Marvelous. And here I thought things were going rather well." He turned away from her.

"It's not that, it's just that you're…" She gasped and put her hand over her mouth.

He turned back. "I'm what?" He moved toward her.

"Nothing. I don't know what I was going to say." She backed away, and he stopped in the middle of the room.

"Fine. You'll want these back." He dropped her keys on the table and walked to the door.

"Where are you going? I thought we were going to the park today?" She stared from the keys to him and back again.

"Seriously?" He walked out the door and slammed it behind him.

Renphor ran down the steps onto the street and walked quickly in the direction of the bus stop. He had gone three-quarters of a mile before he stopped and shook his head. Looking around to see if anyone was watching, he quickly turned down an alley and disappeared.

When he reappeared in his room, his phone was ringing. He pulled it quickly out of his pocket and snarled to see Stefan's number on the caller ID. He stared at it for a second before balling up his hand and flinging the phone with all his might against the bookcase. He stood motionless, staring at the shattered bits of plastic on the floor.

53

The shock from Stefan throwing the existence of his daughter in his face spurred John to action. He spent several hours a day working on the fire vortex, and by early March he had ironed out any remaining issues with the spell. Not only could he consistently produce a working vortex and expand it to ten feet wide with relative ease, but he was able to maintain it for at least ten minutes at a time. The hours of practice he had devoted to it had built up his strength and stamina sufficiently to make the spell useful in a fight.

He continued to keep Julie informed of what his followers were doing, since it was the only topic of conversation that she would actually listen to when he stopped by to see her. David and Jennifer weren't seen at Larch Hill with any regularity, but Nelson dropped by at least twice a week, and Stella was there so often that John caught Joseph rolling his eyes at her retreating form.

One Friday afternoon, when John was engaged in his usual study with the vortex, he received a summons from Stefan to join him in his rooms. There was an inflection of surprise in Stefan's voice when John said he would come immediately, and his eyes narrowed suspiciously when John expressed his delight at the number of people assembled in the room. There were several card tables set up, and John slid into an empty seat at a long faro table. Several of the players looked up in surprise, but the dealer, an emaciated-looking man with white hair and a gold hoop earring in one ear, was more than willing to have him join.

Stefan joined the table as well, to the chagrin of two men at the opposite end. Both were wearing shabby T-shirts and exchanged nervous glances over the addition of both John and Stefan, who were known to play for high stakes. They stuck it out for one more round, then quietly slipped away to play a different game. The conversation flowed readily between the seven players who remained at the table, with the host making repeated attempts to steer the conversation around to John, and John dexterously keeping the others talking about themselves. Stefan finally received some unexpected aid from a man in an expensive-looking suit at the head of the table.

"So, John. I heard something interesting the other day about your mate."

John's eyes narrowed. "Oh?"

There was a sudden scuffle near that end of the table, and the man who had spoken to John looked at his neighbor in surprise. "What the hell did you kick me for, Charles? Anyway. Someone told me that your mate had a young daughter when you met. How did you convince her to give her up to come live with you?"

John clenched his teeth. It was Stefan who responded. "He didn't. Did you, John?"

"Seeing as how I have been mated for nearly seventeen years, I don't see that this is important," he replied stiffly.

"What do you mean?" A vacant-looking man in the middle of the table looked from one to the other.

John turned a jaded eye toward him and sighed. "Do the math, Cholmondeley. Any child of Julie's would be an adult by now. What does it matter?"

While Cholmondeley puzzled over this, Stefan smiled nastily at John. "In this day and age? I thought children stayed at home until their thirties these days."

A man in a purple brocade suit stared at him. "Seriously? What do they do with their spouses?"

"Don't have 'em," another answered.

The man in purple stared.

John looked at Stefan. "I would not allow her to do so, however. Parents these days are far too accommodating. They don't give their offspring any reason to grow up." Noticing several rapt listeners, he firmly turned the subject away from himself.

Stefan interjected again. "And how is Julie these days? I've not heard from her for several weeks. Highly unusual." There was a red glow deep in his eyes, but John was pretending to focus on his cards and didn't see it.

"She's fine. Busy planning her spring garden and reading nonsense as usual."

"I see." Stefan watched him silently for the rest of the hand, then left the table to attend to the rest of his guests. John remained at the party for nearly three hours, circulating amongst the various tables. Word of the conversation at the faro table had spread, and John found himself questioned several more times about the existence of Julie's daughter. He consistently changed the subject when it came up but, unlike at the prior party, did not become the least bit ruffled by the barrage of questions about his family. John finally left around four in the morning but drove off in the opposite direction from Larch Hill. He drove around the city for several hours, mulling things over, before finally returning home around six. He checked on Julie and found her occupied with a book on her rooftop retreat. He slipped back out of the tower and into an unused gallery on the second floor. He put out his arm and smiled with satisfaction as a ball of flame shot from his palm and slowly widened to the height of a man.

Early that evening, he decided he should pay another visit to Julie. It was time for another feeding excursion anyway, and it would give him an opportunity to bring her up to speed. He unlocked the door and handed the key to Joseph before stepping inside. He looked around, but there was no sign of his mate in the first-floor room. He had just decided to look for her on the roof when a fireball flew past his head and hit the shelf just where his hand had been a moment before. He spun around and stared in shock at the sight of Julie standing across the room with her arm raised.

Julie's hair was pulled away from her face by the force of the energy she had just released, and her eyes blazed orange and red. He backed toward the door. "Julie, what the devil—"

"You miserable piece of shit!"

"I don't—" He didn't get a chance to finish the sentence, since he had to dodge another ball of fire.

"All of this talk about protecting me and Arabella, and how worried you were about her being away at school, and then you go and set her up as *bait*!"

"I can't imagine what you mean," he said lamely.

She advanced toward him into the room. "Can't you? Did you honestly think you could set this little trap right under Stefan's nose, and I wouldn't hear about it?"

"Julie, please calm down." He dodged another shot. "You're destroying the books."

"So move." She wound up again. He moved quickly to the door.

"Can we please talk about this?" He put up his hands to shield, finally remembering that he was far more powerful than his mate. The next shot bounced backwards across the room, and she jumped sideways to avoid it. She stood in front of the window, fuming. He walked slowly toward her, speaking levelly. "Please, Julie? Can we discuss this calmly?"

She spoke to him through clenched teeth. "What possible excuse can you come up with this time. Do you deny setting it up?"

He sighed. "I didn't intend to set her up as bait, but Stefan started shooting off his mouth again. I decided it was better to control the situation. I'll have her move back to Larch Hill, where I can keep an eye on her."

"In the middle of the semester? She won't do it!"

"She will if I cut off her rent payments."

"You're forgetting her trust fund."

"She won't spend it on rent when she can live here for free."

"You're a fool."

"Julie, honestly—"

She closed her eyes, breathing heavily. "I don't think I can have this conversation right now, John."

"She's already heavily shielded, and I'll add more. I'm going to go over there today, give her a description of Renphor—"

"Give her…you blazing idiot, Renphor is the least of your worries!"

John's patience finally snapped. "What the hell are you talking about, Julie?"

"I'm talking about the fact that you gave an entire roomful of vampires information about your human stepdaughter. At least if Renphor goes after her, he'll want her alive. Who knows what anyone else might have in mind?"

He blinked, "Why would anyone else go after her? I don't have any other real enemies."

"No, and you also have very few friends," she answered viciously. "I can think of at least half a dozen people who wouldn't mind sticking a spoke in your wheel if the opportunity came along."

"The protections I've given her are powerful. Only a very strong vampire would get around them."

"Right. I've asked Stefan to intervene."

"You what?"

"You heard me. I'm done going along with your little schemes, John. Your sole part of this bargain was to protect

Arabella, and you've set her up to be killed or worse, just to further your own ends." She stalked out of the room without allowing him time to answer, leaving him staring after her with his mouth hanging slightly open. As he turned to leave, his eyes fell on the phone sitting on the writing table, and widened. He picked it up and slipped it into his pocket before knocking on the door and calling to Joseph to let him out of the room.

Once out of the tower, John grabbed his keys from the table and left quickly. He arrived at Arabella's apartment about twenty minutes later and pounded on the door so hard that one of the neighbors poked their head out of the door and told him to shut the hell up. He glared at them and raised his arm to knock again just as Arabella opened the door.

"John! What on earth?"

He pushed past her into the apartment and pulled the door closed behind him. "Where's Sam?"

Arabella blushed and didn't quite meet his eye. "She's staying with a friend right now."

"What do you mean, staying? You mean she isn't living here?"

Arabella quickly dissembled. "She's still living here. It is Friday night, you know." She looked pointedly at him, and he finally noticed that she was dressed to go out.

"Is Ryan picking you up? I'd like to meet him, finally."

Arabella chose that moment to pick her earrings up off the table so John couldn't see her face. "We're not together anymore. I'm going out with a few friends."

"Oh. So you're spending a lot of time alone in the apartment?"

She looked quickly up at him. "Yes, why?"

"It's not safe—a woman living alone in the city like this."

"Sexist much?"

"No need to get offended. I'm just looking out for you. Look, I did come over for a reason other than ruining your social life. You haven't seen any odd characters around lately, have you?"

Arabella stared at him. "Seriously? In Philly? How would I tell?"

"You know what I mean."

She sighed heavily. "No, John. I haven't seen anything weirder than usual."

"I think you should move back home."

"No."

He was startled by the direct refusal. "I am paying your rent—"

She stiffened. "If that's your issue, I'll pay it myself. I'm not moving back there so you can start telling me where I'm allowed to go and when. I had enough of that in high school. Anything else?"

"I'm sorry that trying to keep you safe seems old-fashioned to you. I'm sure most parents are perfectly fine with their daughters' roommates randomly disappearing—"

"Don't start on that again"

John clenched his jaw. "I know you said this had nothing to do with you, and I know you don't really have any enemies. But I do, and it concerns me that the two of you live here alone."

Arabella blinked at him. "You really are concerned about someone coming after me, aren't you?"

"Yes. One person in particular. He's going by the name Ryan Callaghan."

She shot him a startled look. "Ryan—"

"Yes, do you know someone by that name?" he asked sharply.

"I know two guys named Ryan Callaghan. What does this one look like?"

John described Renphor as carefully as he could, while Arabella paced to the door and back. "Do either of the guys you know fit that description?" he asked when he was finished.

Arabella shook her head. "No. Not really, no."

He watched her closely, but she didn't meet his eye. "I still think you should move back home," he said firmly.

"I'm not a child, John. And I was never an idiot."

He walked over to her and took both of her hands in his. "Arabella, I'm serious. I have really good reasons to believe that you're in danger."

"So what are you going to do, confine me to the house for the rest of my life? I'll be careful. Stay away from strangers, travel in groups, all that good stuff."

John looked grim but didn't answer. "I suppose it's all you can do for now." He pulled a crucifix on a chain from around his neck and tossed it over her head. "Promise me you'll wear that all the time."

She stared at him. "Okay…"

"I know it sounds crazy, but I do have some idea what I'm up against, and you're totally in the dark."

Arabella carefully repeated the description John had given her and asked him to confirm that she had it right.

"Yes. He doesn't look like much but don't underestimate him if you see him. Get away as soon as possible and call me."

John pulled his phone out of his pocket as soon as he got back to his car and quickly dialed David's number. He spoke without preamble when the other man picked up.

"David, I have a job for you."

"John—"

"I need you and Jennifer to follow someone. My step-daughter, actually. I don't trust the others—"

"John, for once in your life, stop and listen to someone else."

"What?"

"Jennifer and I don't want anything more to do with this. We signed on for reforms, not some battle to the death. It's not worth getting ourselves destroyed. I'm sorry."

"But, David, I've told you once we get through this—"

"There's no more 'we,' John. Goodbye." He hung up the phone before John could say anything else. John tapped his fingers on the steering wheel for a while before picking up the phone again and dialing Nelson's number.

54

For nearly six weeks after the blow-up in Arabella's apartment, Renphor didn't speak to her at all. Half the time she didn't show up for the class that they were both in, and when she didn't skip she would arrive right at the beginning of class and leave immediately after it was over. Anytime he was in the vicinity, her friends would surround her and hurry her away as quickly as possible.

One day in mid-April, he finally found her alone on a bench, enjoying the warm weather. It was a minute or so before she turned to see who was next to her. When she saw him, she shied across to the other side of the bench and got up to leave. When he grabbed her hand to pull her back to the seat, she sat down but quickly removed her hand from his grasp.

"Do I at least get the courtesy of an explanation?"

"You're the one who walked out."

"Yes, and you're the one who's made it impossible for us to talk ever since."

She looked stung. "I called you every day for two weeks!"

He blinked. "Oh. I didn't have a phone."

"What do you mean?"

"It...broke."

"In other words, you smashed it."

He grinned. "Maybe. Can we start over? Please?"

She shook her head and inched away from him. "Look, Ryan…the timing is just bad right now. It's a month until graduation, I'm interviewing in D.C., and I've got all that crazy family stuff to deal with—"

"What family stuff?"

"Oh. That was after you—"

"Stormed out of your apartment in a rage. I'm sorry, Arabella. What's wrong with your family?"

"Nothing. Just—"

"It doesn't sound like nothing."

She sighed. "Okay, so it isn't nothing. John's acting like a lunatic, and my mother told me not to call unless there was an immediate threat to my life. I tried twice to get her to talk to me. She hung up. I'm still wearing this stupid crucifix, because my insane stepfather asks to see it every time he visits me. Which is at least twice a week. Even Sam isn't returning my calls these days, and who the hell am I supposed to ask for advice about anything?" She dropped her chin into her hand and stared out across the park.

"Me?" he said. She shook her head, and he sighed. "So, you haven't seen your mother at all? When was the last time you actually spoke to her?"

"Last month was the last time she hung up on me. We had the conversation about not calling in early February."

"Shit."

"What's wrong?"

"Nothing. I hope. Look, I get that you don't want to talk to me right now, but do me a favor, okay? Keep calling your mother every couple of weeks, and if she stops answering entirely, let me know." His eyes narrowed as he glanced across the lawn to the other side of the park. "I have to go."

He reached his destination in seconds and sat down on the bench at the exact same time as Nelson. Nelson stared at him in surprise.

"Ryan, right? What are you doing here?"

Renphor grinned. "Just hanging around. You?"

Nelson shifted nervously. "Same." He glanced in Arabella's direction so many times that Renphor could no longer pretend he hadn't noticed.

"She is beautiful, isn't she?"

Nelson jumped. "Who?"

Renphor nodded in Arabella's direction. "She's in one of my classes. It's a bit distracting, to be honest."

He smiled as Nelson twitched nervously. Arabella had risen to leave, and Nelson was hopping up and down on the bench, trying not to lose sight of her while he tried to maintain the thread of the conversation. Once she had walked around the building and out of sight, Renphor managed to keep him talking for another five minutes before he found an excuse to get away. Renphor smiled as he watched Nelson scurry around the corner, knowing that by this time Arabella had already gone into the building for her eleven o'clock class.

Renphor returned to his room as soon as Nelson was out of sight. He pulled Arabella's picture out of his planner and stared at it for a long time before putting it back and slamming the desk drawer closed. He extracted his folder of plans for Larch Hill from their hiding place and tapped his pen on the desk for a few minutes while he stared at the list. Finally, he slowly drew a line through Arabella's name and leaned back in the chair, staring at the list with every item crossed out. He stuffed the folder back into place just as something made a noise by the fire escape. Spinning on his heel, he found Ariliana standing in front of the window.

"What the devil do you want?" he asked.

"You're not seriously still mad at me, are you, Ren?"

She moved toward him but stopped dead at the look that had come over his face. "Mad at you? No, I just can't stand the sight of you. You've got a nerve coming here at all, after you blabbed my affairs to Stefan. Better go back to him."

"I plan to. But he's busy right now, and I don't see any reason why the two of us can't still be friends. I didn't tell him anything really secret about you, you know."

He sneered. "Oh, well, that makes it all okay, doesn't it?"

"Look, I can still be useful to you. Nelson is still hanging all over me, babbling on about John."

"I doubt he knows anything I haven't already gotten on my own at this point."

"No? Did you know that two of his little groupies have left him?"

"And?"

She looked affronted but kept going. "He's down to Nelson and the blond nitwit. Even his mate hasn't been seen around the place for months."

He looked up sharply at that. "What do you mean?"

"Nelson says they haven't seen her since January. Anytime anyone asks John about her, he changes the subject."

"And what does genius boy think has happened to her?"

"I could find out, if you make it worth my while."

"I won't. I'm not interested in 'friends' who betray me the first time I do something they don't like. Now get out, and stay out this time."

She stared at him, and he looked coldly back at her. "You're serious?" she asked.

"Very."

"So it's still the human, is it?" She smiled unpleasantly.

"It isn't, actually. She's out of the picture. And you've got three seconds to be out of it yourself, before I blast you out."

Her eyes blazed red for an instant before she turned on her heel and disappeared out the window. He sat down on his mattress with his head in his hands and stared at the floor.

55

Nelson lay sprawled across his couch, watching reruns of *American Idol*, when he was startled by the sound of his own doorbell. Two o'clock in the morning was an odd time for visitors, even for a vampire. Taking a last quick glance at the TV set, he got up to answer the door. He looked slightly surprised as Ariliana floated in.

"Rilla! What are you doing here?"

She glanced at the TV and raised her eyebrows slightly. Seeing the direction she was looking, he smiled guiltily.

"I know it's not what you'd consider great TV, but it is entertaining. We can watch something else if you'd like." He made a nervous gesture toward the couch.

She sat down on the couch with less grace than she had intended, since she had expected the pillow to be firmer. Slightly ruffled, she blurted out, "I came to tell you about something."

He sat down slowly next to her, patting her knee awkwardly. "You look upset. What's happened?"

She took a deep breath. "That blond guy who was talking to us on the park bench a few months ago—"

He nodded. "Ryan?"

She shook her head. "It's a fake name. I ought to have told you before, but…" She looked down at her lap. "Well, I'm a bit afraid of him."

He put his arm around her, pulling her close to him. "Why?"

Now that Ariliana had gotten started, she picked up steam quickly. "Because he's a lot more powerful than me. And…well…he's threatened me before now."

He puffed out his chest. "Well, he's not going to hurt you here."

She nodded. "I knew you'd protect me." She looked sideways under her lashes to check his reaction and saw that it was exactly what she had been hoping for.

"So who is this guy?" Nelson's jaw was set firmly, and he was scowling.

"His real name is Renphor."

This statement got more of a reaction than Ariliana had been hoping for. Nelson shot straight off the couch and stood staring down at her in horror.

"What?! You've known this all along, and you've let me go along blindly feeding him information?" He started pacing around the room. "John is going to murder me," he said under his breath.

Ariliana's jaw dropped as she watched his progress around the room. "Is it really that bad?"

He looked at her, a hunted expression in his face. "Yes. Look, I have to go. There's someone I have to talk to, before he finds out…"

He ran out of the apartment without a backwards glance, leaving the door hanging wide open behind him.

She looked around her with interest. She had never had the opportunity to explore Nelson's house unaccompanied. Judging that he wouldn't be back for at least several hours, she walked slowly to the door and closed it before starting a thorough examination of all the places where the valuables were likely to be stored. She opened a cabinet in the pantry and smiled at a complete silver service perched on a shelf. Picking a piece up speculatively, she hefted it to check for weight and smiled. *I wonder if he would even know it was gone?*

John looked up from his book in surprise as Joseph led a visitor into the room. "Nelson. Do you know it's three a.m.?"

Nelson shuffled nervously from one foot to the next. "No…yes…I…that is…" He gulped and stood staring mutely at John.

"What have you done this time?" John sighed.

"I didn't…I mean, how…I didn't know…he used a fake name." Nelson tripped over his words.

John sighed and in the voice of one speaking to a toddler asked, "Who used a fake name?"

Nelson gulped. "Renphor."

John nearly jumped out of his chair.

"You've been speaking to Renphor?"

Nelson gulped even harder. "Not really speaking to him…I mean, I've spoken to him, a couple of times, but…"

John took a furious step toward him. "What, exactly, have you spoken to him about?"

Nelson took an involuntary step backwards. "I mentioned a few things…about the security here…about…"

"What!"

Nelson cowered behind the table. "About your stepdaughter."

"What about the security?"

"Well, how some of it works. How all of it works, really."

John flung himself at him, holding him up by the throat and shaking him. "You idiot! You abysmally stupid oaf!" He continued to shake him violently while Nelson tried to remove his hands from his throat. He finally dropped him on the floor and leaned on the bookcase.

Nelson started to speak, but John wheeled around to face him with a look that silenced him in an instant.

"Get out."

Nelson stayed frozen to the spot.

"*I said get out!*"

Nelson scurried through the door that Joseph was holding open.

John was still fuming twenty minutes later when Stella suddenly wafted in. Joseph hadn't gotten a chance to announce her, so she took him by surprise.

"What do you want, Stella?"

She paused on the threshold but started toward him almost immediately. "You don't normally object to my visits," she purred.

"Do you have information for me?" he asked shortly.

"Not precisely. I just wanted to see how you're doing. I know you've been under so much strain lately, and Julie doesn't seem to be offering any support at all." She looked around the room, as if she were amazed at the other woman's absence.

"What would you know about Julie?" he asked sharply.

"Nothing, apart from the fact that she isn't here, and hasn't been for months as far as anyone can tell."

"She's here. Not that it's any business of yours."

Stella seemed to decide something on the spur of the moment. She walked straight up to him and put her arms around his neck. "Julie doesn't deserve all of this. She doesn't do anything for you and never has. I've been devoted to you for years. Can't you see that you're spending your time and money on the wrong woman?" She leaned in to kiss him, but he pushed her away from him.

"My mate is still my mate, Stella. Your opinion of our relationship doesn't change that in the least."

He walked away from her. Stella flounced toward the door.

"Don't expect me to hang around and watch you destroy yourself. If you won't get that bitch out of your life, then I'm not going to stick around to see the consequences."

56

John smiled at the piece of paper in his hand. Nelson had never been the smartest of his followers, but he had turned out to be the most loyal. In the end, it was he who had managed to give John the missing piece of the puzzle. After being thrown out of Larch Hill, he had put all of his efforts into persuading Ariliana to give him Renphor's address. She had finally consented, on the condition that her name never be mentioned in connection with it—a promise which he had broken almost immediately. He had to wait until the next night to bring the information to John, since his activities during the day were limited while he tried to keep tabs on Arabella, but once she was home for the night he had hurried to Larch Hill as soon as he had verified the address.

"Let's go." John grabbed his keys, and the two of them headed out the side door toward the garage. After considering, they decided to take Nelson's car instead—his Mercedes was still too upscale for that part of town, but it would be less noticeable than John's Jaguar. Within half an hour they arrived on the street where Renphor was living.

"You double-checked everything?" John asked Nelson. The other man nodded. Silently slipping out of the vehicle and locking the doors, they crept around the back of the building to the fire escape. Nelson stopped in front of a window on the third floor, reaching for the bottom of it. John reached out to grasp his wrist. Running his hand along the edge, he growled softly to himself.

"Are you certain this is the right place?"

"Of course I am. What makes you think it isn't?"

"Because there's no sign of any protections on the place. Nothing. I can't imagine Renphor being that stupid."

Nelson protested that he was positive about the place, and John reached for the window again, prying it open easily. Both men looked around before stepping inside, making sure none of the neighbors were hanging around. It was unlikely that they would run into anyone at this hour of the morning, but one had to be cautious.

They slipped inside noiselessly, peering around for any sign that the resident would be returning soon.

"Must be hunting," John commented. He looked around the room in disgust.

"Maybe he got invited to a party." Nelson spoke flippantly. John glared at him.

"We could be annihilated at any moment, and that's the best you can do?"

Renphor walked up to the front of his building fifteen minutes later. He had managed to find dinner a block from his house, so he was returning much earlier than usual. After quickly checking his shirt to make sure there was no blood on it, he ran up the steps and opened the front door. He was heading toward the interior steps when someone grasped him by the arm. Spinning around, he found the landlord standing next to him. The man gestured toward his office, and Renphor followed.

He glanced at the gun lying on the man's desk in surprise and shot him a questioning look.

"You have visitors," the landlord said softly.

"Have I, now?"

"Saw 'em go in through the back window. Not that pretty little girl who drops by once in a while, either."

Renphor snorted. If anyone had asked him for a description of Ariliana, it would not have been that. "What did they look like?"

The man described John and his companion in detail. Renphor listened, head cocked to the side.

"You're very observant. I assume you didn't call the police?"

The landlord made a derisive sound in his throat. "Sure. They'll be around next week for their monthly walk-through."

Renphor indicated the gun. "What's that for?"

"What do you think?"

"No point in that. Stay inside for the rest of the evening. I'll deal with the visitors."

John and Nelson searched every nook and cranny of the room, checking for secret hiding places that might contain any vital information about their quarry. They left the window open so that they could make a quick exit if Renphor returned unexpectedly. Nelson became excited upon discovering the map of Larch Hill and the list that Renphor had made and handed it to John without reading it. After smirking over the reference to Nelson, John shoved it back on the shelf. He had already suspected that Renphor was tracking him, and there wasn't anything useful in the folder. It took John an hour to conclude that there was nothing worthwhile to be found. Nelson was a willing participant for the first twenty minutes, but the longer John stayed, the quieter he got. He cast nervous glances at the window and jumped anytime there was a noise in the hallway. John finally indicated that they should leave, and Nelson heaved a sigh of relief.

Renphor emerged from the shadows and watched the two of them disappear around the front of the building before walking slowly up the fire escape to his room.

They got back to Larch Hill more quickly than they had reached Renphor's building. Nelson drove silently, while John continued to congratulate himself on a successful search. When they finally got back to Larch Hill, Nelson didn't get out of the car. John came around to the window to invite him inside, but Nelson shook his head.

"As you like," John said, turning to head inside.

"John, I do have something to say."

"What is it?"

"I—can't do this anymore. I have a nice setup. I don't want to lose it over Renphor."

"Lose…you're not going to lose anything. Once he's out of the way—"

"You can't guarantee that, John." He cut John off as he started to speak. "You can't. We don't live in a 'good guys always win' world. I just can't anymore."

He quickly turned the car around and drove away, leaving John staring after him.

John walked slowly into the house, signaling to Joseph to go down and close the gate behind the Mercedes. He stood inside the door for a few minutes, thinking, before heading to the tower room. He found Julie up on the roof, staring out over the sunrise.

"Where did you and the idiot run off to?" she asked stiffly.

"I've finally found him," he said triumphantly.

"Really? Where?"

"In a filthy little room off Frankford Avenue."

She looked him up and down. "You seem entirely intact, so I assume you didn't run into him?"

He shook his head. He explained the search he and Nelson had made of the room, and the complete lack of any useful information.

"I thought you were waiting to attack him until you had the fire vortex working?"

"I am. The goal was never to run into him this evening. I just wanted to check the place out."

"And you got exactly nothing for your pains. Congratulations." She picked up a book that was sitting next to her chair and began to read.

"Just finding where he lives was crucial. I'll keep an eye on the place. The vortex is ready. I just need to make sure I've got the rest of my plan together before I try anything, and that will take a few weeks."

"How is Arabella?"

He sat back down, smiling at her. "She's doing alright, all things considered. A bit cut up over breaking up with the boyfriend."

"Breaking up...when did this happen?"

He gave her a strange look. "You sound relieved. I thought you liked the guy?"

"I think she's too young to be as serious as she was. And you didn't answer me."

"February. March. Somewhere around there, I think. Does it matter?"

Julie shook her head. "Not really. Just curious."

57

Ariliana spent a week cautiously haunting the campus, trying to figure out if Renphor had been telling the truth about him and Arabella. She finally concluded that they really had split up, after noticing Arabella flirting with other men on several occasions. She smiled to herself. It would make what she was planning to do so much easier. She still needed to get the girl's schedule, though. She hung around the registrar's office that Friday afternoon, surreptitiously observing the one student helper who was still working this late in the day. All she had to do was get a good look at the girl's password and login. She took stock of the office—there was a space between the door and the shelf that she could probably stand in unnoticed for at least a few minutes, but first she would have to get the girl to leave the office and lock the computer for a second. She was considering her next move when she noticed that the girl had stood up. Ariliana held her breath. Was she leaving for the day? She didn't appear to be packing up her work, so Ariliana decided to hang around for a few minutes to see if the girl came back.

She slid behind the door and waited. The crack behind the door was barely wide enough for her to squeeze into. After an agonizing wait that seemed far longer than the five minutes it took, Ariliana saw the girl coming back down the hallway toward the office. Just as she was passing the door, Ariliana accidentally nudged it, and it started to swing closed. She froze, thinking what to do, but the girl caught the door and viciously kicked the doorstop into place under it before sitting down at the computer.

She watched her get settled in front of the computer, then moved softly out from her hiding place to watch. She was close enough to see the keys that were being typed but far enough away not to attract her notice. She committed the information to memory and slid quietly back behind the door. She spent the next hour pressed into the wall, motionless, until the girl finally packed up and left, locking the door behind her. Ariliana slipped out of her hiding place. After gently prying open a window, she slid into the courtyard below.

She arrived back at her apartment several hours later. She had decided to hunt on her way home so that she could do her research without interruption, but she had a hard time finding dinner. It was a game day, so hardly anyone had been out on the streets, but she'd finally caught a man out on a beer run. She grimaced in distaste at the memory—drunks tasted awful. She was always perplexed by this, having consumed her fair share of alcohol while still human. Since it was still too early for what she wanted to do, she flopped down on the sofa with the latest vampire novel for entertainment.

Around two o'clock, she got up from the couch and logged in to the computer. It took her a few minutes to navigate her way around the registrar's computer system. She held her breath, hoping that the information she had gotten really would get her into the scheduling system. The main menu came up a few seconds after she entered the login, and she breathed a sigh of relief as she jotted down Arabella's schedule. Once she had logged off, she leaned back in her chair, steadily regarding the ceiling. She had to come up with a really good plan.

58

A few days later, Arabella was sitting on the ground under a maple tree, absently pulling up blades of grass and picking them apart. An anthropology textbook lay open on the ground next to her, still on the page where she had started. It took her several minutes to realize that someone had silently joined her under the tree.

She jumped at the sight of the dark beauty next to her and eyed her suspiciously. The woman's skin was very pale, and there was something decidedly odd about her eyes. Arabella inched away from her slowly. The woman reached over and touched her arm with an ice-cold hand.

"What do you want?" She tried to sound casual but was pretty sure it hadn't come out right.

Ariliana smiled. "Don't worry. I've already eaten today."

Arabella jumped up, staring hard at her.

"Calm down. I'm a friend of…Ryan's."

Arabella eyed her suspiciously. "And he asked you to come talk to me?"

"Of course not. I don't know when Ren developed this protective streak, but it seems to have kicked into high gear." She smirked. "I'm surprised you enjoy being so well protected. You don't strike me as the submissive sort."

A slight tinge of red appeared on Arabella's cheeks. "I'm not the submissive sort. And Ryan certainly isn't protecting me from anything, since we broke up months ago."

"Such a pity. After all, you knew each other so well…didn't you? I'm sure he told you all about his daily activities. What did you think of his place, by the way?"

Arabella knew this was unanswerable, so she merely continued to glare.

"If I were you, I'd pay him a little surprise visit. Let him know you aren't quite so easily controlled."

"I'm not sure how you can accuse me of being under his control when I haven't spoken to him in weeks." Arabella crossed her arms and stared down at the woman who was still lounging on the grass.

Ariliana smiled and stood to face Arabella. "If that makes you happy, sweetheart. I, for one, would want to know what he'd been hiding all this time." She walked away without waiting for an answer.

Arabella slowly sat back down on the grass. She glanced at the still-open textbook next to her and sighed. If it had been pointless before, it was doubly so now. She reached out and flipped it sharply closed. Hugging her knees close to her chest, she stared out across the park.

She sat motionless for nearly half an hour, staring into the distance. Finally, her eyes seemed to refocus on the grass around her. With a small sigh, she pulled out her phone and dialed the number for the school switchboard.

"Could I be transferred to the registrar's office, please?"

There was a short pause and the phone started ringing again.

"Registrar."

"Jill?"

"Yes. Who is this?"

"You can lose the prim and proper attitude, it's Ella."

"Oh. What do you need? You shouldn't be calling me during my work-study, you know."

Arabella bit her lip. She hesitated before going on.

"I know, but I need you to do something for me while you're there."

"Not you too. No, Ella, I will not break into the computer to change your biology grade."

Arabella giggled. "That wasn't why I called."

"Calculus?"

"What the heck, Jill? I'm an anthropology major—why would I be taking calculus? Anyway, It's nothing like that. Actually, it's a really dumb thing."

"What did you do?"

Arabella took a deep breath. "I lost Ryan's address. I still have some of his crap that I need to send back, and I really don't feel like calling him to get it."

"You know this is completely against the rules."

"C'mon, Jill. It's not like I'm going to stalk the guy."

Five minutes later, she was staring at a slip of paper on which she had written the address.

Arabella turned nervously at the sound of footsteps behind her. She knew she shouldn't be here. Renphor had told her hundreds of times that his neighborhood was no place for her to visit, and she was beginning to see what he meant. The alleyways around her were putrid. Refuse from seedy bars flowed out of dumpsters that hadn't been emptied in weeks. She realized with disgust that the shuffling movement she had noticed among the debris came from rats feasting on the garbage. And the smell was like nothing she had experienced. Half-rotted garbage and urine mingled together with god knew what else. She closed her eyes for a moment to block it out. No wonder he had been so fond of spending time at her apartment. She knew that she needed to stay alert, but she found herself wondering where he was hanging out these days.

She had just forced herself back to the present when a large hand wrapped around her mouth, and another twined around her waist. She tried to scream, but her vocal cords seemed to be stuck together. The hand was ice cold. She felt herself lifted off the ground, and then an odd sensation as if she were being sucked through a tube very fast. She hit the ground hard in what appeared to be the basement of a building.

Arabella's heart pounded as she looked around. How had she gotten here? She noticed five other young women huddled fearfully around the edges of the room. Several of them were pressing their bodies against the wall, as if willing it to give way and release them back into the freedom of the alleyway. She leaned against a wall, trying to collect her thoughts. Some of the other girls were dressed in cheap, ragged clothes, but they didn't show any other signs of having been imprisoned for an extended time.

She approached one of them, who seemed to be the least wild-looking of the group. "My name is Arabella. How long have you been here?" she asked.

The girl stared at her for a moment, and Arabella began to think that she wouldn't answer, but she seemed to find her voice at last. "Eileen. I was the first one they brought in—about two hours ago, I think, but my phone died and I've lost track of time."

"How did we get here? I feel as if I fell through a black hole." Arabella saw a few of the other girls twitch at her words but stayed focused on Eileen. She noticed fear creep into the girl's eyes as she spoke.

"I'm not entirely sure how they're doing it. There don't seem to be any doors here. They just appear with the next girl and then disappear at random."

"Any idea who they are?"

Arabella heard a small voice from near the wall. She strained to see the girl who spoke, but the light in the room was extremely dim. "Vampires. They're going to use us for some kind of rite, I think."

Another girl scoffed. "Where did you come up with that one? It's a sex ring. No doubt about it."

Arabella's mind worked quickly. "Vampires, you say? What makes you think so?"

The second girl spoke again. "Don't encourage the little idiot. And don't tell me you're dumb enough to believe there is such a thing. Biggest bunch of idiocy I ever heard."

Eileen chimed in at this point. "I don't know what the heck they are, but I've never seen a human being that can do what these guys do."

Arabella moved closer to girl, who was shaking with fright. "Why vampires?"

The girl gulped, tears starting to run down her face. "I…" She glanced at the disdainful girl next to her.

"Please go on."

"I saw the fangs on one of them. Blood-red eyes and pale skin. And so cold…" She shrank toward the wall as she spoke and collapsed into tears.

Arabella walked across the room and leaned silently against the wall, her mind working quickly. She pulled out her phone and looked at it. She wasn't surprised to see that the signal had been scrambled but figured it had been worth a shot. She was still leaning against the wall, staring at it, when three men suddenly appeared in front of her. They looked around the room, a strange hunger in their eyes.

"Well, ladies, we've been told to bring you up for the floor show. Come along now." The men started to gather the girls into the center of the room. Suddenly, a memory floated across Arabella's brain. She had copied the contacts out of Renphor's phone months ago, planning to do some research about him on her own, and had never gotten around to deleting them. She scrolled quickly through her contacts until she found what she was looking for.

"Come on, beauty. That phone isn't going to help you, believe me." One of the men leered at her.

"I'm not so sure." She glanced down at the name just before the man knocked the phone out of her hand. She looked coldly at him. "I want to speak to Stefan."

Her tone had been level, but the effect of this simple statement on the three men in the room was profound. They stopped and stared at her, at a loss to respond. The other girls had been struck silent as well.

"Pick up that phone." The man spoke harshly. Arabella walked calmly toward it. Her heart was pounding in her ears, but her pride kept her from showing her fear. She picked up the phone silently and handed it to him. He looked it over.

He started scrolling through the phone, using the same process that she had followed an instant earlier. He paused and showed a phone number to the man next to him.

"Well, Gaylord? Is that it?"

The second man loomed over her. "How the devil did you get that number?" He seemed disproportionately angry.

Arabella quaked inwardly, but her voice remained calm. "From my boyfriend. I copied it out of his phone."

The second laughed derisively. "Your boyfriend? What are the odds?"

"I have the number, don't I?"

The men looked shiftily at each other. "So why ask for Stefan? Presumably he's not the 'boyfriend' you're referring to." The third jeered at her.

"No, but he's the one who owns this place, isn't he?" It had been a desperate bluff on her part, but it seemed to have hit home. A shocked silence greeted her words, and several surreptitious glances passed between the three men. The two on either side eventually settled on staring at the one they had called Gaylord.

"So, what do we do about this?" one of them asked.

Gaylord tapped his foot on the floor for a few minutes, looking at the ceiling for inspiration. Finally, he looked at the others. "I'll go tell him."

He was back almost immediately. "Take the rest of them to the chambers. You, come here." He pointed at Arabella.

She walked toward him, hoping that her knees wouldn't give way. He grabbed her roughly by the arm and turned. She felt the strange sensation of being sucked through a tube again and found herself standing in a very ornate sitting room.

Arabella looked around in astonishment. Everything around her seemed to be composed of either red and black velvet or gilding. A gilded chandelier shone above her head, dripping with crystals, and she stared in amazement at a positively hideous sideboard made of a dark wood with gilded angels on the corners and lion's paws for legs. She wondered at the dim lighting before realizing that the room was lit entirely by candlelight. Ornate porcelain decorations lined the shelves and mantel, where a wood-burning fireplace seemed to be the only source of heat, and a chill lingered in the room. She wrapped her arms tightly around herself to try to stop the shivering, but she found it impossible.

"Cold?"

She looked quickly around as a man stepped out of the shadows. He was only slightly taller than she was herself and looked to be in his early fifties. She reminded herself that this was irrelevant, since he'd probably looked that way for a very long time. His eyes gleamed yellow, and his dark hair had streaks of gray. He was dressed in an old-fashioned style and had wrapped himself in an ornate cloak.

"It is a little cold in here. May I stand by the fire?" She was still making a valiant effort to control her nerves but felt that they were beginning to fail. The goons below she could deal with. This man had a calm air of certainty that completely threw her off-balance.

"Certainly, my dear." Stefan's voice did not match the warmth of his words.

She moved gratefully toward the blaze, stretching out her hands to the fire.

"Gaylord, give me that phone." The man from the basement walked nervously toward him and handed it to him. "Now get out." The man disappeared immediately.

Stefan moved slowly toward her. He stopped a few feet from her and held up the phone.

"How exactly did you come by my number again?"

Arabella swallowed. "I copied it out of my boyfriend's phone while he was running an errand."

"Your boyfriend?"

"Yes. His name's Ryan Callaghan."

Stefan paused, watching her closely. "Would you like a drink?"

"Do you have anything fit for human consumption?"

Stefan smiled. "Ryan—or rather Renphor—seems to have been rather upfront with you, apart from giving you a fake name, of course. How very interesting."

"He didn't tell me anything. But he was practically living in my apartment, so I just…guessed."

"I see. And have you mentioned it to him?"

She shook her head.

"Wine?"

Arabella nodded miserably. Stefan called for a servant. To her relief, the wine that he brought was white. She didn't know that she could have stomached red, under the circumstances.

Renphor was sitting at his desk, idly tracing his finger over the map of Larch Hill, when his phone suddenly rang, startling him out of his reverie. He picked it up and was surprised to see

Arabella's name come up. The surprise turned to panic when the voice on the other end was Stefan's.

"Good evening, Renphor."

Renphor got up from his seat but stood uncertainly in the middle of the room. His inclination was to go immediately to Stefan's rooms, but that would mean hanging up the phone.

"What the devil are you doing with that phone?"

"That's a rather interesting story, actually. If you'd like to hear it, I would strongly suggest that you pay me a visit. Immediately."

Renphor appeared a moment later in Stefan's rooms. He was greeted by a choking sound and turned to find Arabella holding a glass of wine and coughing. She had apparently inhaled some of it when he'd landed in front of her.

"How the hell do people keep doing that! Have you ever heard of using a damned door?" Her voice shook. He laughed and grabbed her to pull her away from the fireplace. He was startled to find that she struggled like a trapped creature.

"Not afraid of me, are you?"

She stopped struggling, and he released her. "I think I am, a little," she said. "I'm not used to you looking so—vampirish."

"You saw the same thing at Halloween."

"That's different. I thought it was fake."

He shook his head. "Well, when you're trying to pretend that you aren't a vampire, looking like one is a bit of a drawback."

She still looked very pale, but the corner of her mouth lifted. "You might want to work on your act a bit."

He blinked. "What do you mean?"

"I mean that I figured it out Thanksgiving weekend. Most people eat. And sleep. And occasionally use the bathroom."

He stared at her. "Oh. Thanksgiving? Really?"

She nodded.

"Hm. How did you get on to vampires from all of that?"

"Once I started thinking about it, your Halloween costume was a pretty obvious clue."

"Fair point." Renphor looked at Stefan, who had glided to the other side of the room when he'd appeared. He looked like the cat at the cream pot, and Renphor felt his temper rising again. "Now, on to other matters. Stefan, would you mind filling me in? What exactly do you think you're doing?"

"Temper, Renphor. She was picked up in a sweep."

"Where?"

"How the hell would I know?"

Arabella swallowed the last of her wine. "I was looking for your rooming house," she admitted.

Renphor turned slowly to look at her, and she took another step backwards when their eyes met.

"Do you understand now why I told you to stay away from there?" He started to walk slowly toward her.

She nodded mutely. A slow smile began to curl his lips.

"Perhaps I should have encouraged you to explore more. I never imagined it would make things so very easy for me. You see, I've been looking for a good excuse to induct you into our little club."

Arabella had backed up as far as was possible without ending in the fire. "I don't want—"

"It doesn't matter what you want," he cut her off. "Your choices now are to become a vampire or be killed by Stefan. And since you are absolutely no use to me dead, I'm not going to leave the second option open."

"Ryan—Renphor—please—" She spoke the words very softly. He struck quickly, deciding that to wait would only prolong her torment. He savored the sensation of her warm blood flowing into his mouth after months of restraint but paid close attention to the strength of her pulse. When he felt it start to weaken, he pulled his fangs slowly away from her throat, running his tongue over the wound before bringing it around his lips to catch the last of the treat. She pushed on his shoulders but staggered and collapsed almost immediately into his arms. He lifted her easily, carried her to a red velvet sofa, and placed her gently on it. She lay there, gulping for breath.

"Sorry, pet. I'm afraid you're in for a bad night." He smiled weakly.

"Renphor?"

"Hmm?"

"Are you very angry with me?"

"I am not the least bit angry with you. You have, in fact, made everything remarkably easy for me."

She tried to speak again but only managed to gasp in pain. He took her hand as her body convulsed.

59

The conversion took hours. Once Arabella reached the point of being totally unaware of her surroundings, Renphor removed to a nearby chair to watch. Half an hour after the convulsions stopped, she finally turned toward him, blinking in recognition.

"Well, my dear?" He stood and walked toward her as he spoke.

"I'm feeling better now." She smiled weakly.

He laughed. "I should think you are feeling much better."

He pulled her to her feet, then took advantage of her proximity to pull her into his arms and kiss her. He caught a brief look at Stefan's interested expression before he felt her body reacting to his more strongly than it ever had before. She suddenly pulled him onto the couch on top of her and reached for the buttons on his shirt. He slipped her t-shirt over her head, finally allowing himself to enjoy being with her without the worry that he would somehow hurt her.

An hour later, they were still lying naked on the couch while he ran his fingers down her cold skin, enjoying the feel of her energy flowing over him. She suddenly scowled over his shoulder.

Noticing the direction of her gaze, he smiled. "Don't mind Stefan. He likes to watch."

He stood up and began to dress. She lay there and watched him for a moment before speaking.

"Renphor?"

"Hmm?"

"I'm hungry."

"I suppose you must be. I've been rather negligent. You should have fed hours ago."

"I don't think I was hungry before." She stood to dress as she spoke, turning her back to the room.

Stefan spoke at last. "I'm sure we have some...leftovers-...from the floor show if you're interested."

Renphor saw a horrified look cross her face. "I...I don't think I could," she said.

He smiled. "I wondered about that. You don't actually need human blood to survive, though over time you'll probably find you prefer it." He looked at his watch as he spoke and pretended not to have noticed when Arabella recoiled at his words. "It's two a.m. We should be able to find some unsuspecting deer in the park, and we aren't likely to be bothered by any human interference at this hour." He put out his hand as he spoke. "Come."

Arabella reached out tentatively and took his hand. In one swift movement he pulled her toward him and turned. An instant later, they were standing in the middle of Fairmount Park. Arabella looked distinctly ruffled.

"Don't like jumping?"

"It's like being sucked through a glass tube."

"True. Let's find you something to eat."

They found the sleeping deer easily enough, although sensing the presence of a predator, they took off as Arabella and Renphor approached. She pulled away from him and leapt for one, catching it easily. She grasped it hard around the throat and sank her fangs into it. Renphor walked away to lean against a nearby tree.

Arabella found him there a few minutes later, glaring up at a squirrel. She giggled. "What on earth is that look for?"

"Hate the little buggers. No use as food, and they've got nasty dispositions."

"This from a creature that lives on human blood. So what now?"

"Still hungry?"

"No."

Renphor suddenly grimaced. "Then our next stop is probably Larch Hill."

"First, I'd like to hear what's going on between you and John."

He nodded. "The best place for that is, unfortunately, my room. We won't be bothered by anyone there, and you won't be tempted to attack anyone either."

"I don't think I would be anyway."

"You only think that because you haven't come across a human yet."

The next moment they were standing in Renphor's room. Arabella looked around a bit, then focused on something on the desk. He followed her gaze to her own picture, which he had propped against the lamp again.

"You kept it."

He smiled ruefully at her. "I've spent months trying to figure out how to wheedle my way back into your life. I'll have to have a new picture taken, though."

"Why?" she asked curiously.

"Looked in the mirror yet?"

She crossed the room and wiped the dirt off a mirror that hung in one corner. She gasped at her own reflection, obviously slightly repulsed by changes that he privately considered to be an improvement. Her skin, which had always been olive, was now ghost white. Her teeth had shifted to allow room for two larger and more extended canines. And a faint orange glow burned at the back of her eyes, which had turned from blue to a deep amber hue.

"How are we going to pass this off as normal?"

"I'm afraid you're going to come down with an extended illness. Mono, probably. While you're hidden from the public eye, I'll teach you to shield the fangs and the change in eye color. The paleness will be chalked up to the illness."

She nodded and looked back at her reflection. "Who came up with the idea that vampires don't reflect in mirrors, anyway?"

He laughed. "Bram Stoker, if I remember correctly."

"I guess the sunlight thing is nonsense, too."

He reflected on this for a moment. "Not entirely. The devil created thirteen original vampires. They were immune to most of the things that supposedly kill us. Vampire power becomes diluted the further away you get from the source, though."

"What do you mean?"

"Vampires made by those original thirteen, or even within two or three generations of them, are pretty much indestructible to anyone but each other. After that, weaknesses start to show. They take various forms, but most of the standard ways to kill a vampire, such as sunlight, are included."

"So, who made you?"

"That was the result of Stefan having a bad day. I was supposed to be dinner. He's one of the originals, which explains why he's such a bloody bastard most of the time."

"So I shouldn't have to worry about any of that—stuff."

"I don't think you have much to worry about. You're only third-generation, and I happen to be fairly powerful."

"You said that John tried to kill you."

"Twice. Speaking of bastards—"

"So what generation is he?"

He sighed. "Third. Same as you."

"Who made him?"

"I did."

Arabella sat down with a thump. "Tell."

60

October 6, 1645

Renphor leaned against a tree trunk, staring up at the house. It had been twenty-five years since he had last passed this way. One of the longer breaks he had taken, since war had made travel more complicated. He assumed that the current master of the house must be in his thirties by now. He smiled to himself. He had mingled in the village for a few days before making the trek out to the manor house, and the stories he had picked up at the inn had been fascinating. John Elder was apparently a strictly religious supporter of Cromwell and was not well-liked in this strongly royalist region. People believed that he had somehow beaten the family curse because he had lived longer than most of his ancestors and feared that he had used some kind of dark magic to do so. John himself publicly disdained the whole notion of vampires. This would certainly be an interesting trip.

As he stood there, Renphor noticed carved markings on the tree. He stared curiously at them, trying to make out their meaning. He was fairly certain they were names. He concentrated on them for a while, then shrugged and went back to watching the fields. One of these years he would learn to read, he supposed. He had always intended to do so, but everything had lost its sense of urgency over the last two hundred years. Immortals could afford to procrastinate. He smiled as he heard hoofbeats on the lane. No doubt this would be his quarry. He slipped silently around the tree to get a better look and stopped dead in his tracks. This was definitely not the master of the house. The woman astride the white stallion was the most stunning creature he had ever seen. Long black hair flowed out behind her as she rode, setting off her white skin. As she rode past him, he saw that her eyes were black as well. He pulled quickly back into the shadows. He couldn't be certain, but she hadn't appeared to notice him.

He heard the horse's hooves retreating into the distance as he leaned against the tree again, staring straight ahead. He realized with surprise that the strange hunger that was overtaking him had nothing to do with blood. He wanted this woman for himself, more desperately than he had wanted anything in centuries. He smiled. Why not? He knew several others of his kind who had made mates for themselves over the years. He would kill the man and keep his wife for himself. He supposed vaguely that the children would be raised by some relative or other—he could come back for the eldest son at his leisure.

He stood for a while, turning things over in his head. He had never made another of his kind but was fairly certain he knew the process. As long as he stopped drinking the blood before life was extinguished, he was pretty sure the rest would take care of itself. He didn't foresee any issues with John Elder. Humans were so easily overtaken. He got up and strolled back into the woods, debating whether it was worth chasing down one of the deer he had seen earlier in the day. He decided it probably was—it would never do to go into this hungry if he was to do a conversion. He went off in search of dinner.

A week later, Renphor found himself in the stairwell leading down to the root cellar at Larch Hill. He had learned that the woman's name was Sophia. After observing her habits for a few days, he knew that she would soon be back from her ride and that once the groom had taken the saddle and bridle she would send him away. He waited patiently, remaining absolutely silent. His hiding place was mostly below ground level, and he had developed a knack for successfully blending into the background so that humans didn't notice his presence unless something called their attention to it.

He stiffened as he heard a woman's voice in the stable yard and waited patiently as she finished her conversation with the groom and sent him on his way. He listened intently to the sounds of her tending to the horse and measured her footsteps toward him when she finally left the stables. When he determined that she must be close, he crept the rest of the way down the stairs and scuffed his foot loudly on the stone floor.

He heard her pause before walking away and hissed in irritation, but a few minutes later she returned. She descended the steps cautiously, and he pushed himself against the wall inside the doorway so that she wouldn't see him until she was already inside. He caught his breath as she walked through the door and turned to face him. She really was stunningly beautiful, although at the moment she was eyeing him with deep suspicion and clutching a sickle in her right hand. He moved to get between her and the exit.

"Who are you?" she asked.

He moved slowly toward her. "My name is Renphor."

She backed away from him. "Where are you from, and what are you doing in my cellar? If you're looking for work, we don't have any right now."

He laughed, revealing the two long, thin fangs that had been hidden from view. "I am definitely not looking for work."

"What is it that you want?" she asked shakily.

"This is a little outside of my usual pattern, but you are so lovely I couldn't resist. I've decided that you are going to join me. Your husband I will dispose of in the normal manner."

"Join you? And if I don't choose to do so?" Her voice was stronger this time, and she clutched the sickle tighter. Renphor smiled to himself. The woman had spirit as well as beauty.

"I don't remember offering a choice." In one swift movement, Renphor grabbed the sickle out of her hand and plunged his fangs into her throat. She tried to scream but no sound came out. When he pulled away, she reeled backwards, momentarily incapacitated by pain and shock. She steadied herself against the wall and looked wildly around.

"What have you done?" She stared at him.

"Started the conversion process. It should only take a few hours." He glanced casually around but jumped as she grabbed the sickle that he had dropped on the floor. She moved into the center of the room, staring at him.

"I will not join you. Reverse the process, and kill me if you want to."

Renphor looked at her in amusement. "I can't reverse it. You don't have to join me, I suppose, but you will become a vampire regardless of what you do."

"Will I?"

He nodded. She suddenly raised the sickle high over her head. He jumped backwards, away from the blade, as she swung it downwards in an arc. He realized too late what her intention was. He leapt toward her as the blade swung inwards, but he couldn't reach her before it did. He watched in horror as she fell to the ground, her throat cut wide open.

He felt as if he were frozen to the spot. A hundred thoughts jammed his brain and combined with the smell of the blood until it seemed to him that he couldn't think of anything at all. He wasn't sure how long he stood there, but he gradually came back to his senses just as a soft footfall sounded on the steps. He looked quickly around at the blood splattered down his clothes and across the wall. There was no other way out of the cellar.

Renphor raised his hand, pointing his palm toward the door. He had only recently discovered that if he focused, he could emit a pulse that would knock over almost any freestanding object in his way. He focused his energy intently on the doorway and felt the power start to flow out his palm. His intention had been to create a short burst and then take off before the person on the steps could recover enough to recognize him, but he didn't anticipate the effect that his panic would have on the strength of the pulse or the control he could exercise over it.

A bolt of fire shot out of his hand, reverberating around the room three or four times before finally dissipating. Renphor, who had instinctively dropped to the ground as the jet of light started its erratic course, leapt up when it stopped and darted toward the foot of the steps where he stopped dead.

He slouched backwards against the wall, staring at the two young boys laying on the ground in front of him. The concussive effect that had preceded the flame had slammed into their tiny bodies, and purple spots were beginning to appear under their skin. For the first time in the two centuries since he had ceased to be human, he felt remorse creeping over him. He knelt down next to the two bodies, stroking the young faces. Suddenly, he snapped to attention, listening to a sound coming from above him. He took off running and was up the steps, through the barnyard, and across the lane in a matter of seconds. Finally stopping when he felt he was sufficiently shielded from view by the woods, he leaned against a tree, thinking over the situation. There was no point in killing Elder now—if he did, there would be no line to continue. He started off through the woods, moving rapidly away from the house.

A few months later, Renphor sat in a dingy basement a few miles from Larch Hill. He had come inside to shelter from the rain, but as he took in his surroundings, he began to wonder if a little water might not be preferable. The room appeared to be a long-abandoned dungeon. Rusty chains hung on the walls, and attached to them at the far end were a few things that he decided not to think about. He had known people who had found themselves chained up in a similar fashion in his past life. He sat down on a stone in the middle of the room and fell into contemplating the water patterns on the walls. The storm raging outside made the atmosphere inside the dungeon seem even more oppressive than it normally would have, and his senses were disoriented by the noise and the smells so that he didn't sense a human presence until it was directly behind him. He whirled around in time to see John Elder swinging a long, sharpened shaft made of oak toward him. He had no time to react, and the stake hit home. It sank into his chest until the sharp end protruded out through his back. Renphor roared in rage and pain. Yanking the stake from his torso, he advanced on Elder.

"That was *incredibly* stupid," he breathed.

John looked back defiantly. "I don't think so," he responded calmly.

Renphor paused, smiling. "And to think, I wasn't going to kill you right away."

John snarled. "Don't do me any favors."

Renphor began his approach again. "Why? Have we decided it would be better to die?"

"As long as I take you with me, death would be welcome."

Renphor laughed out loud at this. "But you won't take me with you, you know. You can see how effective your last attempt was. All you have succeeded in doing is making me very, very annoyed."

"You murdered my family," John growled.

"Yes, I did. Although I have to admit that the children were not part of the plan."

John lunged for Renphor on these words, trying to grab him around the throat. Renphor grabbed his hands and slammed him roughly against the wall. "Temper, Elder. What do you think that will accomplish?"

John struggled violently, but Renphor held him easily with one hand as he looked speculatively around. Finally, he spotted a set of chains that were partially open. Dragging John across the dungeon, he held him with one hand while he forced the rusted chains open with the other. Once he had closed a chain around one wrist, it was an easy task to get the second one in. John glared at him defiantly.

"Leaving me here to starve?" he asked.

"Not at all. You'll be able to escape easily enough in a few days' time."

Renphor saw with satisfaction that fear had finally started to show on John's face. "You shouldn't have told me you wanted to die, you know. I have no desire whatsoever to give you what you want." He searched around until he found a sharp stone. Picking it up, he walked over to John and pressed the edge against his arm, creating an inch-long gash. He reached up and wiped his fingertip across one fang, until a drop of venom glistened on the end of it. Smiling, he rubbed it into the wound and watched with satisfaction as the skin slowly healed around it.

"What have you done?" John asked hoarsely.

"I have given you a gift. One single drop of venom—it will, of course, take several days for that one drop to finish its work. I would imagine it will be a bit unpleasant. But then, so is having a tree driven through your chest." He looked with disgust at the stake lying on the floor. "And now, I'm done with you. In the future, don't attack people with a hundred times your strength."

61

Arabella stood staring out the window for a long time after Renphor's tale had ended. He didn't say anything to interrupt her thoughts but stood behind her with his arm around her waist, looking out over her shoulder. Her eyes suddenly focused on the present again as something shifted in the alley below the window.

"What was that?" She reached for the window, but he stopped her.

"Neighbors. Don't want you going out there right now."

"Why not?"

He smiled. "Because they are almost guaranteed to accost you, and I don't want to have to clean up the mess you would make."

She looked curiously at him, head cocked to one side like a sparrow.

"You have no idea of your own power yet. Give it time. We need to take care of John now, so you have a place to stay."

"And my mother?"

"From what I've been able to find out, she's still alright. He's got her locked up somewhere, though. She should be able to escape on her own once John's out of the way, but if she can't, we'll find her."

She nodded. "We should probably go now, then."

"One thing before we go."

She looked at him questioningly.

"When John goes for me, get the hell out of the way. I'm not sure how long it will take him to process what he's seeing, and I don't want you caught in the crossfire, so to speak."

"You're sure you can win this battle?" She put her hand on his arm and looked up at him as she spoke.

He laughed. "Positive. But if I have to worry about you as well as myself, he might get a shot or two in, and I need to keep the upper hand. Understood?"

"Yes."

"Then let's go."

She shuddered as he reached for her wrist.

"What's wrong?"

"I don't like your method of travel much," she admitted.

He looked at her sympathetically. "It takes some getting used to, but it's efficient. Come."

He reached out for her, and she closed her eyes in resignation.

They entered through the main door of the mansion and found themselves standing in an elaborate entranceway. Heavy tapestries and ornate furniture lined the walls. It looked as if the dust of ages should have covered everything in sight, but the room was strangely immaculate.

Renphor looked around appreciatively. "Joseph appears to be very efficient. I wonder if all the rooms in this ridiculous pile are this clean?"

Arabella gaped. "They always told me this part of the house was falling down."

"Smartest thing to do. I'm sure your mother didn't want you mixing with the sort of guests they were likely to entertain."

"What are you suggesting?" she asked sharply.

"That vampires and human children are a bad mix."

"Oh."

He took a deep breath and reached for her hand. "Might as well get it over with," he muttered as much to himself as to her.

"Should we knock or something?" she asked.

He looked at her quizzically. "You do live here, don't you?"

"Forgot." She giggled.

They walked down the hallway to a door at the end and pushed through it. Arabella looked around the library in awe at the heavily bound leather books lining the shelves and the instruments and gauges all over the tables. She reached out to touch an odd globe-like object. Renphor's hand shot out and grabbed hers just before it made contact with the globe. He pushed her gently away from the table.

"My dear, do not touch anything unless you know exactly what it is."

There was a slight shuffling of feet near the doorway, and Joseph walked slowly into the room. As Renphor looked into the man's eyes, he was startled by the pure hatred reflected back at him. Joseph seemed to fly across the room, with his hands outstretched as if to claw out Renphor's throat. Renphor seemed barely to have moved, but Joseph suddenly went hurtling backwards.

"Down, you fool," Renphor growled. "If John hasn't been able to take me out in four hundred years, what made you think you could?"

Joseph picked himself up slowly, never taking his eyes from Renphor. "Murderer," he breathed. "You killed my mistress. And her children."

Renphor could see the anger starting to build again and decided to head it off. "Where is your master? I have business with him."

"You have no business here."

"I'll be the judge of that." John's six-foot-two frame filled the doorway, and his orange eyes bored right into Renphor. He was too well bred to display the overt rage that had overcome his servant. Instead, his voice was perfectly even and colder than ice. "Renphor. To what do I owe the honor?" He walked slowly to the table. Renphor watched warily as his hand traveled across it toward the long, thin metal instrument that still lay on it. He bowed slightly without taking his eyes off John.

"Get your hand away from that ballomuron gun, and I'll tell you." The tone was casual, but there was an unmistakable warning in his voice.

Arabella had retreated into the shadows when Joseph had entered the room, but she chose this moment to walk back into the light. Whatever response John had been ready to make died on his lips.

62

She walked slowly toward him but stopped several feet beyond his reach.

"Arabella!" The sound was between a gasp and a moan. He moved toward her, but she stepped backwards away from him.

"John." Her voice reflected the coldness with which he had addressed Renphor a minute before. The sound of it cut through him like a knife. He turned on Renphor.

"My daughter, Renphor. Again, you take my child from me." He spoke half angrily, half pleadingly.

Renphor did not get the chance to respond.

"She is not yours. You tried to take her from me, but it never quite worked." Julie had glided silently into the room. John jumped and whirled around to face his mate.

"How did you—"

"Get out of the tower, where you locked me up? In much the same way that Renphor and Arabella got onto the property. I learned to jump some time ago."

A muscle on the side of his throat twitched. "And to get your revenge on me, you gave Arabella to Renphor? Allowed your own child to be turned into a vampire out of spite?"

"I did not give her to anyone. She chose to be with Renphor—by the time I became aware of it, it was already too late."

John looked at her, stunned. "You didn't think to tell me? I could have gotten her away from him."

"Could you? At what cost? You had already brought her to the full attention of our world—how long do you think she would've lasted?"

"I would not have bitten her myself, at least, as he appears to have done. Did you not?" John rounded on Renphor.

"I did. And I might add that you would certainly have done the same."

"I wouldn't have. Not under any circumstances." He turned to Arabella. "You must believe me."

"I do. You would've watched me die instead. Thank goodness Renphor has more sense." She moved away from him to look out the window.

"What do you mean?" John looked from one to the other in confusion.

Renphor smiled maliciously. "Stefan had her. If she hadn't known me and maneuvered herself into his presence, she would've been part of the floor show by now."

John moved toward her again. She turned to him, and even he couldn't misread the look on her face. "You will abandon me for Renphor? That is all that I mean to you?"

Real anger sounded in her voice at last. "Don't you dare talk to me about loyalty. Between you and my mother, did you really expect me to choose you? At least Renphor doesn't lock people up in towers when they annoy him."

"And if I don't choose to let him have you?"

"He'll kill you."

John turned to Renphor. "Is that it, then? A way to back me into a duel?"

Renphor sneered. "What's the matter? Not up for a fair fight? Rather sneak up on me with a little acid shooter and see how much damage you can inflict before I retaliate? I'm done with it, John. Regardless of what you say about Arabella, this ends tonight."

John moved toward Renphor, but Julie suddenly put out her hand and stepped between the two men. They stared at her in amazement. "You're not going to do this in Arabella's presence. Or mine for that matter. Come with me, Arabella."

Arabella walked toward her mother, and together they headed for the hall door. Julie beckoned Joseph as well and forced him to walk out in front of them. She turned as she reached the door and stared fixedly at Renphor. "You remember your promise to me, don't you? Now that you have brought her into our world, you will continue to protect her."

Renphor nodded, and Julie pulled the door closed behind her. He turned back to John as soon as they were gone. The smile that now played across his lips was far from pleasant, and his eyes blazed red as he walked slowly toward his adversary. John stood rooted to the spot, staring at the closed door. Slowly, he turned back to face his attacker.

"And I thought you didn't want me dead. Wasn't that the plan? Force me to live this cursed existence forever?"

"It was, but that was several centuries ago. I'm tired of being attacked anytime my back is turned."

"Were you hoping I would go without a fight once you turned my family against me?" John asked bitterly.

Renphor laughed. "Wouldn't that be nice? No, John, I haven't been counting on anything of the sort." He had begun to slowly circle the perimeter of the room as he spoke. John had to continually turn to keep him in view.

"I think you underestimate me, Renphor. Everyone seems so sure of the outcome of this battle—and what if you don't win?" He raised his hand suddenly, and a bolt of light shot across the room. Renphor deflected it easily, continuing his slow course around the room.

"I don't underestimate you, John. I have made that mistake in the past, but not tonight."

"And you think you can outsmart me, or is your plan just to overpower me?"

"I'm not fool enough to tell you my plan, John."

"No? And I thought you were fool enough for anything." John shot another bolt of light in Renphor's direction as he spoke. It did not come anywhere near its target, and Renphor didn't even flinch.

"Your aim's off," he said conversationally.

John smiled. "But your reflexes aren't. So you've at least learned some degree of self-control. I congratulate you."

"I've learned a number of things, John. I should thank you, really. Being hunted by you gave me far more incentive to study than I would otherwise have had."

John eyed him with hostility for several moments before putting up his hands in a supplicating gesture. Renphor stared. "What is that supposed to mean?"

"That I don't want my library destroyed. We'll go outside." He suddenly turned on his heel and bolted out the nearby window and into the woods. He stopped in a clearing and looked toward the house with narrowed eyes. Suddenly a jet of light hit the tree right in front of him. He spun around to find Renphor standing twenty feet away.

"Don't tell me you forgot about the jumping?" Renphor smiled at the expression on his adversary's face.

"Of course not. I'm surprised you'd waste the energy on it, though. When did you figure out how to do it, by the way?"

"Centuries ago. It isn't that difficult, really."

"Stefan taught you."

Renphor laughed. "Hardly. Stefan only disburses knowledge amongst his minions. Couldn't stop me from learning it on my own, though."

"I should have thought you were counted among his minions."

Renphor twitched. "Then you thought wrong. Truth be told, we don't like each other much. Unlike you, however, he has enough sense to leave me in peace."

"Unless he's kidnapping your girlfriend," John responded drily.

"Arabella, unfortunately, occasionally acts her age. She poked her nose someplace she had no business being, and Stefan caught her at it. I'm merely grateful that she had enough sense to get herself back out of the situation." Renphor watched John with interest as he spoke. The other man had been making slow, circular motions with his wrist the whole time.

John's eyes narrowed. "You consider this getting herself out of it?"

"I do. By rights, she should be dead by now. Instead, she gets the benefit of a long, happy existence with me." This was too much for John. He let fly the bolt of flame he had been so carefully cultivating before it had reached full strength. Renphor expended almost no energy to block it, but it put him fully on his guard.

John backed around a tree, keenly aware of the error. "And you think she will be happy with you? She'll get bored with you in no time."

Renphor sneered. "Wasted tactics, John. While she is enough attached to me to abandon family and friends to join me, I assure you I have not been fool enough to reciprocate."

"I wonder that you wish to keep her, then."

"Why not? She is beautiful and intelligent and will probably grow quite powerful in her own right over time." Renphor was growing bored with the conversation. "Are you planning to stay behind that tree all night?"

"No." John leapt suddenly into the clearing and fired a jet of light that crumbled an oak tree to his right. He stared at it, shocked, then looked back at Renphor standing calmly in front of him. "You redirected that shot."

Renphor smiled. "A useful little shield."

John suddenly shot across the clearing and spun around, sending another jet of light in Renphor's direction. Except that Renphor was no longer standing there. For a moment, he was gone completely, and then John heard a soft laugh directly to his left. He turned to see his adversary standing a mere two feet away. He let loose with another jet of light, prematurely. Renphor seemed to wave it away. John breathed heavily, trying to take control of himself. He saw Renphor's guard falter for a second and let off another shot. This one finally made contact just above Renphor's right elbow. He hissed in pain as it ripped open a section of his upper arm, and quickly fired an answering shot to force his adversary back onto the defensive.

John backed behind the tree again and regrouped while Renphor watched him from the edge of the clearing with a bored expression on his face. John crept around the side of his hiding place and put out his hand. As he did so, a small ball of flame shot into the middle of the clearing and slowly started to expand. Renphor stood up straight and watched with interest as the vortex formed. It faltered a bit on two occasions but finally expanded to the full ten feet across, whirling rapidly.

"Impressive. What do you intend to do with it now?" he asked.

John snapped his head up, and in an instant the vortex was gone. Renphor laughed. "Having a little trouble figuring out that missing page?"

"What the devil do you know about it?"

"Other than the fact that it's in my safe deposit box, not much." Renphor put out his hand, and a similar ball of fire shot from it. It began to swirl rapidly, and the movement seemed to pull the sides of flame away from the center. In one fluid motion, the vortex expanded almost to the width of the clearing as John watched in shock. He stood mesmerized as the vortex moved slowly toward him. Renphor put out his other hand and seemed to wave John toward the center. He realized too late what was happening and pushed backwards with all of his might, but the suction from the funnel had already caught him and was pulling him toward the center of the flames. Renphor heard a piercing scream, and the vortex closed around John's writhing form. He stared at the spot where it had been for a long moment before leaning back against the tree with his eyes closed, then released an extended sigh before opening them again to examine the wound on his arm. He poked an experimental finger into it and flinched. That was going to take a while to close back up. He turned as if to start a jump, then thought better of it and started toward the house at a slow walk.

63

Renphor strolled into Julie's sitting room to find Arabella and Julie perched nervously on the edges of two upholstered chairs. Joseph was seated in the corner of the room, his head in his hands. He stood in the doorway, taking in the scene for a moment. "You all look like a bomb is about to go off," he commented.

Julie jumped several feet in the air. Arabella shot out of her chair and wrapped her arms around him. "Renphor!"

Renphor inhaled sharply before carefully removing his injured arm from her grasp. Arabella looked at the charred hole in horror. "What happened?"

Renphor smiled. "Nothing irreparable, my dear."

Julie strolled over to inspect the wound with an expert eye. "Not too bad. I have something that will tidy it up a bit."

"Thank you."

She nodded as she walked over to a heavy oak cabinet.

Joseph stared from one to the other in shock. "My master..." he moaned.

Renphor looked at him in disgust. "You have no master. I do not keep slaves."

Joseph rocked back and forth. "You will send me away from this house as well?"

"If you can resist the urge to attack me, I don't care what else you do."

"You murdered my master." A spark of anger showed in Joseph's eyes.

"I did not. I killed him in a fair fight."

"Then you should kill me as well."

Renphor stared at the man. "Seriously?"

Joseph nodded. Arabella watched in horror as he kneeled on the floor in front of Renphor. "Please."

Renphor looked at Julie, who sighed and nodded.

"This is truly what you want?"

Joseph nodded again and hung his head. After a moment, Renphor pressed his hands together and pulled them apart. Arabella screamed as a bolt of lightning shot from his fingertips. Joseph crumpled to the ground within seconds, dissolving into dust.

Renphor flopped into a nearby chair but stood up again quickly as a loud, angry hiss emanated from the seat. He stared at it. Ten pounds of black fur and amber eyes glared back, ears flattened and hackles raised.

"Cat," Arabella commented.

"I noticed. Sorry, fuzzy." He picked up the angry animal and put it on the floor before sitting back down in the chair. The cat huffed off into the corner and sat very erect with her tail wrapped around her front paws, glaring at him.

Renphor laughed. "Feisty animal. I'm surprised it stays."

"Cats have too much ego to worry about vampires. We couldn't keep a dog, but the cat doesn't give a shit as long as someone feeds her." Julie walked toward him, carrying a rag soaked in a liquid that smelled slightly of kerosene.

Renphor eyed the rag dubiously as she handed it to him. "Put it on the wound. It will help."

He touched the rag gingerly to the wound and removed it quickly. He let out a yelp as Julie took a firm grip on it and pressed it unrelentingly into place. He felt his eyes go slightly crossed from the sting, but he did not fight Julie to remove it again. Finally, she took her hand off it. "That should do for now."

He removed the rag, staring at the skin underneath. A black mark still stretched across his arm, but the hole had sealed itself. He blinked. "Impressive."

He noticed Arabella giving him a speculative look and put out his hand to her. She took it but didn't move closer.

"Do you always kill so easily?" she asked.

"Our kind? No. To be honest, I was expecting Joseph's reaction."

She curled up on his lap, and he put his arms around her. "It's been a rather rough night for you, my dear."

She nodded into his shirt collar.

"And for you," Julie commented. "You should feed, you know."

Renphor leaned back against the chair, his eyes closed. "In a bit."

Arabella looked at him in concern. "I'm not keeping you, am I?"

"Not at all, my dear." He sat motionless in the chair for another ten minutes before he gently stood her on her feet and rose. "How's hunting?" he asked Julie.

"Depends how far you're willing to travel. Plenty of deer in the woods. You'll have to go a bit further if you want anything else."

"At this point, I'll take the first thing that crosses my path."

Renphor was back within half an hour, feeling far more energetic. Arabella stared at him.

"You know you're covered in blood."

He looked down at the stains covering his chest. "Dinner had some objections. Shirt was ruined anyway."

She moved closer to him. "That's human blood."

"Yes. Came across a homeless person right outside of the gates. Bit of luck, really."

Arabella closed her eyes. "I suppose so."

"I'll go change." Renphor disappeared but was back a few minutes later, wearing a clean shirt. Arabella twitched violently when he appeared beside her. "You really do need to get used to it, my dear," he said soothingly.

"Which? The death, or the jumping?"

"Both." He pulled her into his arms and held her close to calm her down but they both jumped when Stefan appeared suddenly in front of them. Stefan stared at Renphor in surprise. "I have business with John," he said.

"Hope it wasn't important," Renphor said flippantly. Arabella gave him a stern look.

Stefan raised his eyebrows. "Why?"

Renphor's lips twitched. "He's not here."

"I see. Does this mean that you've taken up residence?"

Renphor nodded.

"How interesting. And none of the current residents have any objection to the switch?" His gaze traveled from Arabella to Julie.

Arabella tightened her arms around him. Julie shook her head.

"Joseph?"

Renphor pointed to the dust on the floor.

"You have been busy this evening, haven't you?"

"So it would appear. Anything I can help you with? Wouldn't want you to have wasted the journey."

"In a mellow mood this evening, aren't you? There is a book of John's—or perhaps I should say of yours—that I would like to study. I'll come back after you've had time to settle in."

Renphor bowed his head toward the other man. "Thank you. And now, I believe I shall take a tour of my new home. Arabella, would you like to see all the places you weren't allowed to go as a child?"

A small smile flitted across her face. "I am a bit curious."

He took her by the hand. "Then come."

Julie led them up the main staircase and down a long hallway.

"Where are we starting?" Renphor asked.

"The gallery. Full of portraits that we might as well sell, but the architecture is interesting." Julie pulled open a heavy door to reveal a room lined down both sides with portraits of men and women in centuries-old dress.

"Great Beelzebub. The entire Elder clan, it seems."

Arabella started off down one side of the portrait gallery, while Renphor contemplated a picture of Sophia Elder wearing a long pink gown. His attention was called back to Arabella when she made a small chirping noise.

"Renphor?" she said timidly. "This one looks just like you."

Renphor looked at the picture hanging in front of her. After the briefest of pauses his hand shot out, and the portrait burned to cinders. Arabella stared, open-mouthed, at the hole in the frame and the black mark on the wall behind it.

Julie gawked at him. "Didn't like Damian?"

"My father." Renphor continued down the row of portraits, stopping before one of John as a young man.

"I'd like that one to stay intact, if you don't mind," Julie said drily.

Renphor grinned. "I've no objection."

She looked at him curiously, then nodded her head in the direction of the torched portrait. "What did he do, exactly?"

Renphor's mouth hardened. "He raped my mother when she was thirteen. Then he got angry when she confessed during a fever that he'd fathered me. So he had her killed while I watched. I was seven."

They toured the rest of the house at leisure, looking into long-forgotten bedrooms and salons. Renphor was inclined to think the place was overdone, but Arabella was delighted with all of it. They finally ended back in the library, and Arabella began wandering around the room, staring at the titles of the ancient books. Renphor and Julie sank into the chairs on either side of the fire.

"Out of curiosity, how did you know we'd arrived?" Renphor asked her.

"I can see the front door from the top of the tower. I could tell that you'd been able to enter the house, so I gave it a few minutes and then tried out my jumping skills."

They sat in silence for several minutes.

"I should call Manda," he finally commented.

"Aren't they still in the Bahamas?" Arabella asked.

"The only place they went was Manda's apartment."

She stared at him. "What do you mean?"

He smiled and dialed the number.

Half an hour later, Sam was perched on the edge of John's desk while Amanda paced back and forth in front of the fireplace. Arabella glanced from one to the other. "So I guess the Bahamas trip didn't happen?"

Sam sighed. "No, Ella. Renphor wouldn't let me come near you while you were still human. Seemed to think I lacked self-control. And he's still under the impression that I need a keeper, apparently," she grumbled.

"You're not ready to be on your own yet," he said firmly.

"Get ready for me to move in with you, then. I'm not staying with her."

Arabella opened her mouth to speak, but Julie cut her off.

"Don't bite me for this, but you do still need a more experienced companion. I'm planning to do quite a bit of traveling in the near future. Care to come along?"

"Yes! Anywhere you want," Sam smiled for the first time since she'd entered the room.

Amanda glowered at them and changed the subject abruptly. "Nice digs," she said to Renphor. "Where did you come by them?"

"The house belonged to John Elder."

Amanda stared. "Elder?"

Sam looked curiously at Renphor. "What does John have to do with this place?"

"'This place' is Larch Hill. You've just never come through that entrance before." He said.

"But—wha—" Amanda stammered.

"I've…taken possession, so to speak," Renphor replied.

Amanda blinked. "Is Elder dead, then?"

Renphor nodded. Sam gasped and looked quickly at Arabella.

"It's a rather long story," Arabella said softly.

Amanda looked from one to the other. "Why look so surprised, Sam?"

Sam ignored her.

"Because he was my stepfather," Arabella answered.

She let out a slow whistle. "So that was it, was it?" She looked at Renphor. "I wondered why you were so fascinated with a human girl. You needed her for a shot at Elder."

"I would have gotten him eventually, but it would have taken me longer to work out another plan. This one fell in my lap, so to speak."

Arabella looked miffed. "I hope that wasn't the entire reason you were interested."

He walked up to her and put his arms around her. "Not the entire reason, my dear. But a large part of it." He leaned down and kissed her before she could respond.

She freed herself from him quickly. "Why did you need me?"

"To get into the house. And to take some of the fight out of him."

"Not to be stupid, but I still don't get it. You just walked into the house on your own."

"Your memory is failing. *We* walked into the house. He could bar the entrance against me, but you live here. He had to let you through. The one overrode the other, and I walked right past his barricades."

She swallowed. "I see. Couldn't you have gotten to him outside of the house?"

"I could, but he would've been more on his guard. I'm stronger than he ever was, but Elder was an extraordinarily resourceful man. I needed to get him off guard, where he was vulnerable. And the added jolt of your defection helped as well. Kept his brain reeling in too many directions."

"Renphor, do you—care for me at all?" She looked at the ground. Sam gave Renphor a dirty look. He smiled reassuringly at her before walking over to Arabella and pulling her into his arms.

"I care a great deal for you, my dear. An unexpected bonus, I'll admit, but it makes the victory that much sweeter."

She smiled at him. "You'll help me learn what I need to know, then?"

He laughed at the eager look on her face. "Of course. And protect you from the ill spirits, when needed."

She looked startled. "What would I need protection from?"

Renphor suddenly became sober. "Not from much, admittedly. But I think I will keep a close eye on Ariliana for a while." Arabella gaped at him. "It was her who set you looking for my place, wasn't it?"

She nodded, looking at the floor again.

"I should have anticipated that she'd go for revenge. Stupid girl."

"You're not going to do anything to her, are you?"

He smiled bitterly. "Sadly, no. At the moment she's under Stefan's protection. I don't dare touch her while he still has use for her."

Julie spoke at last. "Not so stupid after all, then?"

"She can look after her own skin, at any rate. I think she's done with me now, but I still don't trust her."

He flopped down in a chair, and Arabella perched on his lap, resting her head on his shoulder. He smiled and tightened his arms around her.

F. Anne Fischer is a biochemist by day, and author, poet, and dragon collector at night. She lives in Czechia with her very opinionated cat, Agatha, and visits the local castles as often as possible.

Her writing covers a range of topics, but a recurring theme is "what would *really* happen if you took these extraordinary creatures, and made them exist in the world as it currently is?" She hopes that her readers enjoy her take on it.

CPSIA information can be obtained
at www.ICGtesting.com
Printed in the USA
BVHW042338060223
658028BV00004B/40